ALSO BY KATIE JENNINGS

So Fell the Sparrow

The Vasser Legacy

Rise of the Notorious
Rulers of Deception

The Dryad Quartet Series

Breath of Air
Firefight in Darkness
A Life Earthbound
Of Water and Madness

Praise for
"When Empires Fall"

When Empires Fall had me hooked from the first page. Katie Jennings does a great job of capturing my imagination and keeping my attention from beginning to end. I felt as though I was a friend of the Vasser family and wanted to visit the hotel. I was so disappointed to get to the last page and not know what happens next. I am looking forward to the next book in this series. Katie Jennings has a five star book that could easily become an award winning movie. Don't pass this one up—it is a true winner.

- Readers' Favorite -

I enjoyed *When Empires Fall*, the fact that you don't know what will happen, you don't know who to love and who to hate, and that it is filled with so much drama. The author did a wonderful job with the flow of the story.

- Christina's Book Review -

This book has it all—murder, intrigue, and romance. Just as in all the great soaps, I was not ready for this episode to be over. I can't wait to get my hands on the next book. I hope that she deals with Linc and his Louisiana home more.

- Voracious Reader -

Jennings' writing is excellent, the formatting attractive, and the pacing spot on. I found myself drawn into their world, an unwitting player in the drama of their lives. The story carried me along all the way to its dramatic conclusion. I loved this story and look forward to more from this wonderful author. Well done!

- Richard C. Hale, author of "Near Sighted" -

Praise for
"Rise of the Notorious"

...a fabulous read. I was involved from the first word to the very last, staying up late into the night. I really wanted to know what happened but I hated getting to the end and leaving my Vasser friends, but I can only hope that the saga continues in many more books. Katie Jennings has written a story that is real, containing all of the good and bad of life in a large and influential family. She made the characters come alive and I laughed and cried along with them. *Rise of the Notorious* will quickly find its way to the top of the best seller list and remain there for many weeks and could easily become the best movie of the year. If you are a fan of a saga with strong family bonds, romance, suspense, passion, deception, betrayal and so on, you must read this book. *Rise of the Notorious* is a hands down winner and a must read book.

- Readers' Favorite -

The writing is superb and not only captures the imagination but also gives you a strong desire to master writing as well as Jennings. The protagonist, Madison, is the perfect female role model, confronting her failures and drawing on her strengths to propel her forward. Beautiful, cunning and undeniably wicked she is the main hook of the story, drawing in the reader to her extremely dangerous life. Jennings has succeeded in creating a world so complicated and—of course—notorious that it offers the perfect escape, while simultaneously reflecting true life in a way that makes you reflect upon your own.

- Elizabeth Wright, reviewer -

WHEN

Empires

FALL

A VASSER LEGACY NOVEL

KATIE JENNINGS

Sapphire Royale
publishing

Published by
Sapphire Royale Publishing

ISBN-13: 978-0615673530
ISBN-10: 0615673538

Visit the author at:
www.katieajennings.com
www.facebook.com/authorkatiejennings
www.twitter.com/dryadquartet
www.katieajennings.wordpress.com

Dedicated to my family,
who have been my biggest supporters from the beginning.

VASSER FAMILY TREE

DIRECT VASSER LINEAGE ONLY
WITHOUT SPOUSES

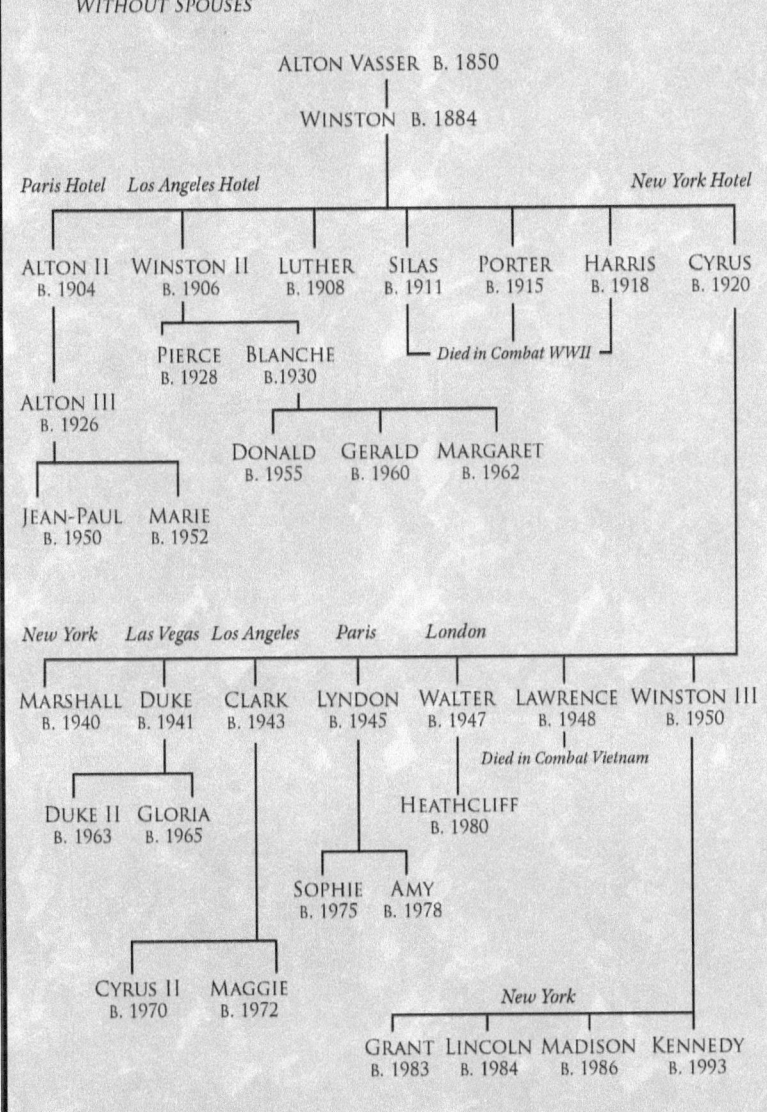

ALTON VASSER B. 1850

WINSTON B. 1884

Paris Hotel   *Los Angeles Hotel*   *New York Hotel*

ALTON II B. 1904   WINSTON II B. 1906   LUTHER B. 1908   SILAS B. 1911   PORTER B. 1915   HARRIS B. 1918   CYRUS B. 1920

PIERCE B. 1928   BLANCHE B.1930

└ Died in Combat WWII ┘

ALTON III B. 1926

DONALD B. 1955   GERALD B. 1960   MARGARET B. 1962

JEAN-PAUL B. 1950   MARIE B. 1952

New York   *Las Vegas*   *Los Angeles*   *Paris*   *London*

MARSHALL B. 1940   DUKE B. 1941   CLARK B. 1943   LYNDON B. 1945   WALTER B. 1947   LAWRENCE B. 1948   WINSTON III B. 1950

Died in Combat Vietnam

DUKE II B. 1963   GLORIA B. 1965   HEATHCLIFF B. 1980

SOPHIE B. 1975   AMY B. 1978

CYRUS II B. 1970   MAGGIE B. 1972

New York

GRANT B. 1983   LINCOLN B. 1984   MADISON B. 1986   KENNEDY B. 1993

PROLOGUE

SOME RISE BY SIN,
AND SOME BY VIRTUE FALL...
MANHATTAN, NEW YORK, NY
FEBRUARY 1957

I f someone compared him to the great Captains of Industry who built America from the ground up, he would laugh. Surely he was no Rockefeller, and he'd be damned if they likened him to Carnegie, the bighearted fool. But perhaps there was some truth to the statement, if one considered hotels to be of equal importance to railways and steel.

And to Winston C. Vasser, hotels were everything.

In his old age, he now understood that hotels hadn't given the country the same benefits that other industries like steel and railroads had, but he and his father before him recognized that where there was money to be made, there was also money to be spent. And the men who profited from luck and good old American ingenuity needed a place to spend the riches they accumulated. Hence, the luxury hotels of America were born.

What started as a single hotel in 1899, housed inside a building that had once been a coat factory in midtown Manhattan, paved the way for an empire the likes of which America was rapidly becoming known for. It was a country for men with big ideas and great dreams, and the willingness and tenacity to make them come true.

Which was why Winston knew he would live out his remaining days right there in New York, the most magnificent city the world had ever seen.

If only he knew how limited those days were to be.

He settled into his desk chair, his eyes drifting to the view of the city lights beyond his window. Outside, the dark scene was spotted with falling winter snow. It was picturesque, as the view always was from the suites of the Vasser Hotel, and rather calming to him despite the circumstances.

He was, in many ways *un*like his father before him, an honest man. Winston prided himself on being straight with people; on his word being as solid as a firm handshake. Which was perhaps why the deception he wove troubled him.

In his prime, he had been sturdily built and taller than most, with a clear, booming voice and enough charm to outwit even the stealthiest of opponents. Generally that charm was used to get what he wanted, and he was damn good at it most of the time.

He had taken what his father started and rode on the growth of the country as it exploded into the 20th century. One hotel quickly become two in the United States, with a third and fourth abroad in Europe. He was thrilled to imagine a day when there would be a Vasser luxury hotel in every worthwhile major city across the globe. After all, the century was only half over. God only knew what lay ahead for the Vasser Hotel empire and for the greatest country the world had ever seen.

Tucking his blue velvet robe closer around his aged body, he turned to face his heirloom oak desk. It was littered with papers, well worn books, glossy black and white photographs, and an ancient deck of cards he'd had since he was ten years old.

He reached for them, running his thumb over the surface of the tattered box. On the front was an image of the American flag, Old Glory. Seeing it brought back the pain, along with the denial and disbelief.

The last time he'd held that deck of cards in his hands was when the Army men arrived, carrying three flags and three sets of dog tags, inscribed with the names of three of his seven sons. It was one of only two times he'd ever cried in his life, the second being when his youngest son, Cyrus, came home miraculously unscathed and a lavishly decorated war hero.

That was the day he'd learned humility and the true measure of sacrifice. The war his generation had fought seemed somehow less frightening, less deadly. He knew Americans could thank film for the violent images of the war that claimed his sons—the scenes of destruction and death, of France and the rest of Europe reduced to rubble. His ancestors came from France, and it was a place he'd known well as a boy. To see it ruined, to know his sons perished protecting it, did more damage to his soul than could ever be repaired.

Feeling sick with grief, he yanked open his right hand desk drawer and tossed the cards inside, slamming the drawer shut again. He didn't want to think about it, couldn't bear to imagine the horror of it now. There was no time for it, not when he needed to act swiftly and secretly to ensure that his legacy, and that of his father, not be tainted. As his father's only child, he was head of the family empire and had been for some time.

He had four surviving sons who had given him ten grandchildren and three great grandchildren, with surely more to come. They all benefited from the fruits of his labor, and from the legacy he would pass on to them when he died.

But none of them would, in the foreseeable future, anyway, take his place as patriarch of the Vasser Hotels. He could not allow it to happen.

Rummaging through the assorted papers on his desk, Winston came across one that was blank and hastily pushed the rest out of the way, clearing space enough for him to write. He grabbed his polished black fountain pen from its holder and pressed the tip to the paper, his mind swirling with hope and regret and fear.

This was serious, that much he was sure of. He could not afford to make mistakes, not when so much was riding on this decision. It had to be Rosalie. She was the only person he could trust, the only person who had never let him down. He owed everything to her for uncovering that dark and heinous secret, the one he shuddered to even imagine now.

His pen scrawled over the page in his practiced cursive, spelling out the new terms for his soon to be rewritten will. Rosalie Owens would, upon his death, take control of the hotels, the accounts, and the employees, including his own children and grandchildren. She would be in charge of ensuring the future of the company and the prestigious reputation of the Vasser Hotels.

His hand paused as he finished the sentence, his pale blue eyes scanning the words through his wire-rimmed glasses, over and over, cementing them in his mind. Yes, this was the only answer, the only solution. His soon to be ex-wife wasn't going to be happy about him leaving the entire family legacy to his mistress, but what did he care? It was not for her to decide, nor to judge. What he did with the empire he and his father single-handedly built was entirely up to him. Certainly it was uncommon for a *woman* to run a company such as his, but he knew without a shadow of a doubt that she could do it. He also knew she was the only one who respected his vision for the Vasser legacy.

He began to scribble down more words when there was a sharp knock on the door to his room. Beyond the entrance of the study, he could see the door to the suite, shrouded mostly in shadows since the only light source came from his desk lamp. A sense of unease settled over him as he wet his lips, feeling the need to moisten his suddenly dry throat.

"Come in," he called out, annoyed when his usually jovial and clear voice cracked with anxiety. Surely there was nothing to fear. He was in no danger. Not yet, anyway.

The door opened slowly and a man walked in, looking oddly calm and collected. The man shut the door until it was merely cracked, then entered the study.

Winston immediately flipped the paper over, concealing the words he'd written. God knew he couldn't let the news get out that his will was to be changed.

"Shouldn't you be at home with your family?" Winston asked, his feathery white eyebrows raised. He trembled once with a bone-quaking fear, knowing he had a right to be afraid. The reasons for it both pained and infuriated him.

"There are some important matters I need to attend to first," the man replied, the light from the desk lamp glowing over the sharp lines of his face. It only served to heighten the dangerous gleam in his cold, calculating eyes and darken the hollows his brows made over them. They were eyes that seemed unnaturally dark now, and eerily devoid of any emotion other than carefully controlled rage.

Winston thought consciously of the .22 Derringer pistol hidden in the drawer to his right, wondering if he would need to use it. Good Lord, use it on his own flesh and blood...

"What sort of...matters?"

The man grinned, though the gesture lacked even the tiniest scrap of humor. No, it was a smile like that of a hunter scenting prey.

"I think you know." Chuckling, the man stood before Winston's desk, his dark trench coat brushing against his legs and his hands tucked discreetly in its pockets. "Then again, you've always been a little slow on the uptake, old man. So perhaps you need a detailed explanation on why I feel you've fucked me. So to speak."

"Now, look here—" Winston began, only to cut off when the man raised his hand to halt the words. His eyes glittered with impatience and a malice Winston had never before seen. Or perhaps he had simply ignored it, all these years...

"I know you plan to leave everything to the whore," the man growled. "You intend to bypass your own heirs to give the bitch everything that should be rightfully mine. After everything *I* have sacrificed, you still choose to dishonor me."

Winston inhaled sharply, his own temper flaring as indignation coursed through him. He glared at the man, suddenly choked with despair and fury over that one, horrific truth...

"Sacrifice? Surely *you* have sacrificed nothing but your soul. God will punish you for what you have done to your own flesh and blood, your *family*!"

"Fuck family," the man hissed, keeping his voice low and level despite the urge he had to tear every inch of the man in front of him to pieces. "If my actions to ensure my success mean I have sold my soul, then surely you have sold yours in the name of that whore, Rosalie."

"This discussion is over," Winston grunted, only to bite back confusion and fear as the man suddenly skirted around the desk to approach him. His face was glazed with a chilling frost, his dark eyes betraying nothing. Those eyes held Winston's as the man came up behind the chair and rested his hands on the top edge of the backrest.

"I don't know what made you think you could cross me and get away with it, old man," the man chided, reaching down to scoop up the paper Winston had been writing on. He read what was written on it before stuffing it into his coat pocket.

Winston only shook his head, understanding what was about to happen. He should have expected it, should have known it would end this way. There was nothing he could do at this point to dissuade the man. Surely he was no match physically for someone nearly forty years younger than he.

This man had killed before. He would easily do it again.

The truth had resurfaced, but now it would perish with him. He would probably target and kill Rosalie, too.

"How could you do it? I just need to know," Winston murmured, his head still shaking in disbelief and dull fear. It was the fear that had him wrenching open his desk drawer and fumbling around for his pistol, only to discover it missing.

The man behind him let out a dark laugh, and pulled the very same pistol from his coat pocket, showing Winston over his shoulder. "I have always been resourceful. I do what needs to be done to get ahead, no matter the cost."

Winston eyed the pistol with a newfound shock racing through his blood. Good Lord, he was going to be murdered with his own gun. What terrible misdeeds had he committed in his life to deserve such a fate?

"You monster," Winston choked out, clutching his robe around his midsection, his eyes glued to the gun. He didn't think he could bear to look at the man's face, only to have the image of those horrifying eyes be the last thing he would ever see.

"Turn your head, old man. And look straight ahead," the man instructed, pressing the pistol to the side of Winston's head. "It'll all be over soon."

"Monster," Winston repeated as he shut his eyes tight, feeling tears brim hotly behind his closed lids. The cold steel of the pistol was like sharp white frost against his temple.

Outside in the hall, a child watched the scene unfold with wide, terrified eyes. When the blast of the gunshot resounded through the room, Winston collapsed over his own desk. His blood spilled to soak through his papers and books.

The child shot out into the hallway, fleeing like a rabbit to safety. A frightened scream was held back only by a pure, unbridled terror that the monster was coming for him next.

It was a fear he would live with for the rest of his life.

ONE

By most standards, Maggie Owens had accomplished very little in her eighty-one years of life. She'd lived in the same two bedroom, one bathroom house since her birth, the one her parents had scraped together a mere five thousand dollars for in the last century. She'd never married, never borne children, and never found the need to work since she lived off the inheritance from her father's rather mild fortune.

She spent her days wandering aimlessly around her little house, nestled in a pleasantly old neighborhood of Queens. She kept herself busy by rearranging things, which wasn't easy in her old age. But she was stubborn enough to ignore the creaks of her tired bones as she putted around, moving vases and lamps from one corner of the living room to another.

Maggie was often told that she lived too much of her life inside her own head. She had an active imagination, which to her thinking kept her mind sharp as a tack. The doctors claimed she had something called dementia, but she dismissed them. She didn't trust physicians anyway.

She had a penchant for collecting trinkets, hoarding her house with anything she could find. Years earlier, her mother had scorned the habit but was helpless to do much about it. From what Maggie could remember, her mother was helpless to do a lot of things in her later years.

Frightened. That's what Rosalie Owens had been. Though Maggie had never learned the reason for the fear, or for the stress her mother was under consistently until her final days.

Maggie remembered many times when her mother would wander around the house without purpose, mumbling to herself about murder, blood and revenge, yet she never explained her ramblings. So Maggie simply did the best she could and took care of her mother physically, unable to fix what was wrong inside Rosalie's mind.

Nearly thirty years had passed since her mother's death during the miserable, sweltering summer of '82. Maggie preferred not to dwell on the sadness she felt when thinking about it, even though the memory was a fading dream to her now.

She let the dark, sad thoughts slip from her mind as she made her way down the narrow hallway of her home. She stepped around the cluttered tables and bookshelves she'd crammed along the walls, filled with layers upon layers of possessions she couldn't live without. Her frail hand skimmed over the surface of the furniture and the various plates, books, and tiny porcelain figurines that covered it. She hummed softly to herself as she went, her glassy dark eyes searching for something to rearrange. She felt that the living room needed something new in it, something big.

Her hand fell over the surface of her mother's old writing desk, which had been locked for forty or so years now. Maggie stared at the dusty oak roll-top for a long moment, fighting to remember if she'd ever seen what was inside of it. As quickly as the thought arrived, it fled, and Maggie's eyes trailed forward onto other things. She continued her hunt down the hallway, her frazzled gray strands of hair catching the light from one of the rooms.

She followed the light and stumbled upon her mother's old bedroom, with its baby blue curtains, faded cabbage rose wallpaper and antique furniture. The room was filled with all her parents' old things, from books to clothing to everything in between. It was a room she mostly stayed away from, as there was so much clutter it was hard to move around.

However, on this day her eye caught something she forgot existed until that very moment. It was an antique vanity mirror that hung over a dusty wooden dresser.

Maggie paid no mind to the dust, nor to the countless items she tripped over and stepped on as she made her way toward the mirror. Her eyes were fixated on it as though it were priceless. At that moment, in her mind, it was.

Biting her bottom lip, she gripped the mirror and attempted to lift it, groaning as she pulled it from the wall. The mass of it tilted toward her and she nearly toppled backward, but caught her footing and tumbled the mirror onto the cluttered carpet. The back of the mirror faced her, and she began to turn it over to make sure she hadn't hurt the glass. Something metal taped to the bottom back corner caught her eye. She peeled off the taped key and held it in her hand, inspecting it in the soft blue light of the room.

It was a curious looking key, certainly not to any door in her home. It was small and pewter colored, with a clover shaped head and long stem complete with two prongs. In the light of her discovery, Maggie forgot about the vanity mirror entirely, and knew she had to find what the key belonged to. She let the mirror fall to the floor and rose to her feet.

With the key at eye level, she wandered up the hallway toward the bathroom, eyeing all the drawers in the vanity cabinet. Seeing nothing that fit, she made her way back down the hallway, nearly passing the old roll-top desk before halting suddenly in front of it. Her eyes widened with flashing memories of her mother sobbing before the vanity mirror, clutching something tightly in her hands. Had she been holding the key?

Maggie's hand trembled as she attempted to shove the key in the roll-top lock, missing it the first few tries. When she managed to slip it inside, it fit with a perfect click. Her breath held frozen in her lungs as she turned the key, her arthritis kicking in and aching horribly in her hand. She managed to open it and pull up the roll-top, eager to see what was inside.

Visions of gold and glittering jewelry flashed in her mind for a fleeting moment, only to be shadowed by her disappointment when she saw nothing but paperwork.

Disgruntled now, she grabbed the top few sheets, noting her father's death certificate, the deed to the house, a few official looking letters from banks and insurance companies. Setting those aside, she got down to a large stack of papers tied together by braided twine. She stared at the cover page for a moment, struggling to comprehend the words. A strange tingling sensation shivered along the backside of her neck.

It was a letter in her mother's handwriting, with tearstains dotting the yellowed page. As Maggie read, the words struck her with a cold, unforgiving chill.

Rosalie told of a vicious murder disguised as a suicide, and how the killer had gotten away with it. She wrote that she was threatened into silence, bought off with money that might as well have been dipped in her dead lover's blood.

Maggie clasped her hand over her heart, her bones chilled to ice as she continued to read the horror that had been her mother's experience with the Vasser family and the killer that resided among them. She'd never known her mother was connected to the famous Vasser family, or the horrific outcome of that involvement. The death that made her a loathed outsider—a smear on the family history that needed to be scrubbed clean off or else tarnish the prestige of the family name. The horror of it disgusted her.

It wasn't until she got to the bottom of the letter that she read about the terrible secret Rosalie had discovered fifty-four years earlier, the disturbing truth that forced Winston C. Vasser to attempt to change his will, leaving everything to Rosalie instead of his own heirs.

Troubled, Maggie flipped through the pages behind the letter, finding documents that provided proof to her mother's claims. It was, essentially, a package that would destroy the Vasser Hotel empire in one fell swoop. Clearly, this was why Rosalie had kept this ticking time bomb locked up safely for so many years. She must have hoped one day it would be discovered-and then everyone would know the dirty, disgusting truth about the Vassers. She had just been too afraid to reveal the truth in her own lifetime.

When she was over the worst of the shock, Maggie placed a phone call to her only living relative, her niece Hannah. She related her discovery in the hopes that justice could be delivered for both her mother and the man she had secretly loved over fifty years earlier.

As she did so, she silently said a prayer to the living heirs of the Vasser family, whoever they were, that they forgive her.

Two

Grant Vasser scowled at the paperwork before him, wondering why it seemed he always had to do things himself if he wanted them done correctly.

It wasn't like the people working for him were incompetent or lazy. Though, given the handling of certain tasks lately, they could have fooled him. He might as well have hired a troupe of dancing monkeys for all the good they were doing.

Maybe his expectations were just too high. Or perhaps he lacked enough sympathy to understand the excuses for not giving a task one hundred and ten percent. He gave everything he did that amount of dedication, so why couldn't everyone else?

What was the point of hiring people when they constantly needed to be reminded to finish the jobs he assigned to them? For God's sake, how hard was it to get multiple bids for a project as costly as remodeling the hotel's indoor swimming pool?

Apparently too hard, since the manager of the hotel gym had received a single, inadequate bid, then presented it as the only option out of sheer laziness.

Grant was more than happy to call the gym manager on his bullshit. And if the idiot felt one lousy overpriced bid was the best he could do, then Grant would simply get the other bids himself.

Clicking into his desktop computer, he looked up the phone numbers of a few well-respected contractors he was familiar with and jotted down the information on a blank pad of paper with his great-grandfather's old black fountain pen.

He'd make the calls himself and handle this the way it should have been handled in the first place. And if the idiot came asking for a raise, he would take great pleasure in knocking him down a few pegs. In his eyes, unless a man earned something, he didn't deserve it.

There was a soft knock on the door to his office, and he called out for the person to enter as he continued to note down phone numbers. He glanced up as Tara, his heavily pregnant soon to be ex-secretary waddled in, her smile bright and cheerful against her rosy skin and short crop of sunny blonde hair.

"I just wanted to come in and say goodbye," Tara explained, biting her lip as her eyes brightened with tears. She glanced around his office wistfully, basking in her memories of the place one last time.

Grant watched her, feeling uncomfortable by the emotions suffocating the air all of a sudden. Damnit, he hated dealing with things like goodbyes. Especially when it was someone he honestly liked, which was saying something since it took a lot for him to really like somebody.

He cleared his throat, searching for something to say at that moment that would both comfort her and get her to leave him alone. Though the sun had already set, he still had hours until he would be heading home. In his opinion, time was money and wasting it was inexcusable.

"I'm sure you'll be very happy," he told her lamely, hoping his statement didn't sound contrived. "Would you like me to see you out?"

"Oh, no." Tara's eyes shot back to his, an appreciative smile on her face. "No, I'll be fine. Thank you for everything. Really. I've loved working here, working for you, for the hotel. It's been a great experience."

"You'll be missed," Grant put in as sincerely as he could, though he remained seated so she wouldn't try to hug him. He was horribly awkward when it came to any show of affection.

"Thanks." Tara nodded, taking in the classy furniture with straight, masculine lines and shades of cobalt blue and steel gray, softened with rich mahogany. It was an office that suited the man only a couple of years older than herself, who had the strength and unyielding stability of steel refined by his reverence of tradition and his dedication to family.

Glancing back at him, she noticed he had the look he got when he was pressed for time but didn't want to hurt her feelings by being rude and shooing her away. It humbled her to be one of the few people he went out of his way to be kind to. It was a very exclusive list.

"I didn't have the chance to meet my replacement, but Marshall tells me she's very nice."

Grant couldn't hold back a grimace at the idea of having to adjust to a new secretary. He wasn't a man who appreciated change.

"Hopefully she's a fast learner," he grumbled.

Tara let out a light laugh and tugged her light blue winter coat tighter over her rounded belly. "Marshall has good judgment. After all, he hired me."

Grant's mouth tugged up at her words. "Yes, he did. Goodbye, Mrs. Sawyer."

"Goodbye, Mr. Vasser." Tara smiled again as she turned to leave the room, shutting the door with a soft click behind her.

For a few moments, Grant sat in the silence of his office, lost in thought. He really was going to miss Tara, or Mrs. Sawyer, as he preferred to call her in his attempt to maintain the professionalism of the office. She was sharp, patient, and reliable. There wasn't much more he could ask of a secretary than that.

His eyes drifted from the door to the framed photographs that cluttered his walls, all depicting his family. He enjoyed having them up there as a reminder of why he worked as hard as he did, a reminder of the legacy that had been passed down to him from a long line of Vasser men.

There were pictures of him and his three siblings when they had been children, both portraits and candid shots of them together. Always together, he mused, knowing as the eldest just how much they relied on him. He knew in many ways he relied on them as well.

Mixed in were shots of his countless cousins and their children, of his fifteen aunts and uncles, and older pictures of those that had come before him, his grandparents and their siblings. There were even a few photographs of his great-grandfather, Winston Vasser, and one rare shot of his great-great-grandfather, Alton Vasser.

But in the midst of all the photographs were three large, professionally painted portraits of Alton, Winston, and lastly his grandfather, Cyrus Vasser, the current head of the Vasser family empire.

Cyrus had a sharp-featured face with high cheekbones, characteristic of their richly European ancestry, and cunning, tawny colored eyes. In his prime he'd had a full head of rich, bark brown hair threaded with silver, wavy even in its cropped length. Now it had gone grayish white and he'd lost many of the hard edges due to wrinkles and sagging skin. But those eyes remained as sharp as ever, and as penetrating as they'd been when Grant was a child. Even looking at the portrait made Grant feel as though Cyrus were watching him right then and there, determining his worth in that calculating and critical way he had.

Grant always thought it was interesting to note the vast difference in appearances between his grandfather and Winston, and then Alton before him. They all looked physically very similar, but their attitudes as captured by the painter seemed so drastically polarized. Where Cyrus appeared impressive and intimidating, his father, Winston, wore an expression of pride and importance, with bright blue eyes that shone with prosperity and happiness. He looked like a man of unlimited charm with a smile to match, and had a relatable sense about him that Cyrus lacked in spades.

Yet Grant had always wondered how a man who looked so full of life in photographs and in his portrait could have possibly taken his own life. From what he'd been told of his great-grandfather, his suicide was the result of a ruinous affair with a devilish woman, who had carelessly broken his heart. A shame, Grant thought, to let any one person have such a hold over you.

It was without a doubt the greatest tragedy his family had ever suffered, and the effects of it were still being felt even though nearly sixty years had passed. He had a feeling that Winston's suicide would be a troubling smear on the Vasser family reputation and name for many years to come.

Shaking his head to rid the thoughts from his mind, his eyes shifted to his great-great-grandfather's portrait. Alton Vasser, who, perhaps since the portrait was much older, looked dry and humorless, cold and shallow. His expression was vacant and unfeeling, his dark eyes emotionless. Yet this was the man that started the first Vasser Hotel and built it from the ground up, making it, with the help of his only son Winston, into the empire that Grant and his family were a part of today. Grant knew he had to throw ample respect and appreciation at his great-great-grandfather simply because of that alone.

Inscribed in a gold plague embedded in the chestnut frame of each portrait was the name and favorite quote of each man. Not surprising, his grandfather's quote read: *The King's name is a tower of strength.*

Cyrus had always taught them that the only reason their legacy held power was because their name was timeless and embedded in the history of the country and of the people who lived there. Quite simply, reputation was everything and tarnishing the name meant losing it all.

But Cyrus was up there in the years now, just past ninety, and Grant knew it was only a matter of time before the old man passed and someone else in the family was crowned with the prestige and burden of the empire.

Not that Grant expected he would be the one. He might have been qualified, but he was one of the youngest in the family and therefore low on the pecking order of seniority. But he didn't mind, as long as he was allowed to continue his duty as general manager of the Vasser Hotel in New York City. It was the original, and in his mind, the best of all the Vasser Hotels. Then one day when it was his turn, he would take over and do the best he could to preserve everything his forefathers had worked for. It was, after all, his legacy and his obligation to do so.

He was jolted out of his reverie when there was a brisk knock on his door once again, only this time the person did not wait for him to beckon them in. But when he saw his Uncle Marshall, he made sure to un-ruffle his feathers and at least attempt something other than a frown.

"I'm sure going to miss seeing Tara's pretty smile every day," Marshall said wistfully as he came into the room and shut the door at his back.

"I'm sure all of us will miss her," Grant replied, warring internally between his work obligations and his family as he eyed his uncle, wondering how he could get out of having a long and winded conversation about the new secretary. He didn't care to hear Marshall's opinions on the woman, especially since his own opinions were likely to vary drastically. Tara had been a fortunate contradiction to the usual difference of opinion between he and his uncle.

Marshall chuckled, his massive frame shaking with it beneath his stylish charcoal gray suit. He rose to a near six foot five, built with broad shoulders and a midsection that had gotten thicker over the years given his impeccable love of fine cuisine and good brandy. With the help of a clever stylist, he kept his hair fuller than it naturally would have been and with only a light dusting of gray against a rich chocolate brown to match his generous and timeless mustache. As a result, he looked a lot younger than his seventy-one years, and he certainly acted younger, too.

He had the same twinkling, charming blue eyes of his grandfather, Winston, and by all accounts he acted very much like the man as well. Marshall was the life of the party at any event and a great poster boy for the Vasser family, a role he had played nearly all his life. He was Cyrus Vasser's oldest son out of seven boys, which meant he was next in line to inherit the family empire. So long as he could outlive the old man, anyway.

"Well, I'm sure you have plenty of work to do, as usual." Marshall winked at his nephew affectionately. "I just wanted to pop by and see if you needed a shoulder to cry on regarding the lovely Tara's departure."

Grant shook his head, trying not to be amused. "I don't cry."

"Of course you don't," Marshall mused as he glanced over his shoulder at the portraits and photographs on the wall behind him, admiring the paintings particularly. "I always said you look more like my dad than your own father, Grant."

"I suppose I should take that as a compliment?" Grant returned to his notepad to scribble down another phone number. "I really am busy, Marshall."

Marshall shoved his hands into the pockets of his slacks and turned, grinning.

"Then I won't keep you." He let out a slow sigh as he admired his nephew, working busily away at the desk that had been both his and Cyrus' for so many years, in the same office that had been Winston's and Alton's before him. Tradition. It was a beautiful thing. "I just want you to know that I'm proud of you, Grant. If I'd had children, had a son, I hope he would've been just like you."

Grant stopped writing and glanced up, meeting his uncle's eyes cautiously. Great, treading on emotional ground again. Even though he felt an odd, deeply buried gratification at hearing the words, he still preferred those kind of remarks be kept inside. All it seemed to do was make him uncomfortable.

"Thanks. Goodnight, Marshall." Grant nodded curtly before turning back to his computer screen.

Marshall only smiled again as he turned away, thinking to himself how lucky they all were to have Grant be the way he was. Sure, the kid could lighten up a bit once in awhile, but there was no one, absolutely *no* one, who worked longer or fought harder for the family business than Grant did.

THE HOLLOW RUBBER ball smacked into the white cement with a deafening thud, then cheerfully rebounded straight for Linc Vasser's head.

"*Shit*," he grunted as he ducked out of the way and swung frantically upward with his racket, barely managing to clip the ball. It sailed back toward the wall and bounced to his opponent, who swung and missed the ball by mere inches.

Both men collapsed into a sweaty heap on the floor of the racquetball court, chests heaving as they gasped for air. But when they met eyes, both had mile wide grins of pure sportsmanship.

"Why do I even bother playing with you? I always kick your ass. It's really not much of a challenge," Linc huffed as he patted his friend on the back with as much force as he could muster, which wasn't much since his arm was throbbing from the last hit.

"Screw you, you don't always win." Greg Carson glared back, fire in his soft brown eyes. His blond hair stuck up in places and his boyishly handsome face was flush from the game.

Linc's teeth flashed in a charming smile, his cobalt eyes glittering with triumph and good humor. "You're in what we call a state of denial, my friend. But it's okay, you're a humble man because you always get beaten. In fact, you should be thanking me."

Greg let out a breathy laugh and shook his head, reaching for the blue rubber ball as it rolled toward him. With a wicked smile, he turned to face Linc and held up the ball suggestively. "I'll humble you, Vasser, by shoving this pretty rubber ball right up your ass."

"I'd like to see you try," Linc shot back, shutting his eyes as he tried to calm his furiously beating heart. He was in excellent shape, but even a good game of racquetball could occasionally kick his ass. "Is that why you're so good on Wall Street? You threatening your clients?"

Greg laughed again, bouncing the ball against the wooden floor of the court absently. "Please, when you're as good at stock broking as I am, you don't need threats to get people to buy and sell. Hell, if you'd ever get over your aversion to investing, I could make you a lot of money."

"I just think real estate's a better buy, my oh so humble friend." Linc got to his feet, reaching out his hand to help Greg up.

"Thanks," Greg said, brushing at the basketball shorts he wore as he followed Linc out of the glass door of the court and into the hotel's gym. "I suppose your obsession with buying property makes sense, being the prince of a hotel empire and all."

"Hey, it's pretty much a guaranteed good investment if you're smart," Linc declared, replacing his racket on the stand just outside the court. "You're just jealous because I bought that incredible plantation house in New Orleans last year."

Greg paused as he put his racket away, eyebrows raised incredulously. "Jealous of a falling apart, beat up old house with holes in the roof and graffiti on the walls?"

Linc frowned. "It has history. And I have old family ties to New Orleans, so it means something to me."

"Yeah, yeah." Greg grinned, thumping Linc on the back as they walked toward the showers, weaving their way through the weight machines and the dozens of people working on them. "I get it, you're sentimental about that stuff. How long have I known you again?"

Linc perked up with a laugh. "Going on nine years now, since college."

"Right. Ah, the good old days..."

"That they were." Linc led the way into the locker room, opening up the locker he'd stowed his gym bag in with a nostalgic sigh. "Back when we lived the high life. What the hell happened to us?"

"We grew up." Greg chuckled, stepping out of his shorts and stripping his sweat soaked t-shirt off before grabbing a fluffy white towel from a nearby rack. He draped it around his waist as Linc did the same. "But hey, at least we stayed friends."

Linc snorted out a laugh as he slammed his locker shut and started toward the sauna, making sure he had his cell phone just in case duty called. "Please, you just stick around for the free gym membership."

"True enough," Greg mused, opening the door to the sauna and settling his tall, lanky body onto one of the bamboo benches. He leaned against the cool tiled wall with a groan. "Ah, heaven."

Linc let out a contented sigh as he took a seat, running his hands through his waves of chestnut hair and shutting his eyes blissfully. He folded his athletic legs in front of him, relaxing as he leaned his head back against the wall. Around him, the steam of the sauna swirled thick and humid, soothing his aching muscles until he felt lax and incredibly calm.

When his cell phone began to ring to the tune of "Uptown Girl," Linc groaned and scrubbed his face in annoyance.

He shot Greg a disparaging glance as he answered the phone, his mouth automatically curving into a strained smile. "Hi, mom."

"*Lincoln.*" His mother's voice came through the speaker in its usual sophisticated and pompous pitch. Despite not being born into high society, Charlene Vasser had mastered the art of sounding pretentious with every breath. "*Where are you?*"

"At work," he lied, though technically it was true. He *did* work at the hotel, just not in the sauna. "What's up?"

"*I asked you a week ago to contact our best clients and invite them to the charity fundraiser, and you have yet to get back to me. I need a list of those who will be attending.*"

He mouthed a silent curse, rubbing his eyes irritably with his free hand. He had completely forgotten. "Mom, I haven't had much time for that yet. But I promise I'll get to it today, okay?"

He heard his mother sigh in annoyance on the other line. He hated to disappoint her, but her stupid fundraiser really wasn't his problem. But he still felt guilty that he'd forgotten, so he knew he had to somehow make it up to her. "Hey, why don't you come down and visit me today so we can get lunch together? I know you miss me."

Though she didn't make a sound, he knew she was probably smiling. Any excuse to visit the hotel usually put her in a less crabby mood. "*Alright. But it's very important that you make those phone calls as soon as possible. I would ask Grant but he's impossibly busy, and I'm sure you can free up an hour or two to take care of it. The fundraiser is great publicity for the hotel, as I'm sure you're aware.*"

"I am aware," Linc frowned, fighting to ignore his mother's deliberate comment about his brother. She slipped in the jab about Grant because she knew it would get under his skin. It was so typical of her. "Now why don't you call up Mads and bug her about the catering list and leave me alone for once?"

She sighed again, though it was a little more affectionate this time. "*Goodbye, Linc.*"

"Bye, mom," he said as he hung up the phone, setting it beside him on the bench once more. He glanced over at his friend, shaking his head wearily. "She knows just how to make me feel guilty enough to give her what she wants."

"That's what mothers do best."

"It drives me crazy." Linc sat back against the tile wall and released a long, annoyed breath. "And then she has to slip in that 'oh, Linc, I would just ask Grant, but you know how awfully busy he is.'" He mocked his mother's voice, chuckling to himself despite the irritation he felt over it.

"In all fairness, you're sitting in a sauna right now while big brother's upstairs buried in paperwork," Greg pointed out with a grin.

Linc shrugged, seeing his point. "I'm not doubting that Grant works hard, but does she have to rub it in my face that he's the pride and joy of the family and I'll always be second best?"

"Think of it this way, you may not be able to do Grant's job, but he certainly can't do yours. See, guys like us, we have the salesman gene in our blood. We can charm ink off paper if we have to. And that's why you're Head of Marketing and Customer Relations, and why he sticks to managing, because that's what he's best at."

Linc considered this for a moment, feeling better. Greg was right; he was being ridiculous. He met his friend's eyes with a grin. "So what do I owe you for the advice?"

"You could put in a good word about me with your sister, see if she'll give me another shot."

Linc burst out laughing. "Seriously? You've got some balls if you're gonna try that again. The woman's a viper and you know it."

"One of the sexiest vipers I've ever seen."

"Did you think she was sexy when she tossed her vodka tonic in your face the last time you tried to ask her out?" Linc asked, delightfully amused by the memory. "If I recall, you called her a disgusting, dirty name and stalked out. I really should've beat you up for it in her honor, but I felt too damn bad for you."

Greg frowned. "That vodka did sting pretty bad."

"Let that be a lesson to you. Madison Vasser is off limits, and it's not just because she's my sister." Linc chuckled. "But then again, you never learn."

"You're one to talk, man. You always date actresses and models with pea-sized brains and then wonder why they can't even name all fifty states." Greg checked his watch distractedly, noting the time. "I gotta get going. Same time next week?"

"I'll be here, like always." Linc held out his hand for a fist bump as Greg strolled out of the sauna, then leaned back against the cool tiles, hoping to enjoy a few more minutes of steam before getting back to work.

He made sure to keep an active social and recreational life outside the hotel for the sake of his sanity, whether it be rock climbing upstate, shooting hoops down the street at Central Park, hitting up the night clubs and bars in the evening, or just putting in a few hours working on the remodel plans for the fixer-upper house in New Orleans that he'd purchased for the simple fact that it existed and he wanted it.

He'd be the first to admit he had an impulsive streak a mile wide. But to his mind, following your impulses was what kept life interesting.

Yet, amidst his wide array of projects and activities, Linc still made sure he gave his best to the hotel that was his birthright. Even he could recognize that he wouldn't be who he was without the hotel, or without his family. He supposed his family recognized in him a likability and charisma that made him a perfect fit for marketing and relations. Hell, he'd been a shoe-in at the New York hotel anyway since his Uncle Marshall, the overseer of the hotel, in many ways considered Linc and his siblings to be more like children to him than nephews and nieces. In the end, it benefited them more than being born to Marshall's youngest brother ever had. Out of college, and upon Marshall's part-time retirement, Grant was made general manager and Linc was made head of marketing. Their sister Madison joined not long after that, and he had a feeling that his youngest sister, Kennedy, would be coming along once she finished college. They would stick together, just as they always had, in what would be their legacy.

Linc had big ideas for that legacy. Well, he'd *always* had big ideas about a lot of things, but finally he'd taken the time to bring these specific ideas together to form what he thought was a surefire way to reinvent the Vasser Hotels in a way that would make them more profitable and open up the field for expansion into even more cities across the country, and maybe even in other, more exotic parts of the world.

America was in the midst of a bad economy with little to no hope of recovering any time soon. Maybe it was time they expanded their client base, building three star versions of their five star hotels that could attract those of the middle class. It seemed a brilliant idea to him, but, then again, he had very little say in his current position.

If he could just get Grant to back him, he had a feeling Marshall would join in, and then maybe they could actually get it done. It was all just a matter of convincing his stuffy, traditional older brother to take a leap of faith and try something new for once.

Rolling his eyes, Linc got to his feet, knowing it was going to take a goddamn miracle. The man was worse than a brick wall sometimes, and if he was ever going to get through to him he'd have to bring as much ammunition to the fight as possible.

CHARLENE VASSER EXAMINED the invitations for the fund-raiser, furious the printers had the gall to misspell her last name.

What kind of impression did that make to her as a client when the worthless printing company delivers invitations to her with the name *Vasar* instead of *Vasser*? God, had they never even *heard* of the hotels?

Frustrated, she lifted the invoice out of the box, fully prepared to call up the company and give them a piece of her mind. She needed to get the invitations out as soon as possible, and now they'd cost her a valuable couple of days because of this pathetic mistake.

Clearly they did not know who they were dealing with, Charlene thought with a haughty sniff, adjusting her reading glasses on her nose as she scanned the invoice for the phone number. She was Mrs. Winston "Win" Vasser III, mother to four of Cyrus Vasser's grandchildren and heirs, and an integral part of the Vasser family empire. Okay, she was technically an *ex*-wife now, but what did that matter? She had married into the Vasser family for a reason and did not intend to let her philandering ex-husband's exploits ruin her long-term goals.

Charlene felt important, affluent, and regal now that she carried the Vasser name. In her youth she'd been nothing more than a mousy girl with boring, forgettable features, stumbling around the East Village longing for a knight or a prince to whisk her away to a better life.

But it had been in that haven of starving artists and drugged out musicians that she met Win Vasser, one of the heirs to the Vasser Hotel fortune and legacy. Initially, she appreciated his whimsical views of the world, along with his hippie idealisms and penchant for experimentation, but what really drew her to him was his name. Once she'd discovered that no knight would ever ride to her rescue, she learned that if she wanted something better, she was going to have to go out and get it. And for Charlene, the best way to get what she wanted—prestige, power, and status—was to marry up and have babies to cement herself in with the family for good.

That was precisely what she did. After giving herself a complete and transformative makeover, she reemerged beautiful and as cunning as any smart woman should be. Then she nabbed her man, and within months was with child.

When she grew frustrated and exhausted with Win's sensitive emotions, impractical dreams and routinely wandering eye, she understood that she unfortunately chose the wrong brother. She should have aimed higher and gone after Marshall. He was the oldest son, ten years Win's senior, and next in line as family patriarch. He'd never married, nor had any kids of his own. But despite divorcing Win and securing herself a comfortable life still ingrained in the family business *just* to keep within eyeshot of Marshall, he never once gave her the time of day.

And oh, how it frustrated her.

But that was neither here nor there, Charlene sighed, pursing her lips and removing her glasses as she stared outside the window of her lushly decorated home office, watching the snow fall in silent flurries. Her meticulously weaved honey blonde hair curled in smooth waves around her face, its short style modern yet sophisticated, and very up and coming with the high society crowd. Her eyes of ice blue were sharp and often times cruel in their assessment of others, though she was rarely wrong about a person's hidden motives or intentions. She learned her skills of reading people while living in the old neighborhood, where, if she didn't want to get shot, mugged, or worse, she had to keep a weather eye out for trouble and thoroughly scan those who surrounded her. And while she no longer lived in that hell hole of a place, but instead in the privileged Upper East Side, she still found her innate talents to be of use. The high society crowd wasn't much different than the people who inhabited the slums; there wasn't a person out there who wouldn't lie, cheat, beg or steal to get what they wanted, and only the strong managed to survive the fray in such conditions.

It was a ruthless world, Charlene mused, her lips curving as she glanced at her reflection in the silver framed mirror that rested on her desk. But she'd survived, and until the day she perished she would see to it that her four children did as well. They were of Vasser blood, after all, and destined for nothing but greatness.

Well, except for one.

Her youngest daughter bounded into the room, excited and peppy, her light chestnut waves of hair bouncing cheerfully.

"Are you going to the hotel today?" Kennedy asked, stopping in front of her mother's desk. She clasped her hands together hopefully.

Charlene turned to her teenage daughter, scanning the girl's eclectic outfit of skintight black leggings, leather cowboy boots the color of raspberries, and an oversized faded and cut up green t-shirt bearing the words *Eat Veggies, Not Friends* in bold blue letters on it.

With a sigh that barely hid her annoyance, Charlene nodded. "Yes, I'm meeting Linc for lunch in about an hour."

"Oh! Can I come? I'm so bored, you have no idea." Kennedy brought her hands up to her mouth in a pleading gesture that, combined with her childish attire, only made Charlene wish to God there was a way she could talk the girl out of acting so much like her damn father. Win used to make that same pleading look to her, time and time again, begging her not to divorce him after she'd uncovered one of his many frivolous affairs.

"It is largely a business lunch, dear," Charlene reasoned dismissively, replacing her glasses and lifting the invoice to eye level. "I don't see how it will be much fun for you."

"Well, I'm part of this family too, aren't I?" Kennedy argued, resting her hands on her hips and attempting to make a stand. "I can handle listening to you guys talk about the hotel. I'm eighteen, mom, not five. Besides, after I'm done at Princeton in four years I'll probably start working at the hotel, too."

"That has yet to be determined," Charlene countered, frowning at the invoice as she started to dial the number on her black desk phone. As it began ringing, she glanced up at her daughter once more, impatience clear in her eyes. "We'll leave in exactly one hour. If you are not downstairs by that time, then I will leave without you. Ah, yes, hello."

Charlene turned away from her daughter, the phone pressed to her ear and her hand restlessly tapping her pen against the desk as she launched into her complaint about the invitations.

Kennedy danced out of the room, too excited to notice her mother's criticisms. As was her way, she chose to ignore whatever momentary feelings of hurt she felt, pleased she got what she wanted.

If she'd learned anything in her eighteen years as a Vasser, it was that life was much easier when lived inside her mind, where nothing and no one could darken her hopes and dreams.

HER FORK SLICED delicately through the sliver of terrine, clicking softly against the white porcelain plate before she brought it up to her lips to sample. She chewed carefully, using all of her senses to evaluate the dish. As expected, the smell, texture, and flavor of the duck paired with marcona almonds was pure perfection.

"Well, Raoul, darling, you have impressed me yet again." Madison Vasser eyed the head chef with a devilish grin as she leaned her hip against the stainless steel counter, tapping her fork lightly against the palm of her hand.

Raoul scowled, as was his way, and brushed off her compliment with little more than a hard eyed glare. "You try the confit so we can be done with this and I can get back to work."

"You are working," Madison reminded him, her lips curving again as she looked back to the elongated plate, which carried three more courses for her to sample. "And while I know it's very difficult for you to come to terms with, I am in fact your employer, and therefore you will do as I say or I will be heartbroken and have to fire you."

Raoul huffed and crossed his burly arms over his chest, though his mouth quirked in a knowing grin when she glanced up and met his eyes. "You don't have the *cojones* to fire me, *cariño*. You love me too much."

"Love is much too strong a word," she chided smoothly, sampling the next course. Her heavy lidded tawny eyes honed in on his jade ones as she chewed, her expression conveying only a mild disinterest. But inside, she was celebrating his culinary skills. Raoul was a master chef and she mentally applauded herself for being the one to discover his talent and personally bring him to the Big Apple.

"Well?" Raoul began, thrusting his hand out in a gesture of impatience. "What is your decision?"

Madison swallowed and pursed her lips, as if giving it serious consideration. After a few more frustrating moments for the chef, she decided to offer him a gem of praise. After all, he did deserve it. "It's lovely, Raoul. Simply divine."

He let out a groan and ran his hands through his striking chin length black hair, his Spanish temper getting the best of him. "I know. Everything I cook for you is divine, is it not? Now try the rest and get out of my hair."

"Don't forget that if it weren't for me you would still be a sous-chef charged with cooking nothing more challenging than chilled lobster bisque in Las Vegas, knowing you were destined for better," Madison quipped, her eyebrows raised in a rare show of good humor at the remark. "You see, darling, we need one another equally."

With a deflated grunt, Raoul nodded, silently acknowledging her point. He was a prideful man nearing forty, with an ego the size of a substantial mountain, but he was the best chef she had ever come across and she knew his insurmountable skills were worth his manic bouts of violent temper characteristic of his Spanish homeland. As much as he may complain and gripe, she knew he respected her just as much as she respected him, and he would remain loyal to her. That, Madison knew, was worth absolutely everything.

As Director of Food and Beverage, she ran the Vasser Hotel's exclusive gourmet French restaurant, *Cherir*, making decisions on new menu choices and handling the details of big events that needed to be catered at the hotel. With a degree from Oxford in hospitality under her belt and a year's training at the best culinary school in Paris, she was more than prepared to take on the position at her family's hotel the moment it was offered to her.

Not that there was any other option. She primed herself for the job specifically and wouldn't accept no for an answer. In her mind this was the best way she could give back to the legacy she and her siblings had inherited.

Madison had none of her parents' looks, but instead looked very much like a female version of her grandfather Cyrus. It was a similarity she held with great pride, as the man was the single most important human being in her life. Cyrus had personally groomed her into the woman she had become. For that, she would be forever grateful to him.

Like Cyrus and her brother Grant, her hair was the color of rich coffee and fell in soft, sable waves just past her shoulders, curling slightly at the tips. Her face was honed at the edges and sculpted, without losing its feminine softness, made compelling by a narrow Anglo-Saxon nose and a full, wide mouth that could both snarl and curve seductively at the drop of a hat. It was a skill she used effortlessly, one that often proved both heartbreaking and disarming.

She had been called ruthless, manipulative, and a cold-hearted bitch more than once in her life. But she'd taken it in stride because as far as she was concerned, maintaining that reputation preserved what she held most dear: herself, and her family.

She cared little about what those outside of her close circle thought of her. The only people that mattered in her life were her family, and those few outsiders she deemed loyal, trustworthy, and worth keeping. Anyone else could rot in Hell for all she cared.

She was about to sample the next dish only to pause mid-motion, her ears honed in on a sound she would have recognized anywhere. Her mother's pristine, bell-like voice, laced with a haughtiness only a woman so hell bent on maintaining false propriety could manage.

Madison shut her eyes for a brief moment, giving herself time to battle back the flash of irritation she felt. Her mother was not the only one in the family who knew the importance of appearances.

"Is she in here? Oh, yes, there you are, Madison." Charlene beamed, her smile seeped in pretense and bravado as she swept into the restaurant's kitchen dressed in a designer frost pink dress suit.

Almost instantly, the smell of Liz Taylor's White Diamonds filled the room. Madison opened her eyes to greet the woman who had given her life, then very little after that.

"Mother. How nice to see you." Madison leaned in to air kiss her mother's cheeks, left and then right, pulling away with a carefully guarded expression. "What brings you to the hotel today?"

Charlene eyed her daughter, who was taller than her by at least three inches, even with both of them in killer sharp heels. She noted the black dress Madison wore, form fitted to every slender and well-sculpted curve. Envy flooded in to settle resentfully in her stomach. "I'm having lunch with Linc, but I wanted to stop by and see if you would like to join us."

Madison glanced over her shoulder to where Raoul was hovering in silence, pretending to be engrossed in re-plating his creations. But she knew him well enough to know he loved a good dramatic moment, and usually when her mother and herself were in a room together there were more than a few cat scratches inflicted.

"Raoul, could you give us a moment?" she asked, keeping her voice level and calm. He gave her a pleading look that abruptly turned to frustration when she didn't waver. Resigned, albeit bitterly, he fled the room, exiting out into the restaurant. Madison watched him go then turned back to her mother. "What are you *really* here for?"

Charlene faked a look of confused hurt, but years of Botox had hampered her ability to show such skilled emotions. "Madison Stella Vasser, why do you always assume I have any motive other than the one I explain to you?"

"Because you do always have an ulterior motive," Madison replied, her lips curving into a dark smile. "Let me guess, you've come to sniff around for the menu you asked me a week ago to prepare for the fundraiser, assuming you would catch me off guard and unprepared."

Charlene pouted, lifting her chin. "Well, if it's ready I would like to see it."

"Of course you would, but you haven't allotted enough time to review the samples that I had Raoul prepare this morning, just on the off chance that you might stop by. Instead, you were hoping I wouldn't be ready and that you could rub my nonexistent unreliability in my face." Madison watched the indignant heat flush her mother's cheeks, and was glad for it. "I know how you love any chance to criticize."

"Ladies," Marshall interrupted as he burst through the stainless steel doors, a cheerful and sunny smile on his face. "I believe it's lunchtime."

Charlene whirled around to face him, her face clear and filled with grace and good humor, though Madison spotted the anxious tick flickering over her mother's left eyelid.

"Marshall, how lovely to see you." Charlene tilted her face up for a cheek kiss. Marshall obliged her, though he maintained a polite distance. "Will you be joining Linc and I for lunch?"

"I'd love to," Marshall beamed, tucking his hands into the pockets of his slacks and winking at Madison, knowing the two women had been up to their usual antics. It was best when stopped prematurely, before too many breakables were thrown. "I'm sure my girl is hungry."

"I am. I hope you don't mind if I join you?"

"Of course not, dear," Charlene preened, avoiding looking her daughter in the eye again. "Let's go find Linc. And maybe we can convince Grant to come down from his cave. That boy could use a good meal."

Marshall chuckled with good humor and placed a hand softly on the small of Charlene's back, leading her out of the kitchen in peacekeeper fashion. As he did so, he shot a knowing look over his shoulder to Madison. She winked at him with a smile as they left the room.

It was all nothing but a game at times, one that had become so normal that none of them even thought twice about it.

"C'MON, JOHN, YOU know your wife loves coming to these things." Linc grinned into the phone while he played with a well-worn metal slinky, his feet propped up on his desk and his tie casually loosened. "It'll make up for all those golf trips you've been taking."

John Berringer, founder and CEO of Berringer Logistics, laughed on the other line, knowing he was caught. Forty years as a loyal Vasser Hotel customer meant he couldn't turn down the invitation to the fundraiser, regardless of how much he hated such events. And the boy was right, his wife would be over the moon delighted to go. Then maybe she'd let him off the hook for forgetting their anniversary the month before. "*You sure know how to play to a man's weaknesses, Linc. You can count me in.*"

"Just looking out for ya, John. Thanks." Pleased, Linc slipped the phone from his shoulder and hung up. He played with the slinky some more as his eyes scanned the list of VIP clients on his computer screen.

Linc glanced up as Walter, his glorified intern slash assistant, walked in looking much too chipper for a guy who was working literally for free.

"Hey man, your mom's here."

Brows furrowed, Linc swung his legs off his desk and sat up, eyes narrowing in on the kid. "Thanks...why the shit-eating grin, Wally?"

Walter froze, his smile faltering as he ran a hand nervously through his hair. "Nothing, man. Just saw your mom and your sister come in and thought I'd let you know they were here."

"Ah." Linc nodded, laughing as he rose to his feet and swung an arm around Walter's shoulders companionably. "Kennedy's here. You know she's my baby sister, right? Ergo, off limits to greasy little college boys like you?"

Walter grinned at Linc and shoved him away playfully. "Hey, she's eighteen."

"And that doesn't make her any less my kid sister." Linc ruffled Walter's already messy cap of russet hair and waltzed from the office, tucking his hands comfortably into the pockets of his designer jeans. Since it was more convenient for him, he kept his office directly behind the front desk of the hotel. Being in charge of customer relations meant, well, being accessible to customers. Linc figured it kept things simpler all around to be closer to the action.

When he swept through the door that opened up to the employee side of the front desk, he spotted Kennedy lounging on one of the lobby sofas, texting away on her cell phone, oblivious to the world around her.

His smile instinctive, he went around the counter and loped toward her. "Hey, stranger."

Kennedy glanced up, her light blue eyes focusing on his as her lips curved into a brilliant smile. "Linc!"

Jumping to her feet, she leapt into his arms as he spun her around once in a big circle before setting her lushly back on the ground.

"I didn't expect to see you for lunch. Or did you just come to torture Walter?"

Kennedy smiled up at him sweetly, adjusting her multicolored patchwork purse on her shoulder. "Walter's nice, I guess."

"Yeah, nice and horny," Linc mused, draping an arm over her shoulders as he spotted his mother, Marshall, and Madison enter the lobby from the restaurant. "Looks like mom's rallied all the troops for lunch today."

Kennedy's face scrunched in annoyance, but she said nothing. She reluctantly released Linc so he could greet their mother with a polite kiss on the cheek.

"Hey, mom." He grinned, staring down into his mother's eyes.

"Hello, dear. I hope you don't mind, but we've got company on our little lunch date."

"Nope. It's rare that all of us get together like this on a whim." He shot a glance to Madison, who smiled at him knowingly before ducking away to answer a call on her cell phone.

Linc lifted his eyes to Marshall, who looked comfortable and good-natured as always. He'd always admired Marshall for his ability to roll with the punches and take things as they were. In fact, he didn't think he'd ever seen his uncle get horribly upset about anything in his entire twenty-seven years of knowing the man.

"If we could just get Grant down here, maybe I'll...oh, good, there he is." Marshall beamed as he spotted Grant emerging from one of the elevators across the lobby, heading for the front desk.

Grant turned when Marshall called out his name and the irritation he felt was momentarily clear on his face. He paused and stared at his family, noting they were all looking to him expectantly. Kennedy was hovering beside Linc, and his mother was standing regally next to Marshall, with Madison off to the side, the rogue. Knowing she would want him to suffer with her through the impromptu family lunch instead of making an excuse and retreating upstairs, he made the decision to join them.

They were his family, after all.

THREE

The minute Quinn Taylor stepped out of the cab and set foot before the grand Vasser Hotel of New York City, she knew she had, quite simply, *arrived.*

Here she was, standing in front of one of the greatest landmarks of glorious Manhattan, taking in the towering forty-floor building complete with glittering windows and Art Deco inspired stone work. All her life she'd heard of the wonders of the luxurious and palatial Vasser Hotel, but never in her wildest dreams did she imagine that she, a small town girl from upstate New York, would be standing there, ready to set foot inside.

Not as a guest, unfortunately. But as an employee, as secretary to one of the Vasser heirs. Her lips quirked into a mile wide grin as she did a self-congratulatory happy dance in her mind, clutching her hands together in delight.

She was here and ready to make her mark. Her ultimate goal of becoming a chef was on the back burner, but her two years of business school and experience in her parents' restaurant had gotten her this job, which was certainly better than nothing. The hotel had three full restaurants, which she could hopefully squeeze her way into once a position opened up.

Things were going to work out for her, she was certain of it. The Vasser Hotel was going to be her ticket to everything she'd ever wanted.

She was a girl with blood that ran almost exclusively Sicilian, with just a dash of Greek that was thrown in somewhere down the line. Because of it, she had a face with high, prominent cheekbones and a strong, squared jaw line that held a wide mouth that was almost constantly moving. Whether she was talking, smiling, laughing, chewing nervously on her bottom lip, or just pouting for lack of something better to do, her mouth was rarely if ever not in motion. Some people considered it a shortcoming, but she preferred to think of it as a gift. What was wrong with a kind word and a cheerful smile now and again?

She was gifted with her grandmother's gypsy eyes of rich hazel, wide and tilted slightly up at the corners, with generous lashes she found no need to use mascara on. Not that she wore much make up anyway—she preferred a natural look without any illusions.

Her hair was rich black and full, falling in spiral curls to just below her chin. Since she, years earlier, discovered it was more trouble than it was worth to straighten her curls, she gave up and wore them natural too.

She was shorter than most, barely rising above five foot three, and the love of food that came with the Sicilian blood gave her a body that would never be super model thin. But her Pilates obsession kept her in shape and healthy, so she felt it would be an insult to God to ask for anything more than that.

And as a born and bred Catholic, insulting God was, as it should be, a sin her mother would flay her alive over.

With an anxious glance at the practical black watch on her left wrist, Quinn noted that she was fifteen minutes early for her first shift. She'd always been notoriously punctual, but she was also impatient. Which meant there was no possible way she could stand around outside gawking at the building any longer. She had to go inside.

Clutching her purse tight enough to make her knuckles white, she made her way to the oversized sparkling glass doors framed in gold, delighted when the onsite doorman greeted her cordially. She paused before him, eyeing his nametag so she would remember his name for next time.

"Good morning, Barry. I'm Quinn." She held out her hand, pleased when he smiled warmly at her.

"Delighted to meet you, Miss Quinn," Barry replied, accepting the handshake. He was a small statured, aged man with dark, weathered skin, warm chocolate eyes and a million watt smile.

"I'm the new secretary," she informed him as he released her hand. "Hopefully if things go well we'll be seeing each other every day."

"I look forward to it. Who're you workin' for?"

"Mr. Vasser," Quinn answered with a proud grin.

"Ah, but which one?" Barry winked. "There are three Mr. Vassers in our New York Hotel."

"Oh." Quinn faltered, biting her lip as she tried to think back. "Well, Marshall Vasser was the one who interviewed me, but I'm not working for him...shoot, I can't remember the guy's name, but he's Marshall's nephew."

Barry laughed. "There are two nephews, Miss Quinn."

"Well, damn." She laughed at herself, then checked her watch again. "I guess I should go find out which nephew it is I work for. It was a pleasure to meet you, Barry."

"The same, Miss Quinn." Barry opened the door for her, and as she walked into the hotel her eyes shot immediately to the tall and expansive ceiling. It was an explosion of intricate coffering and glittering lights, painted in muted golds and pale blues. She thought it was like looking up into Heaven itself, complete with a colossal chandelier that must have cost more than her parents' quaint suburban home, all sparkling crystal and glorious white light.

She'd only been in the lobby the one time before when she had her interview, but despite having seen it then she was still in awe.

The center of the lobby was adorned with plush armchairs and sofas made of gleaming mahogany and rich, buttery leather with royal blue throw pillows. The style was sophisticated and a bit modern, without losing the comfort of traditional and the warmth of antique. Enormous oriental rugs in similar blues and golds layered over the polished travertine floor, giving a homely feel to the area without being impractical.

Against the far wall were mahogany paneled elevators, beyond them what looked like gift shops and another waiting area. To her immediate right and left were the hotel's premier restaurants and bars: on the left, the French inspired five star *Cherir*, and on the right the bluesy New Orleans themed *The Mystic*, a classic Japanese infused sushi joint *Kazoku*, and lastly the hotel's exclusive high end, Paris themed bar, *Amoureux*.

She was positive she wouldn't fit in with the famously chic and sophisticated crowd that frequented *that* place, but maybe one day. Probably far off, she mused, but one day she would be good enough to sit in that damn bar. God help her.

Also off to the left was the front desk, complete with a gleaming mahogany base, travertine counter, and heavenly smelling blue hydrangeas paired with white and green ivy pouring out of slender copper vases. Hanging on the wall behind the front desk was an oversized mural of the New York City skyline at night, with the Vasser Hotel logo in scripted letters that hung an inch or so out from the wall, backlit with a wash of golden light.

Feeling more than a little overwhelmed, Quinn made her way toward the front desk, her eyes on the young man with russet hair and skinny features standing there looking busy. The black polo shirt he wore bore a gold Vasser Hotel emblem.

"Hi," Quinn greeted, startling him as she leaned against the counter.

"Hello," Walter answered, snapping out of his reverie and managing a small smile in return. "How can I help you?"

"Today's my first day. I'm Quinn Taylor." She held out her hand to shake his, and he seemed a bit flustered as he accepted the handshake.

"Oh, okay. Um, what is it you do?"

"I'm Mr. Vasser's new secretary."

"Which one?"

"Honestly, I don't remember." She laughed at herself again, and managed to get a laugh out of him as well.

"Oh man, okay. Wait here." He disappeared into the offices behind him, leaving her alone. She tried to not be embarrassed, and hoped she wasn't going to end up being technically late to her desk, wherever it was, because she didn't know *which* Mr. Vasser she worked for. In fact, had Marshall even mentioned the name of the guy she was working for now? Surely she would have remembered, as her mind was usually a steel trap for things like names.

Just then, Walter reappeared from the offices with another man, who looked at her with a quick grin and cheerful blue eyes set in a roguishly handsome face. He eyed her thoughtfully for a moment, then ran a hand through his waves of chestnut hair and turned to Walter.

"You've been replaced, Walter. She's much prettier than you," Linc joked, causing Walter to look horribly offended.

"No way you're replacing me. I'm awesome and you know it."

"Yeah, but I think you can agree with me when I say I'd rather look at her every day than your greasy mug."

Walter frowned as he looked over at Quinn, whose dark eyebrows raised in amusement. "But I work for free. I assume *she* wants to get paid."

"That's because *she* is what we call an employee. You, on the other hand, are my bitch. Besides, you get something much more valuable than money from me. You get my knowledge and guidance, which, let me tell you, is priceless."

"Boys?" Quinn interjected, waving so they would both look at her. "While I find this all very flattering, I am in fact already employed to work for Mr. Vasser. So if neither of you are him, then please tell me where to find him so I can get started. It's nearly nine o'clock and I *really* don't want to be late for my first day."

Linc flashed her another quick grin, then leaned over the counter with his hand outstretched. "As a matter of fact, I *am* Mr. Vasser. But you can call me Linc."

"Oh." Quinn stared at his hand for a moment, then reached out to shake it, a bit unsure. "You're Marshall's nephew?"

"I am."

"So I *am* replacing him?" She pointed to Walter, who just shrugged.

"Nope." Linc grinned again and winked at her playfully. "Unfortunately, I am not the Mr. Vasser you seek. You're gonna be working for my brother, Grant. He's upstairs."

"So you're nephew number one, got it." She smiled as her eyes shot to the elevators. "Which floor is nephew number two on?"

"I'll take you," Linc offered, already skirting around the front desk to meet up with her. "Despite what everyone says, chivalry is in fact not dead."

Quinn snorted out a laugh, rolling her eyes as he came up beside her. He was less than a foot taller than her, athletically built and quite handsome. But she knew his type. Men like him could be slick as eels and just as dangerous. He was the kind of guy a girl could fall head over heels for in an instant, and then find herself left in his dust as he galloped off to greener pastures.

Or maybe he was just a really nice guy and she was reading him all wrong.

"Alright, but only because I like company, even on short elevator rides." She let him lead the way to the elevators, noting he wore jeans instead of slacks. She wondered briefly if she'd overdressed in her silk plum colored blouse and black dress pants as he punched a button beside one of the elevators and it slid quietly open.

"So does your whole family work here at the hotel?" Quinn asked as he held the doors for her.

He laughed as he followed her in, pushing the button for the second floor. "That would be insane if they did. There's over sixty people in my family."

Quinn gaped at him. "And here I thought I was the one with the obnoxiously large family. How do you remember who's who? I have a photo album I made up with names scribbled on it that I review before reunions and holidays. The only problem is when the young ones get bigger and no longer look like children, then you have me mistaking my cousin Tony for the pizza delivery guy."

Linc eyed her dubiously as the elevator began to rise. "I bet you a million bucks Grant has a photo album with names written in it too, it sounds just like him. Me, I prefer to wing it at reunions and let my sister fill me in on who's who if I forget. What else are sisters good for?"

"Brothers are so helpless. I have four of them myself," Quinn sighed, feeling a dull tinge of homesickness at the thought. Pushing it aside, she fixed a smile back on her face. "So, your brother is an organization freak?"

"Let's just say he's very...serious," Linc mused, content to leave it at that. She'd find out for herself, anyway. He would let her be the full judge of Grant's character, without his influence. "But to answer your earlier question, there's only four of us working at this hotel, and a large chunk of the others work at the other Vasser Hotels across the US and in Europe."

"So it's you, your brother, your uncle...and who else?"

"My sister, Madison. You'll meet her eventually. Oh, and my mom drops by a lot, so you'll probably meet her too." The elevator chimed as it came to a stop, the doors sweeping open at the second floor. "Right this way."

Quinn followed him out into a generously sized waiting area, complete with large windows with partial views of Central Park and similar furniture to what was in the lobby. Off to the right was a hallway that led to what looked like conference rooms, and to the left was another hallway, with two open front office rooms with glass partitions facing the waiting area. Linc led her to the one that was ahead on the right, which boasted a mahogany desk with matching file cabinets behind it, along with a plush royal blue bench to the side and some kind of leafy green potted plant in the corner.

"This is your desk, and Grant's office is right through that door." Linc pointed at the closed door to the left of her desk, which had an embossed gold plaque naming it as the office of *Grant W. Vasser, General Manager.*

"Is he here yet?" She asked, chewing her bottom lip nervously.

"He's been here since six this morning."

Her eyebrows raised. "Is that normal?"

"When you're Grant Vasser, it is." Linc shrugged as he faced her directly. "You should join me for a drink later. If you've never been, *Amoureux* serves a mean martini. I could give you the lowdown on all of your new coworkers, who to avoid and who to suck up to. Let you in on some juicy Vasser family secrets over dessert, then amuse you over another drink with childhood tales of me escaping my driver and wreaking havoc on the poor, unsuspecting citizens of New York."

A charming grin brightened his face. "Did I mention you look stunning in that blouse?"

Quinn blinked, realizing he'd just, as smooth as butter, asked her out after having known her only five minutes. It took all the control she had not to laugh hysterically at him.

"You're a shameless flirt, Linc Vasser."

He chuckled, keeping the mood light and casual. "I am when I want to be."

Despite the obvious come-on, she still found his charm appealing. Maybe it was because she tended to be a straightforward, shoot-from-the-hip kind of person herself, and seeing the same in him made her feel more comfortable than annoyed. "I think the two of us will work better as friends."

"Suit yourself." He smiled to show there were no hard feelings, and she felt she liked him more for it. "Anyway, I'll let him know you're here."

He left her standing just inside the office alcove as he opened his brother's door without even knocking, poking his head in. "Hey buddy, your new secretary's here."

Then he swung back out of the room and patted Quinn on the shoulder, his eyes meeting hers pointedly. "Don't let him dampen that smile of yours, Quinn. It's too pretty to waste."

That same smile faltered as he swept past her and jogged toward an open elevator that a maid had just entered. He waved to Quinn with a grin as the doors began to close, and she attempted one back in return. Then he was gone.

Unsettled by his comment, she turned around and with a jolt spotted a much different man standing before her.

He was taller than Linc and a bit leaner in his trim, professional looking black suit and crisp, no nonsense gray diamond tie. His features resembled Linc's in that they were sharp and European, with dark brows and defined cheekbones, but the similarity ended there. His hair was a darker brown and a bit shorter, in a cut that was both trim and professional. Where Linc's eyes were a warm, cheery blue, this man's were a rich, dark amber, and were honed in on her in quiet assessment. His face was slightly longer than his brother's, with a faintly dimpled chin and firm mouth that, from the faint frown lines on his face, rarely if ever smiled.

Serious. Yes, she could see now why Linc chose that particular adjective to describe his brother. In fact, she bet if she looked up the dictionary definition of the word, there would be a small picture of him right beside it. Go figure.

"Hi, I'm Quinn." She smiled warmly, reaching out to shake hands with him, praying to God her palm wasn't sweaty from nerves. For some reason she had a feeling he wouldn't like that.

He accepted her hand briefly, firmly, then released it. "Right. What's your last name?"

"Taylor. Quinn Taylor." She nodded, though she had no idea why. He was already making her nervous. She was usually such a people person, but there was something different about him, something she couldn't put her finger on. All she knew for certain was that being in his presence was incredibly disarming.

"Alright. This is where you'll report to every morning at nine o'clock. I'm in the office at six, so if you're late I'll notice." He faced the desk, grabbing a stack of papers that were sitting there. "I need you to...please tell me you know how to use a computer and transfer calls? If you don't then there's no point in continuing this conversation."

Surprise hit her first before her temper did, her cheeks flushing with it. "What century do you think this is? Of course I do."

The vaguely irritated look on his face had her cursing silently and shoving her foot in her mouth. "I'm sorry, that was rude. Yes, I ran the office at my parents' restaurant. I know how to do everything."

He handed her the paperwork. "Good. I need you to mark these invoices as paid in the computer. Then, if you open the Word document marked 'daily' on the desktop, you'll find a list of things for you to do on top of answering and transferring calls to me. If you have any important questions, I'll be in my office."

He started for his office door, but before he could disappear inside she called out to him.

"Your brother said your name was Grant, but I need to know what I should call you."

He looked back at her, mildly annoyed. "Mr. Vasser."

He shut himself inside his office, leaving her standing in limbo wondering what the hell just happened.

That had to have been the briefest, least interactive and least exciting introduction she'd ever been a part of. It was like he was so pressed for time that he didn't feel giving her even five minutes was worth the trouble. Never in her life had she met someone so eager to end a conversation before it even began.

Releasing a long breath, she rounded her new desk and stored her purse beneath it, trying not to judge him too harshly. Maybe today was just an off day for him and he really was busy. It was only fair of her to give him the benefit of the doubt, even if Linc's words kept sneaking back in to trouble her.

As she took a seat in her new desk chair, she glanced around at the little space, with its neutral beige paint, small pastoral paintings, and two glass walls with an open doorway that gave a view of the waiting area. It was nice, as far as offices went. And it was quiet as a tomb.

Across the hall was the other glass walled office alcove just like hers, but whoever usually sat there wasn't in. With a quiet sigh, she turned to the sleek desktop computer before her and logged on, hunting for that Word document he'd mentioned.

God help her, she was going to do well here. She had to, really. She'd run out of options and needed to cement a good relationship with Mr. Vasser if she ever hoped to be transferred into the Food and Beverage department of the hotel. Her future was riding on her working relationship with this one man, who already didn't like her.

She'd just have to change that. With a little bit of charm, a warm smile, and a proven work ethic, surely he would come around in time and see how valuable she was. Yes, it had to work, even with him. She needed to believe that.

When it was time to leave for the day, Quinn packed up her things and shut down her computer, stretching her arms behind her head with a soft groan. She'd completed her entire list of duties, fielded a few phone calls, and enjoyed another brief visit from Linc when he came by at lunchtime to check on her. All in all, it had been a pretty good first day.

But what struck her as extremely odd was that her new boss had not left his office once during the day, nor had he even gone out for lunch. He had a few visitors for meetings, including Marshall and the hotel's accountant, Roger, but he never left the room.

And he was still in there, even though it was six o'clock in the evening. That's twelve long hours, she thought dully as she slipped into her coat. The man was clearly the definition of a workaholic. Might as well put his face next to that word in the dictionary, too.

Figuring she should at least let him know she was leaving, she gathered up her purse and walked up to his door, her hand raised to knock. She paused and eyed the gold plaque curiously, an odd feeling coursing through her as she read his name. It was a strange kind of uneasiness, but not altogether uncomfortable. More of a curiosity, a natural intrigue, to learn more. Just what was it like to be him? To be an heir to this great empire?

She knocked politely, then pushed open the door when she heard him call her in. She poked her head in and spotted him seated at his desk, immersed in a pile of paperwork with a cup of coffee at his side.

When he didn't glance up at her, she cleared her throat and spoke anyway, her eyes quickly taking in the décor of his office while he wasn't looking. Traditional and masculine, with modern touches. What an interesting, yet complex, mix.

"I just wanted to let you know that I'm leaving for the day," Quinn said, admiring the photographs cluttering his walls. Family man, through and through, she thought with an approving smile. Interesting...

When he spoke, her eyes jolted back to him, though he had yet to look up from his work. "Thank you, Miss Taylor. See you tomorrow."

"See you tomorrow." She watched him for a brief moment, wondering how he could work such long hours and still be sane. Deciding it wasn't for her to understand, she bowed out of the office and quietly shut the door behind her.

Grant looked up the moment the door clicked shut, his eyes struggling to focus. He'd been staring at the contract for the new swimming pool for the last hour and must have lost track of time. He probably should have at least looked at her when he said goodbye, he realized, scowling to himself. She must think him incredibly rude.

What did that matter, though? he argued with himself. He wasn't there to be her friend, but her boss. And he hadn't been *technically* impolite to her. Or had he? Sometimes it was hard to tell when his brusque nature offended others. Then again, if she couldn't handle it then she had no business working for him. He was the way he was, and it suited him just fine. Even if the weight he put on himself was starting to wear him down.

Sometimes it seemed as though the hours and the days just blurred together. He'd been pushing himself too hard for too long, and it was starting to take its toll. Seeking relief, he reached for his coffee mug and took a generous sip, hoping it would kick in. He still had so much to do...

And on top of all of it was this new secretary. Miss Quinn Taylor. Or was it Mrs? He hadn't bothered to even ask her, he'd just assumed.

Good job, Grant, he grunted as he rubbed his face with his hands, feeling foolish. He'd barely spoken twenty words to her before trumping off into his office to be a hermit for the day. Not that it was unusual, he reminded himself. He just wasn't much of a people person, preferring being alone to mindless chatter. Who needed small talk when there were more important things to do?

But she certainly didn't deserve his callousness. She seemed polite enough, and, thank God, a quick learner without the need for his constant attention.

He knew he should try and be more cordial with her, despite how hard it was for him to adjust to meeting new people, much less working with them. What was the worst that could happen, anyway? He'd liked his last secretary well enough, so there was no reason not to try and have a good relationship with this one.

Though something about her had caught him the second she'd turned around, her face lit with that smile of hers. It was like being caught in headlights, blinded by a brilliance that seemed oddly natural and comforting. If he was rude, it was only because he was flustered and disarmed by her. How else could he explain it, except that she wasn't at all what he'd expected?

And to top it all off, it was Linc who made her smile that way, while all he was able to do was insult her in more ways than one. If it hadn't been so typical, he might have been troubled by it. But he knew who he was, knew who his brother was. Linc possessed all of the charm, humor and empathy that Grant had never been able to tap into. It was no wonder she would smile for Linc—everyone did.

Forcing the thoughts from his mind, he dove back into the paperwork, knowing that if he didn't do it, it wouldn't get done. Maybe he wasn't very charming or funny, but he *was* motivated, determined, and diligent, and work had and always would be the most important thing in his life. Maybe he would die alone, but at least he would have risen to the top of the pile and accomplished greatness.

A couple of hours later, he finalized the last of it and glanced down at his watch. Eight o'clock, on the nose.

With a quiet sigh, he turned in his chair to face the windows of his office, his eyes trailing to the city lights of the buildings around him. He could hear the faint noise of traffic from the street below and the distant howl of sirens, sounds that brought him more comfort than distress. He'd been raised in the city, born and bred a New Yorker. Some said the city life made him tough, but he figured he would be the same regardless of where he lived. The city was not what defined him. His own ambition, strength and fortitude were.

And his luxurious and unfortunately overpriced town house on the Upper East side could hardly be deemed "tough." It was a good investment and a decent place to live, at least when he found himself there. It seemed better suited to call the hotel his home versus the town house, given the percentage of his time spent at work. Even his scruffy gray dog Miles seemed to barely recognize him anymore, and he rarely saw his maid Frieda when she came by to clean up what little mess he made.

Despite the long hours, despite the near constant infighting with his family and the stress that came with being the oldest son, Grant wouldn't have traded his life for the world. This was what he was meant to do, and he was exactly where he was supposed to be.

That had to stand for something, right?

Shutting down his computer, he rose to his feet and grabbed his briefcase, downing his coffee in a last ditch effort to wake up. He shrugged into his winter coat and rinsed the mug out in the tiny sink in the kitchenette he kept in the office before heading to the door.

Prior to shutting off the lights and leaving the room, he found himself staring at the portraits of his family. With a frown, he wondered why, despite having all of them there with him, he still sometimes felt so cut-off and alone.

Perhaps that was what they meant when they said the crown weighs heavy on the head of the king.

MADISON TILTED BACK the long stemmed martini glass, sipping at the vodka and reveling in the welcome frost of it as she sat comfortably at the bar in *Cherir*. It wasn't often that she indulged in the treat of alcohol, but after the day she'd had it was more than warranted.

Raoul had been in one of his foul moods and threw a few pots and pans, alarming some of their customers and causing one of her best souschefs to quit on the spot. It took all of her control and willpower to calm Raoul down and not toss him out for being a pompous jackass. He'd apologized afterwards, as he always did, swallowing the pride that filled that big head of his. But the last thing she needed was upset customers running off to tell their friends about the wild and crazy head chef at the Vasser Hotel's premier restaurant, a fact which she reminded him of as clearly and bluntly as she could. Then she ordered him to find some way to get the souschef back so that she didn't have to go through the trouble of hiring another one, a task he was naturally reluctant to do, but did anyway. It was loyalty that kept him coming back to her. And it was the same loyalty that kept her from firing him every time he went into a tantrum.

Then, after all that, her mother came in to finally sample the dishes prepared for the fundraiser, and had nothing but petty criticisms about each one. The seared tuna was too peppery, the jasmine rice paired with it too bland. The chilled blueberry soup was too purple, and the orange rind garnish excessive. The lemon garlic sauce on the chicken was too soupy and looked cheap, and the accompanying toast points too dry.

Shaking her head, Madison took a long sip of her drink and rubbed her temple, wishing her mother would just leave her uninformed critiques of food at home. Just because the woman had eaten fine dining for the last thirty years did not make her an expert on how it was made or what was *cheap* looking. As if the finest grain fed, organic chicken perfectly sautéed in fresh lemons and garlic was below par. The woman was a menace, who had no idea when she was being obnoxiously conceited.

Then after the inevitable argument over the food, her mother finally threw up her hands and gave in, as usual, and approved the dishes as they were. There was only so much her overly critical nature could get her, and being a snob about excellently prepared food was not one of those things.

With an exhausted sigh, Madison took another sip and glanced over her shoulder toward the entrance of the restaurant, where she could see the hotel's lobby. She spotted Grant emerging from one of the elevators, briefcase in hand and long frame covered loosely by a charcoal grey winter coat. She watched him drop off something at the front desk before heading toward the lobby doors.

Slipping from her seat, she walked swiftly out to catch him, her heels crackling like gunfire against the travertine floor. Perhaps it was the sound of it that had him turning around to face her, his lips curving into a kind smile, one he reserved for so few people.

"You're here late," he commented, noting the soft glow of warmth the drink gave her features, and the faint traces of fatigue under her eyes.

She reached up to adjust his tie and button his coat, her tawny eyes on his. "It was a long, exhausting day, filled with the usual Raoul drama."

"I don't know why you put up with that chef of yours, Mads. He seems to cause more harm than good." Grant watched her closely, sensing the weight on his sister's shoulders. They'd always been close, more so with each other than with anyone else in the family.

"I can handle Raoul, even if the kitchen staff is intimidated by him." She tilted her head back with a soft laugh. "I had another one try and quit today, in fact."

"If I didn't think you could take care of this on your own, I would offer to talk with him."

"Thank you." She rose on her toes to kiss his cheek, fussing again with his coat. "So how is your new secretary? Do you need me to fill her in on how things are done around here?"

"No, so far she's doing alright."

"Is she attractive?"

"No, not at all," he murmured, distracted as he thought of his former secretary, Tara, and the strange guilt he suddenly realized he'd been dealing with the last few days without even knowing it. It was there, nagging just behind his focus on work, just out of reach until his sister's words brought it to the forefront.

Madison picked up on the feeling immediately, knowing him as well as she did. She reached up to touch his face, forcing him to look at her. "You're sorry to see the other girl go?"

"No...well, yes. But in a way I'm relieved." Grant let out a huff of breath, the memories he'd fought so hard to battle back resurfacing to slice little cuts in his resolve, aching points of pain that were pathetic shadows of what had once been in his heart.

"Because she reminded you of Erin." Madison said softly, seeing the truth in his eyes. "It was a long time ago, darling."

"I know," Grant assured her, nodding as he squeezed her shoulder. "I'll see you tomorrow."

She stared after him as he strode out of the lobby where his town car was waiting. The driver hopped out to open the car door, and Grant slid inside and out of sight, taking his haunted memories with him.

FOUR

Ma, don't be stupid." Quinn grinned, the phone tucked against her ear as she sat comfortably in her bathtub, surrounded by frothy bubbles with a full glass of red wine in her free hand. "It's going to take longer than a month for me to get a job as a chef."

"I don't see why you're selling yourself short, working as a secretary. Imagine, all that talent wasted on a job I could do, and I'm not even half as smart as you."

"That's how it works in a bad economy, Ma, sorry." Quinn sipped some wine and laughed when she heard her sister Callie shout something about sleeping with the boss to get ahead.

Her mother chided her in a sharp, thick Sicilian tone. It only got that way when she was stressed, excited, or upset, and the sound of it was like music to Quinn's ears. It'd only been a month or so since she'd left home, but she was already homesick. That was the reason she found herself, nearly every night, chatting away for hours on the phone with her family. They were everything to her and she couldn't imagine a world without all of them in it, as loud and obnoxiously Sicilian as they were.

"Tell Callie that I'm not going to sell my body and my morals just to get a job." Quinn chuckled, wishing to God she could see her mother's look of horror at the idea. In fact, she was probably crossing herself at that very moment. "Maybe she should take her own advice and sleep with old Mr. Taggart so he'll make her manager at the drug store."

Her mother couldn't help but laugh at that one, and relayed the message to Callie and to Quinn's other siblings, four brothers and two sisters, all of whom made audible groans of disgust and horror.

"*Sophie wants to know if this Mr. Vasser is handsome.*"

Quinn thought about it for a moment, pursing her lips and trying to picture his face in her mind again. The wine made her memory a little fuzzy, and definitely made her tongue a little looser than it normally would have been. "I don't think he'd be a very good lay with that stick he has up his ass."

"*Quinn!*" Her siblings heard her comment and were busting up laughing in the background. She imagined her youngest brothers were probably storing that little tidbit to use at school the next day, but she was in too good a mood to worry about them.

"I'm sorry, Ma, that was crude. But still funny." She laughed again and sipped some more wine, enjoying herself. "But to answer her question, he's alright. Not really good looking or bad looking, just...alright. His brother is pretty cute though. He asked me out on a date."

"*A Vasser, of the disgustingly rich Vasser family, asked you out on a date and you waited until now to tell us?*" her mother cried, equally as insulted as she was excited.

"I didn't tell you because I turned him down. He's a nice enough guy, a bit slick. But good friend material, which is where I intend to keep him."

"*I don't care if he's slick, he's rich!*"

"And not my type." Quinn pressed, though she knew her mother respected her judgment enough to be content with that. Her sisters, on the other hand, might just beat her over the head with a frying pan the next time she came into town. "I don't want to ruin this. This job is all I have here in New York, and I need to keep my goal in sight if I'm going to accomplish it. No funny business with the co-workers."

"*Saints be with us, Quinn, you're more moral than I am sometimes.*" Her mother sighed, though there was clear pride in her voice. "*Here, your father wants to speak to you. Love you.*"

"Love you too, Ma." Quinn smiled, her heart aching as she heard the phone shifted and jostled over to where her father, most likely at that very moment, was resting comfortably in his favorite recliner, well worn and filled with the scent of Old Spice, flour and marinara sauce. She suddenly wished for the times long ago when she would curl up in his lap on that very chair and listen to him tell her stories of the old country, where he'd spent the first few years of his life. It was magic to her, the sound of his voice, and the love she felt for him knew no bounds.

Talking to him now, hearing the pride in his voice as he congratulated her on her new job, reminded her of how important it was for her to be successful. Her parents worked endless hours at their restaurant, night and day, in order to provide a better life for her and her siblings. They all owed it to them to make something of themselves, and as the oldest, she figured she better set the example. Even if, at twenty-six, she was getting somewhat of a late start. But better late than never. It had taken years to save up the money to go to school, and working full time while doing so had set her behind. But she was going to reach her goals now.

Damnit, she was going to make her family proud.

Later, when she'd hung up the phone and nestled deeper into the tub, its water gone lukewarm and her wine nearly empty, Quinn let her thoughts drift back to her new job and the family she was now working for.

Was the Vasser family as tight knit as her own? Did her new boss call his mother and father on the phone simply to discuss the day, or the weather, or any range of nonsense she found herself talking with her parents about? And were his parents proud of him, for all the effort he put into the legacy he'd inherited? Did they tell him as much?

For his sake, she sincerely hoped they did.

WHEN GRANT OPENED the email from his mother, he grimaced. Here it was, just after six o'clock in the morning, and already she was asking for money.

It was so typical that he wondered why he was even partly surprised. The woman was the only other person alive that seemed to be up and about as early as he was every morning, and money seemed to be the only reason she or anyone else in his family ever came to him anymore.

While he knew that wasn't *exactly* true, it still felt good to write it off that way and be deservedly crabby about it. He was only human, after all, and allowed to be grouchy when he wanted to be.

Clicking on the email to reply, he began typing out an explanation on why his mother's fundraiser did not deserve an inordinate amount of his time, effort, and money, and that it was her project and maybe she should consider getting the funds to pay the caterers, florist, band, etcetera from her personal accounts. Money was dumped every month into her account from the divorce, so why in God's name she couldn't use *that* cash...

He stopped mid-sentence, already feeling bad and a little bit guilty. Despite how irritating and self-important she could be sometimes, she was still his mother, and he certainly didn't have a reason to be so crass with her. It wasn't like she was asking for money to go buy a new diamond necklace or something ridiculous. She just wanted some cash to put toward the basics needed for the fundraiser, which was being hosted by the Vasser Hotel. As manager, perhaps it *was* his responsibility to see that some funds were thrown at the event despite how little he cared about it. Not to mention the fundraiser was for his mother's breast cancer charity, a disease both of his grandmothers had died from.

Damnit, he really was being an asshole.

With a frustrated grunt, he hit the backspace button and erased what he'd typed, replacing it with: *You have a budget of $20k. No more than that.*

Content with his more than reasonable figure, Grant sent off the email and sat back in his chair, rubbing his face in his hands.

Coffee. He needed coffee the way a dying man needs salvation.

Getting to his feet, he stalked over to the Keurig coffee maker he kept on the counter of the kitchenette, punching the button to get the water hot as he opened the lid and dropped in a new coffee filter cup. Without even glancing at what flavor he was brewing, he shut the lid and grabbed a mug, setting it below the dispenser and pressing the brew button.

Hot coffee poured out in a tedious dribble. He stared at it as he waited, tapping his foot impatiently. It was still faster than brewing a whole pot of coffee, but, damnit, he really didn't like waiting for things. He wasn't necessarily an impatient man, but lately a whole host of normal things had been trying his patience.

It was stress that caused it, he knew that much. He was overworked, running on fumes, more irritable and bitter than normal. And that was saying something, as his usual personality ran on the irritable and bitter side more often than not.

When the coffee finally finished, he yanked out the mug and drank it straight up, ignoring the heat and urging the caffeine to do its job. The day was just starting and he had work to do.

He settled into his office chair and jumped in headfirst.

A few hours passed and he found himself in the same spot he'd been in all morning, but fortunately he'd accomplished quite a bit already. That joyful fact put him in a much better mood, and the energy he'd procured from the coffee was in full swing.

He shot a glance out the window, allowing himself a moment's break, and admired the sunlight that glittered off the buildings and the snow covered streets below.

There really was nothing like winter in New York. It was cold, mean, and at times deadly. But there was something to be said about the way the morning sun hit freshly fallen snow, exploding out in a flash of diamond-like brilliance. The first time he'd seen it, really seen it, it had taken his breath away.

A brisk knock on his office door jolted him from his thoughts, self-conscious to have even thought them.

"Come in," he called out, lifting his coffee mug up to his lips to mask his embarrassment. He'd brewed a second fresh cup only minutes before and the scent of it still hung heavy in the air.

The door opened and Quinn peered in, looking bright and cheerful, her smile warm as a sunbeam.

"Good morning," she greeted, stepping just inside the door so he caught a glimpse of the belted snow-white sweater dress she wore over gray slacks.

He blinked, for a moment caught off guard by thoughts of morning sun and snow, and the woman standing before him. Clearing his throat, he tried what he hoped resembled a smile.

"Good morning."

"I just wanted to let you know that I'm here and ask if you need anything." She grinned again, but this time her eyes sharpened and she sniffed at the air, glancing around his office until she found the source of the smell. "Oh. That coffee smells delicious! I just love the smell of hazelnut and cinnamon in the morning. Don't you?"

Grant stared down into his coffee mug, frowning. "I suppose..."

Quinn came into the room, placing her hands on her hips as she did so. "I mean, I guess it's my sweet tooth talking, but I love a rich cup of hot caramel or vanilla or chocolate flavored espresso in the morning. If I'm being honest, I'm kind of a coffee snob, but maybe that's just because I have an appreciation for any and all things food related. It comes from being Sicilian, I guess."

Grant looked up at her in dull bewilderment. He knew he should be annoyed, but instead was stunned by how swiftly she'd come in and steamrolled him with small talk in his own office. Unsure what else to do, he held up his mug. "Do you want some?"

"Oh, no, thanks." Quinn smiled. "I don't know if you can tell, but I've had plenty of caffeine for the day."

"I had no idea," he replied dryly. He recovered from his initial reaction and set his mug down, shuffling through some of the papers on his desk. He unearthed the one he was looking for and held it out to her. "I need you to send my cousin Sophie a bouquet of flowers. It's her birthday. The address to send it to is on that sheet, along with a list of her favorite flowers. Just have the florist in Paris make up an arrangement of whatever is available of those."

"Paris?" Quinn read the address on the sheet of paper, taken aback.

"They speak perfect English, so there shouldn't be any problems."

"Great, okay." She smiled again, nodding at him. "You can count on me."

"Good." Grant turned back to his computer in a dismissive gesture.

Quinn cast her eyes down and started to leave the room before a sudden thought occurred to her. It was a gamble, but she had to start somewhere. She faced him again, hoping she wasn't about to overstep any bounds. "I noticed yesterday that you didn't get anything to eat for lunch. I'm sure you probably bring food or whatever, but just so you know I have plenty of fresh penne pasta with my homemade vodka sauce. So if you want any, let me know."

He shot her a disconcerted look, unsure how to respond. She was offering him lunch?

"I have something to eat." His voice was colder than he meant it to be, which he realized when he noticed the brief look of disappointment in her eyes. He just found it strange to offer food to someone who was essentially a stranger. Not to mention she was oblivious to his usual "leave me alone" signals. She just kept talking when all he wanted to do was get back to being alone.

"Okay, well, I'll save some in case you change your mind." Quinn nodded as she left the office and shut the door, feeling more than a little stupid. Well, it hadn't hurt to ask, she reminded herself as she took a seat at her desk, thrumming her fingers on its surface as she stared at the paper he'd given her. If she was eventually going to get a job as a chef at the hotel, she had to get the word out that she could cook. Being the general manager and within such close proximity, he was the best candidate. But it appeared all she'd done was make him a little uncomfortable and maybe even annoyed, which either meant he just really didn't like talking to people or he really didn't like talking to *her*. She considered that for a moment, sincerely hoping it wasn't the latter.

She'd never run across someone who truly disliked her before. But, then again, there was a first time for everything.

IT WAS LUNCHTIME when he got the phone call from the hotel's lawyer, Sam Rubenstein, requesting an impromptu meeting to discuss his father's request for an increase in his monthly allowance. Normally Grant would handle it over the phone, but apparently there were critical documents he needed to see in person that could influence his decision. He was tempted to let Marshall handle it, but Grant knew his uncle had a soft side that could be played if the right words were spoken or the right tale weaved.

Grant had no such soft side, especially not in regards to his good-for-nothing father. Which meant he would be seeing to this particular issue himself.

When he rose to his feet to get his coat and scarf, his stomach grumbled and he frowned down at it. He thought briefly about grabbing the day old tuna sandwich in the mini fridge, but decided against it, knowing he didn't really have time. The lawyer had another meeting coming up that afternoon and could only spare a half hour to go over the documents.

Slipping his coat on loosely and swinging his royal blue scarf over his neck, he grabbed his briefcase and swept out of the office, shutting the door behind him and locking it. When he turned around, he spotted Quinn typing away dutifully at her computer, a Tupperware container at her side filled with something that was freshly steaming.

She glanced up at him with a polite smile, but his eyes were on that container, his empty stomach lurching in desperation. Whatever it was, the smell of it was simply incredible.

"Heading out?" Quinn asked, sitting back in her chair and watching him with an amused expression.

"Yeah, out," Grant replied, shifting his weight as he forced his eyes off the food. "I'll be back in an hour."

"Okay." Quinn's lips curved into a devious grin as she reached for the spare plastic fork she kept in her lunch bag, waving it at him suggestively. "You sure you don't want to try some pasta real quick before you go?"

His first instinct, naturally, was to say no. But sometimes, well, in his case, the rarest of times, desires and needs can overtake even the most cautious and controlled of men.

Without a word, he stepped forward and accepted the fork from her. He dipped it into the pasta and pierced a couple pieces of penne, scooping it carefully into his mouth. He handed the fork back to her, ignoring her enormous grin, and chewed.

The fact that it was quite possibly the best pasta he'd ever tasted still wasn't enough for him to dance for joy or anything, but he certainly couldn't hide the surprise from his expression. He definitely hadn't expected her cooking to be *that* good.

"Well?" Quinn asked, beaming up at him indulgently.

Grant swallowed, his mouth twitching as he considered. When he spoke, he fought to keep the enjoyment from his voice. "Good."

With a curt nod, he strode out of the office alcove and disappeared into one of the elevators, leaving Quinn feeling more than a little smug.

Maybe his comment about her cooking hadn't been very eloquent, very thorough or praising. But she'd be a damn fool to not realize that one little word and an honest look of surprise from a man like him was the best compliment any chef could ever receive.

Perhaps chefdom wasn't so far off, after all.

SHE'D WORN HER favorite red suede pumps out of pure female territorialism. It may seem petty when done by some women, but Madison knew herself to be beyond such criticism. She was very protective of her brothers, especially Grant, and felt it was only her sisterly duty to look out for catty and dangerous women looking to cash in on the weaknesses of a ridiculously wealthy man. They existed, that much she knew from her own experience. Who said men couldn't be gold diggers, too?

So she'd put on the shoes to make a statement, along with the slender black pencil skirt and blood red silk blouse with sleeves that barely covered her shoulders. With it she wore an engraved gold locket that had belonged to her grandmother on her father's side, a sign of her bloodline and a respect to those who came before her.

And while it had been a bitch that morning to tread carefully over the slick snow covered sidewalk in four-inch heels and not trip, she'd managed just fine. A real woman could make such an outfit work, even in the dead of winter.

"Carrie, what are my appointments for the rest of the day?" Madison quickly signed off on a few invoices at the front desk, then turned to her assistant, who was standing at the ready beside her.

Carrie, a petite brunette with sharp brown eyes covered by chic black-rimmed glasses, nodded with a polite smile, the appointment calendar already pulled up on her tablet computer. Madison, she knew, put up with nothing less than complete focus, attention and preparedness.

"At one o'clock you have the restaurant staff meeting, followed immediately by final prep for the Lowell Society luncheon at one thirty." The two started toward the elevators as Madison glanced briefly at the slim, gold designer watch at her wrist. "Three o'clock, your mother is coming in to discuss wine and dessert selection for the breast cancer fundraiser, and then at four o'clock you have an appointment for a mani/pedi here at the spa."

They stepped into one of the elevators, held open by a guest who had just vacated it. Madison glared at her own reflection in the elevator doors as they slid shut, pursing her lips in annoyance. This fundraiser was starting to get on her nerves. It was taking up way more time than it deserved. When her mother was involved, it was to be expected. "I want you to shuffle my salon appointment to tomorrow. I'm going to need more than one hour with my mother."

"Will do." Carrie jotted down a notation on the tablet, her fingers sliding over the touch screen expertly.

The elevator rose silently and Madison continued to eye her own reflection, reaching up to fix a stray strand of dark hair. Image was everything, she knew, especially if one intended to get a very specific, very clear message across. And oh, did she ever.

Beside her, Carrie updated the schedule and then stood quietly, knowing that small talk wasn't acceptable. Madison Vasser was all business and a hard woman to work for. But she wasn't unfair, nor was she cruel. She was just...honest. And Carrie, being a driven young woman herself, had been a perfect fit for her position the moment she started two years earlier. She'd learned that with Madison, undying loyalty and a sharp mind were everything, and those who stayed true were rewarded greatly. Again, Madison was the furthest thing from unfair. You had to earn your place at her side, but once you had, it was well worth it.

When the elevator came to a halt and the doors slid open, Madison led the way into the waiting area, her eyes immediately honing in on Grant's office and the glass walled alcove that held his new secretary. She kept her eyes on the woman as she approached, making her assessments quickly and silently with Carrie at her heels.

Quinn glanced up at the two women who approached, and found herself blinking in stunned surprise. She set her fork down and pushed aside her lunch, rising to her feet dully.

The woman's resemblance to Grant was startling. She had the same rich brown hair, lightly curled at the ends, with intense amber eyes that were slightly lighter in color than his. But the bone structure and the serious, unreadable expression were undeniably the same, and Quinn felt more than a little awkward under the woman's stern and very direct gaze. Somehow it was deeper and more intimidating than Grant's was, as if this woman could recognize every hidden secret within a person by simply meeting eyes. It was unnerving to feel so examined, judged, criticized, in a way that was much more obvious than Grant's quiet assessing had been.

Swallowing her discomfort, Quinn held the woman's gaze with determination.

"Hello." She attempted a smile, holding out her hand politely. "I'm Quinn, Mr. Vasser's new secretary."

"So you are," Madison replied, extending her hand in an almost regal fashion, noting silently that the woman held her eyes without yielding. It was interesting to find her either stubborn enough or maybe aloof enough to do so.

"You're his sister, Madison?" Quinn blurted out, too impatient to wait for the woman to announce who she was. It was so obvious, anyway.

Madison smiled, the curve of her lips slow and deliberate. "I am."

"It's a pleasure to meet you. I'm sorry you caught me in the middle of lunch. If you're looking for Mr. Vasser, he's out for another thirty minutes or so."

Madison shot a quick glance down at Quinn's unfinished lunch, disapproving instantly of her carelessness. "Please eat your lunch in the waiting area or the staff lounge next time, darling. We wouldn't want any damage to the equipment."

"Oh." Quinn glanced down at her Tupperware container, embarrassed. "Right, I'm sorry. Will do."

"Thank you." Madison motioned to her assistant, her lips curving again. "This is my assistant, Carrie. On most days you'll find both of us directly across the hall," she pointed to the other glass wall alcove and accompanying office, "so if you need anything, don't hesitate to ask Carrie."

"Okay, good to know." Quinn nodded, smiling at Carrie politely. The woman stood still and quiet as a statue, and nearly as emotionless. Frowning slightly, Quinn turned her attention back to Madison. "If you don't mind me asking, what is it you do here at the hotel?"

"I'm the Food and Beverage director."

Quinn's mouth dropped open at the woman's words, and she spoke before she could contain herself. "Seriously?"

"Seriously," Madison confirmed, a small, carefully restrained laugh escaping her throat. "Does that surprise you?"

"It does, as I wasn't expecting to meet you so soon." Quinn beamed, nearly jumping from excitement, her earlier hesitancy about the woman gone. "You see, I'm something of a cook myself and I was hoping to eventually get transferred into a position at one of the hotel restaurants. Once something opens up, anyway."

"Do you have an education in the culinary arts?" Madison asked, just curious enough to hear her out.

"Not a professional education, per se, but I've been literally cooking all of my life, and my mother and grandmother taught me everything they know. Combine that with years of a manic devotion to the Food Network, an unhealthy obsession with Mario Batalli, Iron Chef, and Rachel Ray, and you have me. Even if it's not for a year or two, I understand, but if something opens up I hope you'll consider giving me a shot. I really am good, I promise you."

Madison lifted one perfectly sculpted eyebrow and eyed the woman with a condescending smile. "I'm afraid I usually require more experience than that. You have one of the best jobs this hotel has to offer, darling. I suggest you make the most of it. Pleasure meeting you."

With that, she swept gracefully from the office, her long legs crossing with the smooth click of her heels as she went to the elevators, her assistant in tow.

Madison knew then that Grant had nothing to worry about from that woman. She was aloof, starry eyed and peppy, traits Madison usually despised, but she certainly was no gold digger. And even if she had been, she was far from being Grant's type. The woman talked too much. Grant was likely to get tired of her within the week, and perhaps he'd transfer her to work with Linc at the front desk. Linc had much lower standards.

Quinn watched the two women disappear into an elevator, then forced herself to sit back down in her chair.

Well, damn, she thought miserably. And here she thought she'd be able to charm the socks off the Food and Beverage Director and convince him or her to give her a job. Apparently *that* wasn't going to happen, not now anyway.

Feeling more than a little angry with herself, Quinn shut the lid tight on her lunch and stuffed it into her bag, not wanting to look at it any longer. Fool, damn fool, she grimaced.

She took a deep breath and shut her eyes, trying to focus. Just because she'd had a relatively crappy first impression with the lofty Madison Vasser did not mean she was never going to go places. Damnit, she was determined to make it in this industry and she would do it whether it was at the Vasser Hotel or elsewhere.

It was pathetic to give up so easily, and Quinn knew it. By God, she *was* talented, and she was going to be a chef. Eventually. All she had to do was remain positive.

And as a positive person, she would make the best out of her current situation and continue pushing toward her goal. After all,

Quinn thought as she clicked back into the computer to resume her work, she still had bills to pay and her own mouth to feed.

She wasn't going to give up. God help her, she'd make her dreams happen, with or without Madison Vasser's help.

ynette Shaw smiled serenely as she stared up at the lobby ceiling inside the Vasser Hotel, admiring the light that shimmered in from the wide open glass doors and countless windows above them, managing to find its way to the golden coffers and sky blue murals. It was, quite simply, divine. In fact, she didn't think she had ever seen anything more beautiful.

In all her previous trips to the hotel whenever her parents were in town, she never paid much attention to the design of the lobby, much less the ceiling. But something about the light had drawn her eyes upward, and now she found herself standing, her feet planted, head tilted back, and her eyes wide with pleasure.

She probably looked like a crazy person, but oh well. This was New York City, and she'd lived here long enough to know that most people paid no attention to anyone but themselves. And she wanted to enjoy this. It wasn't often she had the chance to simply pause and revel in something so simple and beautiful. Not when her life was on constant overdrive and burdened with rehearsals, dinners and performances, tattered ballet shoes and sore ankles, explicit diets and Pilates classes, expectations of her own and of those who loved her.

She was a dancer, plain and simple. Lynette had never considered herself to be anything *but* a dancer, since she'd been three years old and attended her first ballet class. The grace, the beauty and the agility of the professional dancers had left her awestruck with envy and fiercely determined to be just like them.

While it took countless years of dedication, sweat, tears, blood, and a whole lot more that she sometimes wondered if she'd regret someday, she'd made it. She was not only a dancer in the finest ballet company in New York City, but she was a Principal. She had performed all across the world, from Paris to Sydney to Tokyo and back again, in the most luxurious theaters and with the most beautiful people.

It was a life she had earned, a life she had sacrificed for. But in her mind, it was well worth it.

Perhaps she had the advantage of being born to privilege, which meant her parents had been able to afford the top classes with the best instructors and the luxury of a private tutor to guide her through school without her ever having set foot inside a public classroom. She'd grown up largely without friends, without a casual play date, without sipping soda and munching on chocolate chip cookies on a warm summer's day. No, those were the things she had sacrificed.

Again, there were times when she wondered if she would one day regret those things. Until then, however, she was content to enjoy the fruits of her labor. She was at the height of her career and until they told her she was too old to dance, she would keep on doing it.

While Lynette wandered around the lobby waiting for her parents to meet her for lunch, she didn't realize she was being watched.

Walter caught sight of a flash of red out of the corner of his eye, spotted the girl, and immediately his mouth fell open.

Ah, the perks of working in a luxury hotel, he thought, delighted. An endless supply of hot babes as refined as silk strolling in day in and day out.

"Damnit, Wally, where's my stapler?" Linc called from his office, causing Walter to swear audibly.

"I don't know, dude, up your ass, maybe?" he shot back, trying to keep his eyes on the girl.

"Oh, you're gonna get it." Linc chuckled, shaking his head as his hand closed over the previously lost stapler which decided to hide under a stack of invoices. He made his way to the front desk, stapler raised and ready to fire staples at the mouthy intern. "Maybe I should just super glue all of my office supplies to your back."

Walter simply brushed Linc away as he came up beside him. "Dude, I swear that's Rachel McAdams, you know, from *The Notebook* and stuff."

"Get out."

"No, I'm not kidding, seriously. Look." He pointed toward a girl with generous waves of lush copper hair who was wandering aimlessly around the lobby. When Linc spotted her, his eyes narrowed.

"Okay, first off, that girl is much too tall and skinny to be Rachel, plus she's got red hair." Linc's eyebrows raised as he turned to his intern, leaning casually against the counter.

"So, Rachel could have dyed her hair. It's not always the same color, you know."

Linc laughed and patted Walter on the back. "I swear, there must not be any cute girls at that college of yours. You are starved for pretty ladies, my friend."

"Look! She's turning this way!" Walter whispered excitedly, pointing at the girl once more.

This time, Linc really focused on her, and when she turned to face him, he found his hands gripping the travertine counter a bit too tightly and his heart racing a bit too quickly.

"That isn't Rachel McAdams, Wally," he managed, his eyes glued to her now as she strolled along. The sunlight glowed on her cheeks and in her hair, her hands clasped patiently at her back.

"Yeah, you're right. Oh well." Walter shrugged and turned away to help a guest. Linc stayed where he was, resting his chin in his hand now as he continued to watch her.

She was tall and slender, willowy, with ivory skin and legs for days. She wore a casually expensive cashmere sweater the color of soft roses, with an ivory scarf she'd draped comfortably over her shoulders. But it wasn't her clothes that caught his attention. No, they only pegged her as affluent, possibly an heiress to some kind of fortune, here to meet someone for lunch.

It was her face that distracted him, had him taking a second look and really enjoying what he saw. She had the soft and lovely features of an angel, framed by a heart shaped face and graced by big, beautiful eyes. He couldn't see their color, but he could see the way her dark lashes shadowed them as she glanced down at her feet, and the way her copper eyebrows quirked as she noticed something that caught her attention.

But when she was called out by name and turned, her smile nearly stole his breath away.

"Daddy!" Lynette strode immediately to her father, wrapping her arms around him tightly. She breathed in the scent of his cologne, comforted by it. "God, it's good to see you."

"Hello, pumpkin." Senator Warren Shaw beamed as he held his daughter, his politician's smile in place. But at least with his daughter, his smile was always genuine. He had the same copper hair, only his was graced at the temples with flecks of grayish white, giving him a distinguished look. He was tall and burly, but not in an intimidating way. Instead he seemed inviting and warm, in a way that politicians had to appear in order to maintain an election record such as he held. One day soon, he hoped it might even take him to the presidency.

Pulling away from him, Lynette turned to her mother, who was busy fussing around with her purse. "Mama, thanks for coming."

Carol Shaw slipped the clasp closed on her purse, then turned to face her daughter, as usual doing a full visual sweep of her only child. "Honey, you look tired. Have you not been sleeping?"

"I've been sleeping just fine," Lynette assured her, leaning in to kiss her mother's cheek. Her mother was a small, fragile woman, airing on the side of wispy in her prim, pale blue dress suit and heirloom pearls. Her hair was dusty blonde and styled perfectly, as any politician's wife's hair should be, with care and precision. As usual, her eyes were honed in on Lynette, looking for any flaws that needed to be corrected. Her mother, the perfectionist.

Several feet away, Linc watched the exchange curiously. So, the girl was Senator Shaw's daughter. Perhaps he should check in with the Shaws and make sure they're enjoying their stay. They were long time clients of the Vasser Hotel, and on many occasions he'd seen to their needs during their visits.

"I'm sorry to interrupt, Senator. I just wanted to pop by and say hello before you guys took off," Linc greeted as he approached, holding out his hand for the senator to accept.

"Glad you did, Linc! Glad you did." Shaw grinned, shaking Linc's hand with relish. "How's the family?"

"Fine, sir, just fine." Linc winked, then turned to Shaw's wife cordially. "Mrs. Shaw, always a pleasure."

"Nice to see you, Linc." Carol fluttered as he shook her hand. "Have you met our daughter, Lynette?"

With a quick grin, Linc shifted his eyes to the lovely redhead, who was watching him cautiously. "No, I don't believe I've had the pleasure."

He held out his hand for hers, and Lynette, one eyebrow raised curiously, accepted it.

"Honey, this is Lincoln Vasser. His family owns the Vasser Hotels," Shaw provided, beaming at them both.

Lynette inclined her head, taking her assessment of the man before her. He was smooth, that much was certain. She'd seen him swoop in on her parents in a matter of seconds, with the poise and charisma of a salesman or a politician. She should know, having been surrounded by politicians her whole life.

But there was something different about him, she mused. Something honest in his eyes that welcomed trust. That could be a very, very dangerous trait. Or a very fortunate one.

"Lovely to meet you, Lincoln." Lynette smiled graciously, bowing her head slightly.

Damn it all to hell. He had such a weakness for accents, and her lovely southern lilt that was just a little husky around the edges was bound to get him in trouble.

"Please, call me Linc." He smiled again, quick and charming. "Southern Belle, come to New York."

Linc regretfully pulled his hand away from hers, amused by the irritation in her eyes.

"I live here, actually, and have for some time," she corrected him. "My parents are the ones who have come to New York."

"All the way from South Carolina to see our baby girl dance." Shaw puffed up with pride.

Linc noted this, much as he noticed the way Mrs. Shaw was busy fussing with Lynette's clothes and hair. She seemed used to the prodding, to the critiquing, even though it bothered him greatly to see it. His mother was that way too, but he didn't put up with it as patiently as Lynette did.

"You're a dancer?" Linc asked, turning his attention back to Lynette's face. He noticed her eyes were the color of lake water in the spring, coolly calm and endlessly deep. It reminded him of his time at Lake Pontchartrain the year before, when he'd gone to visit the old plantation house he'd purchased. Interesting that she would make him think of that place, and make him realize just how badly he missed it.

Lynette flushed for reasons she couldn't explain. It probably had something to do with the way he was looking at her, as if he'd met her before, even though she was quite certain they never had.

"Yes, ballet," she told him before quickly glancing back to her parents. "So, where do y'all want to have lunch?"

"You're the New York expert, pumpkin. You take us where you like to go." Shaw grinned, winking at Linc as he put his arm around both his wife and his daughter. "Nice talking with you, Linc."

"Same to you, sir." Linc watched as the small family wandered toward the entrance doors, the senator in the middle, his broad arms wrapped warmly around both his wife and daughter. Mrs. Shaw was busy shuffling around inside her purse once more, while the beautiful Lynette smiled up at her father and laughed at something he said.

Charmed, Linc tucked his hands into the pockets of his jeans and watched them go. As he stood there, Walter came up beside him, following his line of vision.

"You know, I saw her first," he said good naturedly, smiling at his boss and patting him on the shoulder.

Linc glanced over at him with a quick grin. "All's fair in love and war, my friend."

With that, he sauntered back to his office, whistling a good old-fashioned southern melody as he went.

THE ROAR OF the crowd still echoed in her ears.

Lord, had they been appreciative tonight, Lynette marveled with a giddy laugh. She was mystified as always by the sheer rush of pleasure she got from sending a crowd to their feet simply because of a performance. Even after the countless years and thousands of shows, she was still humbled to know there were people who would pay to come see her and her company dance and be moved to a standing ovation.

She collapsed into her dressing table chair, her lips curved into a dazed smile and her mind still fuzzy with the thrill of the dance. As always, the beautiful release of losing herself so completely in the music and movement stayed with her, making her steps feel lighter and her heart full and content.

Humming softly to herself, she lifted her right foot and unstrapped her ballet slipper, sliding it off and setting it on the dressing table at her side. Rubbing her toes, she closed her eyes and inhaled deeply, enjoying the comfort of her own fingers massaging away any traces of soreness.

Around her, the rest of the ballet company bustled and chattered, voices light and cheerful, laughter brightly humorous and giddy. The scent of hundreds of roses filled the dressing room, brought in as gifts for the dancers from fans and family alike. At her own dressing table were crisp yellow roses, her signature flower, nestled among the clutter of her stage make up, hair brush, lotion, perfume, and countless other female trappings she went nowhere without.

Lynette shut her eyes again and embraced the familiar surroundings, completely at home. But when she heard her parents congratulating her fellow dancers behind her, she braced herself for what she knew was coming. It was always the same, wasn't it?

"You were magnificent, pumpkin."

Turning in her chair, she faced her parents, her lips curving into a soft smile. "Thank you, daddy."

He was flanked by his two bodyguards, always at his side when he attended public events. Lynette hardly noticed them anymore, and didn't let their presence keep her from rising to her feet to kiss her father's cheek. Beside him, her mother was all smiles and graciousness as the other dancers filtered in and out of the dressing room, distracted by their own friends and family as the night wound down to a cool simmer. When most of the people had left the room, Carol Shaw turned to her daughter and her smile faded to a stern frown.

"You let your chin fall, Lynette. Remember what Madame Marcoux taught you, chin up and neck straight."

Lynette fought to keep the hurt from her eyes, the disappointment. Critics had often praised her fluidity of movement and the naturalness with which she danced, but in truth her mother was correct. It just hurt, as always, to hear the criticism before ever hearing a drop of praise.

"Yes, mama," she conceded, bowing her head and averting her eyes. Better to keep the peace than to ruffle feathers. "So, are you heading back to the hotel? I'm sure y'all are exhausted."

"Nonsense, we're taking our baby girl out." Her father grinned, wrapping his arm around her and pulling her close. "Though perhaps we could go back to the hotel, if you'd like. Linc might still be around."

"Why does that matter?" Lynette asked bluntly, eyebrows raised as her eyes met his.

"He seemed quite taken with you, if I may venture to say so."

"Nonsense," Carol interrupted, bracing her hands on her hips as she glared up at her husband. "That boy is nice and very helpful, but he's nothing but a playboy with a wandering eye. Lynette would be better off not fraternizing with him."

"Playboy?" Lynette snorted, amused as she eyed her mother, who looked appropriately ruffled.

"Yes. Haven't you seen the tabloids? Why just last year he ended a blistering affair with that trashy actress, Jorja Hale. Nasty business if I do say so myself."

"I don't have time for tabloids, mama," Lynette reminded her.

"He's just a boy, Carol. He'll grow up eventually," her husband countered, brushing her comments away carelessly. "Besides, eventually I'd like some grandchildren, and our Lynnie is going to have to get to it soon. 2016 is not too far off, and the public likes a family man with little ones running around."

Great, Lynette thought wearily. Once again, her life was being dictated by a goddamn election.

"Lynette does not need any distractions right now, she needs to stay focused and dedicated to her career. She only has a few years left before they cycle her out for a younger dancer, so she has to make the most of it. The last thing she needs is to get pregnant and destroy her body so *you* can get elected."

"Now, wait a minute—"

"Don't you wait a minute me, Warren," Carol replied coolly, her voice never raising even an octave. There were still a few bystanders wandering around and appearances needed to be kept. "Lynette has sacrificed everything to be a dancer, and I won't let your political ambitions ruin that. Children are hardly worth the sacrifice. The complications of my pregnancy ruined my figure, and my dreams never came true. But I'm going to see to it that Lynette does not make the same mistake I made."

Lynette watched her parents argue with biting words that managed to remain discreet. A clever habit, to be sure, and all the while her chest constricted with a tighter and tighter pain, until she felt like her core was going to implode in on itself like some vast black hole.

Damn the fighting, the constant, never ending bickering over what was in *her* best interests. And wasn't it funny that they never once bothered to ask her what *she* thought might be best? She loved dancing and didn't mind the sacrifices. But it seemed as though her opinion had never once even been considered as viable or worth hearing. Tragic, she sighed. But it was just the way things were.

"Why don't we get going? I'm starved." Lynette swiftly changed the subject, smiling at both of her parents cordially. "Maybe we can try that new sushi bar on Fifth Avenue."

They both looked at her, though neither would apologize. They never did.

"Yes, let's go. Rogers, Eames." Her father nodded to the two bodyguards at his side as he led his wife and daughter from the building, using the back exit reserved for VIP guests who wished to avoid the press.

As they slipped into the discreet town car that would take them the few blocks to Fifth Avenue, Lynette leaned back against the leather seat and closed her eyes. As she did so, it startled her to have the image of her mother's so called "playboy" surface from her memory, his smile upbeat, honesty and compassion so clear in his eyes.

It was curious that her father seemed to think that Linc Vasser had some kind of crush on her. Perhaps it was even more curious to realize that a part of her was oddly flattered by the idea.

If she was being honest with herself, it *had* been over a year since she'd dated anyone. Her schedule was unbelievably hectic and she spent a great amount of time outside the country. So maybe it was only healthy to feel good at having an attractive man look twice at her.

But her mother was right. She was entirely too busy to spare time for dating. So unless by some miracle several more hours of daylight were added to each and every day, she wasn't going to find herself in a position to have a good, lasting relationship with a man until...well, until she could no longer dance.

Ah, sacrifices.

THEY OFTEN SAID he was a man of good humor, with a positive disposition and a carefree, comfortable nature. Despite the pressures of being the eldest son, they'd say, Marshall Vasser continues to remain easygoing and blithe, always the picture of charisma and good faith.

He enjoyed what the media thought of him, of what the society elites thought. He'd worked hard to cement his reputation as both approachable and respectable, as kind but not a pushover. He loved people; he loved talking to them, cracking jokes and making them laugh, enjoying a good story about movies, books, politics, or sports. Give him a topic and he could run with it as skillfully and deftly as the best of them.

Maybe it was his innate people skills that had gifted him with so many friends over the years. God, the people he'd known in his lifetime, both famous and not. Anyone from timeless movie stars to presidents and foreign dignitaries; from great American business tycoons to world-renowned chefs and fashion designers.

It was a list to be proud of, Marshall knew, especially since his father had been known to make nothing but enemies.

Swirling a snifter of brandy, he lifted it to his lips and sampled, leaning back into the comfortable armchair in the study of his Upper East Side town house. Yes, his father had undoubtedly burned more bridges than he'd made in his life, but in many ways it gave him an altogether different reputation than the one Marshall strove for. Where Marshall sought to be loved by all, Cyrus chose to be feared.

And even at ninety, the old bastard was still feared. Even confined to a hospital bed, hooked up to machines to keep his heart beating and his lungs functioning, the man was as ruthless and mean as ever. But even Marshall could admit that it was the ruthlessness and the old man's cunning nature that brought the hotels into full prominence in the latter half of the century, surviving numerous recessions and maintaining a solid and strong reputation.

Cyrus hadn't let anyone take advantage of him. Most were too scared to even try. One whiff of fraud or deceit and the perpetrator might as well chop their own head off for how dead they were going to be once Cyrus was done with them. He was incredibly shrewd and paranoid, and it was because of this that the very few people who did manage to earn some semblance of trust from him ended up very wealthy and successful men.

Including himself, Marshall considered, sipping more brandy and eyeing the photograph he kept of his father and himself on the table at his side. It was taken some thirty years earlier, Cyrus in his sixties, looking callous and bad tempered, and Marshall in his forties, in his prime. In some ways he knew he'd disappointed his father, never marrying and producing heirs being one of them. But marriage just wasn't his style. He preferred a vast selection of women, ever changing to suit his altering tastes. But he'd worked hard and earned his place at his father's side as heir to the empire, even if they didn't always agree on method. They still respected each other, and maybe even loved each other, if there was even room in the old man's shriveled, decayed heart for love.

What little room there may have been, he'd long ago given to the one woman strong enough, or maybe foolish enough, to put up with him. The late, great Stella Waverly Vasser, Marshall's mother. In all his life, he'd never met a woman who could compare to her. She had been one of a kind. Not only a strong woman, but a warm and charitable one who gave everything she had unconditionally. Marshall liked to think he picked up on some of those qualities in the handful of years he'd known her before her untimely death of breast cancer. He'd been just twenty years old.

He had a generous heart, one prone to compassion and forgiveness that very few people could honestly boast of. Perhaps that was why part of him regretted not having kids, a son or daughter of his own to spoil and cherish. But thankfully, in some ways, his youngest brother's kids had become his own. They looked up to him as the man their own father could never be and in that way the void in his life was filled.

He loved those kids with all his heart. He'd been there for each of their births, held them in the hospital when their own father was off getting high or screwing one of his mistresses, and he'd seen the hope and promise in them from the very beginning. Grant, Linc, Madison and even Kennedy. In his heart, they were and would always be his children, and not Win's.

Win. Marshall frowned, drinking more brandy and glancing at a portrait of him and his six brothers, taken when Win had been a broody young man of eighteen. He had always been a handful; wild, reckless and utterly disrespectful to his heritage. It hadn't mattered to Win that the Vasser family name held a reputation of its own, and that by philandering about with drugged out hippies and sex addicts he was tainting the entire family, not just himself. But even when Marshall had tried to explain it, Win hadn't cared. He only made fake promises and apologies, cleaned up for a week, and then fell right back off the wagon. Just what it was that Win was trying to prove, either to himself or to the family, Marshall wasn't sure he would ever know.

What could be done with a bad apple like that? Marshall wondered. The only blessing was when Win divorced Charlene and distanced himself from the family, fleeing to Los Angeles to live off a monthly allowance given to him from the family trust. He, still to this day, had never worked a day in his life. Instead, he mooched off what others would give him and squandered it away on his various vices.

A tragedy, Marshall thought as he stared at the young Win in the photograph, his poetically handsome face filled with ideals and falsehoods, mind a clean slate ready to absorb the nonsense about to be hammered into it from the late sixties radicalism. If only they'd known then just how destructive he was to become, maybe they could have saved him. But, then again, perhaps he just wasn't meant to be saved.

With a heavy sigh, Marshall set aside his brandy and lifted up the day's newspaper, flipping immediately to the obituaries, seeking to take his mind off his foolish brother. It was a daily ritual for him to peruse the obits now that he'd reached the age where many of his friends were passing away. He found himself attending more funerals than birthday parties these days. But it was important to the families of his friends that he was there, to comfort and to speak kind words about the deceased. He was a known great orator, and as representative for the Vasser family empire, his presence was usually considered a great honor.

His eyes scanned the column of names, his reading glasses sliding down his nose. Pushing them back up, he nearly bypassed a name that, once he registered where he knew it from, quite literally stopped his heart.

> Margaret "Maggie" Owens, daughter of Howard and Rosalie Owens of Queens, New York, passed away in her sleep on January 6th, 2011, after having suffered a stroke two days before. She leaves behind a niece and two great-nephews.

Stunned, Marshall looked away from the obituary and his eyes unfocused for a moment, the memories coming back to him in flooding waves. Immediately he thought of the aged deck of cards, worn at the edges and decorated with a faded image of the American flag, that lay tucked away safely in his desk. They had been passed down to him following his grandfather's death, all those years before...

Rosalie Owens was the woman who single handedly destroyed his family. A home wrecker and a whore, not worth the dirt on the bottom of his shoe. She waltzed into his grandfather's life sixty years earlier, tricked him into an affair that ruined his marriage and threatened the very stability of the empire. Then she waltzed out of his life and broke his heart, and in doing so caused his suicide. A bullet to the head, in the study of his suite at the New York Vasser Hotel, back in 1957. Marshall had been just seventeen years old.

The pain of the memory tore through him in one vicious, violent swipe. He was the one to discover the body, to see the pools of dark red blood stain the surface of Winston's prized antique desk. He saw the gun, held loosely in his grandfather's hand, the chrome of the short barrel glinting in the light of the desk lamp. Then there was his grandfather's face, his eyes shut as if in sleep, his features slack and lifeless. He had been a man of great humor, so full of life, even in his final days. Perhaps that was what was so hard to accept about the suicide, Marshall realized. How could such a man ever take his own life?

A woman. Maybe that was part of the reason Marshall had never, in all his life, committed himself to one. Better to avoid the possible heartache and the destructive pain that came from disappointment or from the deceit of a callous woman.

With a shudder, Marshall glanced back down at the newspaper, his eyes finding the obituary once again. Had this Maggie Owens known the damage her mother had caused his family? He hadn't even known Rosalie had a daughter, much less one that lived up until just a few days ago. If he had ever met her, would it have resolved some of the pain in his heart? Would she have been able to provide some kind of apology, some kind of explanation, on behalf of her mother?

Alas, he would never know.

SIX

She knocked politely on the door of his office, then entered when he called her in.

"Here's your mail," Quinn said brightly, a stack of envelopes in her hand as she strode into the room. She spotted Grant staring intently at his computer screen, his nose mere inches away from it. If it were anyone else, she might have laughed and scolded him for destroying his eyes that way, but she had a feeling he wouldn't understand the humor of it.

"Just set it on the desk," Grant murmured, clicking away with the mouse as he filled in the basic information for a new employee health insurance quote, which for whatever reason was near impossible for him to read. Either they made the text on the website extremely small on purpose or he was going to need reading glasses.

"I hear we're going to get another snow storm this evening," Quinn said conversationally as she set down the mail. "Hopefully it won't be too bad. I'd hate to get snowed in, not be able to come in tomorrow... And I know you would just *hate* not being able to come in to work."

"Mmm," he grunted, not really paying attention to her.

"You know, maybe the hotel should put me up in a suite, just to be sure I'm able to be here. In fact, you should put all the employees up in suites for the night, just in case. Can't have a functioning hotel without the staff."

Grant grunted again, then blinked and tore his eyes away from the computer to stare up at her in confusion. "Wait, what?"

Quinn let out a light laugh. "So you were listening. I'd almost given up hope there for a second."

Grant's brows furrowed as he continued to watch her, his eyes hovering a bit too long over her smile. It reminded him of staring into the sun and being blinded by the light of it.

"I apologize, Miss Taylor." He let out a huff of breath and sat back in his chair, rubbing his eyes briefly to will away the strain that had come over them. "I'm just very busy."

"Yes, I know." She smiled, watching him fondly. In the week she'd worked for him, she'd come to appreciate him more with each day. He may not have been as easygoing and funny as his brother, but there was this old-world charm to him that she admired.

At times he was frostily distant, or carelessly blunt in his assessment of her and her work. But then she would catch him staring at the portraits of his family with a soft, nostalgic smile, or gazing out the window of his office, looking as though the entire weight of the world were on his shoulders. It was those few moments that told her more about his character than anything else ever could. Her boss was a tireless workaholic, a man of incredibly few words, and, at the core of it, she had a feeling that he thought himself to be perilously alone at the top of this pillar he and his family had placed him on.

She wondered if he even knew how exhausted he really was. "Would you like me to make you some coffee?"

He sighed, pulling his hands away from his face to look up at her gratefully. "Please."

Quinn smiled before turning toward his kitchenette, reaching up into the cabinet for a filter cup. Before she could get the water hot in the coffee maker, the door to the office burst open and Linc leaned in cheerfully.

"Happy Birthday!"

Grant frowned over at his brother, instantly annoyed. "Is that what today is?" he murmured, fighting to hide the worst of his irritation.

Up until then he'd gone nearly half the day without anyone noticing it was his birthday, which was exactly how he preferred it. Now Linc had let the cat out of the bag. Before he could stop himself, he glanced warily over at Quinn, who was staring at him with wide eyes and a bright grin, the coffee filter cup clutched in her hand. Great, just great.

"Shut up, I know you were just dying for somebody to say something. You always were an attention whore." Linc laughed as he came into the office, holding out a small gift box tied with a neat, emerald green bow. "Now, I know you wanted a puppy, but you're gonna have to settle for this instead."

Grant tried hard not to smile as he accepted the gift. "Too bad. Miles really wanted a friend."

"Mr. Vasser, it's your birthday? Why didn't you tell me?" Quinn asked, her hands clasped together excitedly as she approached his desk. She smiled at Linc before looking back at her boss. "I could have baked you something, a cake, or whatever. You know what, I'll bring you something tomorrow to make up for it. What do you like? Chocolate? Red velvet? Angel food?"

Grant stared up at her for a moment, annoyed that the prospect of her baking for him had some incredibly odd appeal. It was only made worse by the fact that he could imagine her so vividly. Bustling away in her kitchen, singing to herself as she baked with the smell of cinnamon and vanilla in the air. Flour dusting her hands, a smudge of it on her cheek as she smiled up at him. The feel of her skin as he brushed away the flour...wow, okay. Cool it, Grant, he scolded himself. Don't be ridiculous. He averted his eyes from hers, attempting to quell any further absurd thoughts. "I don't really eat cake."

Linc looked over at Quinn and mouthed "chocolate." She winked at him as Grant began to open his gift.

He tore the wrapping paper and lifted the lid off the small box, pulling out the chrome plated harmonica complete with the family name and the current year engraved in the metal. He stared at it blankly for a moment, despising the painful ache it brought to his chest. God, how long had it been? Twelve years? More?

"Well? You do remember, don't you?" Linc pushed, impatient. Beside him, Quinn eyed the harmonica curiously, her eyes darting back and forth between the brothers. The tension in the air seemed to grow as Grant set the harmonica back into the box and looked up at Linc.

"I do. Thank you." He nodded, shutting the box and pushing it aside, not sure he could face it again just yet. "I haven't played in some time."

With a grin, Linc turned to Quinn. "Grant used to be quite the passionate musician, believe it or not."

"Really?" Quinn bit back a smile as she glanced over at her boss. Who knew? "Was the harmonica his favorite?"

"Yep. He used to play to us at night to calm us down while our parents had one of their infamous fights. It helped."

"That's enough." Grant eyed Linc sternly, his disapproval obvious. Not only did he dislike sharing details of the family with outsiders, but he had spent many years forcing those memories from his mind. He certainly didn't want to remember them now, here, in front of the woman who was still so much a stranger...

Quinn took what Linc shared with her and stored it away, adding it to the small collection of things she knew about the Vassers. Because she could tell Grant was upset, and in turn it had put Linc on edge, she didn't push for more and instead returned to brewing his coffee.

Before she could, Madison swept into the office, a lovely crystal vase of grassy green ferns and snow white orchids in her arms. For the briefest of moments she paused, her honeyed eyes sweeping over Quinn in a glance that was undoubtedly territorial. That was all it took for Quinn to get the clear message that she was no longer welcome. As quickly as the look had come, it was gone and Madison was greeting her brother graciously.

"Happy Birthday, Grant." She set the vase on his desk and kissed his cheek as he stood up to face her. "I figured that since the door was wide open and your secretary was nowhere to be found that I would simply let myself in."

Quinn bristled at the woman's words, shocked by the acid in the velvet of her voice. But before she could retort, apologize, or do anything, really, Linc jumped valiantly to her defense.

"She was just talking with us. It's not a big deal, Mads," he told her, tucking his hands into the pockets of his jeans in an attempt to keep his temper in check.

"Regardless." Madison shifted her eyes to Quinn. "I wouldn't want Mr. Vasser to miss any important phone calls, darling."

"Right." Quinn nodded, but before turning to leave she looked to Grant, determined not to lose face in front of his family. She had her pride, after all, and wasn't going to be pushed around by someone other than her own boss just because the woman had some outlandish superiority complex. "Mr. Vasser, do you want me to finish that cup of coffee for you before I go?"

"No, I'll get to it. Thank you, Miss Taylor."

It annoyed Quinn to watch him close himself off, his expression unreadable and his stance dismissive. If only she knew what he was thinking, what he was feeling, then maybe it would give her more insight into how to act around him. Just minutes before it seemed as though he had finally opened up for her, at least just a little. But in the presence of his siblings he seemed to throw up his wall once more.

She went back to her desk, clicking into her computer to resume the letter she'd been typing up before she was distracted. She kept her fingers busy and her eyes locked on the screen as the three of them spoke quietly in hushed, somewhat angry tones. She couldn't hear what was being said, but she had a pretty good idea on the topic of conversation.

She realized this was the first time she'd seen all three of them together in one room. Part of her vehemently wished she hadn't. The tension and electricity in the air when the three of them came together was almost more than she could bear. It wasn't like her family, where she and her siblings may fight, but there was always love just beneath the angry words. With the Vassers, she felt like they were in some kind of constant tug of war for control...

After a few moments, they proceeded past her on their way to lunch.

She sensed Madison brush past her first, who ignored her completely, followed by Linc, who managed a brief and edgy smile when she glanced up at him. Lastly, Grant exited his office, turning around to lock the door behind him. He paused at her desk as his siblings went to the elevators, his eyes betraying nothing of what he was feeling inside, if there was anything. She met them anyway and attempted a smile.

"Have fun at lunch."

Grant bit his tongue, knowing he had no words to say to her, despite how badly he wanted to at least say *something*. She deserved that much, didn't she? But how could he explain to her the complexities of his family, the guarded nature of his sister and the haunting past the harmonica had uncovered that he refused to discuss, even with his own brother? How could she possibly understand the pressure he was under, or how the very need for him to maintain this distance from everyone was a necessary, but at times devastating constraint? She just couldn't understand, being the kind of person she was. So happy, so positive and full of life...surely she had never faced the obstacles or the drama he had or stood up under the pressures of being born into an empire that could not be allowed to fail. No, there was no possible way he could articulate those points to her, because he had never been a man of words and saying what he felt or thought had never come easy. Perhaps it never would. And so he would continue to live with the disappointment of holding back, once more.

"Thank you." He nodded to her before leaving the alcove and joining his brother and sister at the elevator just as it opened. He found himself having to force his eyes away from watching her as the doors slid quietly shut.

THE TENSION THEY carried went with them to lunch.

Grant sat with his family at the best table in *Cherir,* urging himself to relax. It was his birthday. If he didn't deserve to relax today, then when did he?

He laughed to himself at the very notion. He'd relax when he was dead, he thought dispassionately.

"Of the four of you, Grant was the easiest," Charlene asserted, smiling at her children as she lifted her martini for a sip. "The smoothest labor, the least sleepless nights, the most compliments on what a good tempered baby I had."

"Here I was, thinking I was your favorite." Linc grinned, winking at her good-naturedly as he bit into his burger. He'd had Raoul make it up especially for him, given that he was rarely in the mood for the fancy crap the restaurant served. He'd take a good ol' American cheeseburger to a bouillabaisse any day. "Besides, we were raised by a nanny so you collecting pity for sleepless nights is a sham."

Kennedy burst into giggles, while Madison slightly relaxed the stiffness in her shoulders and smiled appreciatively at Linc before turning to their mother. "Grant may have been the best behaved, but you have to admit that Linc and I kept you on your toes."

"You aged me, is what you did." Charlene sighed, shaking her head. "And there were still sleepless nights. Carlotta doesn't work every day, you know."

"Carlotta still makes me French toast for breakfast every morning," Kennedy chimed in, crunching happily into a toast point slathered in goat cheese.

"Too bad you'll miss out on that once you go to Princeton, snotface." Linc reached over to playfully ruffle her hair with a devious grin. "You're gonna have to be a big girl and learn to cook your own food."

Kennedy tried to pout but ended up smiling instead, as always enjoying the time she spent with her favorite brother. "That's what McDonald's is for."

"Oh, Kennedy, please don't tell me you're going to eat nothing but fast food while you're away," Charlene gasped, rubbing her temple in agitation at the idea. "I won't allow it. I just *won't* allow you to ruin your health that way."

"She's right, Kennedy," Madison put in, focusing on her little sister disapprovingly. "The sodium content alone will destroy your complexion, not to mention what the saturated fat and cholesterol will do to your blood pressure."

Kennedy shot a mean look at her sister before rolling her eyes. "Whatever. Forget I said it."

Madison's eyes narrowed, but other than that her expression displayed none of the hurt she felt from her sister's disregard for her advice. Then again, it had been a long time since Kennedy had shown anything remotely resembling affection toward her. In a way, it was her own fault her sister couldn't stand her. Kennedy was soft and naïve, and therefore susceptible to manipulation. Madison only wanted to protect her, but apparently her "tough love" approach over the years had done nothing but drive a wedge further and further between them.

She let the issue be and turned instead to her oldest brother, who was seated quietly beside her, his mind clearly on other things.

"How is the lamb, darling?" Madison asked, wishing she knew what he was thinking. She may have known him better than anyone else in the family, but even she could be shut out from his thoughts if he saw fit. It was just like him to keep his troubles to himself.

Grant looked up from his lunch, startled to find his family watching him expectantly. What had they been talking about? He hadn't heard a word any of them had said. Instead of spending time with his family, his mind had been on Quinn. Damnit, Grant. She's nothing, absolutely nothing but an employee, and it has to stay that way.

But then why could he not erase the image of her face, her smile, from his thoughts?

"The lamb is fine," he assured his sister, attempting a smile for his family. "Thank you all for coming today, for my birthday."

"If only Marshall could have joined us," Charlene sighed wistfully, pouting a bit at the thought. "But he had that funeral to go to. Some woman from Queens, Maggie something-or-other. I've never heard of the woman, personally."

"You know Marshall, he's got friends everywhere," Linc reminded her, polishing off his burger.

"Regardless, family should take precedent over some woman he barely knew," Charlene sniffed, clearly upset. "But I'm sure when he returns later this afternoon he'll stop by to see you, Grant."

"I'm sure he will."

"So, Grant, how does it feel to be two years away from thirty?" Linc asked suddenly, leaning back casually in his chair and eyeing his brother. He still hadn't forgotten how carelessly Grant brushed off his gift earlier, as usual too afraid to even feel the slightest bit of emotion. It was pathetic, Linc figured, to run away from your past when it so obviously defined you.

He didn't like running from things, nor did he like ignoring his own ideas and ambitions for the sake of keeping the peace in the family. Damnit, it was time he pushed back against the family hierarchy that left him helpless at the bottom of the totem pole. He was sick of not being heard, and maybe now was not the right time to bring it up, but he'd be damned if he would sit on his hands any longer. And Grant's dismissal of what was a very thoughtful gift only served to fuel the fire.

Grant eyed his brother cautiously, his eyes narrowing at the tone in Linc's voice. He could tell Linc was still angry with him for his reaction to the harmonica, the hasty way he brushed it off as though it meant nothing. But of course it meant something, he had just been uncomfortable with expressing the emotions his brother needed at that moment, like he always was. He didn't have it in him to deal with things of that nature without shying away from it as a purely instinctive defense. "You should know, Linc. You're three years away from it."

"True, but that one year makes a hell of a difference, doesn't it? I mean, you're the natural assumed leader, the one we all look up to and turn to for guidance."

Grant's brows furrowed as he continued to stare at his brother. "What are you trying to say?"

"What I'm saying is that maybe the rest of us have some good ideas for the company, and those ideas deserve to be seriously considered."

Grant blinked, caught off guard. But because he remembered what happened the last time a similar subject to this was brought up, he fought to keep his voice neutral and indifferent. Linc was in a fighting mood, and Grant refused to take the bait. "This is not an appropriate time to have this discussion."

"Like hell it isn't," Linc shot back, his mouth curving into a grin that was hard and bitter around the edges. "Just hear me out, Grant. That's all I'm asking."

Grant was silent for a moment, all eyes on him as he battled with the guilt and his propriety; warring over the authority in his head and the sympathy in his heart. When he spoke, his voice was as purposely devoid of emotion as ever. "Alright."

Linc wasted no time launching into his pitch.

"I think that we should try and broaden our market share, expand into the three-star or business market instead of being exclusively luxury. The economy's crap right now, and you know people are looking to save money if they're gonna travel. Hilton did it years ago, and look at how well they're doing. With our reputation for excellence, we can branch out and capture that middle class market that's looking for impeccable quality but at a reasonable rate."

He held Grant's eyes with determination, his lips quirked in a salesman's smile, though he knew it would make no difference with his brother. His mother and sisters were eyeing him with mixed expressions, Kennedy agreeable and optimistic, his mother hesitant and unsure, while Madison was looking back and forth between him and Grant, prepared to interfere if necessary. Discussions of changes to the hotel and the company were always a testy battleground.

Grant saw the fire in his brother's expression, heard the passion and the determination in his voice. But there was just no way he could go along with the idea of so drastically altering the foundation of the Vasser Hotel empire and the traditions their forefathers had put in place and expected to be continued faithfully.

"No."

Linc's nostrils flared as his temper sparked, even though Grant's answer had been predictable. "I see, so it's not even worth an explanation on *why* you don't want to give it a shot?"

Grant, determined to hold his ground, shook his head. "We can't compromise our traditions simply because you want to chase a new market share."

"So we're just supposed to live in the dark ages, huh? And never consider growing or progressing?"

"Our business model isn't broken, therefore it doesn't need to be fixed," Grant insisted, his own smoldering temper kept meticulously in check.

"Right." Linc got to his feet then, frustrated. He threw down his napkin on his empty plate and downed what was left of his beer before slamming the glass down on the table. Before any of them could get a word in, he turned to Grant one last time and shoved his fisted hands into his pockets, lest he be tempted to go to blows over this. "One year, Grant. That's all there is between you and I, and yet you have all the fucking authority. How do you think that makes me feel, huh? To know that I will never have any goddamn say in this company for as long as I live, simply because of your seniority over me?"

Grant said nothing. With a disbelieving laugh, Linc shook his head and stalked from the restaurant, shaking with fury. He headed into the lobby, thinking he had to get outside, had to clear his head and go for a walk. He stopped short as he spotted Lynette.

She was leaving, having just dropped off her parents. He took it as a sign from God that she happened to be there, right when he desperately needed to talk to someone, anyone outside of his family. Even someone who was essentially a perfect stranger.

"Hey, Lynette, right?" Linc rushed up beside her, following as she walked through the lobby doors and out into the cold, winter's day.

Startled, Lynette paused just outside the doors and eyed him strangely. Her heart leapt into her throat at the sight of him. He looked nothing like what she'd seen before, the charm and the kindness oddly gone. No, now he looked broody and frustrated and, of all things, miserable.

"Yes. Linc, right?" she returned, noting the shifty way he ran his hands through his hair and the aggravation that was so clear in his eyes. "Are you alright?"

"Yeah, no. No, I'm not," he told her, shutting his eyes for a brief moment and taking a deep breath. "I'm sorry, I hate to do this, but can I just walk with you? I need to get away from here right now, and if I'm alone I might just punch a hole in something."

While she started to say no, Lynette found she didn't have the strength to. How could she turn him down when he was looking at her with so much pain in those honest, open eyes of his? She still had awhile till her rehearsal later that afternoon, so what did it hurt to have some company until then?

"Okay." She started to walk down the sidewalk and he fell into step beside her, his hands still tucked into his pockets. For awhile, neither of them said anything, but instead walked at a consistent and steady pace.

She realized she was nearly the same height as him, only an inch or two shorter, and that when they walked it seemed as though their steps fell into an old, familiar rhythm. Shooting a glance over at him, she saw that his jaw was clenched and his eyes hardened with strain. Just what was it that had upset him so badly?

"Do you want to talk, Linc?" she asked, keeping her hands firmly tucked into the pockets of her coat. Around them, a brisk winter wind shivered through the air.

He sighed, looking straight ahead now as they continued to walk. Though part of him knew it was stupid to unload all of his problems onto a complete stranger, the rest of him found that it just wasn't possible to keep it all inside any longer.

And so he told her. He unleashed all of his frustration over his brother's superiority, the clear lack of respect any of them had for his ideas, the bitterness he felt of knowing that one year was all that separated he and Grant, and yet Grant received all of the authority, all of the praise and admiration while he was left to beg for scraps.

Lynette listened quietly, stunned by just how much animosity he had inside of him. He appeared so carefree before, when really he had all of this building up inside of him.

When he finished, he let out a steadying breath and turned to her, a sheepish smile on his face. "I'm sorry, that was probably too much."

"It is too much," Lynette agreed, meeting his eyes. "Do you not have anyone to talk to, so you unload on a stranger instead?"

He laughed, rubbing his face in his hands. "I have my friend Greg, but he's always looked at me like I'm some prince of a wealthy kingdom. He'd just tell me to shut up and be grateful. Which, hell, I know he's right. I'm bitching over spilt milk like a spoiled kid."

"It sounds to me like you're just wanting to be treated as your brother's equal," Lynette said thoughtfully. "There's nothing wrong with wanting that."

"No, I guess there isn't." Linc stopped as they came to a crosswalk with a red light. He turned to her, his lips quirked into a grin, feeling better after having said it all out loud. Funny how that really worked. "Well, now that I've just poured out all my problems to you, are there any problems you'd like to unload onto me?"

Lynette laughed, shaking her head. "I think I'm okay right now."

"Ah, the introverted type," he mused as they started to cross the street toward Central Park. "Well, if you don't want to spill the beans on any dark secrets, then I guess I can't force you."

"Nope." Lynette grinned, enjoying his company now that he had settled back into what she remembered him being like. Charming, carefree, handsome. Although, if she was being honest, seeing the misery and the frustration in him had disarmed her in a way that wasn't altogether bad. She'd gotten to see the side of him she bet he didn't show too often; the man behind the charismatic mask. "You know, maybe your brother would take your ideas for the hotel more seriously if you were to present them to him in a more practical way."

"Like how?"

"Well, you could do the market research yourself and put together charts and graphs showing how doing what you're suggesting has benefited your competitors, and prove to him that your hotel is behind the curve in the industry and that its time for a change. Have an economist put together figures on projected profits, cost/benefit analysis, etcetera. Once he has all of that, he'll not only see that you're serious, but maybe he'll even agree with you."

Linc stopped dead in his tracks and stared at her when she faced him, her lips curved into a soft smile. He laughed, then swung his arm over her shoulders and kissed her forehead with relish.

"Good God, she's as smart as she is beautiful," he declared, beaming at her. "They teach you economics and marketing in dance school?"

"No, but just because I'm a dancer doesn't mean I'm devoid of intelligence," she countered. "I'm the daughter of a senator, Linc. I know a lot more than I bet you think I know."

"Well that's just scary." He chuckled. "One day I'll have to coax you into filling me in on all those government secrets your dad told you."

"It's a date." She smiled, not realizing what she said until it was already out. She felt her face flush with embarrassment as she turned away from him.

"You know, Lynette, if you're gonna ask a guy out on a date, you should really be a bit more specific about the time and place and all that," Linc told her conversationally, not faltering despite how embarrassed she was. "But since I have a feeling you haven't done this before, maybe I should take the lead."

He came to a stop mid-step and pulled her to him, so they were eye-to-eye and closer than she felt comfortable with. She met his eyes and found it hard to look away.

"I didn't intend to ask you out," she managed, her breath catching in her throat at the direct and predatory look in his eyes.

"That's too bad, because I think it's a great idea. From the second I saw you I was working it out in my head how I was gonna get a date with you. Funny how you subconsciously asked me." He held her eyes a moment longer, then stepped back, tucking his hands back into his pockets. "But since you're having doubts, I'll hail you a cab so you can get home. But the next time I see you at the hotel, I hope you'll reconsider that date."

Lynette blinked, taken aback by the abrupt way he suddenly left her hanging. But as the cab he got for her came to a stop, she made up her mind and leaned in to lightly kiss his cheek.

"Goodbye, Linc." She smiled as she climbed into the cab, shutting the door behind her and leaving him standing on the sidewalk. His lips curved into a mile wide grin as he watched the cab take her away.

Family feud, check. Hotel idea shot down, check. Kissed by a beautiful southern belle, check. It wasn't turning out to be such a bad day after all.

LATER THAT EVENING, Quinn shut down her computer and packed up her things, slipping into her coat and tugging on her scarf. She sang to herself, some old Motown song that had been stuck in her head all day, as she straightened up her desk and prepared to let Grant know she was leaving. Before she could knock on his door, he suddenly swept out of it, startling her.

"Oh!" She jumped, clutching her hands to her heart as she let out a shaky laugh. "You scared me."

"I apologize." Grant watched her laugh at herself, and could feel his lips subconsciously curve into a slow smile. "Was that Marvin Gaye?"

She froze, her cheeks flushing with embarrassment. "You could hear me?"

"I've been listening to you sing to yourself for the last hour."

"Wow, that's great. Just perfect." She smacked her forehead and laughed again, feeling foolish. "Was I any good? Be honest. I can handle the truth."

"You were awful."

"Ouch." She crossed her arms and eyed him deviously. "I'll have you know that I am the reigning shower singing champion in my house and, according to Ma, I have a real shot at the big time."

"There's no possible way she told you that with a straight face."

Quinn's features glowed with humor at the memory. "Yeah, it was actually more like 'Quinn, if you don't shut the hell up I'm gonna send you to the convent and let the nuns deal with you!'"

Grant was bewildered to find himself so amused by her. "You wouldn't fare well in a convent."

"Probably not. I'd talk the nuns ears off until they ran me out of town with nothing but my rosary for company," Quinn mused. "Anyway, I was just about to let you know that I'm leaving. Did you need something else before I go?"

"Yes." He handed her a sheet of paper, almost immediately settling back into professional mode. She missed the humor she'd seen briefly in his eyes. It had been a nice change. "I need you to drop this invoice off at the front desk on your way out."

"No problem."

They stared at each other for a brief moment, both in limbo over what to say or do next. She saw the strain behind his eyes that had been present all week, but accompanying it was something more, something darker and deeper that had been there since he'd returned from lunch. She regretted that he wouldn't want her to pry into his business, when she was sure she could somehow make him feel better.

After all, it was his birthday and as a general rule, at least in her house, everyone was supposed to be happy on their birthday. It was the one day out of the year that was supposed to be a guarantee.

"Mr. Vasser, if you don't mind me asking..." she began, biting her bottom lip to stifle back a smile. "How old did you turn today?"

Grant blinked at her, taken aback by the question. "Twenty-eight."

"Right, interesting..." She was curious to learn he was much younger than she had pegged him for. He just always acted so mature, so serious. "Well, I'm only two years younger than you, so I think it's kind of silly for you to call me Miss...you can call me Quinn, I won't think any less of you."

"I didn't mean to offend you..." he began, feeling unsure. He certainly hadn't expected her to ask this of him; it just wasn't how he'd ever done things. He always maintained a strict professional code of conduct with the hotel staff, and now she was asking him to toe the line and break one of his rules for her. Then again, he'd never found himself standing and chatting with an employee before, either. There was just something different about her, something he couldn't place or understand. It was there in her smile, in her eyes. In the way she talked, the way she moved.

"Please, you haven't offended me at all." Quinn shook her head, not wanting him to misunderstand her. "It's just that it's okay to be more personal, since we're both still on the fun side of thirty and all. And I want you to know that I'm here for you if you need anything. I'm just a phone call or a few steps away, okay?"

"Okay...I—"

"But if you're more comfortable keeping things the way they are, I completely understand. I don't want to step on your toes or anything." She smiled up at him, her hazel eyes patient and kind. God, had anyone ever looked at him that way before?

"Okay."

"Good." Quinn let out the breath she'd been holding, pleased he wasn't angry with her for her suggestion. She still wasn't sure where he stood on the issue, but she could tell he was uncomfortable so it was best to let it be. "Well, goodnight, then."

"Goodnight." He watched her gather up her things before leaving the office alcove. His mind was racing for something, anything, better to say to her. Damnit, why did he have to be so horrible with words?

Before he could do no more than scold himself for being a fool, Quinn turned around and smiled at him once again, just beyond the alcove door.

"Happy birthday, Grant," she said softly, a strange sort of sadness in her eyes. She wished she could give him more than just the words. He desperately looked like he needed a friend. Someone, anyone to talk to.

Grant said nothing as she left, catching the elevator and disappearing from sight. He was left with only questions, doubts, and revelations that did nothing to improve his mood.

Just what was he supposed to do now, when it was impossible for him to deny that he enjoyed her much more than he ever wanted or expected to?

Damn her for being so likeable.

SEVEN

Don Hughes was an uncomplicated man. He was a soft talker with a mountain of patience and the ability to be quietly domineering without appearing forceful or abrasive. He took his time analyzing things, piecing together complex puzzles that most men would recklessly abandon at the first sniff of something easier.

But not Don. No, he enjoyed the long pursuit, the solving of riddles damn near impossible to crack. He reveled in the mystery of times past and the people who were forgotten as the years piled up and more and more crimes were committed, burying unsolved cases under stacks and stacks of the bureaucratic nightmare that was the NYPD. It was up to him to dig into the pile, and bring justice to the forgotten.

He was a cold case detective. In fact, he was New York City's *finest* cold case detective.

And he was, for the first time in his twenty-two year career, at a complete and utter loss for words.

The goddamned Vasser family, he thought as he wearily rubbed his forehead and scanned the documents that were brought to him just an hour earlier, arriving in the hands of a slender blonde woman with worried, grief stricken eyes. How in the hell had they gotten mixed up in something as awful and disturbing as this?

Then again, the documents were old and the murder even older. Few of the living Vasser heirs would know anything about what these papers revealed or of the vile accusations within them.

It was troubling, to say the least.

He supposed the best thing to do was to begin with the woman who'd brought him this joyous little package: Hannah Owens Ashford. Niece of the recently deceased Maggie Owens, who had apparently held this little gem in her Queens home for sixty years without even knowing it. That is, until she discovered the documents a few weeks earlier.

Hannah confessed to him that when her aunt called her up that cold, December afternoon, she wrote her off as having misinterpreted what she was reading or perhaps being confused by the dementia. The doctors diagnosed Maggie with it only a few months before, so Hannah simply assumed her aunt's rant about documents exposing a murder disguised as a suicide by a great hotel tycoon to be a hallucination.

Until, low and behold, her aunt passed away and Hannah went through the old house to clean it up to be sold, only to discover the documents lying on the kitchen table in plain sight. That was the day she turned the papers in to him and wiped her hands clean of it.

Now it was up to him to look through what Maggie's mother, Rosalie Owens, had provided in the way of proof of said murder. He was thrilled, really, at the thought of uncovering what would undoubtedly be one of the biggest crimes in New York City's history. But a part of him was feeling a bit wary about it, a bit uncomfortable.

Maybe he hadn't been born in New York City, heralding instead from the sultry fields of Georgia, but he *knew* about the Vasser family. How could anyone not know, even those tucked away in tiny suburbs across America, nestled in quiet bedroom communities safely removed from the fast paced vibrancy of the big cities. Everyone with a television or, back in the day, access to magazines, newspapers and radio had heard of the Vassers. They were legendary; up there with the Hiltons, Astors, Rockefellers, and the Kennedys.

Countless books had been written about their legacy, along with dozens of screenplays and films depicting their empire. Classes were even taught in universities touting the entrepreneurial greatness of Alton Vasser, his son Winston and the grandsons that had succeeded him.

So yeah, he had at one time or another heard of the Vassers. And the thought of unveiling something of this magnitude, if it could be considered valid, would be a career maker.

It could also be dangerous. After all, the man that Rosalie claimed had committed the murder was, as far as he knew, still alive. Ancient, yes. But alive all the same.

Don tapped his pencil against his desk as he pondered over the documents, his dark eyes scanning the faded paper and written words, his brow creased with concern. Never had he come across a case like this. Or rather, had a case like this dropped in his lap.

Had Rosalie Owens *really* known some dark secret about her lover's death and written it down, stowing it away for fear of being assassinated for revealing it? Or was she simply a woman scorned, looking to destroy the family that perhaps had done nothing more than refuse to acknowledge her, monetarily speaking, after Winston's death? She had been, by her own account, the mistress while Winston was still married, so it was unlikely she would have received anything in the way of cash after his death. So what could be her motive, if not money, for exposing such diatribe as this?

He flipped through the pages, skimming over the countless love letters that Winston had written to Rosalie, some clearly decreeing her as his heir apparent if he were to be killed. But what had he done, or what did he know, to make him think he might be murdered?

He went back to the cover page, the letter Rosalie had written detailing her account of the events that led to Winston Vasser's staged suicide. He read over it again, having only skimmed the first of it before, now reading all the way to the very end. It was a lengthy letter, filled with numerous details, including names and dates of important events. But it wasn't until he got to the very end that he read what was undeniably the most crucial and damning accusation.

What he read in those last few sentences chilled his blood to bitter ice.

Good God. Don's eyes widened as he gaped at the words, reading them over and over again to be sure he read them correctly. In all his years as a cop, as a detective, never had he heard of something as heinous as this...

If what Rosalie Owens claimed was true, then Winston Vasser had been, in his opinion, more than justified in attempting to change his will. If what she described was cold, hard fact, then the Vasser family was in for a very, very rude awakening.

Unfortunately, the only possible way for him to find out was to go to the source and ask some questions. But since the accused murderer was still living and this was undoubtedly going to be a sensitive issue that could not be allowed to leak to the press, he was going to have to be clever on just how much information he revealed from the documents to the living Vasser heirs.

The less he told them up front, the more information he could take from their statements to validate what Rosalie Owens had written.

Then, and only then, would he be able to determine if the patriarch of the Vasser family had indeed committed murder.

Not just once, but four times.

"MR. VASSER, A *detective named Don Hughes is on line one for you.*" Quinn's voice came through the intercom.

Grant stared at it cautiously for a moment, trying to place the name. Thinking it most likely had something to do with his father, who had a habit of hassling cops and getting himself in trouble, he lifted the receiver and let out an impatient breath.

"This is Grant Vasser."

"*Mr. Vasser, my name is Don Hughes, I'm with the cold case division of the New York City Police Department. May I have a moment of your time?*"

New York? Grant frowned, settling back in his desk chair. But his father was in California...

"What is this regarding?" he asked, keeping the anxiety that suddenly bubbled into his throat in check. Was someone hurt? Had there been an accident?

"*It's regarding your great-grandfather, Winston Vasser. I have some new information that I wish to share with you. Are you available to meet with me tomorrow morning?*"

"Excuse me?" Grant frowned, thinking for a split second that this must be some kind of prank. "What kind of information?"

"*Regarding his death, Mr. Vasser. Please, are you available to meet with me?*"

"I'm a very busy man, detective..."

"*Hughes.*"

"Right, Detective Hughes. I don't understand what kind of information you could possibly have. My great-grandfather died over sixty years ago."

"*As I mentioned, I'm with the cold case division of the New York City police department.*"

Grant froze, feeling that anxiety bubble burst in his chest and the cloud of it hover there, heavy and massive.

"*I would prefer to have this conversation in person, Mr. Vasser.*"

Grant's eyes instinctively shot to the portrait of his great-grandfather hanging on the wall across from him. He held them there as he spoke, keeping his voice level. "Be here at nine am sharp tomorrow, detective, and I will give you thirty minutes of my time. No more, no less."

He hung up the phone before the man could respond, his eyes still on the portrait of Winston. The uneasiness he felt settled a bit and quelled, but the suspicion and curiosity remained. Just what was it that this Detective Hughes knew about his great-grandfather's death that hadn't been uncovered in the sixty years since?

"You killed yourself," he murmured to the portrait, his hands clenched tightly around the fountain pen that had been his great-grandfather's, the fountain pen he used nearly every day. It had never really fazed him much to think that the pen had been beside Winston when he had fired the fatal shot, or that his blood had touched its sleek black case. But now he found himself staring down at it, shaking his head slowly. "What in the world could this detective tell me about you that I don't already know?"

Feeling unsettled, he hastily opened the top drawer of his desk and stowed the pen inside, unable to look at it any longer.

He fought to convince himself that it was nothing, and immediately clicked back into his computer. It was most likely some technicality that the police wanted to tie up, and once that was taken care of, he could move on. He had too much to do already without spending time worrying over some cryptic conversation with a cop.

But as hard as he tried, Grant couldn't help but feel as though Winston was watching him from the portrait, dark secrets hidden in his charming smile.

"I'VE ALWAYS SAID you have your grandmother's gift for design." Marshall beamed at Madison, his blue eyes twinkling with humor and pride. "She would have adored you."

"I wish I had known her," she replied, the honesty of the statement softening her words.

They sat beside each other on one of the long sofas in the lobby, discussing minor changes she wanted to make to the décor, including new rugs, fresh flowers, and some kind of water feature near the entrance. It wasn't a professional skill of hers, but even she couldn't deny that she had a knack for it. She had personally redesigned the entire first floor of the hotel just three years earlier and had gotten the hotel listed as one of the most beautifully designed hotels in the United States. Not bad for a novice.

Madison looked over at her uncle, her lips quirking into a playful smile. "*Pépère* tells me all the time that he sees her inside of me reaching out to him. Perhaps that's why he keeps me so close."

"Cyrus keeps you close because you're his favorite," Marshall reminded her, patting her knee affectionately. "You look and act very much like him, but he sees the best of Stella in you. I don't know how it happened that my most irresponsible brother ended up having the best kids. It must be your mother's influence."

Madison snorted, shaking her head. "My mother does what she wants and occasionally it has worked out in our best interest. I think our success has more to do with you and *pépère* than anyone else."

"Well, now." Marshall grinned, pleased by her praise of him. "I did my best by you kids."

"And it was more than we deserved half the time."

"Nonsense, you were good kids, and you're still good now," Marshall insisted. "Though I do worry about Kennedy on occasion."

"She's naïve," Madison declared, her smile fading but her expression carefully devoid of the real frustration she felt. "College may help her grow up, but I wouldn't hold my breath. My mother has let her act like a child for too long. Kennedy's too old to listen to advice and too young to make the right choices."

"Eighteen is a hard age. She's going to need you, Grant and Linc to help her now more than ever."

Madison grew quiet then, keeping her thoughts to herself. Kennedy certainly didn't want *her* help. Definitely Linc, maybe Grant, but the last thing the girl would ever be caught dead doing was asking for Madison's help. It was a truth she'd long ago accepted and fought to ignore.

"I'm thinking of changing out the hydrangeas for irises on the front desk. Maybe throw in some wild grasses for texture," she said, her lips curving even as her eyes revealed absolutely nothing. Such was the gift and the burden of a skillfully closed off heart.

"I think that would be a lovely idea, dear," he muttered, his eyes now trained on a medium build, mid-forties black man who had just flashed what looked like a badge at Walter over at the front desk. Walter then looked beyond the man's shoulder to where Marshall and Madison were seated and pointed to them.

"That had better not be the health inspector. I am not in the mood." Madison's eyes narrowed in on the man as he walked over to them, his expression serious and guarded. Somehow, though, she had a distinct feeling that this man was no health inspector. He carried himself in military style, back rigid and gait purposeful, and the absence of a smile said to her that he took his job much too seriously.

"Marshall and Madison Vasser?" the man asked as he approached, holding his hand out genially.

Marshall accepted the handshake with a polite nod. "That's us."

"I'm Detective Don Hughes with the New York City cold case division. I have an appointment with Mr. Grant Vasser, but perhaps it would be advantageous for all of you to join us."

"What is this regarding?" Madison asked as she shook his hand, her lips curving politely to hide her suspicion.

"I have some information about the death of Winston Vasser," Don said briefly, looking to Marshall as he said the words. By his research, Marshall was the only Vasser in New York City who had been alive at the time of the murder. His reaction would be telling as to whether or not he had been involved.

Don was somewhat disappointed to see what appeared to be genuine confusion on the older man's face, his cheerful blue eyes now clouded with concern.

"What kind of information?"

"I would prefer to discuss this with all the Vasser family members who are present in private, if that can be arranged."

"We'll go upstairs," Madison decided, spotting Linc walking toward them from the front desk. "Linc, please come with us to Grant's office."

"Why? What's going on?" Linc asked, tucking his hands into his jeans pockets as he eyed the detective curiously.

"Detective Hughes says he has information about our great-grandfather that we need to hear." It had been nearly five days since he and Grant argued at lunch and since then the two had not spoken. As such, Madison knew he would be reluctant to waltz into their brother's office but unfortunately he wasn't going to have a choice.

"Alright." Linc kept his eyes on the detective, sizing him up. He looked professional, stone-faced, and quietly patient. That certainly didn't fit the mold of most of the arrogant cops he had seen in his time. "Let's go, then."

The four of them caught one of the elevators and went straight to the second floor. As they exited, Madison led the way toward Grant's office, ignoring Quinn as she knocked on her brother's door. Without a word, she swept inside, the others following her.

Marshall smiled warmly at Quinn, though it was strained. Linc said a brief hello, but it was clear he was distracted. The stranger that followed them nodded once to her and continued inside silently, closing the door behind him.

Grant looked up from his computer screen to stare at his family and the detective, glancing briefly at his watch to note that it was five minutes until nine. At least the detective was punctual.

"Detective Hughes?" Grant asked, rising to his feet to shake the man's hand as he approached.

"Yes, thank you for meeting with me. I know you're very busy," Don nodded, looking official in his black slacks and beige dress shirt. He reached into the inside pocket of his dark coat for his badge, showing it briefly to Grant as a force of habit.

"Please, sit down." Grant motioned to the chairs in front of his desk, his eyes flickering then to his sister, brother and uncle, who were hovering behind the detective. He hadn't mentioned the brief conversation with the detective the day before as he hadn't wanted to worry them.

"I apologize for not being very specific on the phone yesterday, Mr. Vasser, but I felt it was best that I meet with you and your family in person," Don explained, settling into the chair.

"I understand. I've agreed to give you thirty minutes of my time, detective."

"I remember." A brief smile ghosted over Don's lips before he continued. "A woman came to me yesterday with a letter that she discovered in her recently deceased aunt's house, a letter written by her grandmother, Rosalie Owens. Does that name sound familiar to you?"

"Yes, of course it does," Marshall cut in, eyeing the detective incredulously. "I went to Maggie Owens' funeral just last week, but whatever her mother had to say is of no value to us."

"On the contrary, Mr. Vasser," Don began, turning in his chair to glance up at the eldest Vasser in the room. "Rosalie Owens claimed, in the letter, that Winston Vasser did not commit suicide, but was in fact murdered."

The room was silent as they all processed what the detective said. Grant's brow furrowed and Marshall looked flabbergasted, while Madison's face revealed nothing. Linc, however, let out a disbelieving laugh.

"You're telling us that some woman came to you with some letter, that may or may not have actually been written by Rosalie Owens, that claims our great-grandfather didn't shoot himself in the head with his own gun in his own suite in this very hotel almost sixty years ago, but that he was *murdered*? I'm sorry, but that's bullshit and you're wasting your time and ours."

"Linc," Marshall grunted, glaring at Linc disparagingly before looking back to Don. "Detective, I find it hard to believe that you are taking this letter so seriously. If you read over the police report from 1957, you'll find everything in order. It was a definite suicide."

"I *have* reviewed the case file, Mr. Vasser, and unfortunately by today's standards and practices, Winston Vasser's death would not have been filed immediately as a suicide. For example, these days we check for things such as gunshot residue on the victim's hand, the trajectory of the bullet, hair and fiber analysis of the area around the body, etcetera. When Winston Vasser died, the police relied heavily on circumstantial evidence. Since there was no record or testimony from anyone within the family stating any conflicts with Winston, it was accepted that he committed suicide after the fallout with his mistress."

"So why are you here, detective, other than to open up old wounds?" Madison cut in, her arms crossed and her eyes hard as agate.

"If Winston Vasser did, in fact, *not* commit suicide then I am sure all of you wish that the killer be brought to justice. I felt that the information provided by the letter was enough to at least do some digging and see if there's merit to it."

"Rosalie Owens was a tramp," Marshall said heatedly, his face flushing with temper. "I will not have her destroy this family yet again from beyond the grave with some ridiculous accusation."

"Pardon me, Mr. Vasser," Don eyed the older man, his face betraying nothing but a cop's skilled impartiality. "But don't you wish to clear your grandfather's name if he did not pull the trigger?"

Marshall said nothing, gritting his teeth and fighting to calm himself. Beside him, Linc looked equally as frustrated. Madison simply looked suspicious.

Grant watched his family and the detective closely, carefully considering what action to take. Clearly Marshall wanted nothing to do with rehashing the suicide that he suffered from all those years before, which Grant could respect. However, if it meant possibly clearing his great-grandfather's name then how could he not pursue it?

"Detective, I would like to see this letter," Grant said, causing his brother to roll his eyes and his uncle to scoff in indignation.

"Unfortunately the letter is part of a police investigation and I cannot release it," Don explained carefully, knowing he was about to tread on shaky ground. "But I would like to interview those members of your family who were alive when the death occurred and see if I can corroborate what was written in the letter by Rosalie Owens."

"This is ridiculous," Marshall sniffed, outraged. "I better not catch wind of this getting out to the press or I will have your badge."

"The New York City Police Department does not release information regarding ongoing cases to the press, Mr. Vasser, I assure you," Don replied patiently, keeping his eyes on Marshall. "Since I have you here, however, I would like to ask you those questions and get this over with so y'all can get on with your day."

Marshall glowered, but nodded regardless.

"Can you think of anyone who may have had motive to kill your grandfather?"

"Rosalie Owens," Marshall said instantly, earning a half laugh from Linc.

"Can you explain why you believe Ms. Owens would have wanted him dead?"

"I don't know. I only met the woman once when I caught her rubbing up against my grandfather in his suite." Marshall frowned, disappointment flooding through him at the memory. "He claimed she was some consultant, but I knew an affair when I saw one. My guess is he refused to give her a share of the company or perhaps money after he passed away. She could have staged his suicide to shame the family and his name, which is exactly what happened."

"Can you think of anyone else who may have had motive?"

Marshall considered this for a moment, shaking his head. "I don't know, detective. I was only seventeen at the time and not immersed in family politics. My father—"

"Cyrus Vasser," Don confirmed, his face not betraying the flare of adrenaline he felt.

"Yes." Marshall's eyes narrowed, but he continued. "My father was largely in charge of the hotels at that time. I suggest you go speak with him."

"Would you say that your father had the most to gain from your grandfather's death? Since he, after Winston died, was next in line to assume the role of family patriarch?"

Grant watched as Marshall turned an ugly shade of red, his usually cheerful uncle pushed much too far. "Just what is it that you're suggesting, detective?"

"It is my job to look into all of the possibilities, Mr. Vasser."

"Did that bitch say my father did it?" Marshall growled, fists clenched at his sides.

"Marshall." Grant stared pointedly at his uncle, his gaze stern and disapproving before he turned back to the detective. "Detective, I would like you to keep me updated on any new information as you receive it. I'm afraid we've run out of time for today."

He rose to his feet, thus urging Don to do the same. He held out his hand, ignoring the vibrant emotions coming from his brother and uncle.

"Thank you for your time, Mr. Vasser." Don shook his hand before turning to shake hands with the others. Then he swept out of the office and was gone.

"Well, that was bullshit," Linc laughed bitterly. "Just what the hell is this all supposed to mean?"

"It means Rosalie Owens is laughing in hell right now," Marshall scowled.

"You shouldn't have been so rude to the detective." Grant looked at his uncle with concern and exasperation in his eyes. "Don't you see how your reaction may have painted you as a suspect?"

"That's stupid," Linc countered, crossing his arms defensively. "Marshall's pissed off. This is a sensitive subject for all of us, Grant. At least those of us with more emotions than a goddamn rock."

Grant met his brother's eyes and held them for a moment, battling back the anger sparked by the comment. He didn't want to fight with his brother, not now, not ever, and unless this Rosalie Owens business amounted to nothing, they were all going to have to stick together regardless of their disagreements.

"There's more to that letter than what the detective told us," Grant moved on, looking to his sister and uncle now.

"He *was* suspiciously vague about it," Madison agreed, pursing her lips in annoyance. "Regardless, I can't imagine he'll learn anything new by talking with the family. Everyone put this to rest years ago."

"Do you really think he's gonna go all the way to California, Nevada, Paris and London to hunt down the rest of the family and interview them?" Linc asked, trying to brush it off. "I don't think he'll go to that much trouble for something that's probably a lie."

"Even if he does, he won't learn anything new," Marshall insisted, stroking his mustache thoughtfully. "Though I wonder if he'll make a trip to the hospital and have a chat with my father."

"Grandpa Cyrus will gnaw his face off," Linc joked, grinning at the thought. "He won't let some detective push him around with stupid questions."

Grant sat back down in his chair and impatiently eyed his family. "I'll let you know if the detective contacts me again with more information. Until then, I have to get back to work."

Madison nodded before stalking from the office, Marshall following her, still looking upset and shaken. Linc stayed behind, however, his eyes on Grant.

"I'm sorry we haven't spoken all week," he said, his hands finding his jeans pockets.

Grant watched him quietly, guilt creeping into his gut. "I'm sorry, too."

"Look, I know how you are about this hotel, okay? I get it," Linc began, his frustration and eagerness mixing with the passion he felt for his ideas. "But I've been working on a proposal that I want to present to you soon and I hope you'll be a bit more open-minded when you consider it. Can you promise me that, at least?"

Uncomfortable under his brother's intense stare, Grant nodded, wanting nothing more than to be left alone. "Alright."

Linc nodded. "Thanks, buddy. I'll see ya around."

With that, he left the office and shut the door behind him.

"Linc?" Quinn jumped out of her chair as Linc almost swept right past her, causing him to whirl around and grin at her.

"What's up, sweetheart?"

Quinn couldn't help but smile back at him, pleased to see that he and Grant had made up. She had no idea what caused the rift between them, but she noticed Linc had avoided the office all week long and that Grant was hard pressed to avoid any and all mention of his brother. But if Linc's mood was any indication, the two brothers had come to some sort of understanding.

"Walter called from the front desk a few minutes ago. I guess there's someone waiting for you down in the lobby," she told him, biting her lip anxiously. "I didn't want to interrupt your meeting and he said the person was okay with waiting."

"Thanks, Quinn." Linc winked at her before racing off toward the stairwell, not wanting to wait for the elevator. He took the stairs two at a time and made it to the lobby in record time.

When he spotted Lynette sitting primly on one of the lobby sofas, he nearly fist pumped the air like a man who just ran a marathon.

"So you made good on your offer and came back to see me." Linc came to a swift stop before her, his grin a mile wide. "And here I was thinking I'd dreamed you up."

Lynette smiled, blushing a bit as she rose to her feet to stand with him. She was dressed in a knee-length dress the color of storm clouds with her dark coat tucked over her arm.

"I've been very busy," she apologized, feeling foolish as she clutched a ticket in her hand, suddenly wondering if this was such a good idea.

But when she met his eyes and saw the charm, energy and excitement in them that had attracted her in the first place, she thrust the ticket toward him and damned any possible consequences.

"I wanted to give you this," she explained, watching as he stared down at the ticket, her heart racing with nerves. "It's a ticket to see my ballet tomorrow night, if you're interested."

He eyed the ticket, noting that she had written her phone number on the stub. "Is this going to count as that date we talked about?"

"No. Well, I guess. I don't know." She laughed and covered her eyes with her right hand, feeling stupid. "I'm so nervous right now with you, it's embarrassing."

He smiled warmly at her, reaching out to pull her hand away from her face so he could tuck a loose piece of hair behind her ear. Today she had it up in a loose tail, strands of it trailing down in soft copper curls. "I don't know why you're nervous, Lynette. It's just me."

"I don't do things like this...I'm ridiculously out of my comfort zone right now. Being home schooled does that to you." She shook her head with a sigh, pulling away from him. "So have I wasted my time, or will you come tomorrow?"

"I wouldn't miss it." He reached for her hand again, this time lifting it to his lips and kissing it tenderly. She stared at him with both caution and excitement in her eyes.

"Okay." She pulled her hand away and straightened herself, regaining whatever dignity she could manage. "I'll see you then."

She swept away from him, walking through the lobby doors and into the sunny morning light. When it hit her hair and flashed a brilliant fiery red, he clutched the ticket a bit tighter in his hand and marveled at his good fortune.

EIGHT

He preferred that people remember him as a downright mean son of a bitch. It was easier to garner respect when people were so terrified of the very thought of you that to utter even a single word of contempt would be blasphemous.

At least, that was how Cyrus Vasser preferred to see things. He'd lived just over ninety years practicing it and it had yet to backfire on him in a permanent or destructive way. His ruthlessness and at times callous nature had served him well, and he'd be damned if he was going to have some sort of epiphany about "good will toward men" and all that nonsense. He had an empire to run and there was very little room for anything but a clear and level head not tainted by fluffy compassion and open arms.

Call him cold, he enjoyed the term. Say his heart was a shriveled black hunk of coal and he'd thank you. Better that people knew ahead of time not to have any foolish expectations of him. A reputation was the single most important thing a man possessed and one slip up could tarnish years of accomplishment in a manner of seconds.

It was unfortunate that he was chained to a goddamn hospital bed, he thought bitterly, scowling at the machines that pumped oxygen into his lungs and blood into his veins. He'd long ago accepted his fate, but that didn't mean he was happy about it. The nurses were insolent, the doctors even more so, and the orderlies just pissed him off with their stupidity. But they were all scared of him and they kept their distance unless they had to come close. Fortunately for him, he wouldn't have wanted it any other way.

He was a Vasser, damnit, and the name *meant* something to people. It carried with it a prestige, an intriguing kind of wonder and infamy. And the reason it did so was because he made it his life's mission to make it as such. Sure, there had been hiccups along the way that tainted the family reputation, but they were necessary ones that needed to occur to restore order. He wasn't about to start regretting his actions now, not when he'd lived long enough to see the success bred from his choices. He had a legacy, *his* legacy, in his children and grandchildren, and it was him they looked up to, him they admired and revered. Cyrus *was* the Vasser family, and he had single-handedly seen to it that the empire flourished even better than under his father and grandfather before him.

If only he was as confident in his own son as he was in himself, Cyrus grimaced, thinking of Marshall. The man was trustworthy and honest, but he was weak with compassion. He gave in too quickly when pushed and was too frivolous with money. What was worse was the man had not taken the road expected of him and gotten married and bred heirs to inherit the empire. He'd left that task up to his six younger brothers, who had all produced satisfactory enough children, he supposed.

But none had thus far pleased him as well as his youngest son Win's children. Perhaps he was biased because he placed them under Marshall's care at the hotel in New York, therefore keeping the closest eye on them and coming to know them the best. But he saw in them what he had not found in even his own children.

Grant was ambitious and strong-willed, with a serious nature that focused heavily on being prudent and to the point. Cyrus valued Grant's abilities so much so that he'd given him the position as General Manager years before Marshall would have been set to retire. Marshall preferred to ignore the real reasons behind his forced early retirement, but that didn't mean they weren't there, staring him in the face point blank.

Linc was, in his opinion, a bit too much like Marshall, though definitely more driven. Where Marshall had been lazy and ineffective, Linc exuded energy and a passion for the hotel that largely went unmatched by others in the family.

The youngest, Kennedy, was unfortunately a carbon copy of her idiot father, a fact which disappointed Cyrus enough that he preferred not to even speak with the girl. Thankfully, she was much too self-involved to notice he despised her.

And then there was Madison. She was the second greatest love of his life, in a paternal sense anyway, and he was certainly not a man who cherished anyone. But being as vain and narcissistic as he was, how could he not love the girl who was so very much like him. It was uncanny the way her mind worked just as his did and how seemingly without words they could communicate. She was his link to the outside, his link to the empire now that he was bedridden. And though he would never admit the truth aloud, he had never needed anyone more than he needed her.

Thinking of her still, he lifted his worn and tattered copy of *Atlas Shrugged*, his reading glasses perched on his narrow nose and his sharp tawny eyes scanning the words at expert speed. It was the only way to pass the time now, but he wasn't foolish enough to discount the advantages of being well read, especially when one chose his books wisely. There were a whole host of lessons out there waiting to be learned, both in life and through the experiences of others. He was the last man who would spit in the face of history and knowledge, since neither had ever let him down.

He heard the gunfire click of her heels beyond the door of his room long before she swept in, looking pristine and stunning as always, her body dipped in a dress of blood red. She paused before his bed and stared him down, one dark eyebrow lifted skillfully in both challenge and greeting. Her slender arms crossed as her eyes met his, identical in shape and color, and just as disarming.

"Hello, *pépère*," Madison smiled.

"It's been two weeks since you last came to see me," Cyrus scowled, glaring up at her. "Are you too busy to give me your precious time anymore?"

"You know you're not very pleasant company," Madison reminded him as she sat smoothly down on the side of the bed, her hand reaching over to lift the book from his hands and set it aside. "The nurse told me you called her a rotten whore the other day. I know it's hard for you, but sometimes it's inappropriate to speak your mind."

"I'll say whatever I damn well please," Cyrus grunted, holding her eyes as she grasped his ancient hand in her youthful one. He preferred not to note the contrast in their ages. While it didn't seem as though they were so far apart in years, that didn't make it any less a fact. "Besides, it's true. She's been fooling around with that asshole doctor what's-his-name. I've seen them making eyes at each other. Both married, too. Jesus, what has this world come to?"

"Affairs are nothing new, *pépère*, as you and I both know," she reminded him, tilting her head to the side then with a slow, considering smile. "Speaking of affairs, I have some interesting news to report to you."

"Out with it, then, I haven't got all day."

"I pray you will have many more days after today, and you will too after you hear what I have to tell you." Madison frowned, her expression taking on a serious tone that he knew meant something detrimental had occurred.

"The hotel?" he asked immediately, his heart constricting painfully in his chest. When she only shook her head, he allowed himself a brief moment of relief. "What is it, then?"

"A detective came by the hotel yesterday claiming to have received a letter written by Rosalie Owens." She paused, letting him absorb her words before she continued. "In the letter she supposedly wrote that Winston's suicide was a cover up for murder."

"Where did this letter come from?"

"Rosalie had a daughter who passed away recently. Apparently this letter was in her house and was discovered by her niece, who brought it in to the police."

Cyrus said nothing for a moment, his scowl deepening.

"They're reopening the investigation," Madison went on, sticking with the cold, hard facts of the matter and not inputting her own feelings on it. "The detective plans to interview everyone in the family who was alive at the time of the death in order to find out if what they remember corroborates what Rosalie Owens wrote in this letter."

"How could it? Everyone accepted it as a suicide and they wouldn't dare question it now, not with the family's reputation at stake." Cyrus clenched his free hand into a fist, the only outward sign of anger he allowed himself to show.

"He seems to believe he'll find some missing link that was passed up the first time around," Madison explained. "Regardless, I don't see it going anywhere. No one remembers a goddamn thing. It was fifty-four years ago."

"What did Marshall say?" Cyrus asked, eyes narrowed in distaste.

"He was noticeably upset. Outraged, really. He said that the detective was a fool if he wanted to take the whore's word over ours. Grant's worried that Marshall overreacted and made himself appear to be a possible suspect."

Cyrus let out a dark laugh, the thought of his eldest son having the guts to kill humorous to him. "What specifically did that bitch say in this letter?"

"I don't know." Madison frowned, gripping his hand tighter. "The detective revealed only that she claimed it to be murder instead of suicide. But then he had the audacity to ask Marshall if he thought *you* had motive to kill Winston, and Marshall jumped to your defense." She let out a huff of breath, her brow furrowed in a rare show of concern. "I'm willing to bet that Rosalie exposed everything and that the detective was holding back to see what we would say."

"Even if she did, none of it can be proved," Cyrus assured her, shaking his head. "I should have known that threatening her with death was not going to be nearly as effective as simply having her killed."

"That would have raised too much suspicion." Madison reminded him shortly. "No, you made the right decision. Leave this to me. I'll handle it."

"You always do, *mon coeur*." He patted her hand with a heavy sigh, his ancient lungs wheezing from the strain. The machines nearby beeped in a steady drone of noise. "When this detective comes to see me, as I am sure he inevitably will, I will deny any and all accusations in that damn letter. I suggest you maintain the same and instruct the others to do so as well."

"I will." She leaned in to kiss him softly on the forehead, pulling away to meet his eyes once more as she rose to her feet. "Seventeen years ago you entrusted me with your secrets, *pépère*. I, and I alone, will look out for your best interests now. You have my word."

He nodded and silently watched her go, the scent of her perfume lingering after her.

She would do her best, that much he knew. But whether or not she could handle the full extent of what he knew was written in that letter remained to be seen.

At last, it appeared karma was coming to collect his debt. Just what was the price going to be?

QUINN HUMMED QUIETLY to herself as she typed away at her computer, finalizing a letter Grant had dictated to her earlier that morning. Her fingers whisked expertly across the keyboard as she read from her notes, smiling to herself at how formal he was with his word choices. He was clearly far more educated than she was; some of the words she'd never even heard before. She liked thinking of him at some prestigious Ivy League school, all serious and proper as he sat in classes she could only dream of taking. To think of the great minds he must have met along the way, all of whom helped him build upon his character and education.

She'd seen a diploma from Harvard on the wall of his office, though she couldn't read the numerous degrees he had received since the font had to be so small to fit them all on the single, neat page.

There was no denying he was a very, very smart man. Intimidating at times, too, she mused, but she was getting used to him. His frosty silences were usually more out of awkwardness than irritation, and when he did speak he was always kind to her. He never raised his voice, nor did he berate her if she did something wrong. He let her talk to him, even if he rarely got more than a few words in himself. She'd even managed to make him smile a few times.

And he had this way about him, this quietly serious intensity that, while muted by his grounded sensibility, still managed to sneak its way into her thoughts in the middle of the night, when she'd wake up with his face emblazoned in her dreams...

She froze, her fingers hovering over the keyboard and her heart pounding in her chest. God, Quinn, what's wrong with you? She frowned, rubbing her heart. Don't be stupid.

She shook her head, willing the feelings away. She'd be worse than a fool if she, even for one moment, thought of herself as anything more than his employee. No, she was stronger than that, more mature than some stupid crush.

She jolted when the elevator doors slid open across the way. She knew her face must have given away her distress when Linc walked up to her, his smile fading.

"Is everything alright?" he asked, not liking the ghostly pale look on her face or the worry in her furrowed brows.

"I'm fine," she managed, forcing a smile. "What's up?"

He grinned as he shifted the presentation boards under his left arm, a binder filled with figures and projections in his right hand.

"Just wanted to see my big bro," he told her with a wink. "Wish me luck."

"Good luck, for whatever it is." Quinn watched him knock once on the door to Grant's office before letting himself in and shutting the door behind him.

She sat back in her chair, laughing to herself. With a cleansing sigh, she returned to the letter she had been composing, forcing the earlier fantasies from her mind.

About ten minutes later, Madison appeared out of one of the elevators and strolled right past Quinn, sparing her only a passing glance before disappearing into Grant's office. Quinn continued to type for a few more minutes, until she could hear shouting coming from the other room. Her eyes widened as she paused, staring at the door to the office warily as the shouting grew louder and more pronounced. She couldn't make out what was being said, but when she heard the echoing smash of glass followed by instant silence, her hands flew up to cover her mouth in shock.

Before she could do more than rise to her feet in alarm, Linc threw open the door to the office and, boards and binder in hand, stalked from the room looking violently angry. He ignored her as he suddenly whirled around and stared back inside, pointing a finger at his siblings accusingly.

"I don't know why I bother when you don't even take me seri-ously!" he shouted, his face flushed with heated fury. "If what you really want is for me to stop caring, then fine, fuck you both, I'm gone."

He left in a whirlwind of frustrated and furious emotions, leaving Quinn hovering in limbo beside her desk.

Inside the office, Madison turned to Grant, who was seated at his desk with his head in his hands and guilt creeping like acid through his veins. She felt sorry he had to bear the brunt of Linc's frustration, but it was just another aspect that came with the job.

"You're right in this, not him," she said, staring down dispassion-ately at the shattered vase of orchids. She'd thrown it to stop Linc from shouting, and while it wasn't her preferred method of handling situations like that, sometimes it had to be done. Feeling a tension headache brewing behind her right temple, she rubbed at it gingerly and sighed. "I'll have your secretary come clean this up."

With that, she left the office, eyeing Quinn as she did so. "There's broken glass that needs to be cleaned up, darling."

Quinn gaped at the woman as she left. She imagined the worst as she scrambled into Grant's office, her eyes taking in the destruction.

The spread of broken glass was extensive, with water and strewn orchids lying among the shards. But Grant appeared to be unhurt, at least physically, so she returned to her desk to grab the hand broom and dustpan she kept there.

Her breath clogged in her chest as she knelt down on the floor and carefully began sweeping up the glass, her eyes trained on the task at hand and her mouth dutifully shut. More than likely he would prefer not to talk about the incident. He was probably embarrassed, angry or worse over it, and the last thing she wanted to do was upset him further.

So she was incredibly surprised when he suddenly appeared at her side, a towel dangling from his hand.

"I don't want you to hurt yourself," Grant said softly, his eyes revealing nothing when she stared up at him. She accepted the towel with a nod.

"You just don't want a worker's comp claim," she said before she could help herself, relieved when she saw his lips curve into a tired smile.

"No, I certainly don't," he agreed, sorry to see her clean up the mess his family caused. Lord, what she must think of him now. She may not know the details of the argument, but she saw the aftermath and the obvious pain he caused his own brother. He felt sick to even think of her looking at him differently, sneering at him instead of smiling. He couldn't explain why it mattered so much to him what she thought.

She continued to clean up the water and glass as he went back to his desk, sitting down carefully in his chair. He found he couldn't stop watching her, losing himself in his thoughts as he noted the way her sturdy, practical hands diligently cleaned and the way tendrils of her dark hair fell down to hide her face from him.

After she'd gathered up all of the glass she could recover, she left to dump it out in her own trashcan instead of his, somehow knowing he couldn't bear to look at it. Then she returned to the office and lifted the orchids from the floor, hurrying over to place them in a replacement vase Grant kept in the kitchenette.

When she brought the fresh vase over to his desk and set it down beside him, he realized that he'd never been so close to her before and that her perfume smelled exactly as he imagined it would: warm sugar and vanilla, with a hint of cinnamon. It was so different from the rich musk and flower scents his mother and sister wore. Instead, it was much homelier and incredibly more comforting. He wondered if she knew just how well it suited her.

"You know, stuff gets broken in my house all the time," Quinn said suddenly, keeping her hands busy as she arranged the flowers. "One time, Ma and my oldest brother Angelo were screaming at each other over him wanting to buy a motorcycle and her thinking it was too dangerous. She said he was just going to get himself killed on the thing, or worse, paralyzed from the neck down and then we'd all have to take care of him. Well, he got so mad at her that he swung around and drove his fist right through the brand new TV. Broke his hand into a million pieces and taught himself a very valuable lesson."

"What's that?" Grant murmured, his eyes intent on her face as she smiled at him.

"Don't destroy the only means of watching the football game an hour before kickoff." She laughed, amused by the memory as she returned to fixing the flowers. "Needless to say, Angelo never got that motorcycle and his hand has never quite worked the same. But Ma was so distraught by him hurting himself so badly that she fawned over him like a baby for weeks after that and snapped at any of us if we even *tried* to make fun of him. He won't live it down with us girls, though. *Buffy* was on that night."

"How many siblings do you have?" Grant asked. For reasons he couldn't explain, he was determined to keep her talking. Somehow it was easy to lose himself in her words and forget about his own troubles, even if only for a while.

"There's seven of us, four boys and three girls." Quinn turned to him, resting her hip against his desk and smiling as she crossed her arms. "You think I'm loud and talkative? My family is a million times worse. When we're all together it's like a circus. One giant, colossal Sicilian circus."

"Next you'll tell me your father is a member of the Mafia," he mused, humor flashing in his usually serious eyes. She was caught off guard by it for a moment, then let out an appreciative laugh.

"Uh oh, I've said too much," she gasped, feigning alarm as she glanced over her shoulder and then back at him anxiously. "If a man named Al Capone Junior comes knocking, you just tell him you know nothing."

"I'm a little more worried about Don Vito Corleone paying me a visit," he humored her, enjoying himself more than he expected or wanted to.

"Good point." Quinn beamed at him approvingly for the *Godfather* reference. "In all seriousness though, my dad makes pizzas for a living so there's no need to worry about me getting picked off by some mobster in the street looking to score revenge or something."

"That's good to know." Though he didn't know why he was so curious, he continued to press her for information, enjoying the way she laughed with him in that open way she had. "Is that why you like to cook, because of your father?"

"You could say it runs in my family." She held his eyes, her smile warm. "My great-grandmother taught my grandmother how to cook authentic Sicilian food back in the old country, and in turn my grandmother taught my father, and my mother's mother taught her, and consequently they taught us. I've been making marinara sauce and pasta from scratch since I was five, and have gotten to the point where I regularly insult waiters at Italian restaurants when I order a meal to my exact specifications. I can't help it though, food is my life, it's my passion, my everything...I'm sure you feel that way about the hotel."

Grant nodded, unable to take his eyes off her. She had this passionate look when she spoke about cooking, much like the one Linc wore when he spoke about his ideas for the hotels.

Thinking of his brother appropriately doused his mood in ice water.

"Yes, I suppose I do," he murmured, the earlier weight returning to settle upon his shoulders like a ton of bricks. He cleared his throat and turned away from her, needing to reestablish a safe distance. "Thank you for cleaning up, Miss Taylor."

Quinn blinked as she straightened, sensing his dismissal. How was it possible that he could go from being open and pleasant to being cold and dismissive in a matter of seconds? As usual, she had to wonder if it was something she said.

"You're welcome, Mr. Vasser." She backed away from his desk and turned, confused and more than a little taken aback. She glanced over her shoulder before leaving, noting he was intently focused on his computer screen and determined not to look at her.

Yes, she was a fool to think of herself as anything more than just an employee to him. Every time she thought she was close to being his friend, he pulled away from her.

But every time he pulled away, she only became more determined not to give up on him.

THAT NIGHT, LINC sat in the packed audience of the New York
City Ballet Theater, all thoughts of his brother and the family empire
gone from his mind. He was done caring and knew it was best if he
took a vacation and got away from them for a week or two.

But even those thoughts seemed to fade into the background as
he watched the performance. All he could see, all he could comprehend, was the dance. And her.

She moved like she was gliding on water, her movements fluid
and graceful, filled with this latent emotion that sucked him in from
the very start. Her partner and the other dancers were merely filler,
as all eyes were on the angel with the copper hair.

When it was done and she bowed low in a gracious curtsy, the
applause was like a roaring tide rising and then crashing in a monu-
mental and glorious explosion of sound. People leapt to their feet,
but he was already standing, his eyes glued to her as she drifted off
stage and then on again for an encore applause.

At last, when all the dancers left and the curtain came down with
finality, Linc edged his way through the hoards of patrons and weaved
his way toward the dressing rooms. He knew he'd find her there, and
there would be hell to pay if they wouldn't let him in to see her.

Since he'd left the hotel that afternoon, furious with Grant and
done with it all, Linc did nothing but crave her presence. Something
about her was soothing. Her calm, clear eyes, her quiet reason and
sweet smile. She was still so much a stranger, yet he couldn't think
of anyone he'd rather spend time with. He'd never been very good at
being alone.

He didn't care if she thought him too forward or too insistent.
He knew he could convince her to spend time with him, even if it

was only for a little while until he got his bearings and his confidence back. He needed a distraction and it had to be her.

Linc found the dressing room and brushed past security, hoping no one would recognize him. It wasn't that he was necessarily famous or anything, but most people in New York were accustomed to seeing his face in the tabloids now and again, and he had a feeling it would only embarrass Lynette for people to gossip. Thankfully, by the time he made it through to where he spotted her, seated at her dressing table, most of the dancers had drifted off with family and friends.

She saw him in the mirror and her heart jumped into her throat. Instead of turning to face him, she merely held his eyes as he approached, his gaze intense and his movements cagey. He looked like an animal, beaten and raging, ready to bounce back and claim victory. But just what was it that he wanted to win?

"So you came," she said softly, reaching up to release her hair from its bonds, watching him as it tumbled loose over her shoulders.

"I told you I would," Linc murmured, wondering why he couldn't think of a single clever or charming thing to say to her. Either he'd been pushed much too far emotionally that day to be witty, or he'd simply lost all words just by looking at her.

"Is everything alright, Linc?" Lynette asked, turning then and rising to her feet, examining him with concern in her eyes. "You look awful."

"I feel awful," he grumbled, weary now as he watched her. "He said he would listen, but still refused to hear what I was saying. He pretended to be interested, but it wasn't there. His decision was made before I'd even walked in. God, I feel like such an idiot."

Her heart broke a little for him and she reached for his hand. "I'm so sorry. It's my fault. I shouldn't have told you to push him..."

"No, it was time I learned that he's never going to take me seriously." Linc frowned, wanting to forget all of it and focus on the now instead. "I think it's time I take a week or two and get away from that place, clear my head. I have a house down in New Orleans that I might go stay at. You should come with me."

The request was impulsive and spontaneous and so like him that she started laughing.

"Go with you? To Louisiana? On a whim?" She shook her head in disbelief. "Linc, I can't just pack up and go, I have responsibilities here. I have performances and rehearsals and my life...I don't have the luxury to just get up and go."

"Just for the weekend, then. Spare me the weekend," he urged her, reaching out to touch her hair, simply because it was there. "I know you barely know me, and I know you probably don't really trust me, but I promise you that I'm just an average twenty-seven year old guy who loves football games, pizza and cold beer."

"And women," Lynette added, eyebrows rising in good humor as she smiled. "My mother calls you the 'playboy' when you're not looking."

Linc snorted out a laugh, grinning at her. "How did I earn that nickname?"

"Apparently your wild affair with Jorja Hale and several other famous women has given my mother that impression," Lynette informed him, gauging his reaction carefully. "I don't want to be another one of your flings, Linc. I don't have time to deal with that. Well, actually I don't really have time to deal with any of this, but somehow you've forced yourself in and I'm giving you my time regardless."

"Then stop worrying about it and come out with me tonight," he requested, suddenly reaching out to run his hands up and down her arms, a desperate heat in his eyes.

"Where?" Was all she could manage, her heart racing at the idea. He had this ability to make her want to throw all caution and care to the wind and simply *be*. It was undeniably exciting.

"A bar, club, I don't care. Let's just go." He smiled again, cockier now and laced with his natural charm. "I bet you don't get to have a lot of fun, Lynette. Let me show you how it's done."

Lynette bit her lip hesitantly, her mind racing with lists of obligations and responsibilities. But what did one little night hurt? She didn't have to be at rehearsal until eight the next morning and technically until then she didn't have plans. He really looked like he needed a distraction and she felt too sorry for him to not help.

"Okay. Just let me change."

Within the hour, they were at a crowded and noisy blues club called *The Harlot*, complete with hazy blue neon lights, a packed dance floor, and a live band strumming away classics by the likes of Stevie Ray Vaughan and B.B. King.

After sitting for a few moments restlessly at the bar and downing shots of Southern Comfort, they turned to each other and seemed to know exactly what had to happen next.

"I know you've been doing it all night, but that dance floor is calling our names," Linc told her, his grin bright in the blue darkness of the club.

Lynette laughed, then rose to her feet and grabbed his hand. "I hope you can keep up with me."

"I like a challenge," he said as he followed her out onto the dance floor. He immediately pulled her against him and ran his hands down her sides, his hips moving expertly to the music. She matched his movements, her hands finding his as he twirled her out and then back into his arms, her back against his chest as he moved with her, keeping in time with the beat.

"You're better than I expected," she mused, spinning out and then back to him again, her calm blue eyes sparking with heat. "Makes me wonder what else I might learn about you."

"Let's see..." he began, smiling at her. "I'm an avid outdoorsman. I can hunt, fish, sail, rock climb, mountain bike, and snowboard. I love horror movies and rock music and I'm not afraid to get my hands dirty if my car needs an oil change."

"You own a car? In the city?"

"1967 Chevy Camaro." Linc released her to spin again before pulling her back into his arms. This time, her face was just inches from his own and he caught himself staring down at her lips, his heart racing. "I would bore you with the details on why it's the coolest car in the world, but there's something else I want to do."

He caught her mouth with his, enjoying the way she instantly melted against him, her arms sliding around his neck. As they kissed, they continued to sway to the smooth sultry beat of a song about black velvet, losing themselves in both the music and the feel of the moment. It was like being enveloped in a warm wave of molasses, thick and vibrating with drums and bass and a voice raspy with the heat of the south. Nothing else mattered. Nothing existed but each second as it came and went. No thoughts of tomorrow, no regrets of yesterday, only the moment.

Lynette pulled away from him as the music faded, the band switching to some upbeat Doobie Brothers hit about black water. She met his eyes, stunned by the intensity of emotion she saw, knowing he was just as moved as she was.

"This is dangerous," she whispered, so quiet that he only heard it he because he was so close.

"What's life without a little danger." He reached up to cup her face in his hands, leaning in to press his lips to hers once more, softer and gentler this time. Before pulling away fully, he simply hovered there, reveling in the feel of her breath over his own. "I'm leaving for New Orleans tomorrow morning. Come with me."

"I can't, Linc." She pushed back from him and crossed her arms, unable to stand the proximity of being so close any longer. "I'm sorry, but I can't."

"It's okay," he assured her, reaching for her hand to lead her away from the dance floor. "Let's go."

They made it outside the club and stood in the chilly evening air, the sky above them glowing hauntingly with threaded clouds and silvery moonlight.

He turned to her and managed a smile. "I'm still going to go, Lynette. But when I get back, I don't want to find out that you've run off with some other guy."

She snorted, shivering as she laughed at him and rolled her eyes. "As if I have the time."

"Good. I don't want you to forget me." He slipped his dark leather jacket over her shoulders just as a cab pulled up to take her home.

"Don't you want this?" She motioned with the jacket, eyebrows raised.

"I'll come back for it," he said simply, framing her face in his hands once again and kissing her. "Goodnight, Lynette."

"Goodbye." She met his eyes once before sliding into the cab and shutting the door. She couldn't resist turning around and watching him as the car pulled away.

Wrapping herself up tighter with his jacket, she bit back a smile and breathed in his cologne before releasing a heavy, wistful sigh.

NINE

Wyatt Bailey found it ironic that, after having been all across the world, he'd end up right back in his hometown of St George, Maine, doing exactly what he always said he'd never do. Such was the fate of a jaded gambler, he supposed. When the game didn't satisfy the hunger any longer, the best way out was to go back to the only other thing you knew how to do.

And for Wyatt, that thing was boat building.

His father before him had built boats on the weekends, specializing in fishing boats sold mostly to the local area fisherman. During the week, he was one of them; out on the water at the break of dawn, hoping each day was going to be better than the last.

That is, until the sea had claimed him and Wyatt's only brother. That was when Wyatt hightailed it out of Maine, realizing life was too damn short and that the last thing he wanted to do was end up as fish food in the Gulf of Maine.

And so he'd gone out to see the world, playing whatever game struck his fancy in order to maintain a decent amount of spending money. He'd done the backpacking thing across Europe, puttering around Moscow, Prague and Amsterdam, dabbling through Australia one time when he scrapped together enough for the airfare. Then back to the west and up through South America, where the games were hot and heavy, and the cards were usually dusty with traces of cocaine.

Eventually he'd run out of money. Well, what really happened was he wound up in Vegas on a whim and blew every last cent he'd

managed to win while cruising through Mexico, leaving him virtually penniless. He'd even been stupid enough to bet his own car,
which he'd subsequently lost his ass on. His only option then was to
hunker down and get a job. And in Las Vegas, the only real jobs are
in the casinos.

He'd worked his way up from bus boy to dealer, and spent more
time than he warranted in Vegas, losing himself in the lifestyle and
the glamour, the despair and the greed. It was a fascinating and
addictive place for a gambler, and he found he oddly enjoyed being
on the dealing side of the game for once. And it didn't hurt that he
was damn good at it.

But while Sin City may have been a fresh start and a new beginning for him, it also wound up being his destruction. Well, not the city,
really. Like many unfortunate men, it was a woman who did him in.

Shaking away the thought, he focused his attention back on the
fine sandpaper and the hull beneath his hand as he perfected his
creation, a forty-foot wooden yacht built especially for one of the
wealthiest men on the Eastern Seaboard.

At thirty-two, he was well liked among the up and coming elites
who were sick and tired of old men bossing them around. Trust fund
children who wanted to spend their inheritance without dirty looks
from those who despised them for being what they were. Wyatt
passed no judgments and couldn't care less if the client wanted a
kegerator and a hot tub built into his yacht. All he saw was money,
and he didn't care if it came from a trust fund or a drug deal. Cash was
cash and that was good enough for him.

To his right, an outdated stereo blasted out Bob Seger at full
volume and his foot tapped in time with the beat. A freshly opened
Heineken sat beside it, condensation cooling on the green glass while
a chilled ocean breeze whipped in from the wide open doors of his
oversized garage. Late afternoon sunlight streamed in hazily from
the skylights in the ceiling.

Wyatt sat back to admire his work, lifting the beer to his lips and
taking a long sip. Who knew he'd end up building boats, just like the
old man. Funny though how he preferred not to sail in his creations,
not wanting to try his luck when clearly his family had a bad habit of

perishing at sea. Instead he reaped the reward of cold hard cash for a job well done. The gambler in him scoffed at the idea, but the need for money was an absolute and Wyatt wasn't about to shun off an innate skill when it slapped him in the face. Plus he enjoyed working with his hands and building something from scratch that required precision and effort. It kept his mind off the past, which was exactly where it should be.

His cell phone vibrated in his pocket, causing him to scowl as he pulled it free and glared at the caller ID. 310 area code. Los Angeles.

Well, shit. Apparently the past just didn't want to stay buried where it belonged.

"Long time no talk, Win," Wyatt greeted casually into the phone as he shut off the radio and took another swig of his beer.

"*Sorry about that, Wyatt, you know how things get,*" Win said shakily, his voice slurred with drink and his breath uneven. In the background, Wyatt could hear the telltale sounds of a rowdy dive bar at high noon. "*What's it been now? Four years?*"

"Sounds about right," Wyatt confirmed, his lips curving into a slow and cagey smile. "What can I do for you?"

"*I'm sorry to bother you with this, I know you're probably busy... and everything, but I just got to tell you, warn you, really...*"

"Go on." Wyatt disliked the tone of Win's voice. He got extra apologetic and weepy when he was going to ask for a favor, and usually the favor was not one you wanted to be asked for. But they'd been friends once and it would take a crueler man than Wyatt to turn away someone who needed his help.

"*Remember seven years ago when I told you...you know...*"

"I remember," Wyatt said simply, though his interest was piqued.

"*Well, Marshall called me and said there's a detective calling around, asking about the...the thing.*" Win gulped audibly and let out a trembling breath, as if he were on the verge of tears. "*Wyatt, if he somehow gets to you, just pretend you don't know anything, okay? Forget everything I told you. If my father finds out...*"

"Your father's ninety years old, Win. What the hell do you think he's gonna do to you if he finds out?"

"He has people...assassins..." The last word was said in a hushed whisper, as if even the mention of it could get him killed.

Wyatt snorted out a laugh before he could stop himself. "Lay off the coke, Win, it's making you paranoid."

"I'm not fucking around, he's dangerous!" Win shouted desperately, causing Wyatt to purse his lips in irritation.

"Alright, calm down," he insisted, rubbing his temple. "So if this detective happens to somehow find his way to my doorstep, I should play dumb. Got it."

"You're a good man, Wyatt, a good man," Win said as he calmed, his voice slurring again as Wyatt heard him take another drink. *"I knew I could trust you, one of the few...the only, really..."*

"That's me, Mr. Trustworthy." Wyatt sighed, shaking his head and running a hand through his length of bronzed hair. "Get out of that bar, Win, and get some sleep. It sounds like you've had one too many already."

"I didn't want to call from my house...phones could be bugged..."

"That's unlikely, but okay."

Win let out an unstable laugh, the sound tired and worn. Wyatt felt sorry for the man, even though he'd made nothing but bad choices in his life.

When he'd learned the truth, years before, about why Win was the way he was, somehow it seemed justified. Anyone would be screwed up if they'd seen what Win saw when he was just a little kid...

"I know I've said this before, but my daughter should have married you," Win said, regret thick in his voice. *"She loved you the way she'll never love me..."*

Wyatt winced, downing his beer in one final gulp in an attempt to battle back the shame. "Life sucks, Win. But we all get by, somehow."

Leaving it at that, he snapped the cell phone closed and shoved it back into his pocket, feeling restless and edgy.

Great, this was the last thing he needed now that he'd finally gotten his life back in order and his priorities set straight. Sure, he could do what Win wanted and ignore this, and if some detective contacted him he could just shut up and move on. But that wouldn't be right and he knew it. Not now, not when maybe he could finally help Win get over this fear once and for all.

It was time the truth came out. Even though it would cost him a lot more than just gas money and time, Wyatt knew he needed to visit New York and set things straight.

He wasn't sure he could live knowing he'd passed up on this opportunity, not when he'd lived his entire life hedging his bets and taking chances. This was it and he had to take it. And not just for Win, either.

No, he was going to make this trip more than worthwhile for himself, too. If he got burned while doing it...well, at least he'd know he savored the heat of the moment before it came to devour him.

FIRE FLARED IN Madison's eyes as she gripped the phone tighter in her hand. By contrast, her voice through the receiver came out smooth and collected.

"Detective, I don't see the point in risking upsetting my relatives. Many of them are over sixty years old and not in any shape to take such questioning when this is all very likely nothing more than the wild imagination of a foolish dead woman."

"*I understand, Ms. Vasser, but this process is a necessary one if we are to get to the bottom of this.*"

Madison frowned, silently vowing to have the man's badge if he caused her family to implode over this. "You're wasting your time and tax payer money, detective. I hope when you finally realize that, you'll give up this game and do some real police work."

She hung up the phone before he could respond, not wanting to listen to him any longer. She was frustrated with his insistence and annoyed at his blind faith in a dead woman's letter filled with accusations that could destroy her family. Did he not understand the precariousness of the situation? If even a hint of this leaked to the press...God, she didn't even want to imagine it.

She grabbed her coffee mug and sipped, needing to do something with her hands to quell the urge to throw something that would cause a loud crash. She had to control herself if she was going to handle this properly. The detective would have his conversations with the family and tear open some old wounds, but he wouldn't find anything. How could he, when everyone knew exactly what they'd been told and nothing more?

"Your father is on line one." Carrie's voice floated through the intercom, causing Madison to nearly drop her coffee.

She stared at the phone, her eyes wide and her breath caught in her throat. Blinking away the shock, she carefully lifted the receiver and pressed the button for line one.

"This is Madison."

"Hi, princess," Win greeted. His voice was overly cheerful and marred by the drink he used to muster up the nerve to call. *"How have you been?"*

"Fine." She leaned back in her chair, her eyes narrowing. "I see you've decided to emerge from whatever hole you crawled into two years ago."

"I know it's been a long time...things have been rough, Maddie, you know?"

"I don't know. Maybe you should enlighten me on why your life is apparently so rough." Acid dripped sourly from her words and she regretted none of it. "Let me guess, you're contacting me now because you need something. I don't get so much as a Christmas card from you these last two years, but you have the audacity to call me now?"

"I'm sorry, I know I've been a shitty dad to you guys, but I'm gonna make it up to you, I promise...I just need your help, baby, please. I tried to call Marshall first, but—"

"Why? Because you knew he would give you whatever it is you want?" she spat, the vaguest hint of tears threatening behind her eyes, caused more by spiteful hate than pain.

"I just know you're all so busy..."

"Just get to the point and tell me what it is you want," she huffed, furious that she was allowing him to upset her this way. He had no right, no goddamn right to do this to her, not when he'd all but disappeared from her life. Though if she gave it consideration, perhaps she was better off without him.

"I just need a little bit of extra money, sweetheart, just a little," Win told her, desperation in his voice. *"I've come into some troubles, and my income just won't cut it this month..."*

"Income? You mean the monthly allowance we send you simply because you share our blood?"

"Right, allowance..." Win conceded, ignoring the venom in her voice. *"I'm sorry to ask this of you, but I've run out of options..."*

"How much?"

He named a figure and she grit her teeth, sucking in a livid breath. She wished desperately that it was possible to slap someone through the phone. God knew he deserved much more than a slap in the face, but it seemed the man had good enough luck to avoid any and all consequences of his actions. Just how was it her father turned out to be so incompetent when everyone else in the family was just fine? What was it about Win that made him utterly incapable of being anything more than a leech on the family fortune and a stain on their reputation?

"If it's too much, I suppose I could figure something else out..." Win said quietly, misery and hopelessness in his voice.

Despite her better judgment, despite the years and years she'd spent scorning the man for his stupidity as a person and his ineptitude as a father, Madison still felt the strings of loyalty tug at her heart. Underneath it all, he was still her father and a member of the family. And as much as the thought of him lying in a gutter somewhere living with regret and despair for his actions appealed to her more vengeful nature, some tiny part of her knew she couldn't allow that to happen.

Family was family and blood was blood. End of story.

"I'll transfer the money to your account this afternoon." Her eyes shut tight as she spoke the words, hoping to God she was doing the right thing. "But if I find out that you've shot this money straight into your goddamn arm, I will take away everything you have been given and toss you out onto the street. Do you hear me?"

"Thank you, Maddie, thank you," he nearly sobbed, the sound sickening to her as she held the phone away from her ear and shuddered. Men were supposed to be strong and resilient; women were the ones who were supposed to cry. So why was it her father wept while she boasted a spine of steel?

"Goodbye," she murmured into the phone the second before hanging up, not wanting to hear anything more. All that conversation had done was further lower her already rock bottom opinion of him.

Madison rubbed at her temples, fighting to calm the tension there as she furiously bit back the emotions. Because as much as she tried to deny it, she knew there was a time in her life when she'd loved him. When she'd been very, very young, her father was her hero, her king, her everything. But after facing disappointment after disappointment from him, she'd given up faith and lost so much innocence in the process.

Win destroyed any chance she ever had of trusting men with her heart, simply because she gave him hers all those years ago and he carelessly mangled it without even noticing what he had done. And now the man she wanted him to be, the man she needed him to be, was nothing. He was a failure in every single way: a drunk, an addict and a fool. If it wasn't for her uncle and grandfather, Madison may have never learned to place any amount of faith in others, particularly men.

Even then, there was only one man she'd given her heart to. Her time and her body were other things, but as far as her heart only one other man had the honor.

Cursing violently under her breath, she shot to her feet and left the room, leaving her thoughts behind. There was no room in her life for thoughts of those mistakes.

She stormed downstairs into *Cherir*, knowing if she distracted herself enough maybe thoughts of him would leave her mind. But when she reached the kitchens and heard the chaos ensuing within, for the briefest of moments she wanted nothing more than to shrink into a hole and cower.

But she wouldn't do that, couldn't do it. She was made of stronger stuff than that and knew it. Lifting her head up and clearing the weariness from her expression, Madison pushed open the steel doors to the kitchen and instantly made her presence known.

"Raoul," she said simply, her voice steeled with authority and laced with disapproval. Her chef glared over at her, his right arm raised over his head and a stainless steel pasta pot in his hand, ready to hurl at the floor. Its brothers and sisters had already met that fate, as the floor was littered with cookware and the kitchen staff was hovering around in fearful silence.

Madison's eyes swept over the other employees and when she spoke, her voice was much softer. "Please excuse us, everyone. We will regroup and have a conversation once this is settled."

The fourteen or so people nodded and fled from the room faster than she could blink, saying something about how terrified they were of Raoul. Pinching the bridge of her nose, Madison shut her eyes before turning to her head chef.

"Do you care to explain yourself?" she asked, her amber eyes flashing with irritation. "Or should I make my own assumptions?"

Raoul cursed under his breath and tossed the pot he'd been holding down upon one of the counters, reaching up to run his hands through his hair in frustration. He paced for a moment and then spun around to face her, his hands coming together as if in prayer as he met her eyes.

"I am sorry, *cariño*," he said flatly, struggling to preserve his pride despite the apology in his eyes. "You know how I get when I am upset."

Madison frowned, crossing her arms and leveling her gaze with his. "I'm satisfied with our current staff here, Raoul, and I'd be very sore if I lost all of them because you can't control yourself."

"Then tell that Irish boy to get customer orders right the first time and not come begging me to change things last minute. And remind blondie that she needs to wear that gangly mass of hair of hers up or else strands of it get in the food. Oh, and while you are doing that, make sure Jose or Juan or whatever the hell his name is shows up on time or I will escort him out myself!"

Madison said nothing for a moment, amused despite herself. Leave it to Raoul to legitimately have complaints worth noting but somehow make a giant spectacle of it and make himself look bad. Resigned to forgiveness, she uncrossed her arms and stepped toward him, cupping his face in her hands.

"This time, darling, I forgive you. But I still expect you to apologize to the staff for overreacting. I'll have a talk with Ben, Holly and Jesus, and this will all be taken care of. Okay?"

Raoul reached up to grip her wrists gently, nodding. "*Sí.*"

His eyes searched hers for a moment as his brows furrowed with concern. "Something else is on your mind, *cariño*. I know you well enough to see it in your eyes, no matter how well you try to hide it."

Dropping her hands, she turned away from him to take a seat on a nearby bench. She released a long sigh as he sat beside her and wrapped an arm over her shoulders.

"My father called me a little while ago," she said, her tone emotionless even as her throat clenched uncomfortably.

"*Mierda,*" he grunted, shaking his head and kissing the top of her head. "I'm sorry."

"He wanted money." She grimaced, hate simmering beneath the hurt she felt. "Not that I'm surprised. Two years go by and he decides to suddenly call me. How could it be anything but money?"

"I have a third cousin in Los Angeles. I can make some calls, have him killed for you." He looked down at her with a grin. "Solve all your problems, no?"

Somehow, despite everything, she laughed. "What? And then have to pay for his funeral? No thanks."

He laughed with her as she smiled at him, one eyebrow lifting in consideration.

"Seven years ago when I stole you away from Uncle Duke they all said I was crazy," she mused, humor flashing in her eyes. "That psychotic Spaniard, what was I thinking? But while you're still very much insane, none of the other Vasser Hotel restaurants have ever ranked as highly as ours."

He scowled, rolling his shoulders. "I hated that casino. Your uncle, he is a good man, but the people in that city have no class, no refined taste. I could have served slop and they would have known no difference."

"I was thrilled to finally come back to New York." She pursed her lips, something akin to loathing simmering dangerously in her belly. "One year was much too long in that godforsaken desert."

Sensing her mood change and knowing the reason for it, Raoul hugged her close once more and remained silent.

Madison, he knew, preferred leaving that particular part of her past in the dark, never to be mentioned again. He couldn't blame her, not when he'd seen her crumble and build herself back up again, like a phoenix rising from the ashes of its own destruction. Who would want to relive the nightmare that had caused such horrific pain?

MONDAY MORNINGS HAD never meant to Grant what they meant to other people. For most, Monday was the dreaded start to the work week. But he usually worked through the weekend, even if it was mostly from home, and so the horrendous event of trudging to work on a Monday never even remotely fazed him.

Except for this particular Monday morning. It wasn't because he didn't want to work. It was because he knew what awaited him the moment he arrived at the hotel.

The fact was his brother had left. Supposedly only for a week or two, but what did that matter?

Linc had left because of him. It would take a stronger man than him to not feel guilty, as determined as he was not to show it. Already the staff would be whispering, making assumptions and spreading gossip. The only thing he could do was stand tall for his decision.

The elevator opened at the second floor and he stepped out, only to hesitate when he saw Quinn seated at her desk, busy shuffling through a giant stack of paperwork.

She glanced up as he approached, a sheepish smile curving her lips.

"Good morning," she greeted, rising to her feet and wringing her hands.

"Why are you here three hours before your shift starts?" he asked. He gripped his briefcase tighter than normal, unsure why he was relieved to see her.

"I couldn't sleep, so I just came in," Quinn replied, concern in her eyes. "I was worried about you."

"Why?" He fought to keep the surprise from his expression, knowing it would give away the odd spurt of pleasure he felt at her words.

"I don't know. It's stupid, I guess." She tried to laugh it off, but couldn't find the strength to do so. He looked just as bad as she feared. Exhausted and stressed with dark shadows under his eyes. She wished there was something, anything she could do to help him. But, as usual it appeared the last thing he wanted was anyone's help. "Anyway, I won't keep you. Your mother is inside your office waiting for you."

Grant released the breath he'd been holding and grimaced at the door to his office.

"Of course she is," he mumbled, sincerely not looking forward to the conversation he was about to have.

Turning back to Quinn, he watched her for the briefest of moments, taking in her trim and tidy dress suit the color of pears, a color she must have known would bring out the green in her eyes. She smiled at him, slow and warm, and it somehow managed to comfort him more than anything else ever could.

"Thank you, Miss Taylor." He tore his eyes from her and went into his office, shutting the door behind him.

Charlene glanced over her shoulder at her son. She was seated in one of the chairs facing his desk, her slender legs crossed and her back ramrod straight.

She didn't smile, but her eyes swiftly took in his appearance and narrowed. "You look awful, Grant."

"Good morning to you too," he said dryly, stopping to kiss her cheek before setting down his briefcase and sitting in the chair across from her. "What can I do for you?"

"Don't play coy. You know why I'm here," Charlene huffed, clutching her purse tighter in her lap. "As you well know, Linc has decided to take a couple of weeks off."

Grant said nothing and merely sat back in his chair, watching her.

Undeterred, she continued. "Madison has filled me in on the details of the situation, but I must say I'm disappointed you allowed this to happen at all."

"What would you have me do differently?" he countered, keeping his voice level despite the flare of temper he felt. "I'm sorry that not all ideas are great ones. That's a lesson he's going to have to learn, and throwing a fit because he doesn't get his way will get him nowhere."

"Linc feels inferior to you. I think we all can see that." Charlene pointed out, the tiniest hint of worry in her eyes for her youngest son. "And while I agree with your stance on this, I still feel you should have tried harder to convince him to stay. Instead you let him walk out when the fundraiser is fast approaching and the hotel needs him here."

"I'm not his keeper. Why should I stop him from taking a vacation when he wants to?"

"Because as General Manager you are his boss, whether he wants to admit it or not, and therefore you should have handled this as such. How hard would it be for you to explain that you appreciate his initiative and ideas, but at this time you feel it is not in the company's best interests to expand? Then you should have told him that in a year or two, if the economy improves, that he could bring it to you again. Now tell me why that is *not* what you said to him, Grant? Why did you instead so rudely tell him that he was out of touch with the traditions of this family?"

Grant frowned, guilt churning horribly in his gut. Of course he'd gone over the words he used in his head a thousand times since the incident, but it still didn't change anything.

"I told him the truth. I'm sorry if he can't handle it, but I'm not one to sugar coat my words to soften their blow when being straightforward and honest with him is exactly what he deserves."

Charlene looked away from him irritably, knowing she'd just hit his brick wall. He was one of the most stubborn people she'd ever known and one of the last to admit when he was wrong, even if he knew it in his heart. "When your brother returns, I hope you'll change your mind and have a talk with him."

She rose to her feet, her expression grave and concerned. "In the end, family is all we have, my dear. You'll do well to remember that."

She swept from the room, leaving behind only the scent of her perfume and the weight of her words hanging heavy in the air before him.

HE DOVE INTO mindless work in an attempt to ward off his feelings of guilt and frustration, but even after three hours he was still too distracted to concentrate. Throwing down his pen and leaning back in his chair, Grant rubbed his face with his hands.

When his hands fell back into his lap, his eyes drifted to his office door and suddenly he realized where he could find relief.

He grabbed some paperwork from his desk to look official and went to the door, meeting Quinn's eyes as he stepped into the alcove. The second she smiled warmly up at him, he let out a relieved breath.

"I need you to file this paperwork," he muttered as he handed the stack of papers to her.

"What is it?" she asked mildly, looking at it herself.

He paused, realizing he didn't even know what he'd grabbed. When he said nothing for a moment, she glanced up at him and fought back a laugh. He looked like a deer caught in headlights, which made her wonder if he was so stressed out that he was losing his memory.

"Okay then..." She set the paperwork down on her desk and improvised, sensing he wanted to talk to her but didn't know how to start a conversation. Well, she'd never been short of ideas for conversations. "I brought in my specialty today, chicken parmesan. You gotta smell this sauce. It's to die for, trust me."

With a grin, she reached into her lunch bag and pulled out a Tupperware container, which she opened and held up for him to sniff.

Grant hesitated, glancing around to be sure no one was watching before he leaned in to smell the dish, his hands clasped at his back. As he hovered over her, she tilted her head and smelled it herself, not even realizing how close she was to him until she looked up and met his eyes.

While the food smelled incredible, he found he barely noticed it. Instead all he could see was her face and all he could think about was what it would feel like to kiss her.

Quinn was frozen in place, her heart jumping to a wild pace at the sudden intensity in his eyes. He never looked at her that way. He was usually so quiet and reserved, his expression never revealing anything of what he felt inside. But just then, in that moment, it was almost as if...as if he wanted her.

"It smells good, huh?" she stammered, pulling back and turning away from him, fighting to catch her breath and slow her frantic heart.

Grant straightened, part of him curious to see how much he unnerved her while he criticized himself for letting it happen at all. As interesting as it was, it was still unprofessional. But he couldn't deny he felt something, a stirring, a whisper, somewhere deep within that was battling against the rules he lived so prudently by. Something about her charmed him, and while he wanted to despise her for it he couldn't.

"I can't wait to try it," he told her, waiting until she looked up to meet his eyes again. This time, his lips curved into a slow smile, oddly arrogant in a way she'd never seen before. "Your boyfriend is a lucky man."

"I don't have a boyfriend." Quinn blinked, shaking her head in confusion.

Grant continued to smile, saying nothing as he retreated back into his office. She stared curiously at his door, wondering what happened to her serious and impeccably professional boss.

Don't be an idiot, Quinn, she scolded herself, rolling her shoulders and shaking off the sparks of energy that were still tingling through her system. More than likely you're making this into more than it is.

She went back to her work, only to glance up a moment later as Madison and Carrie strolled out of the elevator, looking busy and important as usual. Since she was used to being ignored by them, Quinn resumed typing as the two women disappeared into Madison's office. They reemerged a few moments later, a stack of papers in Carrie's arms.

Madison's heels clicked over the floor as she headed back into the hall, only to stop short as a man appeared out of the elevator with a vase of vivid red, black spotted tiger lilies.

"Madison Vasser?" the man asked, glancing down at the name on the card.

Madison stared dully at the blooms, her heart panging violently at the sight of them.

Instead of saying anything, she only nodded and accepted the vase, her eyes glued to the flowers as she stood in absolute silence. The man smiled politely and left. Carrie looked from the arrangement back to Madison anxiously, wondering if she should say something.

Quinn watched curiously from her desk, holding her breath and waiting for something to happen. What in the world was going through the woman's mind right now? Madison looked white as a sheet and just as emotionless.

Without warning, Madison lifted the vase over her head and hurled it to the floor with a mighty crash, sending shards of glass flying into the waiting area and water and lilies pouring out over the hardwood floor. Her eyes filled with a furious heat that smoldered dangerously as she admired the destruction.

Carrie immediately went to the broom closet to get a towel, which she draped over the pool of water, soaking up most of it so they wouldn't slip. Quinn's hands flew up to cover her mouth as she shot to her feet, unsure what she should do.

Grant bolted from his office, his eyes first going to Quinn, thinking she was hurt. She turned to look at him, her hands falling to her sides and her mouth opening and closing soundlessly, for once lost for words. He noticed his sister and Carrie hovering over broken glass and flowers, and went straight to them.

"Is everything alright?" he asked, meeting Madison's eyes. She was deathly pale, but those eyes were darkened with raging hate.

"It slipped," she said simply, waving him off as she stepped over the mess with Carrie on her heels. She headed for the stairs, not wanting to wait for the elevator.

Grant stared down at the towel, flowers, and the millions of shards of glass. A vase slipping to the floor wouldn't break into so many pieces. But a vase smashed into the floor would.

"Call the janitor, have him clean this up," he said to Quinn as he stepped back into the alcove, his eyes hardened to steel. "I won't have you clean up my sister's mess twice."

Quinn stared after him as he shut himself in his office, bewildered by what she'd just witnessed. Forcing back the shock, she picked up the phone and called the janitor, feeling sorry for the poor guy who sent the flowers.

Though for all she knew, maybe he deserved it.

TEN

Win Vasser crouched in the dingy corner of the Santa Monica Police Department's drunk tank, his head in his hands. He was miserably drunk, beer and liquor sloshing around pitifully inside his head as he swayed back and forth, feeling lost, alone and scared.

It was always this way when the drink took over and burned through the defenses in his mind to unleash the memories, vivid and frightening and horrific. He could see it so clearly when he shut his eyes, when he gave in to the voices and remembered...

He was seven years old the day he witnessed his father commit murder. Even now at sixty he wasn't free of the fear, of the torment that lived within him every single day. In the beginning, drinking helped him forget. Now all it did was enhance the horror and further drive him into madness.

He let out a low groan, willing the images from his mind. His eyes shut tight as nausea swirled dizzyingly inside of him. They wouldn't leave him alone. All he could see imprinted on the walls of his mind was his father, standing over his poor grandfather as a shot rang out into the night and blood spilled in pools of rich red.

His father would come for him next. He was after him. He'd always been after him.

He knew. Somehow he knew that he'd seen him, Win was sure of it. He would kill him.

Just like he had killed his own father, he would kill his own son.

Win shuddered and cried out, sobbing uncontrollably now. He had to run, he had to get away. He was coming...he was coming...

"Win Vasser! Hey, man, how's it going?" A man called out from beyond the bars of the cell, his grin crooked and his dark eyes sparkling with youth and curiosity.

Win's eyes were red rimmed and heavy as he focused on the man, who wore a reporters badge on his gray polo shirt.

"Shit." Win winced, his head pounding as he turned away, wanting nothing more than to fall asleep and escape everything. The idea of tumbling into nothingness was so incredibly appealing at that moment.

"Win. Hey Win, wake up." The reporter jostled the bars, stirring some of the other men in the drunk tank so that they cursed at him bitterly. He ignored them and instead asked the guard to open the door and let him inside.

When the stranger approached and knelt beside him, Win shot him a despondent glare. "Go away."

"Hey man, I just want to talk to you for a minute." The man pulled out a recorder discreetly, but even though Win noticed it he didn't have the strength to care. "So tell me how it feels to be off the wagon once again? Is your family upset with you? Do you think you're an embarrassment to them?"

Win snorted out a half laugh and shook his head, despair leaking in to mix with the exhaustion he felt.

"They hate me," he grumbled.

"Who? Your ex-wife? Your kids? Our readers want details, Win. They're interested to know about your life."

"Fuck you."

"What about your father? How does he feel about you failing to take on responsibilities in the family business?"

Win flinched as if the man had struck him, his blue eyes widening with abject horror. "Did he say something to you? Is he coming for me?"

"Maybe. Does that worry you?" the reporter asked, grinning again, wishing he could get out his cell phone and video tape the old man's expression. It was priceless.

"He's coming. Oh God, help me," Win sobbed again, glancing around wildly as if for a weapon of some sort. His eyes jolted back to the reporter. "You have to help me! If he gets to me, he'll kill me! He knows I know what he did!"

"Whoa man, calm down." The reporter stepped back a bit, suddenly wary of the man's mental state. "What did he do?"

"He killed...he fucking killed him!" Win cried, his voice rising several octaves, his eyes wide with mortified terror.

"Killed who, Win? Who did Cyrus Vasser kill?" The reporter's eyes sharpened, his heart pounding as adrenaline pumped through his veins. "Who did he kill?"

"My grandpa. He shot him. I saw it...so long ago." Win settled down, shame and misery taking over him as tears streamed down his cheeks.

"Wow." The reporter gaped, staring down at the recorder he held in his hand numbly. "Thanks, Win. See ya around."

He raced from the cell and the barred door slammed shut behind him, leaving Win rocking back and forth in the corner once more.

LINC LOVED THE south so much more than New York. The people were friendlier, the climate warmer, the food home cooked and delicious. Not to mention his plantation house was just a stone's throw away from a giant pond to go fishing in, a luxury he'd be hard pressed to find back home.

It didn't get much better than this, he mused, standing on the porch of his fixer upper estate. He held a steaming cup of coffee in one hand as he admired the work he'd done on the yard the day before. He'd ousted all the overgrown weeds and plants and put in all new landscaping, along with a brand new stone pathway that wound up from the dirt driveway to the house.

A full week had passed since he left New York, and in that time he began his remodel on the plantation house. He was still far from finished, but it was a definite improvement. His back was pleasantly sore and his hair hadn't seen a comb in days, but he was happy as a clam and ridiculously proud of himself.

All in all, it was a successful break from the norm and part of him wished he didn't have to leave. But he had an obligation to return home. He had a life to go back to.

Not to mention, Lynette was in New York.

He'd given in and called her once or twice, just to share his accomplishments and bask in her praise. She said she missed him, which did wonders for his ego and made him all the more eager to get back to her.

Going back to her also meant going back to his family and his brother. He'd taken some time to think things over and consider where Grant was coming from. He could understand the desire to want to preserve the tradition of the hotels, but at the same time he couldn't understand why a little bit of expansion would tarnish that tradition.

Maybe the timing was just bad, Linc considered as he sipped more coffee and watched a crane swoop down. It landed gracefully in the pond, its white body catching the morning sunlight. Maybe he'd give the idea a rest for now and ask Grant again in a year. And next time he'd try not to take it so personally. He hated fighting with his brother, who he loved despite their differences. And it wasn't in his nature to hold grudges for long.

He jolted when his cell phone went off in his pocket. He pulled it out and frowned down at the caller ID before answering it. "What's up, Wally?"

"*I know you said not to bother you unless it was important, but, well, I think this is pretty important.*"

"Okay..." Linc chuckled, sitting on the front porch steps and taking another sip of coffee. "Hit me."

"*Maybe it's best if you see for yourself, I don't even know where to begin,*" Walter decided, gulping audibly over the phone. "*Are you near a grocery store that sells tabloids? If you are, go pick up today's copy of* Scandal Source *and read the cover.*"

Linc frowned. "Since when do you read the tabloids?"

"I saw it on the way in this morning. I'm serious Linc, you need to see this."

"And you can't just *tell* me what it is that you read in this stupid tabloid? I have to go all the way down to the damn store and buy myself a copy?"

"I don't even want to say the words out loud, dude. Just do it." Walter hung up, leaving Linc staring down at his phone irritably.

"Okay, kid, I'll go get your stupid tabloid," he grumbled to himself, grabbing his keys from his pocket and heading for his Camaro. After he had a good laugh about the magazine maybe he'd take her for a spin through the country with the top down. Ah, winter in the south, he mused. Odd to think that it was snowing back in New York.

When he reached the grocery store he headed straight for the newsstand by the cash register and perused the titles, looking for the tabloid Walter mentioned. It was one he'd been featured in before, so he was expecting there to be some mention of an ex of his or maybe a picture of him drunk at a bar. That was just a normal part of being in the public spotlight as an heir to an empire as prominent as the Vasser family.

But when he spotted the magazine and lifted it off the rack, it wasn't his face that stared up at him, but his father's face, drunk and frightened looking.

The headline read: *MY GRANDFATHER WAS MURDERED, AND MY DADDY DID IT!*

Linc threw a twenty dollar bill at the cashier, and, tabloid in hand, bolted from the store like a bat out of hell.

HE LEFT HIS car at the airport in New Orleans and hopped on the first flight back to New York City. It was nearing six o'clock in the evening by the time he made it back to the hotel but he knew Grant would still be there. He ran as fast as he could through the lobby and up the stairs to the second floor, bursting into the waiting room. He startled Quinn as he raced past her and went immediately into Grant's office, slamming the door shut behind him.

Grant looked up the moment Linc entered. His breath froze in his lungs at the look on his brother's face.

"Did you see this?" Linc barked, tossing the tabloid onto Grant's desk. Grant stared down at it, then met eyes with his brother, outraged.

"How did this happen?" Grant managed, glaring down at the magazine again, his mind racing with possible solutions to the shit storm he knew was about to hit them all.

"I don't know, but this is bullshit." Linc's hands flew up to grasp his hair as he began to pace, his mouth curled into a snarl. "How could dad do this to us? He must have talked with that detective and gotten these ideas and then sold them to this goddamn tabloid!"

"Detective Hughes hasn't spoken to him yet," Grant informed his brother, flipping open the magazine so he could read the article. He fought to control his anger. "I just spoke with him this morning. He was on his way to Los Angeles but hadn't made it there."

"What?" Linc whirled around. "Then where the hell did this come from?"

"I don't know." Grant propped his left elbow on the desk and rubbed his temple tiredly, closing his eyes. "But I'm sure that once the detective sees this, he'll be all over dad."

"Do you really think he'll believe him though? I read through the transcript of dad's words-and he sounds insane. He was drunk out of his mind and decided to make up this story just to fuck with us."

"He's not smart enough to do that, especially not while drunk," Grant retorted, letting his hand fall away from his face as he met eyes with Linc. "I think he truly believes what he said to that reporter."

"How could he though? He was a little kid when Winston died and he's never led us to believe he thought it was anything but a suicide."

Grant considered this for a moment, trying to remember if his father had ever said or done anything to indicate he believed something so terrible.

"What are we going to do, Grant?" Linc asked. He took a seat in one of the chairs facing his brother, worry creasing his brow as his hands clenched into fists in his lap.

Grant stared at him, realizing they were going to look to him to fix this. If only he knew what to do. "All we can do right now is wait and do damage control if we have to."

Linc nodded, understanding. "I'll call Mads, get her in on this. You call mom."

"Linc..." Grant began, trying to find the words he wanted to say.

"It's okay," Linc replied, reaching for his phone. "This is more important."

Grant tried to smile. "Thank you for coming back."

"Thank you for letting me." Linc rose to his feet, cell phone pressed to his ear as he spoke with Madison.

Quinn's voice cued in on the intercom. *"Your mother is on line one, Mr. Vasser."*

Reaching for the phone and pressing the button for line one, he lifted the receiver to his ear and prepared to tell her the bad news.

"Mother," he said evenly, noticing then the distinguishable sounds of an airport in the background on her end.

"Grant, I'm in L.A.," Charlene informed him, her voice clipped and furious. *"I have your father. I had to bail him out of jail this morning. He's spoken with the press. I can only imagine what the hell they've done with it, but I'm certain it won't be good."*

"It's not good." Grant heard her curse under her breath on the other end, and he waited patiently until she spoke again.

"I'll be back in the city tonight with your father. You can put him up in the hotel for now while he's on bail. The judge agreed to let him come back with me."

"Why are you bringing him here? What happened to his house?"

"Clearly we need to keep a better eye on him. This cannot happen again."

"Agreed," Grant mumbled, leaning back slowly in his office chair. "Have a safe flight."

"Mads and Marshall are on their way up," Linc said, hanging up his cell phone and eyeing Grant strangely. "What's wrong?"

Grant hung up the phone as well before looking at his brother. "Our mother is in California. She's bringing dad back with her."

Linc gaped at him, instantly furious. "You're joking."

"I don't joke," Grant said dryly. "He was arrested again and she had to post his bail. She doesn't feel he should be left on his own right now."

"So she's bringing him here?" Linc growled as Grant nodded. "Well, he better hope you get to him before I do or else I'm gonna beat the shit out of him."

"That won't solve anything," Grant said evenly. "But don't think I'll stop you if you try."

"I may just do it if Kennedy isn't around," Linc ventured, eyes sparking at the thought as he sat back down.

"She's the only one who still holds out any hope for him."

"She'll learn eventually that he can't be trusted." Linc relaxed, arms draped over the back of the chair as he stared out the wide windows and into the night. "We all had to learn that lesson, didn't we?"

"We did." Grant noticed then that the box holding the harmonica Linc gave him was still sitting on his desk, shoved behind his computer monitor. He reached for it and lifted off the lid, pulling out the harmonica. "Did this really make you feel better on those nights?"

Linc watched his brother, his face swimming with emotion. "It was the only thing that helped."

Grant nodded thoughtfully, his eyes taking in the smooth metal of the instrument and the crisp engraving of the family name. Curious, he pressed his lips to the cool metal and blew, his eyes closing peacefully at the sound it made.

"I'd forgotten..." he murmured, emotions stirring as he started again and this time strung together the notes to form the intro to one of his favorite childhood songs.

When he finished, Linc grinned. "I love 'Piano Man.'"

Grant set the harmonica back into its box, eyeing it fondly before turning back to Linc. "So do I."

"Apparently we're not so different, after all." Linc chuckled, feeling oddly relaxed to be sitting there with his brother, content despite all the turmoil about to come crashing down on them. It was like old times, when they'd been each other's only friends.

"I know I've never been very good with words," Grant began, his dark eyes hardening with the guilt he felt. "But I'm sorry if I upset you."

"Forget it." Linc brushed off the thought, smiling. "We're family, we fight, it happens. No big deal."

"When things calm down, you should tell me about the plantation house you bought." Grant decided. "It sounds...interesting."

Linc laughed, reaching into his pocket to pull out his phone. "I took some pictures to show Lynette, but I can show you, too."

"Who's Lynette?" Grant leaned forward to look at the phone when Linc held it out to him.

"A friend," Linc mused. "For now."

Grant glanced up at him, eyebrows raised. "You have a girlfriend? Why didn't you tell me?"

"First off, she's not my girlfriend. Just a girl I've taken an interest in," Linc explained, flipping through to the next picture so Grant would focus on that instead. "Secondly, would you really give a shit if I came to you and said, 'Hey man, I like this girl. Isn't that cool?' I haven't bothered you with girl stuff since prep school."

"What advice you thought I could give you, I have no idea." Grant chuckled, admiring a picture of the refinished kitchen cabinets. "You've always been the ladies man, not me."

"That's only because all those pretty girls who pined after you were disappointed when you ignored them, so they came to the next best thing. Me."

"Shut up."

"I'm serious!" Linc pulled his phone away so Grant would look him in the eye. "You know how many girls I used to see watching you? You were this tall, dark and handsome, strong and silent type, with enough mystery to provoke countless tales of you ravaging girls in the janitor's closet."

"Excuse me?" Grant managed, startled.

"Rumor among the girls, at least from what they told me after I finally swooped in and cured them of Vasser fever, was that you were highly selective but the lucky girls who did catch your attention did not leave unsatisfied. Quite the opposite, actually."

"You're kidding."

"Cross my heart and hope to die, buddy. I'm dead serious." Linc shook his head and laughed again, amused at how flabbergasted his older brother was. "Are you telling me you never ravaged any girls in the janitor's closet?"

"Not a single one."

"Well, you easily could have with the reputation you had."

"This would have been nice to know back then, Linc," Grant told him, even as his thoughts drifted from beyond school years into the here and now. Did he still have that kind of appeal?

Madison and Marshall knocked and came into the office, both harried and upset. Settling back to what was important, Grant got down to business.

QUINN FOUND HIM an hour later, standing before the windows of his office. The only light came from the lamp on his desk, casting soft shadows on the walls. He didn't turn when she came in. Instead he simply stood there, solitary and regal in his quietly expensive dark gray suit, engrossed in his own thoughts.

"Do you need anything before I go?" she asked, chewing her bottom lip. She saw him take a deep, steadying breath.

"No. Have a good night."

She hovered in the doorway for a moment, then instantly made up her mind. She shut the door at her back, closing herself in the office with him. When she approached, he tilted his head to look at her, his expression impossible to read.

"I'm sorry about the tabloid," she began, feeling foolish. "If it makes you feel any better, Ma personally went around our neighborhood and made sure everyone knew it was made up. It's only like forty people, but at least they're on your side. Like I am."

Oddly moved, Grant nodded and turned to the city lights again. If only he could confide in her what the detective said and how part of him actually believed his father. It couldn't be a coincidence that the detective would hint that Rosalie had named Cyrus as the killer, just as his father had. Though he still found the allegation hard to believe because he thought he knew his grandfather so well. He'd been raised to respect the man with all his being. How could some-one he loved so deeply be a murderer?

"This will all blow over," he said, as much for himself as for her.

"Yes, I'm sure it will." She stood beside him and looked down at the streets below. Cars and people drifted by, their sounds muted by the thick glass of the window. Only the glare of lights managed to reach them, and in its luminance she could see his face, just out of the corner of her eye. He looked, for lack of a better word, haunted. "I'm glad to see you and Linc talking again. I can see that he loves you and looks up to you."

Grant frowned, wondering if she could understand that it had always been him looking up to Linc, wanting to be charismatic and easygoing and friends with everyone.

"I know I said it before, but I worry about you sometimes," Quinn continued, keeping her eyes on the view outside the window. "And maybe I just take my job a little too seriously, but I really want to help you. I want you to know that I'm here for you."

"Why?" Grant asked, unable to look at her. "Why do you care so much? This is just a job for you. It isn't your life the way it is mine."

She turned to him, knowing he probably thought she was ridicu-lous. Part of her didn't care. "I give everything in my life all that I have, and that includes you. I've never been the kind of person to consider work over just because I've punched out. If you asked me to pick you up at the airport at one in the morning, I'd do it. If you called me on a Sunday to get your dry cleaning so you can have a fresh suit come Monday, I'd do it. No questions asked."

"That's not required of you."

"You're missing the point." She sighed, trying to figure out how best to explain it to him. "The thing is, I don't only think about you when we're together. You're on my mind, all the time."

He glanced down at her, his eyes haunted with feelings and words he knew he didn't have the capacity to express. That didn't make them any less real, or any less troubling.

"I don't know how to react to you," he murmured, his brow creasing with frustration. "I'm not like my brother. It's not easy for me the way it is for him."

"What do you mean?"

"I've seen how you are with him. It's...easy, friendly." He shook his head, his eyes filled with both envy and regret. "I don't know how to be that for you."

"But you want to be?"

"Yes." He turned to face her, the urge to reach out and touch her consuming him.

She said nothing for a moment, at a complete and utter loss for words. "Wow. I'm tongue tied," she managed with a disbelieving laugh. "That never happens."

"Now you know how it feels." His eyes seemed to darken as he reached for her, one hand brushing a curled ebony strand of hair away from her face. It came to rest just below her jaw line and curved around the smooth skin of her neck. She shivered once from his touch, her smile fading. He continued to stare at her, the slow, deliberate curve of his lips taking on that arrogance she'd seen only once before. "I like knowing I make you speechless, Quinn."

"Oh." She bit her lip as he leaned toward her, his mouth brushing her cheek before hovering over her ear.

"Does it worry you to know that I want you?" he asked softly, his free hand cupping her elbow.

"It floors me...Grant." She ran her hands over the smooth fabric of his suit jacket, staggered by his words, by the sound of his voice saying her name.

He pulled away so he could meet her eyes, his expression sharp and intense. He warred with his own propriety and desires, alarmed to find that for once, his needs were winning. And when he watched her lips curve slowly to one side and her eyes spark with some deep and incredible warmth, there was little he could do to focus on being professional.

"Damnit, Quinn." He pulled her in and crushed her mouth with his, sending them both reeling, breathless and lost. He marveled in the shape of her pressed against him, the smooth and incredible curves, and thrilled at the feel of her practical hands fisting in his jacket, keeping him close. How long? How long had he wanted her like this, wanted her here, abandoning any and all caution? Since he first saw her, he realized. Since the first time she smiled.

She melted into him and gave everything she had, every last ounce of devotion and compassion she had in her. How could he understand just how much she had to give and how desperately she wanted to give it to him, and him alone? He, who had the weight of the world on his shoulders but bore it with this capable strength. He, who stood alone at the top, silent and courageous in his dedication to the legacy he'd inherited. And lastly, he, who so clearly needed someone, anyone, to understand him. Surely there were other women who had filled those shoes, but she wanted so badly to be the one to do so now.

She gasped as his hand dove into her hair and pulled her head back so he could see her face. He needed to see the desire in her eyes, to know it was he who put it there and not his brother or some other man. What he saw did not disappoint him.

He thought briefly of spreading her out on his desk, of pushing his papers and books to the floor so he could have her, unrestrictedly. But the realization that he'd never had such a thought before had him hesitating, wondering what was happening to him. Sex for him had always been straightforward, planned, routine. It had never been impulsive or so intense. Even with Erin. His heart faltered at the thought, at the memory of her face, wondering if even after three years it was too soon to feel so much about another woman.

He was losing who he was, who he'd always been, failing to live up to the rules he chose to live by. All for what? His secretary, who'd completely undone him with little more than a sunny smile and warm, gypsy eyes?

Lord, this woman...what was she doing to him?

His cell phone went off on his desk, startling him. He drew back from her, straightening his suit jacket and clearing his throat.

"I should answer that, it could be important." He winced at the unfeeling frost he heard in his own voice.

Quinn stayed where she was as he skirted the desk to grab his phone. Her arms defensively wrapped around her torso to ward off the sudden chill she felt. When she heard him address his mother, she shut her eyes tight against the hurt and disappointment.

Just before his phone rang, he'd stared at her as if she were a stranger. As though he couldn't understand what he was doing there with her. How could he go from passion to icy distance in the blink of an eye? What had gone through his mind at that moment? What had she done wrong?

Fixing her disheveled clothing, she left the room, needing distance and time to collect herself. As she shut the office door at her back, she leaned against it, her hand pressed against her fiercely beating heart as tears brimmed in her eyes.

ELEVEN

He tapped his hands on the steering wheel of his sleek, black Porsche Boxster to the beat of The Rolling Stones as he breezed through the last stint of his run to New York City. It'd been quite the drive, but Wyatt didn't mind. The end goal was worth any and all hazards he faced along the way.

Snow began to fall as he neared the city, but he paid no attention to it. He was used to the cold, even if it was nicer back in Maine. He'd return to it soon enough. First he had business to see to.

He wondered what her reaction had been to the flowers he'd sent. Knowing her, she likely threw them in the face of the poor messenger, but maybe she'd kept them just long enough to curse his memory. He liked to think that she still did, in fact, remember him, and that she had, even for the shortest of moments, thought of his face and ached.

He usually ached quite a bit at the thought of her face, so why should it be any different for her? They were such similar creatures. He knew her mind better than any other person alive. She was skilled in the art of deception, in ways most people would never understand. But he did. He understood perfectly, if only because he was equally skilled himself. Hell, how could a gambler be successful if he didn't master his poker face?

He rounded a turn and spotted the city looming in the distance. His lips curved into a sharp and eager grin. Then he hit the traffic.

Grunting irritably, Wyatt slammed on the brakes and slowed the car to a steady crawl, remembering in that moment why he despised the city as much as he did. How could she live here, in this tangled mess of towering concrete and steel, surrounded by miles and miles of rubbernecked cars and extremely frustrated people? But maybe that was why he'd been at home in Vegas while she loathed it. She needed New York just as much as New York and her family's empire needed her.

Wyatt needed wide-open spaces. While the strip in Vegas may be crowded, just beyond it was nothing but an expanse of empty desert in all directions. It only took minutes to escape the chaos and find room to breathe. And if he was being honest, he knew the need for space and desire for freedom was partly why he'd lost her in the first place. It was why he'd lost nearly everything that mattered to him. It was an incontrovertible truth that his wanderlust rarely sated others as well as it sated him.

But now he was determined to make things right, both for Win and for the family itself. They had a right to know the truth, and while Win was terrified to speak up, Wyatt wasn't scared in the slightest. Cyrus Vasser didn't intimidate him, had no hold over him. And if the man wanted to pursue some kind of legal action or, if Win's fears were correct, try and send an "assassin" to murder him, then that was how the cards would fall and he'd have to play them as best he could. No use worrying over milk that hadn't even been spilled yet, not when he had a debt to settle.

In a way, that was exactly what this was. He was settling his debt with her, and with the family, by giving them the truth. While he had a feeling they may not appreciate it at first, in the long run it would be best for everyone involved.

Except Cyrus, of course, Wyatt mused, reaching into his glove box for a cigarette as he rolled the window down a crack. Did they throw ninety-year old murderers into prison? He wasn't sure, but at least he'd be alive to witness the mortification this would cause those who loved him.

Most importantly of which, he considered as he flicked on his lighter and breathed the cigarette to life, was Madison.

This news was likely to destroy her.

Rolling his shoulders to shake away any doubts, he continued down the highway and into the city, figuring he'd deal with her backlash and her fury in due time. He'd dealt with it countless times before, hadn't he? And where other men cowered in weakness and let themselves be ruined by it, he fought right back and matched her without faltering. They were both skilled in the art of shooting someone who outdrew them. It had always made for an interesting, albeit destructive, firefight.

Because thinking of it put a bad taste in his mouth, he shot up the sound on the stereo until the blast of Led Zeppelin's guitar broke through his bad thoughts. He swerved into a swifter lane of traffic and gunned the engine, determined to make it into the city before he changed his mind.

He'd never been to the New York Vasser Hotel before, despite having been in the city itself many times. But he knew what to expect, having been to the Vasser Hotel and Casino in Vegas. Hell, he'd worked there. And while the glitz and glamour of the Vegas scene was undoubtedly less sophisticated and posh than the elite status of New York, Wyatt figured he could find his way around. In any case, if he made any inquiries then she might get a heads up he was coming before he actually made it to her. He was a man who valued the thrill of surprises, and this was much too important to leave to chance.

So when he pulled into the sweeping driveway for valet, town cars and limousines, he slipped the young man who approached him bearing a royal blue Vasser Hotel valet uniform a crisp hundred.

"Put it under the name John Smith," Wyatt told the valet, his eyes hidden by the lenses of his mirrored aviator glasses. With a gesture that was both practiced and smooth, he slipped a charcoal gray fedora onto his head.

"Yes sir." The valet nodded once and pocketed the hundred as Wyatt strode away, his gait long and relaxed, not hurried or committed. He grinned and tipped his hat to Barry the doorman as he opened the door, but as Wyatt stepped into the hotel lobby he made sure to keep his head down and his demeanor inconspicuous and leisurely. Linc, Grant and Marshall were likely wandering around, and if they saw him before he made it to her office then he was screwed. He adjusted his hat to shade more of his face and headed toward the elevators.

From experience, he knew that the offices were usually kept on the second or third floors. Since this hotel didn't require the security that the casino did, in all likelihood they fit all the offices onto the second floor. Whether or not she would be inside her office when he found it was one thing, but he'd deal with that possibility later.

When he emerged onto the second floor, his eyes did a quick sweep of the waiting area, hallway and conference rooms to the right, and open glass alcoves with offices on the left. He spotted Quinn, who glanced up at him as he swept in that direction. One quick glance at the plaque on the office door beside her deeming it as Grant's office had him cutting across into the other alcove, where a petite brunette was busy typing on the computer. He noted the plaque on the door labeling it as his destination. Without a word he sauntered right past Carrie and pushed open the door to Madison's office.

She glanced up when he came in, annoyance at the unannounced intrusion barely flashing over her features the instant before she froze. He stopped just inside the doorway and for the briefest of moments simply took his fill of her.

She hadn't changed, he discovered, his heart rioting within the confines of his chest. At least, not really. He supposed that her features had sharpened, hardened in a way that came with experience and age. She'd been eighteen when he'd first met her, still a kid. But it was no coltish teenager that faced him now. No, it was a woman that met his gaze, with a determined strength and a distinctly feminine power. The sight of her quite literally took his breath away.

Her rich honeyed eyes, heavy lidded and sultry, still focused on him with direct intensity, though there was a coldness in them now that hadn't been there before. Her sable waves of coffee colored hair were shorter, but he could still remember what it felt like to run his hands through it. He noted how the smooth ivory skin of her face paled as she stared at him, even as the rest of her expression remained immovable. That, at least, he'd expected. She'd always been talented in concealing any and all emotions from her face, never revealing more than what she wanted others to see. If anything, she'd only perfected her talent in the years since Vegas.

Madison bit down hard on her tongue, forcing herself to not lose focus, to not lose control. She fought to level her breathing, to beat back the violent racing of her heart and the explosion that hit her square in the chest just at the sight of him. Surely he was an illusion. Surely he wasn't really here, not now, not after all this time.

She let her gaze drift over him, taking stock of the man even as her emotions went haywire beneath her carefully constructed shell. She needed a moment to regain the ability to speak, to even fully appreciate the fact that he was here, standing before her.

He looked so much the same, and yet so different. He was still rugged, still tall and wiry with taut muscles rippling beneath tanned skin as though he were poised to attack or run, whichever he decided suited him best. It was his way, she knew, to feign leisure and casualness all the while more prepared than any to defend himself. It tricked others into letting their guard down, while he never, ever would.

He'd kept his golden-bronzed hair long, sweeping just above his shoulders, casually tucked beneath his trademark fedora. His eyes behind the mirrored aviator glasses would be hard as granite and the color of slate, deeply intense and harboring countless secrets he would never share. His faded and worn jeans coupled with the black leather jacket and gray t-shirt spoke of his comfort in the casual, yet she noted he wore a pair of leather shoes worth several hundred dollars. He'd always favored the finer things in life, while at the same time appreciating mundane things. She was well aware that he'd known both outlandish wealth and dire poverty several times over in his life.

He'd been a gambler in those days, among other things. Part of her was curious to learn what he was now.

"Hello, sweetheart," Wyatt drawled with an arrogant, crooked grin as he pulled off his sunglasses. His eyes flashed with humor and something much darker. "How've you been?"

Madison rose to the challenge willfully, almost eagerly. "Hello, Wyatt. I've been quite well, thank you."

She stood and slid around her desk, gliding toward him on sculpted legs, her slender body draped in a silk dress of ivory white.

On any other woman, the effect would have been angelic, a symbol of innocence and purity. But on her it was like a violent contradiction. The woman was the furthest thing from an angel and she knew it, prided herself on it. He wouldn't have wanted her if she were anything other than exactly what she was.

She shut the office door, leaving a confused looking Carrie hovering awkwardly at her desk, unsure what was happening. Then she turned to face him, angling her face toward his, making him wonder if it was in offering or if it was a trap.

Her eyes met his and held, revealing nothing except a vague interest and a quiet simmer of desire. If only he knew the firestorm raging within her and if only she could know of the hurricane tearing apart his own insides. Instead, neither had any assurance of the other's feelings, falling back into the same old game they'd always played.

Her dam was on the verge of shattering and all it took was a quick and stunning flash of violence to race over her eyes for him to foresee the slap before it hit him, wild and deliberate and mean, right across the side of his face. His head whipped to the side from the force of the blow but he didn't stagger, did nothing more than wince from the hot flash of pain. When he tilted his head back to glare at her, he saw the glorious satisfaction and the furious hate in her eyes. Yes, this was the girl he'd known, the red-hot viper that had stolen his heart.

When he started laughing, she nearly blinked, so taken aback by the sudden change of mood. She'd expected him to rage, to storm out, maybe even hit her back. He'd done all those things before, surely he was capable of doing them again. But laughing at her?

"What, may I ask, is so funny?" She crossed her arms, glaring at him suspiciously.

He shook his head and adjusted his hat, buying himself a brief moment of time to finish laughing before he yanked her against him, covering her mouth with his.

At first, he simply acted out of haste and retaliation for the slap. He knew it would hurt her to relive how it felt to kiss him and he wanted to use it against her. What he hadn't known was just how badly it would hurt him, as well.

Not only did she smell the same, like sultry amber and sandal-wood, she tasted and felt the same as well. His hands roamed over her sides and her waist, her hips and the sloping curve of her back, and it was like coming home. Everything about her, from the way her teeth nipped at his bottom lip to the urgent hiss of breath she released each time he dug his fingers into her flesh, was as familiar as his own face.

Her hands clenched into fists, gripping the leather of his jacket as she savored his kiss, her body trembling with the crushing need and horrendous, blood-boiling anger she felt. God, she hated him, hated him so much it ate at her very soul. Yet, despite the hatred she couldn't deny that she would always want him. Damn him for having the power to strip down her defenses this way and release who she really was. He was the only man to ever accomplish it.

Urging back the rush of passion, she broke the kiss and pushed him hard into one of her mahogany filing cabinets, just to get him away from her. He stayed backed up against the cabinet, his eyes unreadable but certainly lacking the arrogance they held before.

Fighting to catch her breath, she smoothed out the ruffles in her dress from where his hands had claimed her and eyed him evenly. There were traces of fury in her expression, less outrageous than before, but just as startling.

"What are you doing here?" she asked, one sculpted eyebrow rising. "I'd hoped you were dead."

He managed a dry smile as he snickered, leaning against the cabinet now and folding his arms casually. "I'm in town visiting a friend. Thought I'd come by and see you."

"Well, now that you've gotten what you wanted, why don't you make my wish come true and go get run over by a bus." Dark humor graced her expression as she continued to watch him. Just how many ways had she imagined him dying? All those painful, inspired ways...

"That's not a very nice way to say you missed me, sweetheart," he mused, his own dark humor kicking in. "Though I suppose I should be thanking my lucky stars you didn't drive an eight inch knife right through my heart the second I walked in here."

"Darling, stabbing you would be satisfying, but much too messy."
Madison stared down her nose at him as her lips curved. "I have a
.357 revolver in my drawer that would work much better."

He didn't doubt she would use it if provoked, so he swiftly
changed the subject. "So I see you've got yourself a nice little
office and a secretary now. Long way from managing the wait staff
in Vegas."

"Nothing good is given to those who don't earn it first." She
turned away from him and went back to her desk, needing to compose
herself as the memories flooded as fast as a roaring river through her,
leaving her unsettled and miserable. She couldn't let him see just
how much she both longed for and scorned those endless, hot days
in Las Vegas. Settling into her chair once again, she looked up at him
and this time, no smile graced her face. "Unless you have something
else to say, I think you should go."

He nodded, backing away from the file cabinet, hating himself
for wishing things were different between them. There was no room
for regrets where she was concerned. He'd done her a favor by leaving all those years ago.

"It's good to see you, sweetheart," Wyatt told her, enough honesty
in his words to hurt them both. "Maybe one day we can be friends."

Madison sneered, determined to hold on to her anger and her
pride. "If you ever come near me again, Wyatt, it'll be the last thing
you ever do."

He said nothing, oddly amused by the fact that this wouldn't be
the last time she'd see him and that he may actually die on this trip.

Hell, it had still been worth it to release Win from his fears and
see the woman Madison had become, savoring her that one last time.
Yes, the risk of certain death was most definitely worth that price.

"I look forward to it. See you around." He tipped his hat to her
with a slow grin before turning on his heel and sauntering right back
out of her office the way he'd come in. He left the door wide open
so she could watch him leave. Her eyes bored into his back, cold
and intense, while her heart pounded violently with both malice
and despair.

Both Carrie and Quinn eyed her curiously, but instead of facing them she got to her feet and slammed the door shut herself.

GRANT STARED UNSEEINGLY out his office window, unable to do anything more than think about her. She had been polite and cheerful enough that morning when she'd come to work, but he could see the darkness that shadowed her expression and the hurt that weakened her smile. He'd made an ass of himself and in doing so had harmed her. The guilt he felt over it had eaten away at his conscience ever since he'd watched her walk out of his office the night before. He'd never felt so awful over anything in his entire life, except for maybe the recent incident with his brother.

Funny how it works that way, he realized sourly. When it rains, it nearly always pours.

Or snows, he considered, watching the flakes of white fall steadily outside. It had snowed relentlessly in the last twenty-four hours, as if nature wanted to reflect his dismal mood.

He jolted at the sudden knock on his door, then felt his chest constrict painfully as Quinn opened it and stepped inside.

"The tile samples for the new pool arrived." She left the door wide open and approached him, a small box and some paperwork in her hands. Her lips curved into a polite, albeit distant smile as she set the box onto his desk and handed him the papers. "Also, your mother faxed these forms over for you to sign regarding the equipment rental for the breast cancer fundraiser."

"Thank you." Grant accepted the paperwork from her and set it aside, struggling to find the right words to say.

"Let me know if you need anything else." Quinn turned to leave the office.

He watched her for a brief moment before he called out to her, knowing he couldn't let her leave without at least attempting to clear the air. "Quinn, please."

She stopped and shut her eyes tight against the wave of dread she felt, knowing exactly what was coming. Turning around to face him again, she blinked back the hurt and stood as tall as she could muster, needing to hold on to her dignity.

"I know what you're going to say, Grant, and it's not necessary," she blurted out. She glanced over her shoulder and lowered her voice, not wanting Carrie to overhear their conversation. She approached his desk and crossed her arms. "Last night was a mistake, I know that. It's done, so now we can both just pretend it didn't happen, okay?"

Grant stared up at her, taken aback. "Mistake?"

"Yes, a mistake. You obviously realized that halfway through kissing me and were more than happy to have the excuse of a phone call to distance yourself. I get it, you regret coming on to me, that's fine. I can handle that. What I can't handle is you trying to let me down gently or placate me and make me somehow understand that you don't think I'm good enough for you. I won't have it. I don't care who you are, but I deserve better than that. From here on out, we'll pretend it never happened and there will be nothing but professionalism between us."

It surprised her to see real anger flash in his eyes as he rose to his feet. "Is that what you think this is? You think I feel you're less than me?"

She felt her lips part in surprise at the heat in his tone, not realizing how badly her words both hurt and angered him. "That was the impression I got, frankly."

"Well, you're wrong," he informed her, leaning over the desk with his hands planted on its surface, meeting her gaze firmly. "I went against my better judgment last night, but I don't regret it. What I do regret is allowing my own personal baggage to ruin the moment we had. Next time, and there will be a next time, Quinn, I won't let it get in the way."

Properly deflated, Quinn sat down into one of his chairs and pouted, unsure what to say to him. After a few moments of silence, she looked up at him sheepishly. "And to think I was about to unleash all matter of Sicilian fury on you."

"Looks like my French temper beat you to it," he told her as he rounded his desk and approached her, his eyes intent on hers. He tilted her face up so he could see her clearly. "I'm not an easy person to be around, but I'll always be honest with you. You should know I've broken several of my own rules between yesterday and today. But you should also know it was worth it to me."

"So what happens now?" she asked, her voice barely more than a whisper. "I don't expect you to compromise yourself for me. This is obviously unprofessional, Grant, I know that..."

"I suppose I could fire you."

Her mouth fell open stupidly. "No, please don't. I have rent to pay, and my bills, and the money I'm saving up for culinary school, and—"

"I was only joking, Quinn." He smiled down at her, amused.

"Good." She let out a relieved breath. "That really wouldn't be the fastest way to a girl's heart, anyway."

"No, it wouldn't be." He looked at her curiously, pulling his hand away from her face. "You didn't tell me you had plans to attend culinary school."

"Oh, well I need to save up the money for it first." She blushed, realizing how foolish it probably sounded to him. "I know I'm a little old to be going back to school again, but I've been giving it some thought and maybe I'm not as prepared as I thought I was for being a chef."

"You're a great cook," he told her, surprised to hear her doubting herself.

Quinn smiled, pleased at his praise of her. "Thank you, but, well, after I spoke with your sister about the hotel restaurant and any open positions—"

"You spoke with Madison?"

"Awhile ago, yeah," Quinn sighed, annoyed by the memory. "I asked her if she would consider me if any positions opened up in the restaurants, and she asked me if I had a professional education, which of course I don't. So she dismissed me. I don't blame her, really, though I do wish she'd let me do a test run or something just to prove that I can handle myself in the kitchen. I've always believed you can learn more by apprenticing than by sitting in a classroom somewhere watching demos."

Disapproval hardened his face. "I'm sorry she was rude to you. I'll discuss this with her."

"Don't you think that will make her a little suspicious?" Quinn shook her head. "Like I said before, I don't want you to compromise yourself for me."

"This is important to you," he said simply. "I'll do whatever I can to make it happen. It may not be for awhile since there are no openings that I'm aware of, but—"

"Stop," she interrupted, rising to her feet with a grateful smile. "Thank you. I can't even begin to tell you how much this means to me."

"I'm just repaying the favor." He leaned in to kiss her, but heard his sister's heels clicking across the wooden floor outside the office. They pulled apart like guilty teenagers just as Madison strolled in.

"Am I interrupting something?" she asked, eyeing Quinn disapprovingly before looking at her brother.

"No," Grant lied, clearing his throat before looking back at Quinn. "Thank you for the fax."

"You're welcome." She smiled, unable to help herself. She swept past him and left the office.

Madison closed the door the second she was gone, then crossed the room and went to stand before the windows, eyeing the snowy scene outside. For a long moment she said nothing.

Wyatt was out there somewhere, she knew. Hopefully driving that car of his off a godforsaken bridge.

"This snow had better let up soon or I'm going to scream," she muttered, more to herself than to her brother. He came up beside her, sensing something was bothering her and knowing perfectly well it wasn't the snow.

"The airport should be cleared by tomorrow. Then they can come home," he assured her, wrapping his arm around her shoulders.

"I'm sure our mother is having a blast being stuck at a fucking Hilton in Chicago with no one but dad for company," she spat, sneering at the thought. "To think I gave in and sent him extra money this month. I even threatened that if I found out he'd used it to get drunk or high that I would cut him off. But no, instead he's being brought here, to live under our roof, after going to the goddamn press and single-handedly turning all of our lives upside down."

"I've already spoken with a real estate agent about selling the house he's been living in," Grant told her, feeling a surge of justice from the thought. "We're going to put him up in a rental, a studio apartment most likely, and severely limit his purchasing power. This won't happen again, Mads. I won't let it."

"He should just kill himself and save us all the goddamn trouble," she said heatedly, vengeance hot in her belly despite the tiniest trickle of regret she had for her words.

Grant said nothing, knowing she didn't really mean what she said. Though it bothered him to acknowledge that yes, their father ceasing to live would undoubtedly make all their lives easier. He didn't even act like a father to them any longer. All he did was leech money from them and the company. But that was going to change from now on.

"Suicide runs in the family," Grant murmured, feeling her tense against him. "Or maybe it doesn't."

"You don't believe him, do you?" she asked, tilting her head to look at him. "We've never been able to trust a single word out of that man's goddamn mouth and you know it."

"I don't know if I believe him or not," Grant replied. "If he'd said this two weeks ago, I would've dismissed it. But now that the police are involved and the case has been reopened...I don't know if it's simply a coincidence or if he really does know the truth."

Madison pushed away from him, stone cold fury in her eyes. "Don't fall for his lies, Grant. This is our grandfather we're talking about, the man who practically raised us, who chose us to carry on his legacy at this hotel. Will you really stand here and tell me you believe he's a murderer after everything he's done for us?"

Grant scowled, feeling restless and uncertain. "I don't want to believe him."

"Then don't," she insisted, shaking her head. "If you value everything this family has stood for in the last hundred years then you'll ignore our father's foolish ramblings and put your faith in our grandfather. He needs you to stand with him right now and deserves nothing less."

She turned to leave the office, frustrated and angry with him for being, in her mind, weak. She was supposed to be able to count on Grant to be strong and consistent, and the fact that he was wavering on this issue disturbed her greatly. Because if Grant was in doubt, that meant the rest of the family most definitely would be in doubt, which spelled trouble for her grandfather and the secrets he entrusted her with. It was up to her to see to it that this issue was snubbed out before it got any worse.

Before she reached the door she paused, her hand resting on the handle, her heart pounding in her chest. She looked over her shoulder at her brother, meeting his eyes in a cold, unfeeling stare. "Wyatt's in town, which could only mean trouble's coming. I just thought you should know."

Grant stared at the door after she left, shock and understanding hitting him. He thought briefly of the flowers she destroyed in the waiting area and realized he should have seen this coming.

His sister was right. Wyatt Bailey didn't just stroll into the city without having a reason to do so, and he was willing to bet it had something to do with his father, Win. And when something had to do with Win, it was always the worst kind of trouble.

TWELVE

L ynette approached the front desk, twisting her purse strap in her hands. She smiled at Walter, noting the surprise that passed over his face the instant he saw her.

"I'm here to meet Linc for lunch, is he around?" she asked, watching as Walter grinned foolishly and dropped the scissors he'd been holding.

"Yeah, sure. Um, let me go get him." He started for the back office before whirling around and pointing an index finger at her. "Has anyone ever told you that you look just like Rachel McAdams?"

Lynette blinked, caught off guard by the question. "No."

"If she had red hair, I swear she could be your twin."

"That's nice, I guess." Lynette frowned, getting impatient with him. "Can you get Linc, please?"

"Oh, right. One sec." Walter grinned again as he skipped off, disappearing into the back office. Moments later a harried and stressed looking Linc appeared, his cell phone glued to his ear as his eyes swept over her. He mouthed a silent apology as he continued to speak into the phone, his words clipped and angry.

"Damnit, Logan, we went to school together. You've known me since the goddamn second grade. You seriously can't persuade your boss to let this lie?"

Lynette watched Linc scowl, his hand clenching tightly on the phone as he ran his other hand through his hair. "Fine. But don't call me for box seats to the Knicks games anymore. You're dead to me."

He hung up his cell phone and for a moment seriously considered hurling it to the floor just to watch it shatter into a million pieces. Instead he took a deep, soothing breath, slipped the phone into his pocket, and turned to face her.

"I'm sorry." He tried to smile, but it was still sharp and bitter around the edges. "Things have been a little crazy lately."

"I can imagine." She walked over to meet him as he skirted the counter, holding out her arms to envelop him in a hug. He went straight to her, the pleasure of holding her again easing the worst of his anger.

"I missed you." He sighed, pulling away so he could kiss her, not even waiting for her to respond. "Did you miss me?"

"More than I wanted to," she joked, enjoying the feel of his lips on hers. "I'm sorry I've been so busy."

He laughed, resting his forehead against hers and shutting his eyes. "You have no idea, Lynette. No idea just how bad it's been here."

"Why don't you tell me all about it over lunch?"

He kissed her again, forcing a smile on his face. "I'm starving. I don't think I've eaten since yesterday."

"Linc, that's awful," she lamented, hooking her arm through his and leading the way toward the hotel's sushi restaurant. "You need to take better care of yourself."

"What I need is another vacation." He held open the restaurant door for her. "And a shot of sake. Maybe two."

They took a seat at one of the high bar tables next to the sushi bar. Lynette watched curiously as Linc greeted the chefs in perfect Japanese. Amused by him, she settled into her chair and glanced at the menu.

"So what do you like?" Linc asked, checking off items on his own menu list expertly. "Lemme guess, you like the safe stuff like California Rolls and salmon sushi."

"Now what makes you think that?" she asked, smiling as she began to check off a few items. "You don't wish to offend me, do you?"

"Not intentionally." He grinned, reaching over to tilt her chin up so he could see her face. "So then are you a wild, culinary risk taker? Trying any and all varieties of exotic cuisine without hesitation?"

"No," she replied, eyebrows raised. "I like to think of myself as somewhere in the comfortable middle. Not too safe, but not too risky either. Just...moderate. Oh, but I can't have rice. So that unfortunately limits my selection regardless."

"What's so bad about rice?"

She laughed. "I'm a dancer, Linc. I have to follow a very strict diet in order to maintain my figure."

"So no starchy white rice?"

"No starchy white rice."

"What about rice wine?"

She blinked, considering the notion for a moment. "I don't know. I don't really drink that much, but I suppose a little bit wouldn't hurt."

"Great." He gestured to the waitress, handed her both menu lists, and ordered four shots of sake. When the waitress swept away, he reached over to hold Lynette's hand, releasing a heavy sigh. "I really did miss you."

"I know." She avoided his eyes, unused to seeing so much honesty just in a person's expression. It was a trait of his that had unnerved her from the start. "So tell me about what's been happening...I heard about the tabloid."

"Yeah, it's a goddamn nightmare." Linc grimaced. "I found out about it while I was in New Orleans. I left my car down there and flew back as soon as I could, but there hasn't been much I can do about it. My mom is with my dad. They're flying in tonight."

"Have you talked with him about it?" she asked, sorry to see the worry and frustration in his eyes.

He shook his head, his temper sparking. "I haven't talked to my dad in over a year."

"Oh...I see."

"Yeah." He sneered, sincerely not looking forward to the reunion. "He's an asshole, plain and simple. I think he did this just to get attention and maybe some quick cash, but Grant thinks...well, Grant thinks he might be telling the truth."

"What?" Lynette gaped, startled. "But it's your *grandfather*."

"I know. It's crazy." He took another deep breath and met her eyes, wondering if he should confide in her about the detective. As of yet, only those within his family knew about Don Hughes of the New York City Cold Case Division sniffing around the family asking questions. But he had trusted her with key information before and she kept it to herself. "I really don't know what's going to happen. I've kept our statement limited to 'no comment' until we can talk to dad and find out what the hell he was thinking. But until then it's my job to fend off hungry reporters and columnists looking for a hot story. I was just talking to one of them on the phone when you got here. Old friend of mine, Logan Schultz. Bastard works for the goddamn *New York Times* and he won't stick his neck out for me and tone down the story. Instead he's going to run the full thing, front page, because he wants a promotion and doesn't care if it ruins my life."

"Some friend," she managed, squeezing his hand in hers. "It'll blow over, Linc. These things always do. Something else scandalous will happen and then everyone will forget about this."

His expression hardened as doubt filled his eyes. "I don't think we'll get off that lucky this time."

"Why not?"

He paused as the waitress dropped off their sake. After he thanked her he grabbed one and downed it gratefully, needing to quell the fury and suspicion exploding in his gut. Once the waitress was out of earshot, he set down the glass and leaned over the table toward Lynette, lowering his voice, his eyes intent on hers.

"A few weeks ago, a detective from the cold case division of the NYPD came to see us. He claims he has evidence that my great-grandfather was murdered. A letter from some long dead mistress of his from the fifties that apparently knew it wasn't suicide. He made it sound as though the letter names my grandfather as the killer, but he wouldn't say specifically. The detective was making the rounds meeting with my entire family when my dad talked to the press, but he never made it to Los Angeles. So it's possible that my dad actually does know the truth and got anxious knowing the detective was coming for him so he blabbed to the press."

"Good Lord." Lynette covered her mouth with her free hand, her eyes widening.

"Or, it's possible that he's full of shit, and this is all just some crazy coincidence," Linc added, scowling.

"Have you spoken with your grandfather? Gotten his side of the story?"

"My sister usually goes to see him, so I imagine she will once we figure out what's going on with dad. She won't want to upset our grandpa unnecessarily, so she'll want to have all the facts before she goes."

"You're sure he hasn't already seen this on TV?"

"He's ninety years old. He couldn't care less about TV," Linc mused. "The old man reads the same ten books over and over again. That's all he does."

"Well, that's a good thing, at least." She let out a sigh and sipped one of the sake shots curiously. When she felt Linc's hand stiffen in hers, she glanced up and noticed he was staring over her shoulder, cold, hard fury blazing in his eyes.

"You've got to be fucking kidding me," he grumbled.

Startled, she turned around to see what he was staring at and spotted a tall, vixen looking woman walking toward them, long legs exposed beneath a trim black leather dress, ice-pick black stiletto heels gracing her feet and a fluffy gray chinchilla sweater wrapped casually over her shoulders. Her straight dark hair was cut razor sharp at her chin and her bright blue eyes were honed in on Linc with sultry intensity. Lynette watched as the woman's lips curved into a dangerous feline grin. Lynette's brow creased as she realized she'd seen the woman before. But where?

"My, my, Linc Vasser. Didn't expect to run into you here." The woman purred as she stopped by their table, her hands resting on the smooth curve of her waist, her generous cleavage all but spilling out of her dress.

"This is my hotel," Linc muttered, eyeing her with the deepest, darkest disdain. "What the hell are you doing here, Jorja?"

"Oh, just meeting a friend for lunch." Jorja glanced briefly over at Lynette, scanning the girl up and down. "Who's your girl, Linc?"

"None of your goddamn business."

"Oh, well now, that's no way to treat an old girlfriend, honey." Jorja smiled again, focusing back on him. "I was just trying to be friendly."

"Jorja Hale," Lynette murmured, looking over at Linc curiously before turning back to the woman. "The actress."

"Mmm, yes." Jorja pursed her lips and disregarded Lynette as an ignorant, wide-eyed southerner as she reached out to run her right hand through Linc's hair. He batted her hand away furiously before rising to his feet, fighting not to lose his temper and cause a scene.

"If you don't get the fuck out of my hotel, I'll have you thrown out on your goddamn ass, Jorja. So help me God, I'll give your entourage of paparazzi enough pictures of you lying in the muddy snow to last for months."

She only smiled. "I dare you to try, Linc. How do you think your customers will feel watching you lose your temper and forcefully throw a well-respected actress out of the hotel when I've done nothing wrong? And don't forget, you screw with one of us, you screw with all of us. Remind me, how many of your clientele are members of the Screen Actors Guild?"

"A few." His hands clenched into fists at his sides as he glared at her. "Just get out of my face. I have enough shit going on right now without you adding to it."

"Like that tabloid article?" She smiled, enjoying the angry flush that came over his face. "You know, I'm inclined to believe poor Win. He always was an awful liar."

"You should know," he said through clenched teeth. "Goodbye, Jorja."

"See you around, honey." Jorja blew him a kiss and grinned devilishly at Lynette before swaggering off, her hips swaying and her head held high. Linc noticed she left the restaurant instead of staying for lunch. The bitch had always been a liar.

He settled back into his chair and rubbed his face in an attempt to beat back the urge to scream and shout and rage. God, that woman drove him crazy.

"Are you okay?" Lynette asked, unsure whether or not she should try and comfort him. She'd never seen him look so furious. Even when he'd been angry with his brother, he hadn't looked like this.

Linc let his hands drop away from his face, remorse eating away at his gut. "I'm sorry you had to see that, Lynette. That was embarrassing for both of us."

"I'm not embarrassed," she insisted, trying to offer him a reassuring smile. "Just shocked, is all. It's not every day that I get to meet a celebrity."

"She's scum," Linc spat, reaching over for his second shot of sake and downing it gladly. He slapped the glass back onto the table and sneered. "Hell, she's lower than scum."

"She's not as pretty in person as she is on the big screen," Lynette said, hoping to lighten the mood. "She wears a *lot* of make up."

"When you're ugly inside and out, it takes a lot to cover it up." Linc leaned back as the waitress dropped off platters filled with the sushi they'd ordered. "Let's drop it. She's not worth talking about."

"Well, if you don't mind me asking just one quick, tiny question?" Lynette began, lifting her set of chopsticks and passing them through her fingers.

He looked at her warily. "Okay, shoot."

"Why did y'all break up?"

Linc sighed, gritting his teeth again as he opened his own chopsticks. "She fucked my dad. And that was the end of that."

Lynette froze, wishing she hadn't asked. Feeling sorry, she reached over to touch his arm. "I'm sorry. It wasn't my place to ask that."

"No, it's better that you know."

"So that's why you haven't talked to your father in so long?"

He selected a piece of spicy tuna roll, dipping it generously into a tiny bowl of soy sauce. "It's exactly why I don't speak to him. And he knows what he did, though I doubt he feels the least bit sorry about it. He's always been selfish and childish enough not to realize when his actions hurt others."

"I understand that," Lynette said as she took a tentative bite of seared tuna. "All my father can think about is getting elected. He actually had the nerve to suggest that I marry you and have babies right away so that, come the 2016 election, he can run for president and the public can woo over his adorable grandchildren."

Linc nearly choked on the roll he was chewing on. "Excuse me?" He half laughed and half coughed, wondering if he heard her right.

"Apparently, having little ones running around will ensure he wins the election. And according to him, I really shouldn't be selfish and deny him that. Even though having babies right now would destroy my figure and consequently ruin my career."

"Tell him to adopt a baby from Africa or something," Linc suggested, his lips quirking into a half grin.

Lynette shook her head. "He's impossible. And my mother is even worse. She lost her chance to be a dancer because she got pregnant with me, so now she's made it her life's mission to see to it that I fulfill all of her wasted dreams. Luckily for the two of us, I love ballet."

"That's pathetic, Lynette." Linc frowned, reaching for her hand again. "You need to tell them that they're not in control of your life."

"I'd rather not cause a fight." She waved the thought away, pulling her hand from his and poking around at her food, feeling foolish. "It's not easy for me to talk to them. I'm always steamrolled into compliance before I even get a word in."

"Let me talk to them, then."

She snorted out a laugh, briefly picturing him riding gallantly to her rescue and saying all the things she'd always wanted to say to her parents but never had the guts to say. "No, it's not your problem. Besides, I love my life, my career...there's no reason for me to stick a wrench in things when it's all going so well."

"It's up to you," he said softly, feeling sorry for her. "But if you change your mind, I'm here for you."

"That's sweet." She met his eyes again as her lips curved. "But your issues are much more pressing. If you need anything, Linc, even just an ear to bend, don't hesitate to call me. If I'm busy, just leave me a message and I'll get back to you as soon as I can. I want to be here for you, too."

He grinned appreciatively. "You have no idea how badly I needed to hear that."

CHARLENE ROLLED HER eyes as she stared out the window of the discreet, black town car as they cruised into the city, wishing to God she'd thought to bring a Vicodin so she could tone out her ex-husband's pathetic whimpering. Three days she had to spend with him and his obnoxious excuses, which was three days much too long. And if his turbulent mood swings were any indication, things were only about to get worse.

"Char, please, please don't make me go back there," Win pleaded, shifting constantly in his seat and fidgeting, scratching his head, rubbing his face, clawing at the cloth of the black tailored pants she insisted he wear. He was nothing short of a goddamn mess. "I don't want to be here. Take me back to L.A."

"No," she spat, glaring at him. "You got yourself into this mess, Win. Now it's time to face the consequences of your actions."

"I'm sorry, Char, please," he whined, his knuckles whitening as he clutched the edge of the leather seat. "I made a mistake, but don't make me go back there, don't make me do this."

"Your *mistake* has cost this family a lot of heartache and stress. Especially our children, Win. Or do you honestly not care about them?"

"I care..." He frowned as he chanced a look out the window. His eyes trailed over the view of New York City's skyscrapers, shrouded in heavy, thunderous clouds, and he felt a convulsive shiver race through his body. "But why can't I just go home?"

"You're clearly incapable of handling yourself without causing trouble. You're going to have to stay here for awhile."

"No." Win's eyes widened with fear, his hand jerking out to grip the door handle, seriously considering vaulting himself from the car and ending it. But when he tried the handle, he realized they had turned on the child safety locks and that he was trapped. Panicking even worse now, he reached out for his ex-wife's hand desperately. "I'm begging you, don't make me do this."

Charlene ripped her hand from his. "Don't you dare touch me."

He stared at her for a long moment, his heart aching, his emotions flashing from fear to misery. It had always been that way with him, his moods fleeting and rapidly changing, which led some in the family to assume he was bipolar. He'd always simply considered it to be part of his nature.

"You used to love me, Charlene," Win murmured, anger mixing in with the despair he felt. "A long time ago, you looked at me so differently than you do now. Why did that change? Why did you turn on me?"

"This is ridiculous," Charlene huffed, though her throat clenched uncomfortably as she looked away from him. "I've told you before that I only married you for your name. And I would have stayed with you happily had you not screwed every bimbo you came across, sullying both my reputation and your own. You were an awful husband and you're an even worse father. Just look at what you're making your children go through now."

He felt heavy hearted and weak as he turned away from her. He knew what he was, though sometimes he forgot until someone reminded him of the things he'd done. But when he heard it put so bluntly, so coldly, as his ex-wife and children were prone to do, well, it made him wish he were dead. At least then he wouldn't have to live with the shame.

A few minutes later, the town car came to a stop in front of the Vasser Hotel. Win stayed where he was and waited for the driver to open the door. When he stepped onto the sidewalk, he kept his head hung low and sulked all the way into the lobby, fear slipping in to stab hotly into his gut. It'd been years since he had been to the New York hotel, so long that he knew he wouldn't recognize it. He held way too many bad memories of the place to ever feel comfortable there. Even the atmosphere, the smells and the sounds of it, brought back the demons and ghosts of his past.

"Stop sulking, Win. Or do you want your children to think even less of you than they already do?" Charlene barked, smacking his arm and causing him to lift his head and see his family, waiting in the lounge area of the lobby for him. He tried to smile, though he knew by the hard looks on their faces that he was in deep trouble.

Grant, Linc, and Madison stood together as a solidified unit, while Marshall hovered behind them, cautiously protective. In front of them stood Kennedy, who actually smiled and waved. When she bolted toward him and flew into his arms, Win let out a startled breath and held her closely, spontaneously thankful for her.

"Hi, daddy!" Kennedy pulled away and beamed at him, not wanting to be such a downer like her siblings. "How was the flight and stuff?"

"Just fine, baby." Win pressed a kiss to her forehead and smiled, noticing how much she'd grown and how much she looked like him. It brought a lot of regret and pain to his heart to know he'd neglected her, while at the same time he felt this wild hope that she could be the one saving grace left in his life. "How's high school going?"

Kennedy's smile faltered as her eyebrows knit together in confusion. "I graduated high school last summer. I start Princeton soon. I told you about it in the email I sent you."

"Last summer? Did I miss your graduation?" Win asked, frantically trying to remember as Kennedy backed slowly away from him, suspicion in her eyes now.

"You said you had the flu and that was why you couldn't be there."

"Oh." He paused, suddenly remembering the real reason why he hadn't made it out to see her graduate. He'd taken a trip down to Jamaica with some blonde he couldn't even remember the name of now. They'd gotten wasted and made love in the sand, then did lines of coke on the bathroom sink. Forcing the memory from his mind, he tried to smile at his daughter. "Yeah, I was really sick, baby, you wouldn't have wanted me to be there."

"I suppose not..." Kennedy mumbled, wondering why she had the distinct feeling that he was lying to her.

Win turned his attention to his other three children and, as he approached them, he blinked back guilty tears from his eyes. He looked to Grant first, his oldest son, and tried not to focus on how much the boy looked like Cyrus. If he started making that correlation, he knew he might just bolt from the hotel like a bat out of hell.

"Grant," Win greeted, holding out his hand. Grant shook his father's hand, but the contact was cold and brief, as was his silent nod.

He turned then to his other daughter, and again tried not to see his father in her face. "Hi, princess."

Madison angled her head as she eyed him frostily, taking in his expensive clothes, most likely forced on him by her mother. He'd washed his hair and didn't look nearly as disheveled as she had imagined, though one look at his eyes gave away the truth. He'd been using. Recently, too. Most definitely alcohol, and given the way he trembled and the jittery, scattered look in his eyes, he was probably on some kind of uppers as well. Disappointment lashed through her in one violent swipe.

"I hope you understand that your life is about to change dramatically," she said, keeping her voice down so only her family could hear.

Win's eyes widened at her words and his forehead creased with worry. "Did he say something to you? Is he going to hurt me?" he stammered, one quick shudder racing over him at the very thought.

Madison glared at him. "We're not going to have this discussion here. It can wait until you're settled in and we can speak in private."

"Grandpa Cyrus doesn't know about the tabloid yet, if that's what you're asking." Linc put in, his arms crossed tightly and his expression pitiless as he stared at his father.

Win looked to his youngest son and let out a relieved half laugh. "Good. I hope you all can understand why I'll want protection while I'm here."

"I say we throw you to the wolves," Linc spat viciously. "It's about time you took responsibility for your actions."

Before Win could respond, Marshall cut in and placed a hand smoothly on Linc's shoulder. "There is certainly a lot to discuss. Why don't I show you to your room, Win, and you can get settled in before dinner?"

He led Win toward the elevators before more angry words could be exchanged, a bellhop following them with Win's luggage. At the same moment, Madison's cell phone rang. She glanced down at it quickly before answering.

"Hello, Detective Hughes. How are you?" she answered, staring pointedly at her brothers as she spoke.

"*I'm just fine, Ms. Vasser. Is your father with you?*"

She considered his question, wondering if they were going to need more time with her father before they handed him over to the detective. Deciding it was best not to lie, she told him the truth. "He just arrived here at the hotel. He's going to be staying here for awhile so we can get this all straightened out."

"*I will be by tomorrow morning to speak with him. Can you please let him know I'm coming?*"

"Certainly. Goodbye, detective." Madison hung up the phone and eyed her family. "Detective Hughes will be by tomorrow morning to speak to him. I suggest we get this straightened out this evening and have a concrete story for all of us to adhere to before he arrives."

"We'll give him two hours to settle in, and then I'll talk with him in private," Grant decided, glancing over at Linc. "You can have your words with him later. He may feel more comfortable talking with just me at first."

"Whatever." Linc shrugged. "I've got work to do."

"I've got an errand to run. I'll be back in a couple of hours." Madison rose onto her toes to kiss Grant on the cheek, then kissed Linc as well. "Be good, boys."

She said a brief goodbye to her mother and sister before leaving the hotel, knowing she couldn't put this off any longer.

It was time to tell him.

THE MOMENT DON hung up the phone Wyatt Bailey took a seat in the chair across from him.

"Detective Hughes?" Wyatt held out his hand, his smile quick and direct.

"That's me," Don replied, shaking the stranger's hand. "What can I do for you?"

"I believe the real question here is what can *I* do for *you*."

Don leaned back in his chair, casually tapping his pencil on the surface of his desk. "I'm listening."

"My name is Wyatt Bailey." He tilted down the edge of his hat to the detective in greeting. "I'm an old friend of Win Vasser's."

"If you're here about the tabloid article—"

"I'm not. In fact, I only just recently found out about the tabloid, long after I'd made the drive out from Maine with the intent of giving you a heads up on your case." Wyatt's smile was dark as he remembered the shock he'd felt when he spotted Win's face on countless magazines in the newsstand that morning. "I know for a fact that he is telling the truth in that tabloid."

"How do you know?"

"Because seven years ago, when the two of us became friends in Las Vegas, he told me he witnessed his father murder his grandfather."

Don's eyes narrowed. "And how do I know you didn't just read the article and decide to make this up to get your own name in the papers?"

Wyatt only smiled, the movement bordering on aggressive. He wasn't a big fan of cops or their ingrained habit of always assuming the worst of people. He was here to do this man a favor, yet there was not an ounce of appreciation being thrown his way. Yet, anyway.

"Winston Vasser was killed with a .22 derringer pistol which was registered in his name and usually kept in the right side drawer of his desk. The killer stood at Winston's left side and held the gun against his left temple before pulling the trigger. When Winston slumped over, his nose hit the desk and broke. Those are all facts that were not included in the tabloid article, nor were they included in the original newspaper reports from the 1950's. They are facts that Win gave as he related to me what he witnessed when he was seven years old."

Don was silent for a moment, digesting the information Wyatt had given him. All of the facts were in line with the original police report, which made him both intrigued and suspicious. He didn't feel inclined to trust the man, but he supposed it didn't hurt to at least give him some consideration. "What else did Win Vasser tell you?"

"Only that he's terrified of his father and has been ever since that day. That's why he's the black sheep of the family. He's largely tried to stay out of his father's way and as a result has never amounted to anything more than a beggar, living off the money his kids earned."

"You don't sound as though you respect Win very much, Mr. Bailey," Don concluded, eyeing Wyatt curiously. "But you consider him a friend?"

"We had some good times." Wyatt shrugged. "Win's not a bad guy, he's just troubled. Wouldn't you be if you'd seen what he saw when he was just a kid? Pardon my French, detective, but that'd make anybody fucking crazy."

"I don't doubt that it would," Don agreed, rubbing his chin thoughtfully as he continued to watch Wyatt. "How did you know to come to me?"

"Win said Marshall told him to expect a detective knocking on his door, that the case had been reopened. Consequently he called me up and told me that if you somehow found your way to *my* door, that I should play dumb and say I don't know anything. Obviously, I felt it was better that I come to you with what I know and air this out once and for all. After a few phone calls I had your name, your office hours, and your expected date of arrival back from the west coast. And now here we are, enjoying this little chat."

"Resourceful." Don's lips quirked into a vaguely impressed smile as he sat up in his chair and shuffled some of the paperwork around on his desk. "This investigation has not yet leaked to the press, Mr. Bailey. I would prefer it stay that way, for the sake of the family. If you truly care about them, as you've made it sound, then I urge you to keep this to yourself."

Wyatt thought briefly of Madison and relished in the image. He grinned at the detective and rose to his feet, reaching out to shake Don's hand. "I've kept the secret this long, detective."

"I'm going by the hotel tomorrow to speak with Win and the family about his accusations. Would you prefer it if I left your name out of the discussion?"

"Win's in town?" Wyatt asked, his interest piqued at the thought. "I'll be damned. Here I thought he'd never set foot in New York City until the old man croaked."

"So I take it that you don't mind if I mention your name to them when they ask me who it was who corroborated Win's story?"

With a conspirator's wink, Wyatt backed away from the desk and tilted his hat once more at Don. "You do whatever makes you happy, detective. I'll be staying at the Waldorf through the weekend if you need to reach me."

Don watched Wyatt leave, the wheels turning in his brain as he figured all the angles. It was possible this man had some ulterior motive and he was merely trying to spice up the investigation. But what Wyatt Bailey didn't know, or at least hadn't mentioned, was that there was a letter that implicitly named Cyrus Vasser as a killer. Wyatt seemed to be trusting Win's word alone, and clearly he hadn't been told the reason for the case being reopened. It appeared as though he didn't care what the reason was, he just wanted the opportunity to set things straight.

If anything, at least the man presented himself as another rung on the ladder toward a conviction. Now he could counter any attempt by Win Vasser to deny the validity of the tabloid by simply bringing up his conversation with Mr. Wyatt Bailey.

THIRTEEN

D id you know, *pépère*? Did you know that he knew?" Madison asked, her arms crossed as she sat at the foot of her grandfather's hospital bed. Cyrus eyed her contemptuously, his mouth twisting into a scowl.

"Of course I didn't," he spat, his hands clenching around the soft blue blankets of the bed. The machines beside him beeped faster as his heart rate elevated. "If I'd known, do you think I would've let him live?"

"If you'd done something as drastic as killing your own seven year old son then I would not be here," Madison reminded him, rising to her feet to pace the room, her heels tapping hollowly over the smooth hospital floor. "Who would have run your hotel if not for my brothers and I?"

Cyrus pursed his lips bitterly as he watched her pace. Even he couldn't deny the irony of *that* scenario. No Win meant no witness, but it also meant no Madison, Grant, or Linc. If he'd been a more humorous man he may have found that funny. Instead it only infuriated him.

"Marshall would have had children."

"And?" Madison spun around to face him, one eyebrow arched. "Would they have been as loyal to you as I am? Would they have kept your secrets as their own the way I have for seventeen goddamn years? Don't forget that I branded myself for you and considered it an honor to do so."

On impulse, she shoved the bulky silver and sapphire bracelet up her right forearm, exposing the tattoo on her wrist for him to see. It was the Roman numeral IX, for the number 9, simple and discreet in plain black ink no larger than a nickel. They both knew the significance of it.

"I was nine years old when you put your faith in me." She watched him as he stared silently at the tattoo and saw a brief flash of intense emotion run over his stony features. As a result, when she spoke again her voice softened. "I haven't forgotten the words you spoke to me that day. You said—"

"You will be my ideological vessel and my ardent defender. You will carry my vision and my methods into the next generation, ensuring my legacy and the prosperity of this family and our empire. I trust you with my secrets and my wisdom in the hopes that you will persevere against those who will attempt to drown you in deceit and coercion. Our name is only as strong as we fight for it to be. I need you to fight, and fight ruthlessly, child, because in this life, the Vasser legacy is the only thing worth fighting for."

Madison slowly sat down on the edge of the bed, her hand reaching for his. She held his gaze, never wavering, even as the emotions coursed through her. All fiery rage, dark despair and golden reminiscence. She squeezed his hand, needing to ground herself, to hold on to reason and control. The last thing she would do was crumble, not when he needed her now more than ever.

"Tell me what you want me to do," she whispered, ashamed at the tight grasp her emotions had over her throat, making it hard to breathe and even harder to speak. But she wouldn't cry, not in front of him, not ever. He despised tears.

Cyrus took a deep breath, more to settle his own rioting heart than to buy time for words. He knew what needed to be done, had known it the second she told him of the tabloid. He also knew it was going to hurt her, and hurt her very, very badly. But there was no other option, no other way. He wasn't going to let her take the fall for this, not when he'd been selfish enough to burden her with his sins all those years ago.

It was odd how differently he looked at his decision to take her under his wing now, when the truth was on the edge of release and all he'd lived for was about to be dealt a vicious blow. Madison didn't deserve to bear the consequences of his actions. If the police or the family found out she'd known the truth all along and did nothing, it would destroy her. Not only would her reputation be tarnished, but his legacy would be as well.

There was only one solution, one course of action that would keep her safe and preserve as much of the empire as could be salvaged.

He glanced down at their joined hands and seeing her youth, her vitality, her *strength*, gave him a contentment he hadn't felt in more years than he could count.

"I want you to carry on as though you know nothing," he said sternly, looking up at her again.

"But once the detective talks with my father, he's going to come to you looking for answers." Madison pushed, frustration hitting her. "With my father's testimony and that letter, I don't see how you'll be able to convince the detective that you didn't do this. They'll arrest you, put you in prison. Don't you see that?"

"Let me worry about that, *mon coeur*." He squeezed her hand once more before pulling his own away, reaching for the old, tattered novel that sat beside him. "Now, you're going back to the hotel to continue on as normal. I want you to support your brothers and keep them focused. They need you more than ever now."

"It's not them I'm worried about," she murmured, urging him to look at her. "You've made me strong, *pépère*, but without you I don't know what I'll be."

"You'll be exactly as you are now," Cyrus replied, his scowl deepening. "Nothing and no one can take away your power unless you let them. If you fight tooth and nail to keep it, then you will survive. But if you give up now then you're not the child I raised. She would do whatever was necessary to keep our empire strong. Are you still her, *mon coeur*? Or are you now too weak to follow in my footsteps?"

Madison's eyes flashed with heat even as her lips curved into a tenacious smile. "If not me, than who? I'm all you've got." She rose to her feet and stared down at him. "And lucky for you, I have no intention of letting you down."

"Good." Cyrus' mouth shifted into a proud smile. "When the devil finally comes to take me down to Hell, I'll go gladly knowing I left the best part of me right here, in you."

Madison leaned in to kiss his forehead. She hovered there, her eyes shutting tight to hold back the sudden influx of tears. Taking a deep breath, she spoke softly into his ear, her heart aching. Somehow, for some reason, this felt like goodbye. "When you see him, tell the Devil he'd be smart to prepare himself for me. We're going to rule Hell together, you and I."

Cyrus said nothing as she pulled away and left the room, unable to face him or else he'd see the tears falling from her eyes. But he knew. He heard the suffering in her voice regardless of how well she tried to conceal it. Her words haunted his old, calloused heart and made him only more sure that what he was about to do was the right thing.

He leaned over the side of the bed and wheezed as he grabbed his notepad and pen from the bedside table. Settling back against his pillows, he began writing. His hand shook as he wrote, more from old age than fear. He wasn't afraid, no. In fact, he was eager. He'd known one day his sins would come back to haunt him, and he also knew he was lucky to have lasted as long as he had. It seemed the old adage 'only the good die young' was the stone cold truth. He'd lived much longer than his blackened soul warranted.

Then again, he'd sacrificed more than just his soul in order to rule the Vasser Empire. Now it was time to pay the Devil his due.

A couple of hours later, after he'd seen to it that the letters he wrote were notarized and sealed, he slipped them between the pages of his favorite novel and set it on his bedside table. He then reached down on the right side of his bed toward the wall outlet, where all of the machines he was hooked up to were plugged in.

With a grunt, he yanked all of the plugs free and let them fall to the floor. The monitors and machines clicked off instantly. He felt the assistance they had provided for his lungs cease and his heart thudded weakly in his chest of its own accord.

Content, he laid back against the pillows and shut his eyes, a smile curving his lips as he waited patiently for death.

"ARE YOU UNCOMFORTABLE being here?"

A half laugh escaped Win's throat as he buried his face in his hands, shaking his head. He sat on the edge of one of Grant's desk chairs, fighting to soothe his rioting nerves and beat back the bite of withdrawal clawing away at his insides.

His hands fell away from his face as he leveled his gaze with his oldest son, who was eyeing him with quiet patience and stern disapproval. Funny how he felt more like the child in this scenario, with his own son as the father. Then again, it had always been that way.

"What? You mean in this room, with all those pictures of people who wish I was dead?" Win let out a huff of breath and leaned back in the chair, urging himself to relax. "No, I don't feel comfortable here. I never have."

"I'm sorry there's not a better place for us to have this conversation, then," Grant said, averting his eyes from his father to look out at the heavy rain that fell from sinister, tumultuous clouds. The office itself was silent as a tomb and oddly calming despite the nerves of the man who sat before him. He considered his words carefully before speaking again, maintaining a businesslike tone he hoped suited his father's mood.

"I need you to tell me about the tabloid," he began. He kept his gaze glued to the window so as not to come across as accusatory.

Win sighed, watching the rain fall for a moment before he opened his mouth, even then silently mouthing words before choosing ones that seemed right. When he spoke his voice was hollow, haunted in a way that disturbed Grant more than he cared to admit.

"It's all true, Grant. All of it," Win murmured, his eyes wide and glassy as he stared at the rain, not really seeing it at all. Instead he saw, replaying over and over in his mind as it often had throughout his life, the image of his father standing with a gun in his hand.

Grant inhaled deeply, his hand clenching over the fountain pen that had been his great-grandfather's until his knuckles were white. "Please start from the beginning, then, and tell me everything."

"Okay." Win swallowed the bile that rose in his throat as he tried to think of where to start. Shutting his eyes, he put himself back in that very hotel, only fifty-four years earlier. As he did, the memories flooded through him like water through a cool, easy stream. "I was seven years old. My mom brought Walter, Lawrence and I to the hotel after school, and we had to stay until dad was ready to leave, but it took hours. I got tired of waiting in the lobby so I wandered upstairs, hoping I could find him and get him to come home. I went to his office, this office, actually, and didn't see him. His secretary said he'd already left, but I knew he hadn't been downstairs. So I thought maybe he'd gone up to talk to grandpa in the suite upstairs, so I went up to go look. I remember walking down the long hallway toward grandpa's suite and hearing voices. It felt dark and terrible up there, as if something bad was going to happen, though I don't know how I could have known that. When I got to the door of the suite, it was cracked open and I peered in, and that was when I saw him. He was standing next to grandpa, who was seated at his desk, and he was talking. I don't remember what he said, but I do remember the look in his eyes. Evil. A bad man's eyes look like that, I thought. Then they were arguing, and dad pulled the gun from his coat pocket and put it up to grandpa's head. I wondered if maybe they were just playing a game, maybe this was all for fun. But when he pulled the trigger and grandpa's blood went everywhere, I knew it wasn't a game. I've never been so terrified of anything in my entire life. He had the Devil in his eyes, the goddamn Devil..."

"Did he see you?" Grant asked, his voice rough from the dryness in his throat. He had no doubt his father was telling the truth. The reality of it frightened the living daylights out of him.

"No, I don't think so," Win replied, grinding his teeth together as he considered the possibility. "I'd always wondered, though. I always thought he was biding his time and that one day he'd find the perfect moment to come after me, to kill me for what I'd seen. It's haunted me all my life, Grant, you have to know that."

"I understand." Grant looked over at his father then, meeting his eyes. "I believe you, dad."

Win nodded, his lips tightening together as he blinked back tears. "I'm sorry it had to come out like this. I've burdened you kids with my demons...it isn't fair that you should have to pay the price."

"It is what it is." With a heavy sigh, Grant looked beyond his father at the portrait of his grandfather. He held the eyes in the painting with his own for several long, silent moments.

How could you? I trusted you. We trusted you.

"There's a lot of things in my life I regret," Win said with a saddened smile. "Hell, most of the shit I've done has only given me grief and heartache. I've been a selfish man my whole life and ignored you kids. I'm sorry for that."

Grant looked away from the portrait and back to his father, startled by the contrast in the two men. Where Cyrus was strong, ruthless and powerful, Win seemed broken, like a beaten dog terrified of its master but still hungry enough to beg for food. Pity washed over him as he stared into his father's eyes and recognized what he'd never before noticed in them. The desperation and the all encompassing fear he'd lived with all his life. Fear of his own father. Grant couldn't imagine being afraid of *his* father. But then again, his father never had the chance to become what Cyrus was. Maybe he wouldn't have even if destiny had played different cards. The fact remained that while Cyrus had remained powerful through the years, Win had succumbed to weakness.

"I'm not going to forgive you for everything," Grant began, making sure to remember the long, anxious nights with his siblings, doing everything he could do to comfort them while their parents waged wars with each other in the other room. He could distinctly remember the shouting, the vile accusations and violent threats, the desperate pleading and cold pride. The only thing that could drown out the sound had been the harmonica, and so he'd learned to use it for the sole purpose of keeping his siblings calm. It was his parents' inevitable divorce that forced him to take his father's place for his brother and sisters. They had no choice but to rely on him and he had no choice but to step up to the plate. Once he did, he understood his father was as good as useless. "You were a bad husband, but it's not my place to forgive you for that. Maybe one day my mother will, but that's up to her. Before the divorce, when you were around, you could be a good father. But as we got older and the 'around' time became less and less, we all gave up on you. You chose women, drugs, and alcohol over your own wife and kids and *that* I won't forgive you for. What I will do is forgive you for not having the strength to come forward with this sooner, as I understand you were afraid. I'll forgive you for needing to distance yourself from the hotel and consequently from us, because I know you couldn't stand to be here because of what happened. And I suppose I'll forgive you for leaving me no choice but to take your place, since I don't regret doing so."

Win absorbed his son's words carefully, digesting them with both guilt and relief. He glanced back out the window and watched the clouds shift, allowing a few thin rays of sunlight to peak through and highlight the sky. "Thank you, Grant. Lord knows I don't deserve your forgiveness, but thank you anyway."

Unsure what else to say, Grant followed his father's gaze toward the sunlight, wondering if it was a sign of good things to come.

If only he could have known just how horrifically wrong he was.

AS QUINN LOGGED off her computer, Madison exited the elevator. She watched as Grant's sister stalked past, curiously sensing the other woman's distress. Usually Madison was a master of deception when it came to her feelings, but today it seemed even she couldn't hide them fully. When she breezed past Carrie without a word and slammed her office door shut behind her, Quinn shrugged and figured it was stress caused by their father being at the hotel.

She'd met him earlier when he came up to Grant's office. He seemed sad, she remembered, her brow creasing. Sad and lost, in a way. But when she smiled and greeted him, he managed to smile back and she liked the poetic innocence of his expression. He was clearly worn out from the years of abuse to his body and mind, but there was still some sensitivity and idealism in his features to give her an insight into the man he'd once been.

It was most shocking to note that *this* man was Grant's father. Grant, who was larger than life and disciplined, had come from this man, who looked as though life had dealt him a particularly rough hand. She knew very little about him other than what she'd gathered from Grant and Linc, but she knew Win was not well liked by the Vasser family.

She wondered if it was because what he'd said in the tabloid was true. If it was, then what would happen to the Vassers? What would happen to Grant?

The office door swung open and Win wandered out, looking happier than before. He'd entered looking like a frightened puppy and came out looking like he got a treat instead of the vicious beating he expected.

Grant emerged from the office after him, sparing her a moment's glance before turning to his father and holding out his hand cordially.

"Get some sleep. Tomorrow's a big day for all of us," Grant said, startled when Win pulled him in for a bear hug.

"Thanks again, son. I owe you one." Win smacked Grant on the back before pulling away. He sent Quinn a quick wave and a grin before wandering off to the elevator.

Quinn watched him go, charmed. When she looked up at Grant, he was still staring after his father, his expression hard to read. He looked like he was caught between pleasure and disapproval, and couldn't decide which one to choose.

"Well, it's six o'clock," Quinn said cheerfully, rising to her feet and grabbing her purse. She set it on the desk and reached for her coat. She paused when she saw Grant watching her. "Do you need anything?"

You, apparently, Grant thought soundlessly, startled as always that just being in her presence calmed him. Yet, at the same time, looking at her put wild thoughts in his mind he knew didn't belong there. Then again, he *had* told her there would be a next time.

"Let me help you," he offered, pulling her bright red peacoat from her hands and wrapping it around her shoulders. He held it out so she could tuck her arms into the sleeves.

He was close enough to smell her, all warm vanilla and sugared cinnamon. It took all of his control to slow his blood from rushing to merely flowing.

"I hope it's stopped raining outside, I forgot my umbrella." Quinn laughed, shrugging into the other sleeve of her coat and pulling the front together so she could button it. She kept her eyes on the buttons as she hooked them, her heart pounding in her chest as she realized he wasn't going to move. Because it both unnerved and thrilled her, she did the only thing she was capable of doing. She started talking. "Back home I used to purposely walk in the rain just to feel it on my skin. Ma used to get so mad at me when I'd get home, drenched and spilling puddles of water all over the kitchen floor. But I loved it. It was the one thing she could never convince me to stop doing. Somehow I got lucky and never got pneumonia. Now that I think about it, it's been awhile since I've done that." She hooked the last button and glanced up at him. Her breath caught in her throat at the look in his eyes, all warmth and dark intensity. "I guess I outgrew it."

"I could listen to you talk for hours," he murmured, reaching up with his left hand to cup her cheek.

"That's a first." Quinn couldn't help the giddy half laugh that escaped her throat as he leaned in to kiss her. She tilted her face up to his in invitation, her hands drifting up the lapels of his suit until they rested on his shoulders. She rose slowly onto her tiptoes, guiding her mouth toward his, her eyes closing.

Suddenly, a deafening scream and a violent crash resounded through the offices, jolting them apart. They looked at Madison's office where the sound had come from. Before Quinn could do so much as blink, Grant was rushing to his sister.

He bolted past an alarmed looking Carrie and threw open Madison's door, stumbling into her office only to find her collapsed over her desk, all of her belongings pushed to the floor. She was sobbing harder than he'd ever seen, her hands clenched into white knuckled fists and her hair strewn over the surface of her desk in wild brown waves. Beside her elbow lay her cell phone, broken into pieces from being battered against the mahogany surface of her desk.

He gathered her into his arms, pulling her down with him as he knelt on the floor beside her desk. She only buried her face into his neck and continued to cry.

"What happened?" he asked, his heart an explosion of nerves and horror in his chest. "Mads, what is it?"

"*He's dead!*" she cried, clutching at his suit jacket, her entire world in a state of Armageddon.

Grant didn't need to ask who she meant. There was only one person in the entire world whose death would destroy her this way. He took a deep, shuddering breath and held her tighter, pushing aside his own grief to deal with hers.

He spotted Carrie and Quinn hovering in the doorway, looking distraught and confused. He met Quinn's eyes without hesitation. "Quinn, get Linc and tell him to come up here. Miss Lewis, call Marshall and my mother and tell them to come to the hotel immediately. It's about our grandfather."

Carrie nodded and rushed immediately to the phone at her desk while Quinn bit her lip and left, the image of the grief in his eyes staggering her. Oh, Grant, she thought sadly, tears in her eyes as she took the stairs two at a time. I never, ever want to see that look in your eyes again.

When she emerged out into the lobby, she ran as fast as her heels would take her to the front desk, pushing past Walter and heading straight into Linc's office. She found him with his legs propped up on his desk and a stack of forms in his hands. He glanced up the second she entered, his smile instinctual but fading when he saw the look on her face.

"What's wrong?" he asked, already jumping to his feet and tossing the paperwork aside.

"Grant needs you upstairs. It's your grandfather," Quinn said, successfully maintaining her cool long enough for him to get the message, thank her, and race upstairs. She let out a heavy breath, needing to slow her rapidly beating heart. Pulling herself together, she left his office and headed into the lobby, intending to go back upstairs to make sure Grant was alright.

When she swept out to the front desk she spotted a pretty redhead talking to Walter.

"Linc's busy, Lynette, I'm sorry. Something happened." Walter was saying, his voice apologetic. Lynette looked a little disappointed, but certainly more worried.

"Is he alright? Was he hurt?" she asked, her brow furrowed with concern.

Seeing this, Quinn made up her mind instantly on what she had to do.

"Come with me, honey, I'll take you to him," she said, waving for the girl to follow her toward the elevators. Lynette did, shooting a confused glance Walter's way before racing after Quinn.

"Can you tell me what's going on? Is he okay?" Lynette asked, pausing before the elevator as Quinn pushed the button.

"He's fine." Quinn assured her, distracted as the elevator doors slid open. Both women clambered inside and Quinn pushed the button for the second floor. Once they were moving, she turned to face Lynette and held out her hand. "I'm Quinn, by the way. Grant's secretary."

"Oh, nice to meet you." Lynette blinked, taking in the other woman fully. She was pretty, in an exotic, gypsy kind of way, Lynette considered, admiring Quinn's dark curls and warm hazel eyes. Her smile was weary, which made Lynette worry even more.

"So you're Linc's girlfriend?"

Caught off guard, Lynette let out an embarrassed laugh and ran her hand nervously through her length of red hair. "We're...seeing each other, I guess. But it's not very serious yet."

"From the look on your face, I'd say you care about him," Quinn observed, her smile warm. "That's good. He needs someone right now, especially after this."

"What happened?"

"From what I gathered, their grandfather passed away," Quinn told her. "Madison's not taking it well."

"Is that their sister?" Lynette asked as the elevator came to a stop and the doors opened.

Quinn nodded as she rushed out of the elevator and back into Madison's office, relieved she could no longer hear crying.

Linc was sitting on the edge of Madison's desk, holding her hand as she stood wrapped in Grant's arms, her eyes red rimmed but no longer shedding tears. When Quinn and Lynette came into the office alcove, Linc glanced over his shoulder and spotted them. His emotions were at a severely dangerous boiling point, but seeing Lynette had him taking a deep breath and rising to his feet.

He murmured her name as he went to her, gathering her into his arms. "I'm sorry, I forgot you were coming by."

"That doesn't matter." Lynette pulled away so she could see his face more clearly, her hand coming up to slide over his cheek. "I'm so sorry."

"It's okay," he said firmly, looking up as Marshall rushed in, his face creased with dark grief. "Uncle Marshall."

"Linc." Marshall nodded to Lynette absently as he patted Linc on the shoulder, nodding also to Quinn before heading straight for Madison. Grant released her so she could go into Marshall's arms. He held her tightly for a long moment, tears sliding hotly down his cheeks.

"It's going to be okay, dear," Marshall said quietly, more to calm his own nerves than to help her. He knew she was much stronger than he was, as much as he didn't readily want to admit it. But right now, it was as much her holding him as it was he holding her.

Grant looked away from his uncle and sister and spotted Quinn retreating back toward her desk. He was pushing back his grief as best as he could, but there was nothing more he could do for his family. For now, at least, his siblings were taken care of.

As he brushed past Linc and Lynette, he met his brother's eyes and nodded. Linc nodded in return, a silent acknowledgement passing between them. They both knew that Cyrus' death was likely to change things, and change things drastically. Now they would never know his side of the story, and so Win's account would be the only one the family would have.

Grant approached Quinn's desk, watching her gather up her things. When she looked up from her purse and met his eyes, he noticed the traces of tears in hers. He froze, unsure what to do, what to say. He'd never known how to deal with his own emotions, let alone anyone else's. With Madison it had been instinctual; he needed to protect her. But with Quinn he had no responsibility, no ties, no connection other than being her boss. So how was he supposed to comfort her? Or should he allow her to comfort him?

"I'm sorry, Grant," she said, sensing his discomfort. He often had the appearance of a man who wanted to say something, but had no clue how to say it. "If there's anything I can do—"

"We'll be alright," Grant interrupted, feeling foolish for craving her company so badly that he was letting himself be distracted by it. "There are arrangements to be made, family members to call. You're free to go home, I don't need you."

Quinn wondered over his choice of words for a moment before speaking. "Okay...do you mind if I ask what happened to him? Your grandfather?"

Grief and anger over the situation flashed in his eyes, his hands clenching at his sides. She noted both as she watched him, wishing more than anything there was something she could do for him.

When he spoke, his voice was hard and unfeeling, such an extreme contrast to his words that it took her violently by surprise. "He pulled the plug on the machines keeping him alive. He killed himself."

"Oh." Her hand flew up to cover her mouth. "I'm so sorry."

"Don't be," he insisted, despising himself for burdening her with the horror of it. Though she was likely to find out eventually as it would be all over the news by morning. "Go home, get some sleep. I'll see you tomorrow."

With that, he turned to go back to his family. Quinn followed him out and they met up with Linc and Lynette in the hallway.

"Mom's on her way," Linc told Grant, his arm wrapped tightly around Lynette's shoulders.

Grant looked once at the redhead and realized abruptly that she was something of an anchor for his brother, a buoy for him to cling to in this rough time. Did he have that with Quinn? Despite how much he tried to deny it, maybe he did.

Linc gestured to Lynette, attempting a smile. "This is Lynette, by the way."

She held out a hand to him, her eyes filled with a wariness he didn't understand.

"Nice to finally meet you," she greeted, her voice tinged with a defensive frost. She wouldn't let herself forget this was the same brother that hurt Linc just a week earlier. Even though current circumstances forced the brothers to concede their differences, she still held some amount of reserve for the man who stood before her.

"Nice to meet you," Grant replied, distracted by Quinn standing beside him. Avoiding looking at her, he turned instead to his brother. "I suppose I'll go let dad know."

"Let mom do that," Linc said, nodding to Quinn. "Thanks for bringing Lynette up here, Quinn."

"You're welcome." Quinn attempted a smile for both Linc and Lynette. "I can tell she cares about you."

Lynette blushed as Linc grinned. "I like to think so."

Linc noticed curiously that when his brother met eyes with Quinn, something passed between them, some kind of quiet spark that suggested intimacy. He knew his brother well enough to know Grant never looked at his employees that way, much less his secretaries.

Before Linc could ask the two of them to confirm his suspicions, Madison walked over and touched both his and Grant's arms.

"I'm afraid I need to steal my brothers away, girls," she said firmly. "There are arrangements to make. You understand."

Grant nodded politely to Quinn, saying nothing as his sister pulled him aside. She watched him go, equally as silent, as lost.

Linc pulled Lynette against him for a kiss before releasing her. "I'll call you when shit settles down, okay?"

"Try and keep your head above water," Lynette advised, waving as Madison shut the door behind them.

Left in the hallway alone, Lynette and Quinn both let out heavy sighs and faced each other awkwardly.

"I picked a very turbulent time to get involved with the Vassers," Lynette mused, attempting a smile.

Quinn laughed. "Me too, honey. Me too."

THAT NIGHT HE called her, needing refuge.

When he showed up at her front door, darkness hollowing his features and his eyes sparking with emotion, it took all she had to stay focused.

"Linc, are you—"

"No," he muttered. He shut the door and pulled her tight against him, burying his face in her hair. "Not tonight. I don't want to talk, Lynette. I just needed you."

Shaken, her hands slid up his back and clutched at his shirt. Her lips parted in a quiet moan when he kissed the soft curve of her throat.

"Needed me?" she asked breathily, arching against him as he tugged the straps of her dress over her shoulders, revealing the smooth, lightly freckled skin for him to taste.

"Mmm hmm." His mouth continued to torture her, gaining a fevered momentum as he reached her mouth again, crushing it with his own. "God, life sucks. Except for you. Everything sucks except for you."

"Spoken like a true romantic," she said, laughing as he suddenly scooped her up and carried her over to her plush sofa in shades of neutral beige and gray, much like the rest of her quaint apartment in Uptown. "And a Yankee to boot. Lord, my grandmother must be rolling over in her grave."

He smiled, blue eyes bright. "I guess I'm just gonna have to show you the Yankee way, Lynette. To hell with grandma."

"Oh, she's probably there anyway. Crazy old biddy."

He laughed as he laid her down on her sofa, sliding over her and meeting her eyes, marveling at her. "Where the hell have you been all my life?"

She returned the smile, her eyes softening. "Does it matter?" She tilted her head up to kiss him, teasing his lips with her own. "I'm here now."

He gripped her waist and held her closer, deepening the kiss. As he lost himself in her, pushing aside all thoughts of his grandfather, his family, his hotel, the only thing he could do was thank God or fate or whatever it was that had brought her into his life.

She was the only solace he could find in the storm raging around him, like a lighthouse shining through the darkness of a violent hurricane. And now that she was his, he was going to do everything within his power to make sure she stayed that way.

Later, they lay together on the carpeted floor of her living room, wrapped together and comfortable. She sighed as she trailed a hand down his bare chest, her eyes heavy and sultry in the candlelight as she watched him.

He turned his head and caught her staring. A quick grin flashed over his face. "What?"

She cuddled closer to him, her hand resting just over his heart. "Nothing, just thinking."

"About what?" His hand lazily brushed through her waves of copper hair.

Biting her bottom lip, she shook her head. "It's stupid. You'll just laugh at me."

"Okay, now I have to hear it. Spill."

"Okay, fine." She sat up on her elbow so she could look down at him as she smiled. "I was listening to the radio the other day and heard one of my favorite Randy Travis songs. It reminded me of you."

"Okay, and?" He stared at her, eyebrows raised.

"Well, it's this classic country love song, that's why you'll think it's stupid," she admitted, laughing at herself and blushing at the look he gave her. "But I don't know, something about it put your face in my mind as I heard it."

"How does it go?"

"Oh, Lord, I can't sing, Linc. Don't ask me to." She laughed again, feeling foolish. "I'll tell you what he said though, in the song. The part that made me think of you."

When he only smiled, she continued. "He said something about no longer being the type of guy to kill time with a woman." She shrugged, avoiding his eyes when he only continued to look at her, processing her words. "I guess I just hoped that was how you felt, and that I could prove my mother wrong about you."

Sitting up now, he reached for her, tilting her chin so she was forced to meet his eyes. The seriousness of his expression startled her. When he spoke, his voice was softer, more endearing than she had ever heard it. Perhaps that was what scared her the most.

"I don't think you're ready to hear just what it is that I feel for you, Lynette," he murmured, his eyes intense on hers. "But rest assured, this, what we have, it means something to me. I don't want to lose it."

She nodded, her heart swelling inside her chest until she could hardly breathe. Letting out a slow release of breath, she kissed him, aching for him even though he was right beside her. God, was she in love with him? It certainly felt that way.

The urge to tell him, to surrender under the full impact of just what it meant to love him washed over her, but she held back, unsure if it was the right time. He himself said he was holding back from expressing his feelings for her, maybe because he felt there was too much going on in his life to worry about something as silly and mind numbing as love.

Needing to change the subject before he succumbed to his own rioting emotions, Linc pulled away from her and forced a lighthearted grin on his face. "I think my brother has a thing for his secretary."

Lynette managed a smile, her curiosity piqued. "Really?"

"I've never seen him look at anyone the way he looks at her. It's weird," he added, frowning at the thought. "Very weird, actually."

"But she's so *nice*," Lynette protested, her brow furrowing. "And he's...not."

Linc laughed and ran his hand through her hair again, just because it was there. "He's not all bad. He's a good person at heart. Just trust me."

She pursed her lips, unconvinced. "If you say so."

"And it's been three years since Erin died..." His eyes darkened with an old ache for his brother at the thought. When Lynette looked confused, he elaborated. "She was his fiancé. She died a month after he proposed, in a car crash. Drunk driver. I still don't know how he got through it, but then again he's always been the strongest person I know."

Lynette softened, remorse clouding her expression. "I'm so sorry. How awful."

"That's why it's so weird to see him attracted to Quinn. It's been three years since I've seen him even give a passing glance to a woman."

"He must really see something in her, then," Lynette mused. "It's actually kind of romantic."

Linc snorted. "Of course you think that. Girls are all the same."

"You wouldn't be so sarcastic about it if I said I thought *you* were romantic," Lynette countered.

"True, but I already know I'm romantic." He grinned, grasping her hair and lifting her face to his. "And speaking as a true romantic, what do you say we hop into the shower and you can sing some good ol' country love songs for me?"

"Oh, Lord." She laughed, eyeing him playfully. "I can't promise that I'll be any good, but I'll give it my best shot."

He grinned and rose to his feet, reaching for her hand. "Then what are we waiting for?"

FOURTEEN

Walking into the vacant room in the hospital was like returning to an old, sacred place and finding it desecrated.

Madison didn't know what she would feel when she returned, but witnessing it now tore through her in one toxic swipe. She'd never known the room without him in it. Now it would be passed on to another long term patient, with his or her own family, and the hospital staff would soon forget about her grandfather. The room would no longer harbor his intense presence, bear the scent of his favorite cologne or the rich smell of his aged books. The television he had removed would be returned, and the room would never again be filled with the sound of Debussy or Mozart from the old fashioned record player in the corner, a gift from her grandmother before she died.

Madison took a moment to embrace the fact that he was really gone.

She stood silent as a statue in the doorway, taking in the haunting stillness of the neatly changed and folded bed, the lifeless machines pushed diligently against the white wall. The curtains were spread open to let in the early morning light. It was cold in the room, and not just physically. It was emotionally cold, devoid of anything that suggested the greatest man she'd ever known had lived there for the last few years of his life. The only traces of him were his belongings, few as they were, which were stacked on the armchair by the bed. She eyed her grandfather's possessions, stacks of books and some clothing, with his record player resting closed beside them. It took all she had to not storm out of the room and never return. It would be easier, she knew, to let her mother come and deal with going through Cyrus' things. But it wouldn't be right and it wouldn't be what he wanted.

She closed the door behind her and moved slowly toward the bed and the armchair, trying to adjust to his absence. She sat on the edge of the bed in the same spot she had the last time she'd spoken with him. Her left hand trailed over the blankets where he normally would have laid.

"You said that without you I would still be the same person," Madison murmured, tears welling in her eyes as both fury and misery filled her. Her hand clenched into a fist as she gripped the soft blue blanket, a single tear escaping to slide down her cheek as her lips curled into a snarl. "Damn you, you godforsaken bastard. Damn you."

Shutting her eyes, she sucked in deep, soothing breaths of air in an attempt to quiet her emotions. Even as she did so, her broken heart ached and bled miserably, throbbing with vibrant, red-hot pain. It wouldn't heal, she knew. Not this time. How could it, when he'd left her willingly, had taken his own life. He'd wanted to die, wanted to leave her alone. If this was some kind of test of her dedication or her strength of will, then it was a damn trying one.

Opening her eyes, she rose to her feet and stood before the stacks of books. Beside them lay an empty cardboard box one of the nurses must have provided, which made Madison wonder if they were happy to be rid of Cyrus Vasser. He had been a hard man and not one that most could handle. Perhaps the offering of a box for his possessions was a final kick out the door and a sign of good riddance. Either way, she lifted the box from the floor and set it on the bed, beginning to pile the books inside.

Her eyes scanned the titles, some nearly impossible to read through the tattered and worn covers. Many were books he'd lent to her over the years, hoping to gift her the life lessons he found useful within their pages. When she grabbed one of the last books, she accidentally knocked another one to the ground. She bent to pick it up, noting it was the same book he'd been reading the last time she'd seen him.

It caught her interest, her fingers running over the faded cover and creased spine. Just knowing he'd read passages from the book shortly before dying fascinated her in a strange and unearthly way. What had gone through his mind? Had he been angry, remorseful? Had he been at peace?

She realized the irony that for years her grandfather maintained the story that his own father committed suicide, when in the end suicide was what ultimately claimed his own life. Did he consider such a paradox before pulling the plug?

She opened the cover of the book, only to discover two envelopes tucked neatly inside. One was labeled *Detective Don Hughes* and the other *Mon Coeur, my Madison.* Stunned, she set the book aside and sat slowly on the bed, staring at the two envelopes. Curiosity urged her to tear open the letter to the detective, the desire to discover its contents insatiable. But respect for her grandfather won as she set it aside and focused instead on her own letter.

As she opened it, her heart raced wildly in her chest, though her hands remained steady as she unfolded it to read. It was a lengthy letter, written in his own handwriting and notarized on each of its three pages.

She read through it at first somewhat calmly, collectively, figuring it was the goodbye he hadn't been able to give her in person. But as she got to the end, her mouth fell open and her eyes widened. Her hands trembled with disbelief as a chill spread over her body.

She felt nothing, heard nothing, could experience nothing at that moment other than pure and unbridled shock. And when she read his last words, the letter fell to the floor as she fought the urge to scream.

CHARLENE PERUSED HER to-do list for the fundraiser as she sat in her favorite corner booth of *Cherir* for breakfast, her reading glasses perched on the end of her nose and her blonde hair meticulously styled. She wore an all black, knee length dress suit with soft water pearls at her throat and ears to soften the moroseness of it all. To the press and any curious passerby, she looked exactly like she wanted to appear: a woman in mourning over the tragic loss of her father-in-law.

Not that she really gave a damn that Cyrus was dead. The old man had despised her just as much as she despised him, but it wouldn't do to celebrate the tragedy in public, not when the family reputation lay so precariously in the balance. Once news of Cyrus' suicide spread around the country like wildfire, the scandal over Winston's murder was likely to flare up from the ashes it had temporarily dissolved into and all hell was going to break loose. Surely it looked suspicious that the man commits suicide shortly after being accused of murder. Innocent people didn't do such things.

Even if he was guilty, Charlene was determined to play this out as carefully as possible. The upcoming breast cancer fundraiser was now going to be transformed into not only a charitable event, but a public show of family unity, strength, and remorse over what had happened both fifty-four years ago and now.

It was important, she knew, to distance her children's reputation from their grandfather's as swiftly and cleanly as possible. The public had to understand that Cyrus Vasser's immoral choices had nothing to do with his grandchildren, plain and simple. And if any asshole reporter or socialite even dared bring her children into this, heads were going to roll. She still had enough ferocity in her from the old days before she'd ascended the social ladder and she wasn't afraid to unleash it if her family was in danger. Words were weapons, ones that Charlene was a master at utilizing. She'd use them to drive figurative daggers through the hearts of any paltry miscreant who doubted her willingness to do so, and they would be resorted to nothing but shamed and despicable mush afterward.

A smile lifted the corners of her mouth at the thought, allowing herself the pleasure of imagining the damage she could do. It was common for people to underestimate her, including her own children and especially Marshall. But Charlene was no fool and she was not about to wither into horrified silence while the family name she'd worked so hard to latch on to descended into disgrace.

She glanced up as Win wandered into the restaurant, looking much too cheerful for a man whose father just died. She glared at him as he slipped into the seat across from her, earlier traces of her dark humor fleeing, replaced only by disdain.

"Good morning," Win greeted, smiling as he lifted the white porcelain coffee pot that rested on the table and poured himself a generous cup.

"Stop acting like you just won the goddamn lottery, Win," Charlene scolded in a harried whisper. "Your father just passed away."

"I know, it's great, isn't it?" Win took a sip of coffee and sighed. "I'm finally free."

"What you are is a disgrace," she shot back, removing her reading glasses. She made sure to conceal the worst of her anger from her expression, and kept her voice low so no one nearby would hear. Though for breakfast, *Cherir* was filled mostly with business professionals from the nearby high rises and guests at the hotel, and none of them were paying her or Win any attention. "First you get drunk and publicly accuse your own father of murder, leaving me no choice but to bring you back here where I can keep an eye on you. And now, before this detective has even had the chance to speak to you or to Cyrus, he offs himself and you're chipper about it. I won't have it, Win, I just won't have it."

"Calm down, Char," Win told her, avoiding her eyes and reading from the menu, his smile still in place. "Everything's going to be fine now."

"How so?" She scowled, clutching her napkin in her lap to keep from throwing something at him. "You and Cyrus have potentially destroyed everything this family has worked so hard for. Our reputation is at stake, and if we get swallowed up by this scandal then we will not only lose market share, we'll lose our standing in New York. So tell me again how everything is going to be just fine, Win?"

He said nothing for a moment as the waiter interrupted them, taking the menu and Win's order. As the young man walked away, Win folded his hands on the table and hunched over, lifting his eyes to meet his ex-wife's. What he saw there brought a quick bite of panic to his gut, but he pushed it aside. He was safe now, he just had to get used to the idea. No one could hurt him anymore.

"When the detective comes today I'm going to tell him the truth. He'll probably believe me since the suicide shows my dad was guilty, and so he'll close the case and this will all be over."

"And what of the negative press? The damage is being done as we speak to our reputation, and it can take several years if not decades to recover from something like this. We could lose everything, Win. That means no house in the Hollywood hills, no luxury cruises to the Caribbean, no barely legal tarts with more breasts than brains, and no Lamborghinis for you to cruise the Boulevard in."

"You know, I was thinking maybe I wouldn't go back to all that anyway," he said. "I thought maybe I could start over, ya know? Here in New York. Get an apartment, maybe work at the hotel or something. I've been away for so long, but now that he's gone I can finally come home."

Charlene blinked, speechless. She started breathing again when Marshall came up beside her and leaned down to kiss her cheek.

"Good morning, Charlene. Win," Marshall mumbled, clearly distracted and stressed. Charlene nodded as Marshall slid into the booth beside his brother and poured himself some coffee.

Win beamed at his brother and patted him on the back. "Hey man, it's a beautiful day, isn't it?"

Marshall's lips pressed together to form a tight, disapproving line as he finished pouring his coffee and set aside the pitcher. "It's raining outside. Again."

"So what? A little rain never hurt anybody." Win grinned, pausing as the waiter delivered his plate of strawberry crepes and took Marshall's order. As the waiter left, Marshall frowned at his youngest brother.

"The detective should be here any minute. I hope you're prepared."

"To what? Tell the truth?" Win asked, aloof to Marshall's weariness and frustration. "I can't wait to tell him, to be honest. Then this will all be over and I can move on."

"It may be over for you in one sense, brother. But this will not be over for the family for some time."

Win's smile faltered and he glanced over at Charlene. "That's what Char thinks too, but c'mon. Once the case is closed, no one will care anymore."

"Americans always care about a scandal and one of this magnitude will not pass us by without causing irreparable harm." Marshall took a tentative sip of coffee to shield the emotion from his voice, his grief insurmountable. Not only for his deceased father, who he had loved and respected, but for the beating he knew was coming for his family. It was up to him to protect them, yet he worried he was too tired and too old to do enough. And sensing defeat after a lifetime of success and triumph was breaking his entire soul to pieces.

Charlene noted the sadness in Marshall's eyes and her lips curled in anger. Win was always destroying everything, and now Marshall, the man she should have married in the first place, was grieving and Win couldn't care less. It was so typical.

"Just before you arrived, Marshall, Win was telling me he would like to relocate back to New York. He said he wants to work for the hotel," she said conversationally, watching Marshall to gauge his reaction. The flash of shock and fury that passed over his face did not disappoint her.

"Damnit, Win," he grunted, turning to face his brother accusingly. "You can't just avoid responsibility for a lifetime and suddenly expect to be included. Any position you may have qualified for has been passed on to your children, who are doing a better job than you would have anyway."

"But Marshall, you know now why I stayed away, why I didn't want to get involved," Win reminded him, his brow creasing with frustration. "I was scared of him. He was evil. Don't you see that?"

Marshall's gaze hardened, his temper rising to mix dangerously with the grief. "The man has barely been dead fifteen hours and you have the audacity to speak ill of him when nothing has been proven? I for one won't believe anything you say until the detective confirms it. For all I know, you made it up just to punish him, to punish all of us for ignoring you."

Win paled to a ghostly white, staggered. "You don't believe me? You have to believe me."

"Why? Because you've been so goddamn honest in the past?" Marshall growled, tossing his napkin down and rising to his feet. "You can't even be honest with your own little girl on why you had to miss her high school graduation."

"She doesn't hold that against me."

Marshall shook his head, disgust rising in his gut. "You said that about all of them, Win. And each time you were wrong."

"Hey, mom. Marshall," Linc greeted as he walked over, his voice gruff from lack of sleep and his eyes shadowed by dark circles. He leaned down to kiss his mother's cheek and patted Marshall on the back, attempting a small smile at he met his uncle's eyes. He'd watched the exchange from outside the restaurant and knew he needed to intervene.

With obvious disdain, he turned his attention to his father. "The detective is here. He went upstairs to speak with Grant first but he's expecting you up there in about twenty minutes."

Win stared hopelessly at his youngest son, regret and guilt pounding through his brain from Marshall's words. Did all his kids really hate him? "Okay, Linc. Hey, you know, maybe when I move back to New York we can hang out or something. Maybe make a fresh start of the mess I've made of things."

Linc's jaw clenched as he tucked his hands into his pockets. "Who said you're allowed to move back to New York?"

Win froze, confused. "I..."

"Let me put it this way, *dad*," Linc said, an edgy smile curving his lips. "You were dead to me the moment you decided to fuck my girlfriend. That was when I officially wrote you out of my life. Don't you ever wonder why Grant, Madison and I don't bother to talk to you? And Kennedy won't be far behind, trust me. She's been pissed off at you ever since she found out the real reason you dodged her graduation."

"How did she find out?" Win stammered, eyes wide.

"You think I don't have access to your expense account? You think I can't put two and two together when you're reserving a hotel room in the Caribbean, buying two sets of overpriced lobster dinners and ordering a five hundred dollar bottle of champagne and chocolate strawberries that you're not with some woman? Well, now she sees you for what you are and it's done. You've successfully lost all of us. Congratulations."

"Linc, wait—" Win tried to reach for his son across the table as Linc stalked away. As he watched his son disappear into the lobby, Win felt despair and misery wash over him. He settled back into his seat and stared numbly at the table.

Marshall left without a word, having seen and heard enough. He had his own grief and anger to deal with and seeing his brother in pain was doing nothing to help.

Charlene remained where she was, replacing her reading glasses as she returned to her to-do list, proud of her youngest son.

"It's like you said, Win. Everything is going to be just fine."

"I'M SURE YOU'RE wondering why I came to see you first," Detective Don Hughes said, his voice solemn and businesslike as he met Grant's eyes. He sat in one of the chairs in front of Grant's desk, just as he had weeks earlier when he'd first come to tell the family about the letter. Funny how so much had changed in that short period of time.

Grant frowned, leaning back in his chair and eyeing the detective thoughtfully. In his hands, he held his great-grandfather's fountain pen and he passed it between his fingers idly as he spoke. "I suppose I am curious, detective. My father's the one with the testimony you need to close this case."

Don considered Grant's words for a moment, a manila folder containing all of Rosalie Owens' documents in his lap. He ran his hands over its surface, pondering just how best to explain the disturbing truths that lay inside.

"I still intend to get your father's statement, Mr. Vasser," he began, choosing his words carefully. "But before I do so I wanted to share with you the rest of the information that was included in Rosalie Owens' letter. Now that your grandfather is dead, there is no longer a need for me to hold out the details from your family."

Grant's eyes narrowed, his knuckles whitening as he gripped the pen he held tighter. "What sort of *details* have you been withholding?"

"I needed to find out if anyone in your family could corroborate what Rosalie Owens claimed. Luckily for me, your father is a witness, and a man by the name of Wyatt Bailey came to me to confirm that your father had not just recently made up his eyewitness account."

Grant stiffened, anger hardening his face. "Wyatt Bailey, detective?"

"Yes, he said your father told him about it seven years ago. Mr. Bailey was very specific, so I'm inclined to believe him."

"So that's why he was in town," Grant murmured to himself, remembering Madison telling him that Wyatt had come to see her. Shaking his head, he pushed the thought away. "So what is this information?"

"Fairly extensive proof, Mr. Vasser, I must say."

"Proof of what, exactly? That my grandfather murdered his father? I think we can assume that his suicide confirms his guilt." Grief flashed briefly in his eyes to mix with the resentment he felt.

"Unfortunately, Mr. Vasser, there is more than just the murder of your great-grandfather that Cyrus Vasser was accused of committing." Don lifted the manila folder so Grant could see it, but he did not open it. "In her letter, Rosalie described what Winston told her about the war and how Cyrus came back a hero. But three of his brothers were not so lucky."

"Silas, Porter, and Harris." Grant's eyes shot to one of the photographs on his wall that showed the three brothers in uniform, arm in arm, on an Army base in the Carolinas back in 1942. "They were in a bunker that was hit by a German howitzer. My grandfather was the only one who managed to escape. They weren't even all supposed to be there, but they refused to let the Army separate them."

"Did you ever wonder why your grandfather managed to get out in time, along with the rest of the men in that bunker, but his three brothers didn't?"

"I never really gave it much thought, no." Grant stared once again at the detective, impatience flashing in his eyes. "Why is this important?"

"It's important, Mr. Vasser, because Rosalie Owens *did* wonder why Cyrus was the only one of the brothers to get out alive, and she did some research into military documents through a friend of hers in the State Department. She learned that when they found the bodies behind a stack of what had been wooden crates, they discovered traces of rope around their wrists and ankles. They'd been bound and gagged and probably drugged, though we'll never know. That particular area had been bracing for a German attack, and so it was no surprise that the bunker was targeted. Which was why most of the soldiers were ready to vacate the building the second the threat arrived. Except for Silas, Porter, and Harris Vasser."

"If they found the rope, then how come there was never an investigation?" Grant asked, his forehead creasing as his eyes narrowed. "Why was my family told it was an unfortunate accident?"

"More than likely the person in charge was bought off." Don shrugged as if it was obvious. "It made it into the file, but whoever would've been notified of the possible foul play afterwards decided not to pursue an investigation."

"That's impossible," Grant challenged, though doubt circled miserably in his gut. "Why did no one else question why the bodies were found tucked behind some crates?"

"It was war, Mr. Vasser," Don replied, his eyes hardening. "Men don't waste time standing around asking a lot of questions when there are bullets and bombs flying at them from every which direction. They accepted, and they moved on. And from what I understand, most of the men who managed to escape that day were not so lucky just five days later when the Germans attacked again. It seems your grandfather picked an excellent setting to dispose of his brothers."

Grant said nothing for a long, haunted moment. He stared at the detective, his breath caught in his lungs and his heart a stone cold weight in his chest. When he finally blinked, he felt a chill settle over him.

"I don't believe you," he managed, his voice quiet and hollow. The pen slipped from his fingers and tumbled onto the desk. He didn't even notice. Instead he saw, in his mind, thousands of memories of the man he'd known, the grandfather who'd raised him, who'd always been a source of respect, strength, and admiration. It was bad enough to come to terms with that same man murdering Winston in cold blood, but having also taken out his own brothers in the heat of war? He'd known Cyrus to be ambitious, ruthless, and at times cruel, but the man he'd known his entire life could not be responsible for such vicious acts of hate.

Don's mouth set in a grim line as he watched Grant, knowing this to be one of the hardest parts of the job. Oftentimes people chose to dismiss the claims against their loved ones and live in denial. Other times, people collapsed into puddles of inconsolable grief. And, in the rarest of cases, people believed him, and accepted. He could see now by the dulled expression on Grant Vasser's face that his mind was urging him to accept the truth. It was a troubling thing to witness.

"Now you understand why I wanted to come to you first."

Grant nodded slowly, at a loss for words.

"I've researched the Army's files myself and confirmed that what Rosalie included in this package is factual. The Army is, as of this moment, informed of the oversight and they're conducting their own investigation. Within a few weeks, the files on your three great uncles will be updated to show the true cause of death. Since your grandfather is already deceased, there will be no charges filed."

Grant nodded again, avoiding looking at the photographs on his wall, not yet ready to face them. "Is that all, detective?"

"Not quite, Mr. Vasser," Don said evenly, patient as always despite the irritated stare he earned from the man across from him. "When Rosalie discovered the truth, she told Winston and showed him the proof. By her own account, he didn't want to believe her, but she was convincing enough to place some measure of doubt within his mind. Then she confronted Cyrus and told him he wasn't going to get away with it, and that his father was going to change his will and leave the hotels, the money, and the power to her instead. She said she wanted to see the fear in his eyes, but he wasn't afraid of her. Instead, he was cold, and as she described it, amused. The very next day, Winston was dead and she was followed home from work by a stranger, a man with a gun who threatened to kill her if she didn't disappear. Right after that, Rosalie claimed she received a letter and a hefty chunk of cash from Fern Vasser, Winston's soon to be ex-wife, urging her to silence for the remainder of her life. Evidently she fulfilled the bargain, only leaving behind this file for someone to eventually find after her death."

"Alright...but I still don't understand why he would kill his own brothers. Isn't it possible that it was someone else?"

"I've done some research into your family tree, Mr. Vasser, and it appears as though Silas, Porter and Harris were the only ones standing in the way of Cyrus becoming next in line to run the family estate and business. His other brother Luther, according to public record, relocated to the USSR in the 1930's and never returned. And above him was Winston II, who was busy establishing the Vasser Hotel in Los Angeles and was not in competition for the New York hotel. And lastly, the first and oldest son, Alton II, had died five years earlier of tuberculosis."

"But other than speculation, you have no proof that this is true. Just because he stood to benefit from their deaths doesn't make him their killer," Grant argued.

Don nodded, opening the folder to pull out a plain white envelope that bore his name on its face. He stared at the letter for a brief moment before passing it to Grant, leveling his gaze with the younger man before he spoke.

"This was dropped off at the precinct this morning by your sister. Your grandfather left it in one of his books and she found it while she was going through his things."

Grant accepted the envelope and frowned as he opened it and pulled out the letter. As he read, his hands tightened on the thin sheet of paper until his grip nearly tore it in half. It was impersonally straightforward and to the point, and outlined the crimes Cyrus admitted to having committed. Included were the murder of his father, Winston, and the murders of his three brothers during the war. Grief and denial settled hotly in Grant's gut, but he pushed them aside in order to maintain his composure. Control had always been his strongest skill, after all. It was one he'd inherited from the very grandfather he now knew was a cold-blooded killer.

"Did Madison read this?"

"It was sealed when she gave it to me, so I'm going to assume she didn't," Don said, accepting the letter as Grant handed it back to him. Before he spoke again, Don rose to his feet and held out the folder. "Inside you'll find copies of everything Rosalie Owens wanted to be found. I urge you to look through it all and carefully consider how best to inform your family."

Grant accepted the folder and met Don's eyes. "What happens now? With the case?"

Don slipped the confession letter into the inside pocket of his coat. "I go and get your father's testimony, then I go back to my office and close the case."

"That's it?"

"That's it," Don replied, his expression professionally distant and yet still sympathetic. "I can personally promise not to deliver news of this to the press, Mr. Vasser. But as I'm sure you're aware, this will not be kept under wraps, either."

Grant nodded, understanding. "I'll take care of the press." He rose to his feet and held out his hand. "I should probably thank you, detective, but I hope you understand it's halfhearted."

With a small, measured smile, Don bowed his head. "I'm hired to discover the truth, Mr. Vasser. Good and bad. Take care."

As the detective turned and left the room, Grant settled back into his chair, his gaze reluctantly finding its way to his grandfather's portrait. He stared at it for a long, silent moment, unsure how to react to the whole situation.

His grandfather had written out a confession to both crimes and then he'd killed himself. It was so incredibly *un*like the man he'd known all his life that he wondered if this was just some insane nightmare he would soon wake from.

Had his grandfather really felt the only way out was death? Had he thought at all about how his actions were going to impact the rest of the family and the hotels? Surely he had some kind of plan, something in motion that would protect the empire from imploding. But what? What kind of plan could he enact from beyond the grave?

"Grant?"

His eyes shot almost guiltily to the doorway where Quinn stood, a small brown paper package in her hands. Her lips curved into a sunny smile, and he felt the heavy lump in his chest lighten at the sight of it.

"Hi." He pushed the folder containing Rosalie's documents aside, knowing he couldn't share it with her, no matter how badly he wanted to confide in someone with an outside, objective point of view. She wouldn't have any answers, anyway. It would just worry her.

She walked to his desk and handed him the package. "I made you my world famous cannolis. I thought maybe you could use a pick me up today."

He accepted the package and set it on the desk, a half laugh escaping his throat. "If only you knew."

His cell phone rang, his mother's name on the caller ID. He lifted his index finger to motion for Quinn to hang on as he answered the phone. "Mother."

"*I wanted to remind you that the fundraiser is tonight. Are you bringing a date?*"

"Why do I have to go?" he asked, shutting his eyes and rubbing them tiredly with his free hand. "I really don't have time for this."

"*You will be there, Grant, and that's final,*" Charlene snapped. "*This is not just a fundraiser. It's a show of strength, unity and mourning, and we must all be present.*"

Because he knew she was right, he let his hand fall from his face and let out a slow, measured breath. "Fine. I'll be there."

"*Good. Are you going to bring a date?*"

"Who would I bring?" he scoffed, even as his eyes rose to Quinn, who was busy plating a cannoli for him in the kitchenette. "Never mind. Yes, I'll bring someone."

"*Excellent. See you tonight.*"

He hung up the phone as Quinn set a paper plate in front of him with one of her cannolis on it.

"If you don't try the first bite in front of me, I'll be very disappointed," she informed him, standing back with her hands clasped together. "Go ahead, try it."

"Let me ask you something first." Grant met her eyes, annoyed that, even at twenty-eight, he still felt the fear of being rejected. It was downright pathetic. "The fundraiser is tonight and I need a date. You'll need to meet me in the lobby at eight o'clock sharp."

Quinn blinked, her mouth falling open stupidly. "You want *me* to be your date? To a fancy New York City fundraiser? Where all the elites hang out and drink several hundred dollar champagne and eat beluga caviar? Really, Grant? You can't do better than me?"

"There is no one better than you," he said simply.

She considered that for a moment, but the thought of pretending to be classy and rich for an evening distracted her from his comment. "You don't know what you're asking. People like me don't go to parties like that because we get nervous and laugh too loud or say stupid things or trip over our own feet or use the wrong fork for our salads...oh God, you can't possibly want me there, seriously."

Amused, he sat back in his chair and smiled. "Actually, it sounds like you'll make the evening much more enjoyable for me."

Flabbergasted, she wrung her hands together in front of her and chewed her bottom lip, alarmed by the humored look on his face. Great, he thought her misery was funny. Just great.

"And if I don't want to go?" she asked, lifting her chin stubbornly and crossing her arms.

"That's up to you. I'm not ordering you to, I'm simply requesting."

But the look in his eyes told her that he would be disappointed if she didn't go with him, and the last thing she wanted to do was put him out like this when he needed her. After all, she had told him she would do anything for him. With a heavy sigh, she let her hands fall to her sides in defeat.

"Alright, I'll go. But I can't promise you that I won't do any of the aforementioned embarrassing things, thus making you regret this very moment."

"I think we could all use a good laugh right now, so if you feel inclined to fall down some stairs, be my guest. Just don't sue me if you break a leg."

"Such a nice guy," she said sarcastically, shaking her head. "Now eat your damn cannoli before I change my mind and take it back."

FIFTEEN

S o let me get this straight," Greg began, his hand clenched around a ten-pound weight as he did bicep curls. "You guys get visited by some detective saying he has a letter accusing your grandpa of murder. Then your dad comes out and publicly announces that he witnessed said murder. Then your grandpa pulls the plug; bam, he's dead. And now everyone is going to naturally assume that he did in fact commit the murder because a suicide is as good as a confession."

"That's pretty much it," Linc huffed, his hands behind his head as he methodically did crunches, annoyed that the gym around them was depressingly empty. Clearly the hotel was already taking a hit from the publicity of the scandal. "Hell, it's still fucking surreal to me. I don't even know what to make of it all."

"You could change your name and move to Iceland."

"That's your answer to everything."

"Because it's a good escape plan," Greg argued, switching the weight to his left arm. "I really don't see a positive way for you to spin this one. It's pretty bad."

"Tell me about it," Linc grunted as he fell back onto the mat, sweat pouring down his face. "But if I don't come up with something soon, we're all screwed."

"Isn't that fundraiser thing tonight? I'm sure that'll give your top clients the chance to see that you're holding things together. Word on the street is that the Vasser hotel company is going to implode and collapse because of this, but if you can put on a good face and convince everyone that it's business as usual despite the, ya know, *murder*, then I think you'll be okay."

"Shit, that is tonight, isn't it?" Linc rubbed his face with his hands and groaned. "The last thing I want to do is deal with the goddamn press. You know they're going to be there, swarming the place like sewer rats."

"Just show up with some bombshell on your arm and maybe they'll forget," Greg suggested jokingly.

Linc rose up on his elbows and managed a weary grin. "That's actually not a bad idea. Though I don't think even bringing Megan Fox would distract that crowd. But it might make me feel better."

"You thinking of bringing that redhead you told me about?"

Linc shrugged, reaching for his water bottle and gulping down half of it before speaking again. "I don't know. I really shouldn't put Lynette through all this. It isn't fair to her."

"She's a senator's daughter, isn't she?" Greg asked, earning a nod from Linc. "Well then she's used to the press. She'll be good with it."

"Yeah, but being a politician's daughter also means that her face means something to these psychos. And next year is an election year, so associating with me is probably not going to put her in her father's good graces right now."

"You make it sound like you have the plague." Greg rose to his feet and dropped the weight onto the rack with a loud crash that echoed through the gym. "If she likes you, she'll go."

"That's what I'm worried about." Linc scowled, accepting Greg's hand to help him to his feet. "She may not be thinking very clearly about the consequences of associating with me."

"You don't give her enough credit, man," Greg countered, patting Linc on the back as they headed toward the showers. "Hell, I still stick around, don't I? So you can't be nearly as bad as you think you are."

"Yeah, but even now being around me improves your social status. You're just the son of a farmer from Iowa with bad teeth."

"You sure know how to put a man down when he's just tryin' to help you." Greg chuckled, slapping his friend on the back. "Now call your girl before I call her up myself and steal her from you. Bad teeth and all."

Linc laughed and reached into his pocket for his cell phone. "Can't risk that. I'll be there in a second."

Greg walked off as Linc pulled up Lynette's number and called her, still laughing to himself. When she answered, he felt his smile grow ten times bigger.

"Hey, beautiful. Put on something sexy tonight and meet me in the hotel lobby at eight. I'm taking you to a fundraiser."

SOULFUL JAZZ BOUNCED off the walls of her town house as she slipped into a dress as dark as night. Her fingers skillfully located the zipper at the back as she slid it up, enveloping her slender body in a color appropriate for a mourner.

And Lord, was she mourning.

Not visibly, Madison contended proudly, her eyes meeting her reflection in the floor to ceiling mirror in her bedroom. No, to anyone else she appeared melancholy, but steady; grieving, but calm. She was a woman who had lost a family member who had meant very much to her, who had to adjust to the newfound knowledge of the horrific acts he had committed in his past. Of course, most of that knowledge was not actually new. But no one else would be permitted to know that.

Her room, and her town house on the Upper East side, suited her tastes and her personality. It was a décor that referenced heavily on the oriental palate, with vibrant red and bold black covering nearly every surface. But the reference stopped there, and instead ventured into metropolitan modern and sophisticated, with hard, straight lines and sharp edges. Her furniture reflected her passion for equal parts comfort and chic, begging to be sat upon and yet daring to be tarnished. Where there was wood, it was mahogany, a rich red toned wood that filled both her kitchen and her bathrooms, covered beautifully by stark black granite.

She disliked excessive patterns, preferring instead sleek, bold solids and textures that urged a second look and a reverent touch.

As such, her enormous four poster bed with its red canopy and mountains of textured pillows, all in black, spoke as much about her belief in luxury as it did about her darker views of what went on in a bedroom. Sex had never ashamed her, nor had her need for it. She was a woman who knew the game of love like the back of her hand and in her experience love was rarely, if ever, a part of it.

Except, of course, in that one case. But she'd damn herself to hell for even giving one more thought to what it felt like to have Wyatt Bailey's hands on her.

To distract herself, she lifted her rounded glass of rich, dark cabernet to her lips, savoring the flavor on her tongue for a moment as she analyzed the fit of the dress on her figure. It infuriated her to notice that she'd lost weight from the stress of the last few days. It was only in times of extreme emotional disturbance that her control over her eating habits wavered, and it was notably a bad sign. It was also maddening to acknowledge that the entire situation was going to get far worse before it got better.

Her eyes shot to the plain white envelope resting on her nightstand, her name scrawled in shaky cursive over the front. What lay inside both alarmed and revolted her. It would surely do the same, and more, to her family when she presented it to them.

But that would have to wait until tomorrow, after the fundraiser. She wanted her brothers as attentive and positive as they could possibly be this night and then, only once the public display was done, would she reveal to them what she had learned.

She wondered briefly if Detective Don Hughes had found a similar confession in his own letter and if he had seen fit to share it with her brothers. Perhaps he had.

How would Grant, so honorable and loyal to the family, take the news that their grandfather had murdered not only his father, but his own three brothers just to climb to the top of the ladder of control? And how would Linc, goodhearted and honest, deal with knowing the lies that had been hidden for over half a century by a man he had admired and loved?

It would break them both. But it was time the truth came out.

In some ways, she was relieved to not have to hide the few secrets she herself had known any longer. While part of her was outraged that her grandfather had hidden the worst of his secrets from her all these years, the other side of her wondered if she would have felt the same had she known then what she knew now.

She had been able to justify, in her mind, Cyrus killing Winston. It was over Winston's mistress, Rosalie, and the threat that the woman was to inherit everything, the money, the hotels, all of it, simply because Winston was smitten with her. Madison had understood the necessity to preserve the empire and keep it within the family, not allowing an outsider to benefit from years and years of Vasser blood, sweat, and tears. So it had seemed only right to snuff out Winston, as he was, in a way, committing treason against the very family that had made him. Yes, she had truly, wholeheartedly, believed that.

Now none of that made any sense. Now it appeared the reason for killing his own father had not just been about reclaiming the family empire. It had been about covering up a crime. Rosalie had uncovered the truth and told Winston. Cyrus would have lost the position he had killed for because of this woman, so he made her so terrified of him that she would never again utter the name Vasser. He killed her lover in cold blood and displayed to her just how far he was willing to go to preserve his reputation.

And as practical, cool-headed, and merciless as she sometimes thought herself to be, Madison still could not stand behind such heinousness. She could never, ever envision killing her two older brothers simply to rise within the ranks of the family hierarchy. It was unimaginable.

But Cyrus had. And the betrayal and stunning fury she felt was burning through her like a raging, out of control fire. It burrowed into her very bones and tore through her heart, making a mockery of her principles.

He'd made her believe, for all these years, that he'd done the right thing. He'd convinced her to honor him, to trust him, to fight for him. He'd given her what she had always considered a gift: his trust, his secrets, his goals. What did any of that mean now?

It meant it was now up to her to pick up the pieces. And the detailed instructions on how to do so were laid out in that very envelope.

Ignoring the shiver that ran down her spine, Madison took another sip of wine and went to her vanity table. She set her glass down and opened the top drawer of her mahogany jewelry cabinet. She lifted out a three tiered, diamond studded white gold necklace that sparked like fire in her hands. As she encircled it around her neck, her eyes lifted to watch her reflection. Against the smooth ivory of her skin and the elegant black of the strapless dress she wore, the diamonds were strikingly opulent. With practiced movements, she added matching diamond earrings, large studs that caught the light.

As she reached for a gleaming tennis bracelet to slide over her right wrist, her eyes fell upon her tattoo and held. Her breath caught in her throat, but she refused to shed any tears. The stark black outline of the IX stood out like a glaring, pitiful mistake against her skin. There was a time when she had put all her faith into that symbol, all her hopes, dreams, and fears. It gave her strength when she nearly succumbed to weakness, showed her the path when she felt lost.

Now it took all she had not to claw it from her very skin.

In time she would come to terms with the disaster her grandfather left her. She had specific instructions on how to fix the mess her family was in and needed to trust him this one last time.

The next step was to attend the fundraiser, looking vibrant and focused. Grieving, but strong as a rock and just as formidable.

She would see to it that her family pulled through this catastrophe, even if she had to beg, steal and borrow her way into hell to do so.

QUINN SAT IN the lobby of the Vasser Hotel, feeling as out of place as a mutt in a kennel full of purebreds. Men and women breezed past her, heads held high and bodies donned in clothes fit for royalty. Armani suits and Versace gowns with glittering diamonds, sapphires and rubies assembled into jewelry she could only dream of even touching. Oh, and the *shoes* on these women...Quinn sighed as she watched a particularly dreamy pair of silky, scarlet red pumps waltz by on the legs of a woman who belonged on the cover of *Vanity freaking Fair*.

She ran her fingers through her hair anxiously, frowning down at her own pair of plain black pumps. She'd had them for four extremely long years and they were entirely more practical than elegant. She would have splurged for new ones, but it just wasn't in the budget right now. She was still trying to save for culinary school on the off chance Grant couldn't secure her a position in the kitchen of the hotel.

A smart girl always had a back-up plan.

What she had done, however, was make a quick trip after work to the local department store to scour the clearance dress rack. After several frantic minutes of searching, she found a respectably pretty cocktail dress that thankfully suited her curves and didn't make her look too short. She pulled at the hem of the emerald green dress, tugging it further down her thighs, wondering if Grant would find it acceptable. When standing, the full skirt hovered just above her knees and the cinch at the waist accented her figure nicely. The heart shaped bodice with halter straps that tied in a bow at her neck were a nice touch, as was the pretty bow at her lower back where the dress dipped low enough to reveal some skin. She tried not to feel inadequate in a thirty dollar department store dress while surrounded by women in designer gowns that must have cost thousands.

Her mother had always taught her that coveting was a sin, so she dismissed the feelings of envy as best she could.

A waiter wandered by and handed her a glass of champagne. She accepted it with a numb smile, too nervous to drink. She spotted Lynette as she wandered through the lobby doors, looking lovely in a rose pink off the shoulder gown of lace and silk, her long waves of copper hair piled elegantly on top of her head.

Waving to her, Quinn saw the pleasure and relief chase away the nerves on Lynette's face. It made her feel better to know she wasn't the only one who was uncomfortable.

"Hey," Quinn greeted, hugging Lynette with a grin. "Of course you look just as gorgeous as the rest of them. Is it okay if I hate you for awhile?"

Lynette laughed, her smile kind as she looked Quinn up and down. "I should be hating you. I can't pull off a dress like that. I'm all scrawny legs and no curves."

"I guess we're even, then," Quinn decided, grabbing a glass of champagne for Lynette when a waiter passed by. "Here, might as well make a toast, don't you think?"

"To what?" Lynette accepted the glass and eyed Quinn. "Seems as though we're both here as distractions."

"Mmm...yep, distracting the Vasser brothers does seem to be our specialty." Quinn smiled deviously, considering the thought. "We should toast to having the guts to put up with this crowd for the evening. Hopefully we make it out in one piece."

"Amen." Lynette giggled, tapping her glass against Quinn's. "You'd think I'd get used to them, being in the political spotlight after so many years. But the judging, the spitefulness, the drama...it never gets easier to bear."

When Quinn only looked confused, Lynette elaborated.

"My father is a senator back in South Carolina, where I'm from, so I've been dealing with social elites all my life. Even after I moved here to work as a dancer for the New York City Ballet, I still couldn't escape it." She pursed her lips, irritation flashing in her eyes. "In some ways they're worse, though, because they take something I love so passionately and turn it into nothing more than politics."

"I know how you feel. All I wanna do is cook for a living, but you wouldn't *believe* the hoops they make you jump through just to get into the business," Quinn said as she took another sip of champagne. Her lips curved as she spotted Grant and Linc coming through the lobby doors. Their heads were together as they spoke to each other in hurried whispers. "Looks like our dates are finally here."

Lynette spun around, surprised to feel so nervous. Hoping to distract herself, she leaned in to speak in Quinn's ear. "So I just *have* to know...are you and Grant more than just boss and secretary?"

Quinn kept her eyes forward instead of facing Lynette, worried what she would give away if she did. "No, we're just friendly, that's all."

Lynette nodded and pulled away, but noted the flush that came over Quinn's cheeks and wondered just how involved they really were. She and Linc had their hunches, certainly. But maybe there was more to this than even they theorized.

A few yards away, Linc stopped walking and put his hands on his brother's shoulders, turning to face him. "You're holding out on me, I can tell. That detective told you something that you won't tell me."

Grant grimaced, feeling uncomfortable. "This is not the time or the place to discuss this."

"Damnit, Grant. You're being selfish by keeping this to yourself."

Grant blinked in surprise. "That's a new one. I don't think you've ever called me selfish before."

"Well, I'm saying it now," Linc sighed, running his hands through his hair. "Look, I—"

He paused as he spotted Lynette and Quinn. He let out a slow whistle, a pleased grin curving his lips. "Would you look at that?"

Grant followed his brother's gaze and saw Quinn. He watched in stunned silence as she walked toward him, a sunny smile glowing over her face.

"Didn't your mother ever tell you not to keep a lady waiting?" she joked, her gypsy eyes glittering with humor.

Grant frowned, taken aback by her words. He glanced down at his watch, earning a laugh from her.

"Grant, I'm only joking." She reached out to touch his arm. He stared down at her hand for a brief moment before meeting her eyes again.

"You look beautiful," he said impulsively. He cleared his throat when he realized his brother and Lynette were both staring at him with curious grins on their faces. But he wasn't lying when he said it. He was completely and unexpectedly floored by her. She'd done something clever with her makeup, darkening around her eyes to highlight the green in them, honing her Sicilian bone structure with blush and painting those lush lips of hers an alluring rose color. Her hair was left loose and curled nearly to her shoulders, and the ebony mass of it tempted his hands to run through and stake claim.

Not to mention that smile of hers was going to be his undoing.

"Thank you," Quinn beamed, rising on her tiptoes to kiss his cheek. It was a move that appeared remote and professional, given

the distance between their bodies and the casualness of the movement. But the spark hit them both as her lips brushed his cheek and
her hand clenched tighter on his arm.

The scent of her engulfed him and it took all he had to politely
push away from her.

"We should be heading upstairs," he said, straightening his tie
and holding his arm out courteously for Quinn to take.

She accepted, and tilted her head to smile and wink at Linc. "Grant
thought it would be funny for me to make a fool of myself and trip
down some stairs, but the joke's on him. We're taking the elevator."

Linc and Lynette laughed and Grant tried his best to prevent his
mouth from twitching into a smile. He'd been right that having her
around for the fundraiser would greatly improve his mood. Already
he felt calmer, more centered. Just having her beside him gave him
something he thought he'd never find again. She was a source of light
to combat the darkness he was facing.

The four of them made their way to the elevator and then up to
the third floor, where the hotel's exquisite ballroom resided, once
home to countless celebrity weddings and elite social and political
events, all spanning the ballroom's fifty year history. From icons like
Marilyn Monroe and Grace Kelly to political movers and shakers like
FDR and Eisenhower, the hotel had served them all, and had done
so with impeccable class and a dignified ambiance that guests had
come to expect of the Vasser hotels. Grant wanted their reputation
for excellence to remain intact, in spite of how damaging the scandal
with his grandfather would be.

At one time they'd come in droves, with events booked up to
three years in advance. Would they still, with the scandal tearing
apart his family's name? Would the hotel continue to be a prestigious
New York City landmark?

Only time would tell.

He led Quinn off the elevator and down the hallway toward the
double door entrance of the ballroom, where the doorman, Barry,
stood to accept coats and greet the guests.

"Hello, Miss Quinn." Barry smiled, bowing his head to Quinn as she approached with Grant beside her. "And Mr. Vasser. It's going to be a lovely event tonight, sir."

"I expect it will be," Grant murmured, handing his coat to Barry. He nodded politely and headed into the ballroom.

Quinn held him back and grinned at Barry. "If you'd like, I can sneak you some dessert later. Whaddya want? Chocolate? Cheesecake? I'm sure they've got it all in there."

Barry laughed and met eyes with Grant before clasping Quinn's hand affectionately in his own. "Sugar, you just go on in and enjoy yourself. I'll be fine right here."

Quinn winked. "Cheesecake it is."

She patted Grant's arm and they walked into the ballroom, Linc and Lynette directly behind them. She fought to take it all in at once but found it was simply impossible.

The room was wider than it was deep, with a tall, coffered ceiling resembling the gilded one downstairs. But here, instead of the quiet, stately elegance of the lobby, blatant extravagance was on full display. Three chandeliers, two small and one large in the center, descended from amidst the elegantly carved coffers. Each was a glittering mass of lights that were as luminous as diamonds in a smooth, rounded shape that radiated golden light.

The four walls of the room were draped in rose colored fabric graced with an intricate damask pattern, all set between equally spaced pillars with carvings that referenced the coffering of the ceiling. Floor to ceiling mirrors replaced the fabric along the wall in between every other pillar, reflecting light and movement to bring the entire room to life.

Perfectly arranged circular tables of ten chairs each were scattered around the room, adding up to what Quinn knew to be a few hundred guests, the majority of which had yet to arrive. Atop each white tablecloth were intricate arrangements of soft pink orchids and hibiscus, paired with leafy ferns that draped from tall glass vases to the table.

Along the back wall was a small, low-level stage complete with an elegantly dressed band. She watched, charmed, as they played soothing music with violins, flutes and cellos.

"Our table is near the front," Grant said, leading her through the room.

"This is incredible," she managed as he pulled out a chair for her at their table. "I feel like I've been smuggled into a royal palace. Any minute the guards are going to notice and they're gonna kick me out."

Grant smiled, amused at how nervous she looked. On impulse, he knelt down to meet her eyes and brush a strand of hair from her face, his hand lingering on her cheek. "You belong here just as much as the rest of them do."

She stared at him, wishing she could believe his words. But she didn't, and never would. "I'll do my best not to embarrass you. I promise."

He nodded as he straightened, his hand falling from her face. "I'll be back in a few minutes. Drink some champagne, relax."

"Okay." She watched as he walked away, sorry to see the stress and anxiety stiffening his shoulders and clouding his eyes. She wished there was more she could do for him. But until he allowed her in fully, there was little she could do but wait patiently outside for his invitation.

Linc leaned in to kiss Lynette as she sat beside Quinn, his hands resting on her shoulders.

"I have to go talk with my uncle, find out how much press is here," he told her, tweaking her nose as she smiled over her shoulder at him. "Don't let some guy come and sweep you off your feet while I'm gone, or I'm gonna have to start a brawl and I didn't bring any back up."

"Well, if he happens to be a better dancer than you then I can make no promises," she joked.

"I'm the only Yankee that can dance so I wouldn't hold my breath." He kissed the top of Lynette's head and winked at Quinn before walking away.

Quinn watched Lynette with her chin in her hand and her elbow propped up on the table, a smug smile curving her lips. "You pried into my business earlier, so I think it's only fair I pry into yours. Are things between you and the hunky Mr. Vasser number two getting serious, or what?"

"Oh, I don't know," Lynette admitted, fumbling with her napkin as she gave Quinn's words some thought. "I mean, this all happened so fast. It's like he suddenly stormed into my life and now he refuses to let go."

"But from the look on your face you don't want him to," Quinn noted, tilting her head curiously. "You're so smitten with him that I bet a deaf, dumb and blind person could even recognize it."

Lynette looked pointedly at Quinn, eyebrows raised. "That's a colorful way of putting it."

"I'm just stating the obvious." Quinn smiled, lifting a fresh glass of champagne to her lips. "I think you're good for him. You seem like a smart girl, seem to have your head on straight. He needs that structure and security now, especially with everything that's happened and will happen to the family. He's going to need you, honey. I just hope you're ready to be there one hundred percent."

"I'm here, aren't I?" Lynette replied dryly, sipping her own champagne in an attempt to settle her nerves. "I love him."

Quinn froze, her eyes widening. When she found the words to speak, she reached out to grip Lynette's hand in her own. "That's wonderful, Lynette. Have you told him?"

"No," she admitted, embarrassment flushing her cheeks. "With all the stress he's been under, he doesn't need me getting all sappy on him. He probably doesn't want to be tied down, anyway. I know what kind of man he is."

"Don't sell yourself short, honey. Or him for that manner." Quinn squeezed her hand tightly, urging Lynette to look at her. "There is a lot more to him than meets the eye, as I'm sure you're well aware. He'll appreciate the honesty if you tell him the truth about how you feel."

Lynette nodded, her lips curving into a slow, considering smile. "Aren't you being a bit of hypocrite?"

Quinn laughed. "I suppose I am, in some ways. But my situation is much different than yours."

"How so?"

She released Lynette's hand and leaned back in her chair, lifting her champagne to her lips as she thought it over. Her gaze drifted past Lynette to where Grant had disappeared into the adjoining kitchen area. She couldn't help the unsteady sigh that shivered out of her. "He has this habit of opening and closing for me like a steel door. When I'm allowed to enter, I get a glimpse of his passion and his ambition, his courage and his strength. But then he shuts it in my face and I'm left doubting his intentions, struggling with his coldness and apparent disinterest. It's like being on a circus wheel, going round and round in this circle of moods, never knowing what to expect."

"But you care about him," Lynette put in.

"More than is probably healthy, I'm sure." Quinn met the other woman's eyes. "Since pretty much the first day I met him, I've respected him. Admired him. What I saw was this man, so brazenly honorable, reverent of tradition and family. He carries this weight around on his shoulders, like Atlas with the world, this empire that he guards and protects with courage and unshakable conviction. I've never known anyone like him."

"The way he looks at you, Quinn, I don't think he's ever known anyone quite like you, either," Lynette mused, enjoying the surprise that flickered over her friend's face. "Maybe we're both being a bit silly by denying that the Vasser men are crazy about us."

Quinn let out a laugh that echoed through the half empty ballroom. "Maybe. God help us."

"God help us," Lynette agreed, lifting her glass in salute.

Across the room, Grant hovered behind his mother and sister inside the adjoining kitchen, prepared to bash their heads together if they continued bickering. A tension headache was already blooming behind his left eye and the goddamn fundraiser hadn't even started yet. He wanted nothing more than to get the entire ordeal over with and then take a long, hot shower and crawl into bed.

But until that happy moment, he was going to have to push through like a good soldier.

"Go help Marshall greet the guests as they arrive," he ordered his mother, inviting no room for rebuttal in his tone. Charlene bit off her intended snide reply to Madison and tilted her head to stare up at her oldest son.

She met his eyes and held, then let out a smooth, reluctant breath. "This is my event, after all. Perhaps I will."

But before she left the room, she shot a glance at her daughter, as though daring Madison to comment on how easily she had followed Grant's orders. But Madison said nothing and only met her gaze with mild disinterest. Furious, but refusing to show it, Charlene left the room in a flourish of black skirts and shimmering diamonds.

Once she was gone, Grant let out a long exhale and turned to his sister, measured impatience in his eyes. "Are you feeling alright? You haven't seemed yourself since you came back from the hospital."

Madison held firm, even as her heart skipped and shuddered in her chest. "I'm right as rain, darling."

But Grant wasn't convinced and she knew it, so she diverted the subject from herself and onto him. "I should be asking you if you're alright. You seem troubled."

He frowned, thinking of the file folder tucked safely in his brief-case upstairs. "I'm worried about you, Mads. You were the closest to him."

She felt the sharp pang of horrified grief wretch through her body, but any trace of it barely flickered over her face. Instead, she let her eyes fill with the quiet, cool sadness that was expected of her.

"He was one of the great loves of my life," she declared. "After you and Linc, and Uncle Marshall. Of course I'm sad. But this will pass."

"And the scandal?" Grant asked, his dark eyes searching hers. "Doesn't it spoil your memory of him?"

They both thought of Cyrus' confession, each thinking them-selves alone in knowing there was not just one murder admission, but four. They both understood that things were about to get a whole lot worse for the very family they were sworn to protect.

"Let's just get through tonight and worry about it tomorrow," she decided, rising up to kiss his cheek softly. "Tonight we'll mourn him. Tomorrow, we'll do what needs to be done for the family."

Grant hugged her closely, pulling from her strength as much as she pulled from his.

"The goddamn press is a fucking zoo out there," Linc grumbled as he prowled into the kitchen. Grant and Madison pulled away and turned to face him. "Most of them are outside the hotel by the lobby, but there's a few that'll sit and watch the event. I swear, if any one of them lies about what happens tonight, I'll kill them."

"Calm down, Linc," Madison said, grasping his shoulder. Her other arm remained around Grant. "We're here together. We don't have to deal with this alone."

Linc attempted a grin for her, then looked up at his brother. "You're right. I love you guys."

Marshall poked his head into the kitchen. "Show's about to start, kids," he said, his smile strained. "Best to go sit down."

SIXTEEN

The three of them made their way out into the ballroom. Grant noted that every one of the three hundred seats was filled. Either they'd all come out to support the family, or, more than likely, they simply wanted a chance to see its demise.

Most of those present were family friends and long time recurring guests, while scattered among them were the mayor of New York, a few celebrities with ties to the family, prominent business partners with the hotel, and reporters primed with voice recorders and notepads. He ignored the curious stares as they weaved their way toward their table. Assuming his natural born role, he kept his hand supportively placed on his sister's lower back and on his brother's shoulder as the three of them walked, knowing their every move was being judged, weighed, and monitored. There could be no slip-ups tonight.

The band continued to play soft music and most of those around them chattered away so that the drone of voices carried throughout the room. It wasn't until Grant sat down beside Quinn and finally released the breath he'd been holding that he noticed the noise. To him, it had seemed as though they were walking through a silent minefield, moments away from being hit by an explosion of distrust and hate. But in reality, it hadn't been nearly as bad as he assumed.

"I got you a beer. I hope that's okay," Quinn told him, motioning to the slender glass filled with amber colored liquid and a generous foam head.

Grant managed a tired smile and reached for the beer gratefully.

"This is perfect. Thank you." He sipped, pleased to note she'd chosen a brew he would've easily picked for himself.

Quinn smiled, her hand reaching for his free one under the table, sensing his unease and weariness.

He set his beer aside and tilted his head to look at her. His eyes met hers silently, his expression unreadable. He wished he could tell her how much it meant to him to have her there, holding his hand.

Beside her sat Lynette, and next to her Linc, who was vibrating with adrenaline, jumpy nerves and anticipation, almost to the point of being electric to the touch. Lynette thought briefly of reaching out to comfort him, but decided against it, knowing now would not be the time. Everyone would be watching them tonight, and watching her as well. More than likely the reporters were already noting that it was she, the only daughter of Senator Shaw, sitting beside the Vasser playboy as his date. Imagining the headlines made her feel a little sick, so she pushed the thought away and focused instead on Marshall, who had just made his way onto the stage.

The band slowly eased to silence as Marshall reached for the microphone. He was dressed in an impeccable suit of solid black, with a demure black vest and tie to match. On his lapel was a pin, a golden *V* that had been his grandfather's. He wore it as both a symbol and a tribute.

"Good evening, ladies, gentlemen, we're so delighted you all could make it," he began, his smile solemn beneath his thick mustache and his eyes respectfully grim. "When we first planned this event, we wanted to honor my mother and my grandmother, Stella and Fern Vasser, both who died tragically of this awful cancer many years ago. We wanted to raise money in their name, and hopefully assist the Cancer Society in its research to combat this disease and save as many lives as can be saved. All of you, as you know, by simply appearing here tonight are doing your part in ensuring Breast Cancer, and other cancers like it, remain a strong initiative among those of us who have watched loved ones lose the tragic battle that comes with it. So I thank you, on behalf of my family and families across the world, for giving what you can in the name of life."

The crowd applauded politely as Grant, Linc, and Madison scanned the sea of faces, gauging reactions, moods, intentions. As of that moment, everything appeared as it should be, but all three of them knew better than to feel relieved just yet.

Marshall continued as the applause died down, his tone slightly more solemn, traces of his grief now edging through his composure. "Now, as many of you have likely heard, our family has recently lost one of our own...my father, Cyrus. Some of you knew him well, while the majority of you may have never had the pleasure. While his death may signal the end of an era within the Vasser family, it reminds us all just how precious life is. We stand before you tonight, united and strong and ready to persevere through this tragic loss. We thank all of you for standing with us, and it is my sincerest hope that you will remain beside us as we go forward, pursuing our destiny as hoteliers and as friends." He paused as a staff member approached him with a half filled champagne flute, and as he accepted it he raised it with a smile. "A toast to my father, Cyrus Vasser. *Santé.*"

As the crowd lifted their glasses and repeated the cheers, Linc's eyes continued to scan the room. When he noticed the doors to the ballroom open and his father step in, looking disheveled despite the expensive Armani suit he wore, his eyes narrowed. And when the tall, leggy brunette in a skin tight black dress riding high on her thighs stepped in beside him, Linc's hand tightened so hard on his champagne flute that it may have shattered into dust had Lynette not released his hand from it.

"What's the matter?" she whispered, her brow furrowed with concern.

Linc, keeping his gaze on his father, merely grumbled out a barely audible "be back" as he rose to his feet.

Quinn and Grant noticed the exchange, but it was Grant who spotted his father and immediately knew the reason Linc was outraged. Without a word, he left the table and followed his brother, keeping a few steps behind him as Linc skirted the outside edge of the room and made his way to the entrance. The second he reached his father and his date, he shoved them right back out the doors and into the hallway.

"What the hell do you think you're doing here?" Linc growled, his hands clenched into fists around the lapels of his father's suit jacket, his face mere inches from the older man's.

Win went ghostly pale at the look in his son's eyes. The second his other son came through the doors and shut them discreetly behind him, he saw his chance and took it.

"Grant, get him off me!"

Grant's arms crossed in disapproval. Beside him, Jorja Hale hovered dispassionately, her heavily painted eyes bored.

"I think you have some questions to answer before we allow you inside, dad," Grant said evenly, keeping his voice down just in case those inside could hear. As he stepped forward, Linc released their father but kept within punching distance, just in case he had the urge.

"What? I'm not even invited to my own family's fundraiser?" Win choked out, angry now at the hostile reception he hadn't expected from his own sons. "I thought we were moving past all that old shit between us."

"Unbelievable," Linc spat, throwing up his hands in frustration. "You just don't listen, do you?" When Win said nothing, Linc turned his attention to Jorja. Her lips curved into a sly grin as he stalked toward her, his hands in fists at his sides. "Did you do this on purpose? Did the two of you come here together tonight just to rub your affair in my face? To embarrass me in front of hundreds of people?"

"Not at all, honey," Jorja purred, reaching out to run a finger down the front of his suit jacket. "We ran into each other this morning and thought it'd be nice to drop by tonight. I assumed my invite had been lost in the mail or something."

"It wasn't lost because you weren't invited," Linc said through gritted teeth, tucking his hands deep into the pockets of his slacks in an effort to avoid using them to throttle her. What a headline that would make, he thought bitterly. Hotel Playboy Strangles Hollywood Slut Ex-Girlfriend On Eve of Family Event. Just peachy.

"It's too late to send them away now, Linc. Everyone inside has seen them." Grant pointed out, his demeanor much more controlled than his brother's and his temper kept dutifully under wraps. They could not afford the mistake of showing weakness tonight, and unfortunately Win was the family's weakest link. But he was there, as was Jorja Hale, who without a doubt had been instantly recognized by everyone inside, including the reporters. They had no choice but to allow them back inside.

Linc scowled at his brother, then nodded. "You're right. I don't like it, but I know you're right."

Grant turned to his father, his eyes hard and his voice level and direct.

"You and Jorja will remain low key for the remainder of the evening and don't speak about the murder or Cyrus. Don't give the press any reason to make a story out of you again. Am I making myself clear?"

"Crystal, Grant." Win nodded as Jorja slid under his arm. She winked at Linc, who grimaced in response.

Before the four of them could make their way back inside the ballroom, a man came through the elevator and made his presence instantly known.

"Don't tell me I missed all the fun." Wyatt grinned as he walked toward the Vasser men, his arms spread out in greeting. He wore a tailored gunmetal gray suit with a black vest and tie, his trademark fedora perched at an angle on his head. "I came all this way for a good time and I expect to get my money's worth."

"Christ," Linc swore, his face lighting up with a grin as he went straight to Wyatt for a back slapping hug. "What the hell, Bailey, you lose my number or something?"

"Been busy, my friend." Wyatt pulled away, his hands on Linc's shoulders as he looked his old friend up and down. "Life's been good to you, Linc."

"It's been something, that's for damn sure," Linc said as he patted Wyatt's shoulder and stepped back, giving him room to greet the others. He went to Win first, embracing the older man with relish. He nodded and tipped his hat politely in Jorja's direction, then turned to Grant.

The oldest Vasser brother stood firm and resolute, disapproval clear in his eyes. Unlike Linc, he'd never really cared for Wyatt Bailey or for what he'd done to Madison. And now that he knew

Wyatt had been privy all along to the truth about his grandfather, he felt even less inclined to trust him. "I don't recall you being on the guest list, Wyatt."

"Good to see you too, Grant." Wyatt nodded, knowing he would encounter an obstacle here. "I was in town and Win forwarded an invitation to me."

"It was not his invitation to extend," Grant replied, his gaze hardening to a rich, dark amber that had in the past successfully intimidated lesser men. Unfortunately for him, Wyatt knew the game and was well versed in its rules.

With a stance that appeared casual, he tucked his hands into the pockets of his slacks and smiled. "Would you really send away a loyal supporter of the Vasser family who parted with a sizeable sum of money just to attend this event? Even I don't think you're that stupid, Grant."

Grant said nothing, carefully considering Wyatt's words. If Wyatt had indeed donated to the fundraiser, which would only take a few moments to confirm, then he was entitled to attend. Even he didn't have the power to turn him away, nor did he want to risk the bad publicity likely to come if Wyatt talked with the press.

But Madison was inside and he didn't trust that Wyatt was here for any other reason than to see her. Just what he had in mind, Grant wasn't sure, but he did know Madison was likely to tear the idiot's heart out before the evening was done.

With that thought, his lips curved into a slow, deliberate smile. "You're the one who's stupid if you think she'll let you out of there alive. But be my guest." He bowed his head, his eyes on Wyatt's in direct challenge, vague traces of humor in his expression. Then he turned his attention to the others. "Gentlemen, Ms. Hale. Shall we go back inside?"

Marshall was just wrapping up his speech as they trailed back into the ballroom. Win and Jorja took a seat at one of the back tables and Grant, Linc and Wyatt made their way to the front.

Back at the table, Madison was watching Marshall closely, noting the tone he used as he discussed standing for conviction, rising above criticism and judgment, taking life's hardest tests and surviving. It was an excellent speech, she had to admit. One she'd helped him write herself. It was meant to convey that the Vasser family was going to remain strong and unified. And while Marshall made sure not to mention the tabloid or the murder, it was implied that the family was moving past the scandal and prepared to go on, sturdier than ever.

Little did anyone know that the scandal was on the brink of becoming cold, hard fact that the family would no longer be able to ignore. It was sure to be a test; a savage and severely demoralizing test that she couldn't stop any more than she could stop a moving train.

She had noticed Linc and Grant leave to deal with her father and that whore Jorja Hale, but she hadn't worried herself with it. When they returned silently to their seats, she kept her eyes on Marshall, her attention dutifully focused.

The chair beside her was pulled out and someone lowered themselves into it. Someone wearing Giorgio Armani cologne, a scent she would have recognized anywhere.

Her hackles rose instantly, her hands tightening on the napkin she held in her lap. When she felt his hand brush her shoulder, felt the heat from his skin as his face hovered next to hers, she nearly whirled around to strike him. Instead, she remained composed and disinterested, knowing it was likely to frustrate him the most.

But inside, hidden from view, her heart jolted and panged, then sighed with relief at his touch.

"*Bonjour, ma belle,*" Wyatt murmured into her ear, his own heart galloping wildly just at the sight of her, diamonds layered like forbidden treasure over the smooth, ivory skin of her neck. But he kept his demeanor lax, calm, controlled. If she knew, even now, how much she affected him, she would surely use it against him. She certainly had in the past.

At that same moment Marshall finished speaking and the crowd applauded, so Madison took the brief second to soothe her wracked nerves from his sudden assault to her system. As the applause slowed and the music began once more, she tilted her head over her shoulder to eye her ex-lover with a cool, level stare.

"My, my, aren't we daring." She all but purred the words, her sultry voice rolling over them like smooth water in the darkest of nights. It took all he had to remember how to breathe.

"You look stunning. But then again, you always did, even then." He reached out to trail a hand slowly down her neck, caressing over her shoulder and sliding smoothly down her arm. The brief flicker of fury in her eyes told him he was treading on very testy waters. He'd known the risks when he decided to show up. "I'm sorry to hear about Cyrus. Well, not too sorry." He added with a dark smile, his eyes sharpening with an old, long held distaste.

"What are you doing here, Wyatt?" she asked him, ignoring his statement. Clearly he'd read the tabloid. Big surprise, everyone had.

"I wanted to show my support for your family, sweetheart. And for you," he said, his eyes betraying nothing as he watched her. He drank in every movement she made, unable to help himself.

"That's nice, darling, but we don't need your support." She smiled, the edges of it sharp with poison. Despite it, he knew he needed to have a taste of it before the evening was done.

"You always were so strong on your own two feet." He fought to keep the nostalgia from his voice, the longing he knew he couldn't deny existed in the darkest corners of his very being. For her. Always for her. "But who's going to reach for you when you fall?"

The amber in her eyes hardened with contempt. She lifted her chin, displaying the hate that years of suffering without him had given her.

"I won't fall," she said coolly, turning away from him as a waiter arrived to deliver the first course.

"SO YOU'RE A boat builder?" Quinn asked, her eyes lit with interest as she rested her chin in her hand and leaned over the table, intent on Wyatt. They had finished the dinner courses and dessert was on its way, giving her time to grill him for information. She found him fascinating, which made her wonder why both Grant and Madison were doing their best to avoid him. Linc and Lynette were having a good time, so he couldn't be all bad. And she was never one to shy away from meeting new people and having a good conversation.

"Yachts, mostly," Wyatt told her, chuckling as he sipped his beer. "My old man built fishing boats back in the seventies and eighties. Guess I just thought I'd continue the family tradition."

"That's great." Quinn smiled, enjoying herself. "What's it like in Maine? I've always wanted to vacation there but Ma insisted on getting as far away from Utica as possible, which usually meant the Grand Canyon or somewhere boring. But Maine...Oh! Do you eat lobster all the time? I bet the seafood is to *die* for."

He laughed again, admiring her. "It's the best damn seafood in the country. You'll have to come up some time to visit. I'll take you sailing."

"I've always wanted to go sailing." She glanced over at Grant with a smile. He looked at her with raised eyebrows, his mouth curving at the delight on her face.

"You? Sailing?" Grant mused, the image of her tripping over a rope or something on the boat flashing in his mind. But when she arched an eyebrow at him playfully, he could almost see the ocean wind whipping her dark hair back from her face and hear her laughter mixing with the roar of the sea. His smile faded as he held her eyes, then disappeared completely as he turned away.

"I'm sure she'd make a fine sailor, Grant." Wyatt grinned, leaning casually back in his chair. His arm snaked around the back of Madison's, his hand lightly caressing her shoulder. To her credit, she didn't flinch, but he did sense her rage, deeply hidden within the confines of her excellent self control. Getting under her skin had always been one of his favorite pastimes.

Ever the actor, he kicked up the sociable side of his nature and turned to Lynette, who he had carefully watched throughout dinner. She was quieter than Grant's gypsy eyed secretary, subtler in a way that suggested good breeding and likely conservative manners. And, loving all women as he did, he wasn't about to let her squeeze by without giving him some insight into what made her tick.

"So tell me where you found the lovely redhead, Linc, so I can get myself one."

With a laugh, Linc wrapped an arm over Lynette's shoulders and pulled her close, kissing her forehead with relish. "Hands off, Bailey, she's mine."

"For now." Wyatt grinned, winking at Lynette. She merely eyed him with a cool, refined stare before addressing his question.

"My parents are regular guests at the Vasser Hotel. One day I went to visit them and Linc swooped in like a bird of prey and I haven't been able to shake him since," Lynette told him with a dry smile, earning a hoot of laughter from Wyatt and an appreciative one from Quinn.

"Who would want to shake off handsome here?" Quinn asked.

Linc immediately turned to her. "You did."

"Oh." Quinn blushed, having forgotten the first time she met Linc. Embarrassed, but determined to roll with it, she let out a light laugh. "I must've skipped my coffee that morning or something."

She felt Grant stiffen beside her and knew he was revisiting his old worries of her liking Linc better than him. Not wanting him to dwell on it, she poked him in the arm just as the band changed over from classical to a romantic song originally by the Righteous Brothers.

"C'mon, let's go dance." She smiled, amused by the dark look he sent her.

"Seriously?"

"Seriously. It'll be fun." She rose to her feet and pulled at his arm.

He stood up and fought to keep the humor from his expression. "If you think I'm any good at this, you're in for a big surprise."

"Good. Because I suck at it too." She winked and dragged him onto the dance floor, which was already populated with a few couples swaying back and forth. She positioned herself in a typical waltz pose, one hand on his shoulder and the other in his hand. Because she was as clueless about fancy footwork as he, they stayed relatively stationary and instead swayed in a tight circle.

His gaze shifted around constantly, taking in the crowd of people who were watching with vague interest. He knew if he stumbled over his own two feet it would be all over the papers. Even now he noticed a few reporters taking snap shots of him with Quinn, undoubtedly wondering over his choice of date and her importance in his life.

Unlike his brother, he was hardly ever in the media unless it involved the hotel as a business. His personal life was largely a mystery to the public and he preferred to keep it that way. But with the scandal that was about to become public record, there was little he could do to keep himself, or Quinn, free from wagging tongues and vile rumors.

"Why don't you like Wyatt?" she asked suddenly, interrupting his thoughts. He turned his gaze to her, brows furrowed.

"Does it matter?" he asked, irritated she brought it up. Though he supposed she was just naturally curious.

"I can tell you don't trust him."

"No, I don't."

She nodded, considering the unusual heat that tinged his words. "He's a man of many secrets, many faces, many lines. I get the impression that at one point he held the family's confidence and then abused it. What did he do?"

Grant was silent for a moment, wondering just how much he could tell her. He tried to tell himself that it was none of her business. But then again, if he didn't explain to her just what kind of man Wyatt Bailey was then she may fall victim to his traps like the rest of his family had.

Resigned to finding a happy medium, he told her as much as he felt comfortable with.

"About eight years ago, Madison spent a year working with our cousin Duke at the Vasser Hotel and Casino in Las Vegas. Wyatt was a dealer there and they began seeing each other. About a year later, he broke it off and left the city. Up until a few weeks ago, she hadn't seen him since that time. I hadn't either."

"He was the one who sent flowers to her office?" Quinn asked, connecting the dots.

Grant nodded, staring over her shoulder as the memory of his sister's display of violence flashed in his mind. Wyatt was the only man to ever give her that type of flower.

"And then he had the gall to walk into her office unannounced, and then to show up here..." Quinn murmured, shaking her head. "I can't believe she's taking this so well. I would have thrown him out on his ear by now."

"She's hurting, but she won't show it. She won't give him the satisfaction." Grant let out a slow, uneasy breath, truly sorry for his sister. Meeting Quinn's eyes again, he tried to smile. "She can take care of herself. You don't need to worry about her."

"So how come Linc likes him so much?" she asked, her hazel eyes troubled.

"As far as I know, Wyatt and Linc have stayed in touch over the years. I think he chose to believe whatever story Wyatt came up with about why he ended the relationship as opposed to taking Madison's side. My dad is also good friends with Wyatt, so apparently there's something good about him. I can't say I've ever seen it." He added with a scowl, annoyed at the thought.

"Thank you for telling me. I know it's none of my business."

"You're welcome." He held her eyes, his own softening as he pulled her closer. "Are you enjoying yourself? I'd hate to think I made you suffer."

With a languid smile, she tilted her face up to his. "I'd hardly call this suffering."

"Good," he murmured, his eyes trailing down to her lips. She noticed him staring and felt her blood heat.

"If you were to kiss me now, here, in front of all these reporters, what would the headlines say?" Quinn asked, biting her bottom lip. His hand gripped tighter over hers and her breath caught at the look in his eyes.

"Again, does it matter?"

She shook her head, unsure how to react to the heat in his gaze. The passion. Again, he'd gone from cold and illusive to powerful and direct. Her heart shuddered from both nerves and need.

"Can we slip away?" she asked breathlessly, gripping the lapel of his suit jacket in her hand, her eyes bright and uncertain.

He rested his forehead against hers for a brief moment, indulging himself.

"I wish we could, Quinn." Pulling away, the intensity in his expression slowly faded, replaced by his dignity and sense of duty. She lamented the loss, but understood even as he fought for some way to explain it to her. "If things weren't so complicated..."

"I understand," she assured him, attempting a smile as she tried to cool her own crushing emotions. "Family first is a motto we both share."

He nodded, regaining his composure as they continued to sway together. Having her there in his arms distracted him from the worst of what was to come. As she changed the subject and rambled on about dinner and the decorations and grabbing Barry some cheesecake, he breathed a sigh of relief.

"YOU NEVER TOLD me you flirted with Quinn," Lynette mused as Linc led her expertly through the waltz on the dance floor.

Linc grinned sheepishly. "Ah, yeah, about that..."

"Am I just a consolation prize after she turned you down?" She let him spin her around, her lips curving as she came back into his arms.

"You're nobody's consolation prize, Lynette." He pulled her closer, his face mere inches from her own. She arched against him as his hands trailed down her back. "You are, however, mine. And I intend to see that you stay that way."

"Is that right?" she asked, trying to stay amused even as the hunger in his eyes distracted her. "Linc, people are watching."

"So?"

"So you look like you're going to devour me in one bite."

He laughed, his eyes wicked. "That's because I want to."

She blushed, averting her eyes from his in a last ditch effort to keep her knees from giving out. He had this way of speaking that just about ruined all of her careful years of etiquette school.

"My parents are supposed to be coming. If they see us like this they're going to make assumptions."

"Let them."

She eyed him again, one eyebrow arched. "You do remember that my father suggested you should marry and impregnate me, right?"

"And maybe I will," he said easily, returning to the dance as casually as if he'd just told her the time.

She blinked, unsure she'd heard him correctly. "You don't really mean that."

"Maybe I do." He smiled again as he spun her around, enjoying the way her silk and lace gown shivered over those long legs of hers. "I already told you that you're mine and I have no intention of letting you go."

"We barely know each other."

"On the contrary, Lynette, I feel I know you very well," Linc told her, leaning in to kiss her nose playfully. "I know that you're a ballet dancer with the New York Ballet. I know that you're from South Carolina and that your father is Senator Shaw, a staunch Republican, who's considering running for the presidency in 2016. I know that you enjoy old movies, maintain an impeccable diet, love architecture and yellow roses. You keep current on classical music to please your parents, but are incredibly talented at belting out country tunes in the shower."

"That's enough." She laughed, lifting her hand in retreat. "I get it, you know *some* stuff about me."

"And the rest we have a lifetime to learn about." He kissed the palm of her hand, his eyes meeting hers. When she blushed again, he smiled so warmly she felt its impact straight down to her very bones. "Maybe I should stop wasting time and just ask you."

"Ask me what?" She trembled against him, her eyes widening.

He smiled coyly, making her heart pound in her chest. "Do you love me like I love you, Lynette? Or are you just playing with this fool's heart of mine?"

Unable to do more, she laughed, hysterical, bubbling laughter that rose out of her throat in waves. Shaking her head, she looked at him as if he was mad. "Good Lord, Linc, you need to slow down."

Pride bruised, he frowned. "Why?"

Seeing the hurt in his eyes, she cupped his face in her hands. "Please, don't misinterpret my words." Delicately, she leaned in to press her lips to his. "You frighten me, Linc. You fell out of the sky and came into my life and I haven't been the same since. And I don't mean that in a bad way."

"But this is moving too fast for you," he murmured, his eyes searching hers. "And my impulsiveness scares you."

She nodded. "My life is very structured, and I prefer it that way. But if you must know, I do...I do love you."

He let out a breath of relief and pulled her in for a swift kiss. "Good. Because I was willing to go to Hell and back to convince you to love me if you didn't."

"That won't be necessary," she said dryly. "But I better not catch wind of you hitting on Quinn again."

He grinned. "What? And deprive my brother of the first woman he's fallen in love with in three years? Even I'm not that cruel."

Seventeen

There was a time when she wouldn't have hesitated to drive a knife straight into Wyatt Bailey's traitorous heart. Which was probably why she was so surprised to find herself refraining from doing so now.

She had held a knife in her hand throughout dinner, slicing through the chicken on her plate without even once imagining hurling it into his chest.

Madison figured she was either drunk, distracted, or, better yet, completely over him.

But no, none of those things were true. As a rule she never allowed herself to get drunk, so she had sipped at her single glass of wine throughout dinner. And she rarely found herself distracted, despite the scandal and her family troubles. Maintaining a clear and level head had always been her strong suit, especially when it was important.

So that left being over him. Which she knew was a bold-faced lie.

She was as over him as she was a goddamn nun. And the fact that he was parading himself around her, waiting for her to take a bite out of him really grated at her already testy mood. She *wanted* to destroy him and teach him a lesson for daring to show his face to her again. But it appeared that her *want* to hurt him was surpassed by her *need* to enjoy him.

Damn him to hell for it.

"You realize of course that I'm never going to forgive you," she said quietly, running her fingers up and down the stem of her wineglass, her eyes following the movement. Beside her, Wyatt leaned back in his chair and studied her, wishing he could give her the world and yet knowing she would never accept it. Not from him, anyway.

"I never suggested I wanted your forgiveness, sweetheart," he replied.

"Then why are you sitting here, desperate to touch me and yet smart enough to know what will happen if you try?"

He smiled, slow and catlike, as he leaned over to run his right hand down the exposed skin of her back. When she did nothing more than tense and shift away from him, he laughed.

"Looks like your bark is louder than your bite this time."

Shooting him a disdainful glare, she rose to her feet and leaned down until her face was level with his. She met his eyes, hot amber into cold steel, and smiled predatorily.

"Is it my bite you want, Wyatt?" she purred. She leaned in as if to whisper in his ear, but instead nibbled on it. He gripped her arms, losing himself in her scent, in the feel of her clever mouth on his skin. She'd always been intoxicating; a drug to his system that he'd been addicted to from the very start.

Knowing he was on the brink of caving in to her wiles, he let his hands fall away from her. His eyes filled with dark humor when she stared at him. "What I want is another drink."

He rose to his feet and walked away from her, leaving her standing frozen in place, stunned and furious. She watched him go into the Men's room and immediately turned away, cursing herself for playing right into his game.

Inside the restroom, Wyatt stormed over to one of the gleaming porcelain sinks inlaid in rich tawny colored granite and flipped on the nickel faucet. He set his fedora on the counter and splashed water over his face. Bracing his hands on either side of the sink, his head lowered and his eyes shut tight. He fought to slow the rushing of his blood.

Damnit, what was he even doing there? He wasn't sure he knew any longer. His original intentions had become inconsistent with his actions and he was beginning to lose his mind over it.

He'd wanted to help relieve Win of his painful secret, and he'd done so. He'd given his corroborating statement to the detective and saw to it that Win, for the first time in fifty years, felt free and safe. He had even followed through on his intention to see Madison, to check out how she was doing without him after all this time. But that was supposed to be the end of it. He wasn't supposed to see her again and fall back into the possessive need for her that had gotten him into trouble in the first place. No, he'd originally planned on getting the hell out of Dodge before it would even be possible.

But he was a damn fool for thinking he could see her and not want a taste of her, smell her and not crave her presence, hear her and not fall to his knees at her feet. The fact that she was even more stunning now than she'd been at eighteen was something he hadn't expected, though he should have known. Like a fine wine, she'd aged with grace and vitality, so beautiful it hurt. Especially when he saw the hate she felt for him, could sense the hostility and fury radiating off of her despite the coolness of her gaze.

And he deserved it, he thought as he lifted his head to eye himself in the mirror. He deserved every last ounce of hatred that resided in her heart for him.

Even though she had been better off without him all these years, could he deny he was still completely in love with her?

No. Her face would haunt him until the day he died.

Unless he found a way to get her back.

SHE MADE HER way through the room, greeting the guests and making polite conversation. Playing the gracious host had never been difficult for her, despite how much she hated nearly every person present. It was a gift, she knew, to portray one emotion on the outside while feeling a different one on the inside.

Madison smiled warmly, bowed her head graciously, held and shook hands sociably, and accepted condolences with a brave, albeit sad look of appreciation.

All the while on the inside she raged with fury and spitting distrust.

Just why the hell was Wyatt there, anyway? Who did he think he was, coming back into her life after all of these years? He had to have some reason other than the pathetic excuse of wanting to "support the family." Bullshit. Wyatt had never given a damn about her family, so why should he now? He famously looked out for himself alone, and if he did anything kind it was always somehow beneficial to him. Why should that have changed?

She stopped as she reached her father's table where he was seated beside Jorja Hale. Win glanced up at his daughter, his face flushed a bit from the vodka tonics he'd been drinking, his smile affable and carefree.

"There's my princess!" He laughed as he rose to his feet to give her a sloppy hug. Madison carefully peeled him off her, her nose crinkling at the heavy scent of alcohol.

"I think it's time to cut you off," she said coldly, averting her eyes from him to glare at Jorja. "I suppose it's too much to ask that you don't allow him to have any more alcohol."

The woman merely crossed her long, slender legs with a haughty smile. "He's a grown man, honey. He can take care of himself."

"I'm fine, Maddie, just fine," Win insisted with a lazy grin. "You look pretty tonight. Black always suited you."

Madison turned her attention away from Jorja and stared at her father. "You may not be in mourning, but the rest of us are."

Win managed a light laugh, the alcohol swimming in his head. "Everything's gonna be alright now, you'll see. Besides, you should be happy. Wyatt's here."

She bristled, but kept the worst of her fury from her expression. "Contrary to what you may believe, he doesn't make me happy."

"Oh." Win frowned momentarily, only to smile again as he beamed with pleasure. "He came all this way to help me, ya know. Such a good friend to me, that Wyatt. Don't know what I ever did to deserve him. Wish you two could've worked it out, made him part of the family..."

"What do you mean he came all this way to help you? How?" Madison said slowly, keeping her voice down so the other guests nearby couldn't hear. Her honeyed eyes bored into his, intense and unnerving.

When he faltered, realizing somewhere in his drunken haze that maybe he'd said too much, he cleared his throat and tried to smile again. "I told him a long time ago about what I'd seen. He came out here to talk to the detective, to let him know I wasn't making it all up."

Madison froze, her eyes flashing dangerously as her blood began to boil. "He knew? All these years, he knew the truth?"

"Yeah." Win patted her shoulder, needing to sit down. The room was starting to spin. He collapsed into his chair and wrapped an arm around Jorja, his eyes lifting to his daughter. "He kept my secret for me, all this time. Damn good man."

Madison tore her eyes from his and stalked off without a word, pushing past the doorman on her way out of the ballroom. She needed time to think this over, to figure out what she was going to do now that she knew the truth.

Biting back the worst of her anger, she went straight to one of the windows that overlooked the city streets below, resting her hands on the windowsill and closing her eyes. She could hear the muffled sounds of voices, laughter and music from inside the ballroom, but out in the corridor she felt removed, peaceful. Her entire body loosened, the stiffness in her shoulders relaxing and the lines on her face smoothing as she calmed herself. When the worst of the fever subsided and her heart slowed to a softer, more controlled pace, she took a deep breath and opened her eyes once again.

So he hadn't come back for her, after all. For some reason, knowing it frustrated her more than seeing him had. She'd wondered if he was still suffering over her, missing her, regretting his heartless, callous decision to sever all ties with her on a whim. Now she had no idea what he was thinking or what his intentions were. She was shooting in the dark, blind and lost, scrambling for some semblance of understanding. The fact that he still had the power to make her feel so helpless grated on her very soul.

From the moment he'd charmed his way into her life, she'd suffered over him. Suffered through all the heated passion and violent battles and furious accusations. And then when he'd left, she suffered even still, without him.

Even though she'd taken back her life, she'd never forgotten him. His face still haunted her dreams, his voice an echo in her heart, his touch unforgettable on her skin. Whenever she would try to move on, she would see his face on another man's, pretend it was his hands claiming her. But it hadn't been, and there was no possible way she could ever let it be again.

Wyatt had to be punished. He needed to know how it felt to lose everything, abrupt and cold, without feeling. The only choice she had was to make him suffer as she had suffered.

It wouldn't be hard, she mused, her lips curving as she considered. He still wanted her. Toying with him could be enjoyable on both ends, only she wouldn't just be toying with his libido. Oh no.

She would make him fall in love with her, all over again. Only this time she would be the one to end it, leaving him with the broken heart while she laughed all the way into the depths of Hell itself.

It was brilliant. And would be oh so satisfying.

"SO WHAT'S THIS one called again?"

"*Framboise au Chocolate*," Quinn supplied, grinning. "It's a very decadent, very fancy version of a chocolate cake. This one has layers of milk and dark chocolate ganache, with feuilletine thrown in for a nice crunch." She slipped her fork into the dessert and sampled another bite, brow furrowing as she chewed, tasted, dissected. "Yep, and it has some raspberry puree in there too, which pairs really nicely with the glaze on top."

"Oh God, I bet this has a million calories." Lynette grimaced as she ate another bite desperately. "But I have *never* tasted anything this good."

Beside her, Linc laughed and continued to run his hand lazily up and down her back. "So what? Live a little."

"You tell that to my ballet master when I can't fit into my dress for *A Midsummer Night's Dream*."

"To be fair, the portion is rather small, so I think you'll be okay," Quinn reasoned, reaching over the table for a plate that held a single chocolate éclair. She set it down between her and Grant and smiled at him. "Now this little beauty I think you'll enjoy."

"Is that right?"

"It's a classic French dessert, an éclair," Quinn told him, slicing into the dessert carefully with her fork. "Choux pastry with vanilla flavored custard, dipped in chocolate. Here, try a bite." She scooped up a small piece and held the fork, fully intending on feeding it to him. When he hesitated, she only laughed. "Oh come on, you won't look that stupid."

"According to you," he grumbled, even as he leaned in and sampled the piece on her fork. She watched as he chewed, his face skeptical. But when she saw the surprise flash in his eyes, she knew he was hooked.

"It's to die for, isn't it?" she said indulgently, resting her elbow on the table and leaning closer to him, her eyes lit with pleasure and delight. This was her realm, her passion, and she loved sharing it with him more than he could ever know.

Grant's mouth lifted in a subtle smile. "Almost as good as your cannolis."

She beamed, pleased by the compliment. "Why thank you."

As she turned away to talk with Lynette, he let out a slow, quiet sigh of relief. Sitting there with her, forgetting his worries for even the smallest of moments was the greatest relief he'd ever felt. And on this night, on the eve of what was sure to be the biggest hell storm he and his family had ever faced, he needed any ounce of relief he could get.

Across the table, Linc watched his brother proudly. He had no idea how it had happened or when, but it was clear to him that his brother had fallen for Quinn. Not just a passing interest or a crush, but head over heels love. Best of all, she was remarkable, funny, cheerful, and stubborn enough to ride through any storm with her head held high. She'd need to be all those things in order to make it through what was happening to their family.

They had their differences, but Linc could see what his brother found in Quinn. Hell, hadn't he found exactly what he needed in Lynette?

Where Lynette was his anchor, Quinn was clearly Grant's light. Where Lynette steadied him and cooled the flames of his temper, Quinn provided the warmth and understanding that had been missing from Grant's life since Erin.

Funny how in the midst of one of life's biggest tests, they'd been gifted with something neither of them thought they could have again.

But maybe that was just how life worked, Linc mused, watching Lynette as she joked with Quinn. It dealt you a hard hand, only to throw you an ace just when you least expected it.

Or, as he was about to discover, a joker card could abruptly slip in and muddy the waters.

"Lynette, honey, there you are." A delicate, breathy southern voice said from behind them. They whirled around, spotting Senator Warren Shaw and his wife approaching their table.

"Mama, daddy." Lynette smiled as she rose to her feet to greet them, brushing cheeks cordially as was expected in the environment they were in. "I thought you weren't going to make it."

"Nonsense," her mother chided, waving the thought away.

Linc stood up to shake the Senator's hand. "Good to see you, sir."

"And you, Linc." Senator Shaw smiled as he gazed around the room, taking stock of who decided to show up. The group surprised him. Perhaps things were not as deteriorated as he'd assumed. "I'm sorry we missed the dinner, but we had a check sent for the fundraiser. It's obviously a good cause."

"Thank you very much." Linc grinned, wrapping his arm around Lynette. She stiffened against him, her eyes averting to the ground as her cheeks flushed. He ignored her discomfort, wanting to display his affection for her openly and without shame. "Did Walter book you in the usual suite? If I'd known you guys were coming I would've reserved it for you personally."

The senator and his wife hesitated as they glanced at each other. The look that passed between them was some parts guilt, other parts distrust.

"Linc, we're at the Waldorf for the evening," Shaw replied, his casual southern drawl touched with discomfort.

Linc's brow furrowed as he stared at them both, unsure what to say. "I don't understand, Senator. You always stay here."

Lynette hovered at his side, uncomfortable and uncertain.

"Well, Linc, you know how it goes..." Shaw began, trailing off vaguely, not really wanting to elaborate.

Instead, his wife stepped in, her voice curt and filled with the southern nobility of her bloodline that she felt made her infinitely better than any Yankee.

"With all the negative press surrounding the hotel and your family, Linc, we felt it was best to stay elsewhere," she said simply, a cold and empty smile curving her lips. "I'm sure you understand why we only dropped by instead of staying for the duration of your fundraiser. We couldn't risk associating ourselves too closely until this quiets down."

"But you'd donate money? I'd say that associates you pretty damn well with my family," Linc argued, fighting to keep the worst of his temper at bay.

"The money came from a trust fund under my maiden name. It can't be easily traced to the Shaw name but will still make for a nice tax write-off."

"Unbelievable," Linc growled, releasing Lynette to run his hands through his hair as he digested the disloyalty, the abandonment. If the Shaws felt this way, how many other patrons were doing the same? Some of them were there at the fundraiser, but how many of them were planning on cutting all ties at another whiff of trouble for the Vasser family?

Though he didn't want to take the Shaws' caution and blatant self-interest personally, he found it impossible not to. Turning to the Senator, he jabbed an index finger in the older man's chest, fire in his eyes. "We've been nothing but good to you, Senator. Is that worth nothing anymore? Is one goddamn bump in the road all it takes to scare you away?"

"Settle down, Linc," Shaw insisted, his voice dark with disapproval and embarrassment. "This isn't the place for a scene."

Grant rose to his feet but held back, watching the scene unfold cautiously. Most of the guests seemed oblivious to the tension between his brother and the Senator and he wanted it to stay that way.

"Apparently we're losing our best clients regardless of what I say or do, so why should I pretend that I'm okay with this? Because I'm not, Senator. I and my family have been dedicated and honorable to you and this is how you repay us?"

Shaw leaned in closer to Linc, his voice lowering dangerously. "I'm sorry, Linc, but next year is an election year. It's not personal, son, not at all, but if you don't settle down now, I'll make it personal."

"Daddy," Lynette hissed, her eyebrows knitted together with worry and disgust. She stepped between her father and Linc.

Shaw frowned at his daughter, his eyes narrowing. "I know you like this boy, pumpkin. I like him too. But this is just politics. It isn't personal."

"Like hell it isn't," Linc interrupted, only to be cut off as Lynette touched a hand to his shoulder, her eyes meeting his disparagingly.

"I don't expect you to fully understand, Linc," she said softly, defensively. His eyes hardened as he stared back at her, his mouth set in a grim line as she continued. "One bad press circuit can ruin a politician. The media can do major damage...you know this as well as I do. You need to consider the cost my father will be paying if he continues to openly support your family."

"Jesus, Lynette," Linc murmured, eyeing her as if she were a stranger. "It's not like I'm asking him to declare me a saint or anything. I just don't want this stigma out there that we're bad people not worth doing business with."

"That's not at all what he thinks." Lynette shook her head, trying to maintain reason.

"The Vasser name is now associated with murder, rumor or not. The damage is done," Lynette's mother chimed in, waving the declaration off with an air of disdain. "In fact, Lynette, you may want to reconsider your involvement as well. Your ballet master may not tolerate his principal dancer being involved with one of the Vassers, not if it means damaging the reputation of the New York Ballet itself."

Lynette's eyes widened, her lips parting as she considered her mother's words. Uncertainty warred with every last defense she had in her for Linc. Could her relationship with him seriously hurt the ballet company?

Linc watched Lynette, noting the doubt that flashed over her features. Fury filled him again as he turned to her mother. "This is just some bullshit tactic to keep me away from your daughter."

"I'm only letting her know what may happen if she continues down this dangerous path she's on," Mrs. Shaw said frostily.

Irritated, he turned to Lynette. "She's reaching, Lynette. You can't seriously believe her."

But some part of her did, or at least doubted enough to worry her. Lynette let out a slow breath as she met his eyes. "I don't know," she murmured, shaking her head.

He sneered, his words heated and careless. "The snobs at the ballet company will get over it."

Her brows furrowed, stunned he could be so callous. "*I* am one of those snobs. The ballet is *everything* to me, Linc. I can't lose that, not even for you."

Betrayal hit him, sinking in and burrowing under his skin. He glared at her, all heat and outrage, his hands clenched into fists at his sides. Anger, disappointment, and misery mixed in his gut as he turned away, unable to look at her any longer.

"It's best that you go." His hands trembled as he fought back the worst of his temper, struggling to maintain control. Grant stepped immediately to his side, placing a hand on his shoulder. He eyed the Shaws coldly.

"Thank you for your donation, Senator. Enjoy your stay at the Waldorf," he said, closing the argument.

Shaw nodded, then wrapped his arm over his wife's shoulders. Turning to his daughter, he reached out with his other arm. "Come along, Lynette. We'll take you home."

Lynette hesitated and glanced at Linc, who still refused to look at her. A sinking feeling settled heavily in her stomach. She caught Grant watching her and the coldness of his gaze bothered her, as did the questioning, worried look on Quinn's face.

Feeling torn, confused, and shaken, Lynette said nothing and went to her father, who led her and his wife from the ballroom. Before he could get more than a few steps, Charlene approached them, her blue eyes lit with icy disdain.

"I didn't realize you had been invited, Carol," Charlene said, eyeing Lynette's mother directly.

Carol bristled, more from an old, deeply rooted hatred than from insult.

"Charlene, how awful to see you," she chimed, her voice dripping with acid but maintaining an air of southern dignity. "Our daughter invited us. Or did you not know that she was dating your son?"

Charlene's eyes narrowed and she glared at Lynette, noting the humiliation that lined her face. Her gaze then shot behind the Shaws to her own children. She saw Linc and Grant watching her, both edgy and cautious. Making her own calculated assumptions, Charlene turned back to her old enemy with a degrading smile. "Why don't you get back to your plantation. I'm sure the cotton needs to be picked or some such thing."

Outrage flashed over Carol Shaw's face and her mouth opened to retort, only to have her husband step in and stop her.

"Not here, Carol," he said in a low growl, his hand tightening on her shoulder as he eyed Charlene warily. "We were just leaving, Charlene. You get on back to your party and we'll get out of your hair."

Charlene crossed her arms and stared after her old rival as the Shaws left the room, taking their daughter with them. She waited until they'd gone before turning to face her sons.

"What was that about?" she demanded, looking from Linc to Grant.

Both of them shrugged guiltily. Linc spoke first, feeling the need to take responsibility. "Just a friendly disagreement, nothing major."

"That wasn't what it looked like," Charlene said, keeping her voice down so the other guests wouldn't notice. Fortunately, the entire altercation had gone off without much notice from the surrounding crowd. "Why didn't you tell me you are dating the Shaws' daughter, Linc? I would have encouraged you against it."

Linc laughed darkly. "*Was* dating. Don't know where we stand now. And it's not like I know everyone you have beef with, mom. The list is pretty long."

"Carol Shaw is just an old southern inbred wannabe," Charlene spat. "I don't know her daughter, but I can't imagine the girl is much different."

Rolling his eyes, Linc fought back the urge to defend the woman who'd just walked out on him. He was still exhausted from the fight itself and the last thing he felt like doing was fighting some more. "What did she ever do to you, anyway?"

"She caught her husband flirting with me twenty years ago at a gala in Chicago," Charlene informed him with a dismissive wave of her hand. "I didn't return the advance, naturally, but Carol decided to smear my name by calling me a home wrecker anyway. Then her husband got deeper into politics and she had to give up the name calling in order to save her husband's reputation. Pathetic."

"Right." Linc ran a hand through his hair and turned to his brother. His lips curved into a grin that was sharp around the edges. "I promise to be a good boy for the rest of the night, okay?"

Grant watched his brother silently, feeling sorry for him. He understood how hard it was for Linc to reign in his temper and not go after Lynette to finish the argument they'd started.

Before he could respond, the sound of a microphone being flipped on stopped him. He turned to face the stage and spotted his father, clearly drunk, microphone in hand and a jovial grin on his face.

"Everyone! Hello. I just wanted to say something, before this is over," Win began, his eyes scanning the crowd lazily as he continued to smile. The ballroom settled into hushed silence as all eyes turned to him. He gestured to the crowd with his drink and joyfully delivered his bombshell. "What you've all heard is true. My father murdered my grandfather."

EIGHTEEN

Stunned silence hung like a heavy shroud over the entire ballroom. Win only continued to smile, his balance precarious as he teetered onstage, vodka sloshing in his head.

Then, as quickly as the silence had fallen, the slow simmering rumble of voices started up again. The crowd buzzed with confusion, excitement and intrigue all in one massive wave.

Without wasting another second, Grant stalked to the stage and took the microphone from his father, replacing it in its stand. Quinn and Linc watched him escort Win out of the ballroom, while Marshall and Charlene went to the stage together to try and smooth over the chaos Win created.

Marshall attempted a laugh as he lifted the microphone, smiling out at the crowd and shrugging his big shoulders.

"And that, ladies and gentlemen, is a lesson on why you don't get drunk at a function," he joked, earning a few laughs but barely making a dent in the chatter and gossiping happening among the guests. He cleared his throat and tried again, his booming voice echoing throughout the room as he spoke. "Quiet down, please. Let me be clear, before this gets out of hand. My grandfather's death fifty years ago was an unhappy accident, nothing more. There is absolutely no proof that it was anything otherwise. So please, let us not ruin our evening because of my brother's delusions. Join me, if you will, in another toast to my sister-in-law, Charlene, your hostess for this evening."

He continued on with Charlene beside him as Grant pulled his father to the doors. The people they passed stared curiously but Grant forced himself not to look at any of them as he dragged his father out into the hallway.

Madison was already there, her back to them as she stared out the window. The moment she heard the doors open she glanced over her shoulder. Her eyes narrowed at the stone cold fury she saw on Grant's face and the drunk grin on her father's.

"What happened?" she demanded, approaching her father and brother.

"Everyone's so uptight." Win laughed, shaking his head. "I don't get it, it's the truth and they're all gonna find out soon anyway. What's the problem with me saying it?"

Grant glared at his father. "I told you not to."

Linc, Jorja, and Wyatt emerged from the ballroom, shutting the doors behind them.

Because the urge to beat his father to a bloody pulp was violently strong, Linc shoved his fists into his pockets and snarled instead. "Good job, dad. Nice going."

"What did he say?" Madison asked, staring from Grant to Linc.

"He told the truth," Wyatt interrupted, looking casual and misplaced in the background. His arms crossed as he leaned against the wall, his expression both dangerous and disarming. "They were all eventually going to hear it."

Madison stared at him for a long, silent moment. A dozen emotions stirred violently within her. How dare he get involved? How dare he even show his goddamn face when this was *her* family, *her* problem?

Without a word, she whirled around and slapped her father hard across the face, her fury over Wyatt fueling most of the power behind the act. Win toppled over from the blow, not having seen it coming. He yelped, clutching the side of his face as he fought to process what had happened.

Madison only glared at him, her lips curled into a snarl. "You ruin everything," she said, her voice hauntingly level and filled with contempt.

He stared up at her, bewildered. "W-what?"

"Leave him alone, sweetheart. Can't you see that he's been through enough?" Wyatt growled, pushing away from the wall. "For Christ's sake, he saw his goddamn father murder a man. Show some sympathy." He paused, a dark grin twisting his features. "Oh wait, I forgot. That heart you used to love me with is all black and withered now. You can't feel a goddamn thing."

"Don't lecture me on sympathy, darling," Madison responded, keeping her fury in check as she stared at him. Her knees trembled beneath her, but she wouldn't fall. Under no circumstances would she give him that pleasure. "I wonder what my father gave you in return for this allegiance of yours. Was it Vasser money? Was it property? A new car?" She sauntered toward him, her lips curving in a dark smile. "Tell me, Wyatt. Did you only pretend to love me for my money? And then when a better gig came along you left town without even an explanation?"

She was close enough now that he could both smell and feel her, electricity roaring like a live wire just under her skin. She was primed for the fight, fearless and raging, with fire in her eyes and a façade of stone cold resolve over her face. It was an incredible contradiction. But then again, she'd always been exactly that.

Her words had shaken him. She'd swiftly turned the tables on him, making him the target and her the sharp and poisoned arrow. For a few moments, he fought with himself over how to respond, on what to say. Hell, he couldn't tell her the truth, not here, not in front of her family. It wasn't the right time to explain the reasons he'd left all those years ago.

So he would wait. He would wait for as long as it took for the right moment to arrive. Patience, after all, was a virtue.

"I never pretended to love you, sweetheart," he said simply, his eyes revealing nothing as he walked past her. He approached Win, who stood wide-eyed with Jorja at his side, supporting him as he struggled to stay upright. "Let's go, Win. I'd say we've overstayed our welcome."

"You're all crazy," Jorja muttered, shaking her head as she led Win down the hallway. Win glanced over his shoulder at his kids, misery and confusion in his eyes.

They disappeared into an elevator and were gone.

Grant and Linc stared awkwardly at the elevator. They shot each other a swift, nervous glance before facing their sister.

Before they could say anything, Madison tilted her chin up, one eyebrow cocked arrogantly as if daring them to comment.

Linc spoke first, clearing his throat and reaching into his pocket for his cell phone. "I better call Rubenstein, fill him in. Get his take on what we should do."

As he walked away and dialed the family lawyer, Grant turned to Madison, his expression hard to read.

"Marshall lied to those people in there. He told them there's no proof that Winston's death wasn't a suicide."

"But we know better, don't we, darling?" She met his eyes, her own softening as she went to him, seeking his comfort.

He held her tightly, warring with the uncertainty and the fear in his heart. His sister sighed against him, and when she spoke her voice was almost too quiet for him to hear.

"What are we going to do, Grant?" she asked, even though she knew the answer. She knew exactly what needed to be done. But that didn't mean she wanted to be the one to have the burden of it. Cyrus' letter was hidden in her purse and she dreaded the moment she would have to reveal it to her family.

Grant thought of the file folder upstairs in his office, the one containing all of Rosalie Owens documents and letters. The contents proved his grandfather was not only the murderer of one man, but of four. How would his family take the news when he finally told them? And how much damage would it cause the hotel?

While he'd planned on waiting until the next day to share the file with his family, he had a feeling it would only be detrimental to put it off any longer. They had to know the whole truth so they could prepare themselves for what was coming the minute the press got a hold of the official police report.

It was going to be a long, exhausting night and, without a doubt, a game changing one.

"I don't know, Mads," he murmured, pulling away from her. "Let's go back inside. The night is almost over."

AN HOUR LATER the guests began to leave.

Charlene and Marshall stood at the doors to personally thank everyone and to say goodnight. Grant, Madison and Linc stood with them, shaking hands and offering words of gratitude.

When the last of the guests made their way to the door, Grant broke away and went to Quinn. She was standing alone in the hallway, staring out the same window Madison had been plotting at hours earlier.

Quinn sensed him as he came up beside her. She tilted her head to offer him a warm smile.

"How are you?" she asked, sorry to see the strain and exhaustion in his eyes.

He tried to return her smile, wanting to give it to her as some kind of consolation for staying through the entire evening and not running away like most women would have. How could he blame her if she had? "I'll be fine. Why don't I walk you downstairs? There's going to be press everywhere. I don't mind escorting you."

"Oh, no, I'll be okay." She turned to face him, her hands twisting together anxiously in front of her. "The press doesn't know who I am, anyway."

He nodded, glancing over as the last few guests disappeared inside the elevators. His family retreated into the ballroom, most likely to give instructions to the wait staff. Which meant he was finally alone with Quinn, something he hadn't realized how badly he needed until that very moment.

Without a word, he closed in and pressed her against the wall beside the window, his hands in her hair as he leaned in. His mouth was a breath away from hers as his eyes closed on a long sigh.

He reveled in the feel of her against him, in the softness of her hair under his hands. Intoxicated, he closed the gap between their mouths and kissed her, diving in without reservation, needing some sort of relief to quell the chaos raging in his mind and in his heart.

She was eager against him, her hands running up his back as she gave him all she had, seeking only to comfort him. Her heart ached as she screamed her love for him over and over in her head, knowing it would only complicate things and yet understanding it was undeniably true. He was everything. What good was she unless she could be for him?

He murmured her name as his mouth trailed over her face, drinking in her scent and her breath like water. When her eyes flew open and met his, the green in them bright and heavy with need, he saw the dedication and the love she felt as clear as day.

Seeing it staggered him. Could she possibly love him? After everything that had happened, the scandal, his callousness to her, his sister's rudeness. Could Quinn seriously still want him, despite all of it?

She saw the humility and disbelief come into his eyes as he stared at her. Basking in it, she reached up to touch his cheek. "I'm here for you, Grant."

He only pulled her closer, burying his face in her hair and accepting her offer without words. She held on, biting back what she so wanted to say at that moment. Maybe sometime soon, she'd tell him. But until then all she could offer him was this.

On impulse, she backed away and reached into her purse for a piece of notepaper and a pen. She scribbled her cell phone number on the paper, then handed it to him. "If you want to talk or need anything, just call me, okay? Anytime, day or night."

He stared down at the number dully, unsure what to do about the grasp she had over his heart. It hurt and at the same time soothed. What madness...

"Thank you," he said quietly, leaning in to kiss her again, slower this time, drawing it out so he could commit her taste, the feel of her, to memory. When he pulled back and straightened, he tried to smile. He wanted to reassure her that everything would be alright, even though he knew better. "Goodnight, Quinn."

"Goodnight." She kept her eyes on him as she walked away, wishing more than anything that she could stay. But his family needed him more than she did at that moment.

When she stepped into the elevator and the doors closed, she felt the tears begin to fall.

THEY MET UP fifteen minutes later in one of the conference rooms on the second floor. Grant sat at the head of the thirty person conference table, his brother to his right and his sister to his left. Marshall sat beside Madison and their mother next to Linc. They watched him quietly, waiting to hear what they should do. Knowing how much they relied on him was a responsibility that weighed heavily on him, especially in that moment.

In front of him was the file containing Rosalie's evidence, and he tapped his fingers against it as he determined where to begin.

With a heavy sigh, he got down to business.

"I think we can all agree that tonight did not go over as well as we'd hoped. It wasn't a complete disaster, but it wasn't perfect, either."

"Goddamn Win." Marshall scowled, clenching his fists in front of him on the table.

Charlene pursed her lips. "You should have never let him in."

"At the time it would've looked worse to force him to leave. The press had already gotten a look at him and Ms. Hale," Grant told her, dismissing the indignant snort Linc made at the mention of Jorja. "Regardless, it's done. Now we need to determine our next course of action."

"Take cover," Linc suggested wryly, feeling useless and frustrated. "Before the shit hits the fan tomorrow. Goddamn press."

"What's in the file, Grant?" Madison interrupted.

He met her eyes silently before passing the folder to her. As she began to look through it, he addressed the rest of his family.

"When the detective came to meet with me yesterday, he admitted he hadn't told us everything. He didn't just have a letter from Rosalie Owens detailing the murder. He had an entire file filled with evidence."

Charlene gasped, covering her mouth with her hand.

Linc stared at Grant incredulously. "Is he allowed to do that? Withhold evidence from us?"

"Yes," Grant replied. "He wanted to find out how much we knew before he revealed everything he had. Apparently dad's testimony paired with Wyatt's corroboration was enough to confirm the murder allegation."

"Wait, Wyatt knew about the murder, too?" Linc asked, his eyes narrowing. "Why didn't he say anything to us?"

"He was keeping dad's secret," Grant replied. "The reason he came into the city was to meet with the detective."

"Why don't you tell them the rest, darling," Madison said, her eyes still scanning the documents carefully. She wasn't surprised Rosalie Owens had known about Cyrus' other crimes, though it made more sense now why he'd killed himself. He didn't want his family to endure a trial, not when the proof was so substantial.

"What else is there?" Charlene pressed, eyeing Grant apprehensively.

Grant's jaw clenched, wishing he didn't have to be the one to deliver the bombshell that would destroy everything.

"There's evidence that Cyrus is responsible for the deaths of his three brothers during the war," he said, noting the disbelief flash over his uncle's face. He held Marshall's eyes, knowing he would need to hear the news the most. "He drugged them, tied them up, and when the Germans attacked the bunker, he fled with the rest of the men, leaving his brothers to die in the explosion. They found traces of rope around their wrists when they discovered the bodies. There was a subsequent cover up, so an investigation was never conducted. Cyrus came home a hero, and was next in line to inherit the New York hotel."

"No," Marshall whispered, his face ghostly pale. Memories of his long lost uncles and the grief the family had gone through flashed painfully in his mind. "It's...it's outrageous. Sickening. He couldn't have..."

"He did," Grant insisted, troubled at seeing his uncle suffer under the heavy weight of the truth.

"Dear God." Charlene rushed to Marshall, wanting to comfort him. He let her wrap her arm over his shoulders as she sat beside him.

"Great, so not only do we have to explain away one murder, we have to explain away four." Linc realized, revolted and disturbed. He stared at his brother, shaking his head wearily. "When does it stop? I seriously can't take much more of this."

"None of us can," Madison put in, shutting the file folder and pushing it across the table to Linc. "Tell them the last part, Grant."

Linc reached for the file but didn't open it. Instead he stared at it numbly as Grant continued.

"Rosalie found out that Cyrus killed his brothers. She went to Winston and showed him the proof she'd found. He was going to change his will to write Cyrus out completely. Unfortunately, Cyrus found out about his intentions and killed him before he could. He scared Rosalie out of town, threatened her, and our great-grandmother gave her money to ensure her silence. The truth was covered up for five decades after that. Now we're left to clean up the mess."

"Goddamnit," Linc cursed, mostly without feeling, his heart sinking in his chest. "I'm sorry, guys, but I can't think of a single positive way to spin this one."

"That won't be necessary," Madison told him, reaching into her purse for the letter from their grandfather. She waved it in the air in front of her, eyeing her family with heat in her eyes. "Our grandfather left this letter for me after he died. I think you'll find its contents both shocking and comforting."

Marshall glanced over at his niece, his eyes filled with angry tears. "What does it say, dear?"

She passed him the envelope casually, then eyed her mother and brothers.

"It says that, according to Cyrus' will, I am now in charge of all the hotels and the entire family estate."

"What?" Marshall blinked, bristling as he tore open the letter and reviewed it himself. "You must have misread, my dear, there's just no way..."

He cut off as he found the will, enclosed in the envelope along with the letter. Madison's name was at the top, along with the endowment of full control of the business and the estate. Stunned, Marshall eyed his niece, his lips parted in speechless shock.

She turned her attention away from him and focused instead on her brothers. "I know this sounds strange and perhaps unfair, but let me reassure you that I did not have any say in this."

"Like hell you didn't," Linc snapped, rising to his feet angrily. "Jesus, Mads, how could you do this to us?"

She stared at him silently for a moment, digesting his anger with her, knowing it was to be expected. He was going to have to get over it because nothing he said or did would change the fact that she was now in charge.

"It is what it is, Linc." She looked to her oldest brother, who was staring at her with narrowed eyes, as if trying to figure out if she was somehow responsible for ensuring he would never have the legacy he'd been born to. Linc's burst of fiery anger was easy enough to deal with, to understand. But Grant's quiet, stern distrust was burning holes through her very heart. "Read the will yourself, Grant. You'll see it's all in order."

"I intend to," he replied in a low, dangerous voice. He continued to stare at his own sister as if she were a stranger, and couldn't help but feel like she'd betrayed him. "If this was the shocking part of the letter, then what was the comforting part?"

"He left me explicit instructions on how to get our family out of this mess. A list, if you will, of actions we, I, need to take in order to preserve our family's reputation."

"This is outrageous," Marshall snarled, throwing the letter and its contents across the table toward Grant and rising from his chair. "I need a goddamn drink."

He stormed out of the room. As Madison watched him go, her heart broke.

One door, closed.

"I have to call Rubenstein again, make sure this will is legit." Linc glared at Madison as he stood, his eyes filled with disgust. "For all I know you're trying to bypass all of us for a shot at control of the family. Is that what grandpa's been teaching you all these years? How to get rid of us so you could take over, just like he did?"

Madison's eyes widened and her horror at his words flashed brilliantly over her face. When he saw it, he despised himself for what he said. Nevertheless it was out there and didn't change the betrayal he felt.

When he turned and stalked from the room, Madison did her best to clutch her shattered heart together.

Two doors, closed.

"I for one think this is very exciting," Charlene said, rising to her feet regally. "Though I would have preferred for Grant to have been given this opportunity, at least one of my children will now be in charge."

She left as well, intending to find Marshall in order to make him see reason.

When she was gone, Grant let out a long, measured sigh, unsure just what to think or say to his sister.

She watched him cautiously, fighting a losing battle to keep the pain from showing in her eyes. She had to be strong, had to show them that this was the way things were and that they would not convince her to back down from it. But seeing Grant look at her with so much distance, so much coldness, was destroying her. He'd always been on her side, had always been a sturdy rock for her to seek support from when she felt weakened. Now she had to wonder if he would ever forgive her.

"I don't know if you've had this planned from the start or if he sprang this on you as suddenly as you've just done to us, but it doesn't change the fact that this undermines the traditional order of things in this family," Grant said quietly, his expression impossible to read. "I don't know if I can trust you anymore. We've always been close, but this has and will come between us. I think you know that."

Leaving it at that, he rose to his feet and swept from the room, not even sparing her a look as he left.

Three doors, closed.

She stayed where she was for a long while, adjusting to this newfound feeling of emptiness inside her heart. Never had she felt so alone, so lost, as she did now, knowing that her family was breaking away from her.

But it was her duty to the entire Vasser family to carry out the instructions her grandfather had left her and to ensure they didn't lose their foundation.

She needed to push aside her own broken heart, her fears and doubts, and focus solely on preserving the empire. Even if it meant a future that looked like an incredibly long and solitary road.

LYNETTE OPENED HER front door cautiously, her pride and defenses primed and ready. But one look at his face had worry and doubt replacing the anger in her eyes.

"Can I come in?" Linc asked, the dim golden light from the hallway casting dark shadows over his face. He held her eyes without wavering, but she could tell he was on the verge of collapsing right there in front of her.

Unsure what to say, Lynette backed away and let him wander in, staring after him as he headed straight for her sofa. He settled into it, tilting his head back against the cushion and shutting his eyes wearily.

She shut the door and walked over to sit beside him, curling her legs under her. She carefully brushed his chestnut hair from his forehead, her fingertips cruising over his skin. When he let out a long, slow sigh and seemed to relax, she folded her hand into his, hoping to comfort him.

"I think we're both sorry for what we said earlier," she murmured, squeezing his hand gently. "Let's forget it happened."

He nodded, his eyes opening but only to stare forward blindly. He looked deeply haunted, and a quaking shiver coursed through her at the thought.

"Talk to me, Linc." She slid closer to him on the sofa, troubled by his silence.

"Your parents are right, Lynette. You shouldn't associate yourself with me," he said quietly, flatly, his face expressionless.

"What? Why?" she asked, her brow creased in confusion. "If this is about my ballet master…"

"No." He shut his eyes again, pain flashing over his face as he fought back the grief, the betrayal, the madness of all he had learned that night. "It's not just that. God, Lynette, my grandfather didn't just kill his father. He killed his three brothers, too. In the war…he made it look like an accident."

"Oh." She let out a stunned huff of breath, digesting his words.

"That was why he killed his father. He found out about the other murders and was going to change his will, cutting my grandfather out completely."

She said nothing, sorrow for him etched over her face.

"And now he's left everything to my sister." Fire flashed through the exhaustion in his eyes as he finally turned to look at her. "He put Madison in charge of the hotels, the estate, everything. He bypassed all of us, and gave it to her."

"Oh, Linc," Lynette managed. "I'm so sorry."

"I said something despicable to her," he winced, loathing himself. "The look on her face, Lynette, it killed me. I know this isn't her fault, but, damnit, it pisses me off."

"I know," she murmured, wrapping her arms around him and pulling him close. "You'll get through this."

"Grant's probably more pissed off than me. He deserves this more than anyone, and now it's hers. We don't even have a say in it unless she steps down, which she won't."

"Then you accept it and move on with your life," Lynette told him, pressing her lips to his forehead. "Put yourself in her shoes and imagine what she must be dealing with. Her whole family is angry with her for something she presumably didn't ask for, and now she's probably looking at the whole situation and preparing herself to face it all alone. She's going to need all of you supporting her, Linc. And as much as it hurts you to be bypassed like this, part of you must be relieved. Leading the family out of this crisis is not going to be easy. She'll be the one facing sleepless nights from now on and she'll do it for the sake of your family, because it means more to her than anything else in the world."

Linc considered her words for a long, silent moment. When he spoke, he realized that she couldn't have said it any more perfectly to make him understand.

"You really *get* people, don't you?" He attempted a weary smile as he shifted away from her so he could frame her face with his hands.

She smiled in return, lifting her hands to rest over his. "That's what Libras do, Linc. We never just choose one side; we have to have balance."

He snorted out a laugh and kissed her, relieved she wasn't still angry with him. He didn't think he could stand it if she was.

"Whatever it is, this is the second time it's helped me. I don't know if I deserve it, though." His smile faltered, anger flashing in his eyes. "Your parents certainly wouldn't think so. Part of me still thinks they're right."

"My parents don't control my life, Linc. They try to, but I'm breaking free of them. I can't promise they'll stand behind you, but you shouldn't for one second doubt that I will."

He gathered her close, his hands roaming over her back. "Thank you."

She nodded, her breath catching in her throat as he tilted her head back, his mouth capturing hers with an intensity she should have come to anticipate from him. It was full of emotion and a fervor that shook her to the very core, stunning her into assent without question, shuddering through her like a wildfire rages through the forest. He was spontaneous and impulsive, and despite what she'd always assumed, it seemed to suit her just fine.

She returned the kiss, grasping his shirt and pulling him closer. As he leaned back against the sofa, she fell with him, her hands everywhere as she gave in to the madness he sparked within her, the wild freeness she'd never before let herself experience.

Except while dancing. Good Lord, only ever while dancing had she felt as alive as she did at that very moment. With him.

If the sky fell and the Earth cracked open and the demons of Hell paraded around in the streets, she couldn't have cared less.

She had Linc Vasser, and that was all that mattered.

WHEN GRANT ARRIVED home that night, he did his best to settle into his usual routine.

He set his briefcase beside the front door on an old, antique oak bench that had been passed down through three generations of Vasser men, its intricate carvings indicative of classic French Rococo style.

His dog Miles trotted into the parlor, shaggy gray and white body trembling as his tail thumped happily back and forth. With an instinctive smile, Grant bent down to rub his hands over fur and muscle, accepting slobbery kisses over his cheeks and mouth in greeting.

"Life's so rough, isn't it?" he asked dryly, straightening and heading into the kitchen to get dinner for Miles. As he walked, he continued to talk with his dog, a habit he didn't even realize he had. "You get to sleep all day, get all your meals served, have someone else clean up after you..."

He reached up into one of the upper cabinets of his kitchen to grab a can of dog food, which he opened and dumped into a bowl. Miles dug in the second Grant set the bowl on the slate tile floor, wasting no time devouring every last bite.

With a slow sigh, Grant leaned back against the black granite countertop and watched his dog and best friend. "If you had to spend a day in my shoes, you wouldn't last one second."

Miles looked up at him with a doggie grin, and Grant snorted and pushed away from the counter. He went to the wet bar in his living room for a drink. After pouring himself a glass of scotch, he gratefully collapsed onto his black leather sofa.

Taking a generous sip, he eyed the room around him tiredly, his mind already falling victim to thoughts of the events that night. As much as he tried to push them away, they continued to beat their way into his brain, over and over, like a record on repeat. God, would he ever find relief?

It was at least a small comfort to finally be home, in familiar surroundings that suited him. His tastes at the office largely translated to his taste in furnishings at home, favoring traditional antiques as focal pieces while still maintaining sleek, sharp lines and modern edges for the rest of the space. Steel grays and rich golden oak accented with subtle hues of blue reigned throughout his town house, from the muted sapphire walls to the sturdy oak floors of his living room, covered partially by an oriental rug in shades of cobalt and gray.

A slate framed fireplace graced the wall across from him. Above it was a large flat screen television that he realized he'd only watched a handful of times since he had it installed three months earlier. The few times he actually found himself at home that he wasn't sleeping were spent in his home office.

Maybe now that there was no goal, no future to work toward, there would be no reason to work from home any longer. In fact, maybe he'd just let Madison handle the stress and the weight of responsibility he'd burdened himself with for so long, since she seemed so keen on accepting the challenge.

But no, he couldn't do that. Work was his life and he cared too damn much about the hotel and the family empire to stand by while someone else did all the work. He didn't know what Madison's role had been in deciding her fate, but he still felt wounded by distrust and jealousy.

And, damnit, he'd never been a jealous man. He'd never craved what another man had without figuring out how to get it for himself as well. But this time, with her, with his sister, the girl he'd grown up protecting, confiding in, relying on...this time it was different. He wanted to give her the benefit of the doubt, felt she deserved at least a moment of his time to explain herself.

But part of him, the stubborn, immovable, and frigid part of him, doggedly refused.

And until he came to terms with his own obstinacy, there was little to do except sulk.

Feeling suddenly constricted and uncomfortable, he set his drink down on the coffee table and shrugged out of his suit jacket. He tossed it on the sofa next to him and loosened his tie, relieving the pressure gratefully. With a sigh, he set about emptying the pockets of his coat so he could send it out for dry cleaning the next morning, only to freeze as he pulled out the tiny sheet of notepaper with Quinn's number written on it.

He stared at it silently for a long moment, wheels turning in his head as he considered his options. Sure, she'd said he could call her anytime, and he knew it would comfort him to hear her voice. But he didn't want to burden her with any more of his problems. She still was, essentially, an outsider. How much could he really trust her?

When Miles padded over and sat beside the sofa, long tongue lolling out in a satisfied grin, he instantly made his decision.

Grabbing his cell phone from his other jacket pocket, he dialed the number and held the phone to his ear impatiently, his heart racing with anticipation. When she answered, his eyes were on his dog and he spoke without thinking.

"I was looking at my dog, and when he smiled it reminded me of you," he told her, only to blink a second later as he realized what he said. Mortified, he smacked his forehead and cursed himself for a fool. "Wow, that sounded awful."

She burst into laughter on the other line, full-bodied, delighted laughter, and hearing it had a sheepish smile breaking over his face.

"*Grant, you really need to get some new pick up lines if that's the best you've got,*" Quinn informed him in between more laughter.

"Yeah, well, I'm a bit rusty." He sighed, leaning back against his sofa and shutting his eyes, relishing in her voice. He'd done the right thing by calling her.

"*I'm happy you called, I was worried about you,*" she said, concern replacing the laughter in her voice.

"It's been a long night." He hesitated, unsure how much he wanted to tell her.

"*Do you feel like talking about it?*"

He thought for a moment, weighing all the pros and cons in his head. It would be a relief to share the two awful truths he'd learned that night with her, but it would only upset her. Or it might scare her away, a thought that terrified him. What if she wanted to quit her job and leave the company because the truth about his grandfather was too disturbing to bear? What would he do without her, now that she'd imbedded herself in his life, in his thoughts and feelings?

He couldn't rule it out as a possibility. If she wanted to leave when she found out the truth, then it was her decision. He couldn't make her stay.

But he could postpone revealing the truth, at least for one night. It might be the one and only thing he had to hold on to now.

"No, I don't want to talk about it."

"*Okay.*" He could hear her smiling on the other line, and the cheerfulness she put into her voice calmed him in a way only she was able to do. "*What kind of dog do you have? I've been thinking about getting one myself, but...*"

She rambled on with him interjecting only when necessary, until the eastern sky began to glow with morning light.

NINETEEN

The next morning, they faced the first of the media backlash. Being a Saturday, the news was subdued on television due to news programs being few and far between on the weekends. By contrast, the internet was alive with it, with websites like TMZ and the Associated Press running wild with every little detail they could scrape together from insiders present the night before. It was a dirty sort of madness that was only funny and intriguing when it was happening to someone else.

The newspaper reporters who'd been allowed inside the fundraiser spared no details in writing their columns on the juicy and scandalous subject, and surprisingly even reputable reporters seemed to be having a field day with the shocking confession made by Win Vasser during the event.

However, what little coverage there was of the scandal on television was by far the most demeaning, demoralizing, and destructive.

The giddy blonde television reporter on channel five indulgently described the alarming way Grant Vasser dragged his father off the stage after the big confession and flew from the room in a flurry of righteous outrage and disgust. Which of course was wildly exaggerated, but the public wasn't going to know that. All they would hear would be a reporter's wild imagination running with whatever would get the highest ratings.

Grant clenched his teeth, steeling himself from the worst of it as the reporter finished her commentary with an excited flourish, stating that perhaps the Vasser family was in over their heads.

Madison hit the off button on the remote, refusing to watch any longer. Linc sat beside her on the sofa in Grant's office, his face buried in his hands.

"This is only the beginning," he murmured, lifting his head with a sigh. "On Monday when all the networks get their hands on that police report the shit is really going to hit the fan."

"We have one thing going for us," Madison began, crossing her legs as she glanced to her left and right at each of her brothers. "We know the whole truth now and are in a position of power because of it. First thing Monday morning, we will send out a press release explaining where we stand on our grandfather's crimes and death and how we are determined to move on and remain committed to excellence in serving our guests. We can't stop the media from hyping up the murders, but we *can* present our usual and potential guests with reassurance that we aren't going to let half century old crimes destroy us."

"And for God's sake we've gotta keep dad under fucking wraps," Linc put in heatedly, rising to his feet. He stared down pointedly at his sister, his expression filled with equal parts fatigue and resentment. "Since you're in charge now, I guess I'll leave dealing with him up to you. I'll just go work on that press release like a good soldier."

He stalked out of the room and shut the door, leaving Grant and Madison alone.

They sat in silence for a long moment, neither sure where they stood with each other. That morning they'd come together with Linc to discuss the family business, but any emotions had been pushed aside so that the focus would be on handling the situation. They'd been coldly polite with each other, but now that Linc was gone, there was only room left to speak their minds.

If only they could decide who should forgo pride and speak first.

"I've scheduled the funeral for Friday afternoon," Madison said, the tone of her voice emotionless. She shuffled through the stack of newspapers in her lap, pretending to look through them even as her eyes saw nothing. It was simply an attempt to buy time. "Ferncliff cemetery, of course. I've arranged for him to be buried in the plot beside our grandmother, as he requested in his will." She paused, setting aside the newspapers and turning to face her brother. He sat still as a statue, his arms resting on his knees as he leaned forward, his eyes focused on his hands. She would give anything to know what he was thinking, to know what he was feeling. But he was as closed off as ever. "I've also contacted everyone in L.A., Vegas, London and Paris. They're making their flight arrangements as we speak, and I took the liberty to book them rooms here in the hotel. Seeing as we've been in a lag since this whole scandal broke out, there were plenty of available rooms."

Grant nodded slowly, acknowledging her words without looking up from his hands. After a few more moments of silence, he finally spoke, his voice just as void of emotion as hers had been. "You're adjusting well to being in charge, Mads."

She fought back the urge to take a swipe back at him and instead folded her hands in her lap. "Why would I waste such a gift? Or, maybe it would better be described as a burden. Either way, it's mine to bear now. And if you don't wish to work under me and continue as general manager of this hotel, then I'll just have to take on that as well."

She cursed herself silently and bit back the flash of guilt she felt at her own words, knowing they were unnecessarily cruel. On instinct, she reached out to hold his hand, urging him to look at her. When he did, she let the regret she felt show. "I know you feel betrayed, Grant. But I want you here beside me. You and Linc both. If I had to do this on my own, I could find a way to manage, but I don't want it to be that way. I need you to trust that I have only the best interests of all of you in mind as we move forward, and that I would give my very life for this." She had to pause, her emotions strangling her throat and forcing unwanted tears into her eyes. She watched the change that came over his face as he noticed her pain, and he squeezed her hand to show he was listening.

When she continued, there was a tenacity in her voice that impressed him, but didn't come as a surprise. Madison had always been the strongest person in any room, why should this situation have changed that? "This hotel, the legacy we inherited, it needs to be protected. I know you love it as much as I do. So please, don't let your anger over this situation cloud your judgment. We need to stand united, now more than ever."

Grant weighed her words against his own feelings, only to find the stubbornness he'd been battling before had now been ground into dust. Damn it all, she was his sister and he loved her. Just as he loved the hotel.

He slipped his hand from hers and wrapped his arm over her shoulders, pulling her against him. She rested her head on his shoulder and released a long, overdue sigh of relief.

"The three of us have always stuck together," he murmured, staring up at his wall with all the family photographs he'd collected. His eyes hovered over one that showed the three of them as children standing side by side in the lobby of that very hotel, holding hands. It startled him that his throat tightened uncomfortably from the memory, and only made him hold her tighter. "This won't change that."

"Thank you," Madison whispered, kissing his cheek as she pulled away, her eyes meeting his. The gratitude in her eyes faded as curiosity replaced it. "You brought the secretary as your date last night. Are you seeing her?"

Grant avoided the critical look she gave him and shifted away. "Not exactly, no."

Her eyebrows shot up as she gave his words consideration. "This is certainly an odd move for you. Falling for the secretary. Interoffice romance. It's very scandalous."

He shot her a dark look, irritated that he felt even a drop of guilt over it.

"I suppose I could tell, though," she continued, tilting her head to the side as she watched him, amused that he was so touchy about the subject. That meant only one thing, that whatever he felt for this girl was serious enough that her stern, impassive brother was losing his cool and getting all flustered. Very, very interesting. "Obviously I was dealing with my own demons last night, but I did notice the two of you together. She makes you happy, doesn't she?"

After a sidelong look, he nodded. "She does."

Her face lit with a slow, considering smile. "Well, she's not my first choice for you, but she seems nice enough. I hope to find that she's deserving of you."

He nodded again, relaxing his shoulders as he faced her. "I want you to consider allowing her to intern as a cook in *Cherir*, Mads. She deserves the chance to prove herself."

One eyebrow arched curiously as she considered his request. "I suppose it wouldn't hurt. Though I'm surprised to see you sticking your neck out for her this way. She must be very important to you."

"I believe in her," he said simply, his eyes glowing with pride.

Seeing it had her smiling again. Yes, this *was* interesting. "Then she'll have her shot, Grant. Once things settle down and I have time to think, I'll arrange it."

"Thank you." He nodded, avoiding her eyes uneasily as other memories from the night before resurfaced in his mind. "Has Wyatt left town?"

"I wouldn't know," she bristled. "Though I don't see why it matters. There are more pressing issues at hand, darling."

She rose to her feet and leaned in to press a soft kiss to his forehead. When she straightened, her amber eyes were hard and remote. "I'm going to hire a guard to watch our father's room to make sure he doesn't leave. Until the worst of this settles down, I don't want him setting foot outside of that room."

Grant's brows furrowed. "I don't think that's a good idea, Mads. He won't do well locked up like that for the few weeks it's going to take for this to quiet down."

"He's made his own bed. It's time for him to lie in it," she retorted before turning from him and leaving the room.

He sat in silence for a long while, gazing up at the images of his family, wondering where in the hell it had all gotten so extraordinarily out of control.

"WAKE UP WINNIE... it's time to get up."

He heard the voice, the words, but they seemed lost in the darkness. He could feel his body attempting to move, trying to wake up, but his mind was groggy and disoriented and failed to follow through for several moments. It wasn't until the slap hit him hard in the face that his eyes flew open.

He sat up and let out an incoherent grunt of confusion, staring around for the source of the slap. His eyes found Jorja seated beside him on the bed.

"I'm sorry, honey, but you need to wake up now," she purred, a kittenish smile curving her lips as she leaned in to kiss him lightly on the forehead.

Win winced and fell back against the pillows, rubbing his groggy eyes. "What time is it?"

"It's nine am, Thursday morning. The funeral is tomorrow, and I've brought you your suit. And your crutch."

"Thank God, I ran out of grass and pills yesterday..." he mumbled as he sat up and reached for an opened, half empty beer on his nightstand, chugging a few sips to soothe his dry throat. As he set the beer down, he angled his head to look at her, an admiring gleam to his dusty blue eyes. "You're so damn beautiful. Why the hell do you hang around with a guy like me?"

Jorja smiled and sidled closer to him on the bed, reaching over to run her hand down his thigh, cruising back up the denim of his jeans to tease him tortuously. "Honey, you and me, we're just so much alike. I understand you, know you for what you are and what you can be. No one will ever have as much faith in you as I do."

"Really? You believe in me?" Win managed, his eyes widening as he stared at her, honestly taken aback. "No one's ever said that to me before. Ever."

"With my help, Win, we're going to do great things." Jorja leaned in, her lips sliding over his throat and her tongue hot on his skin. "You're my ticket into the Vasser family empire, honey, pure and simple. And I'm your ticket to realizing your dreams."

"What dreams would those be?" He grasped for her desperately, his hands greedy as they fumbled over her body.

"To open a Vasser luxury hotel in Miami, one to call your own. To make me your wife, your partner...think of the money, the glamour, the prestige. We could have it all, Win."

He rode on the image she created, and on the knowledge that the marijuana she brought would relax and comfort him the minute she left. Since he couldn't leave his room, what else was he supposed to do to loosen up? Madison would flay him alive if she knew. But then again, maybe he could make her understand. A man had a right to relax, didn't he? There was only so much alcohol could do for him anymore. He needed something else to help him get through the days, the hours, the fucking *minutes* he had to spend in this cramped, pitiful room.

No daylight, other than what little managed to come through the north-facing window. No fresh air, since the window didn't open. And a security guard at his door at all hours of the night and day, preventing any hopes of escape.

It was downright humiliating, but he was helpless to do anything about it.

Other than get high. And thanks to Jorja, who graciously kept the supply of booze and drugs coming, he was managing the days as best he could.

An hour or so later, she tugged on her dress and sauntered out of the room, promising to return later with food. He waved her off, already lighting up the single joint she'd gotten for him.

Later, after the joint was diminished and his system was smoothing out from the drug, he settled into the shower with the water steaming all around him. He sat on the cool tile floor and rested his head back against the wall.

Only, instead of the numbness and calm he had anticipated and expected, something else began to creep its way into his system, skittering along his skin like millions of ants, bubbling under it like acid. His breathing accelerated as he stared down at his arms, his vision blurring and the steam of the shower burning his eyes until he had no choice but to shut them tight. Fear hit his bloodstream and chilled him against the heat. Something was wrong, horribly wrong.

Within seconds, the voices started.

306   KATIE JENNINGS

Being the seventh son of the seventh son was supposed to mean something, goddamnit! But you're just fucking pathetic!

He rubbed his temples frantically with his hands, willing the voice of his father to go away, to leave him be. But it didn't let up. No. Cyrus only spoke louder.

How the hell do you expect to live up to my expectations when all you do is parade around like a pansy boy with your hippie music and anti-war traitor friends? I served my country, as all Vasser men have done. But you...no, you would rather spit on everything I've made, everything I am!

"Shut up," Win groaned, smacking his forehead. His eyes closed against the fear he felt, the anguish. "Leave me alone."

Don't you know what I can do to you, boy?

"Stop it." Win clawed at his face, his hands shaking feverishly as the memories came flooding back into his mind. It often happened when he gave in to the momentary comfort from his vices, when he pushed the envelope too far and was overwhelmed by the fear. Only something about this was different than those other times.

He felt haunted by his father, infested by the monster he had feared all his life. If he'd had the ability to do so, he would have screamed. Instead, fear seemed to have a lock grip on his throat, choking him, strangling the life from his very body.

You're trapped, boy. You think you can escape me?

Dear God, he was trapped. Trapped like a goddamn rat.

Panic jolted through his system like a speeding train and all he could do was fumble his way from the shower. The water was slick under his feet, causing him to grip the shower door to keep from crumbling to his knees.

Paranoia had him reaching for the baggie of pills Jorja had brought him. Without thinking he tore open the bag and dumped the remaining pills into his palm, knocking them back with relish, eager to stop feeling, to stop thinking. If he could get his mind numb enough, maybe the voices would stop. Dear God, he had to make the voices stop...

But Cyrus didn't go away. Instead, he instructed Win to do the very thing that had been nagging at the back of his mind for decades, always there as a welcome way out, an easy escape.

And when he latched the belt around his neck and the frame of the shower door, he tumbled into a dark, numb unconsciousness. Win was, at last, at peace.

GRANT SAT BACK in his office chair and watched the sun ascend over the buildings of New York. He sipped his coffee, oddly at peace with the world, with his life. It was a feeling he wasn't used to or ready to embrace. But it was there nonetheless, and part of him enjoyed the comfort it gave.

There was no doubt in his mind where his newfound contentment came from. If he'd been a foolish or arrogant man, he may have attributed it to his own actions or his own carefully constructed mindset. But no, it was neither of those things.

It was Quinn.

She'd buried herself underneath his skin and projected warmth and a sense of quiet relief through to his very core. He didn't know how she'd done it. He was still trying to sort through the details of it himself. Somehow she'd slowly but surely chipped away at his defenses, at his fortified wall, and slipped into his life.

And, though the thought worried him, into his heart as well.

Since the night of the fundraiser, not a single day had gone by without him seeking her out, needing her close by, even if only to see her smile. It was a smile that brightened even his darkest hours.

Not a single night had passed without him calling her up, craving the sound of her voice, needing her to take his mind off the chaos that had descended upon his family. In the rare moments when he needed to vent his frustrations about dwindling reservations or bad press, she was there to listen. To comfort.

He'd never needed anyone in his entire life. Not even his family, who he loved unconditionally but never *needed* just to get through the day.

But it was becoming clear to him that he desperately needed his secretary.

With a heavy sigh, he set his coffee mug aside and closed his eyes, picturing her face in his mind.

"Good God, is he *actually* taking a break?" Her voice rang out as she sailed into his office, all smiles and dressed in a knee length spring dress the color of lilacs, her dark curls bouncing just over her shoulders.

His eyes flew open as he faced her.

"Just for a second." He frowned, clearing his throat. When he met her eyes, he felt the worst of the awkwardness fade. His gaze flicked up and down her body as a grin twisted his lips. "Is it spring already?"

Quinn let out a light laugh as she walked to his desk, pulling at the skirt of her dress self-consciously. "It's work appropriate, right? I mean, with the warm weather we've been having this week, I've seen a lot of people breaking out their spring clothes. Figured I'd go along with the trend."

He said nothing as he rose to his feet and rounded the desk, approaching her slowly. His tawny eyes flashed with something that was wholly unprofessional.

"It's up to me to decide what's appropriate and what isn't, Quinn," he said softly, tilting her chin up so her eyes were on his. Slowly, deliberately, he closed the distance between them and kissed her.

Quinn released a long, slow breath as she melted into him, her hands finding their way to the front of his white dress shirt, clutching at the fabric. He deepened the kiss and pulled her closer, his hands sliding over her back.

When he broke the kiss and pressed his lips to her forehead, savoring the sunny warmth of her, he felt the walls surrounding him come crumbling down in glorious flames. This is it, he thought wildly. Thank God.

"Grant?" Quinn murmured, her entire body shivering against his as she relished what he gave her, this sense of security and wonder.

How in the world did she ever manage to convince this man, of all people, to want her? One of the heirs to the great Vasser Empire, a man who could have any woman in the entire country. Yet somehow, unbelievably, he'd chosen her. At least for now. She prayed with everything she had that he never changed his mind and gave up on her. Because right now, in this moment, it was undeniably clear to her that she was in love with him. Desperately, helplessly, in love.

"Yes, Quinn?" he said in response, his hands sliding up her arms and winding their way into her hair, stoking the fire that was already burning rampant inside of her.

"I think the phone is ringing," she managed. "Or it's in my head, I don't know."

But sure enough, the moment she focused on something other than the sensation of his hands on her, she heard the phone shrilling obnoxiously from her desk.

"I better get that." She tried to smile, though it was a bit weak and delirious around the edges. As she made her way from the room, his lips upturned in a feral grin.

It was probably misguided, but he got a kick out of seeing her flustered and breathless. Especially when it was he who caused it.

Moments later, she came back into the office, worry and anger clouding her eyes. Concern flushed out the pleasure in his system.

"What is it?"

Quinn hesitated, pursing her lips in a gesture that was as protective as it was instinctive. "That was Marshall. He wanted me to let you know that he isn't coming by the hotel today, or any day in the near future. He said that since he's being forced out of the picture by his dead father instead of being passed the torch, then there's no need for him to be a part of running the business any longer. He's decided to retire. Oh, and he said good riddance because he was sick of all of us anyway. Then he hung up on me."

Grant scowled, his temper sparking. "He told you all this instead of coming in here to speak to me like a man?"

"That's what it looks like," she huffed, crossing her arms. "I just don't understand it. It's not like you asked for Madison to get control of everything, so why the hell is he acting like it's your fault? You're being bypassed just as much as he is."

Irritated, Grant sat down on the edge of his desk and stared at his meticulously waxed dress shoes, his mind working through how to deal with his uncle. Marshall was understandably upset. But he was acting childish which did nothing but hurt the family. How could Marshall not see that?

Then to bark at Quinn about family business, when it wasn't her burden to bear? It was unprofessional, outrageous, and cruel. And if it was the last thing he ever did, he'd make sure it never happened again.

"I'm sorry he put you up to this," he said, glancing up from his feet to face her. "I won't let him talk to you that way again."

She waved him off, feeling sorry and mad and frustrated all at once. "It's not a big deal. He was just upset and took it out on me because he didn't have the backbone to talk to you face to face. He'll get over it, Grant. Just give him time."

Because she could tell he needed it, she went to his kitchenette to brew some coffee. When she was finished and the warm smell of roasted grounds was filling the room, she turned to face him again, her smile back in place.

"I should get to work. Go ahead and enjoy a cup of coffee, and once lunchtime rolls around you're in for a treat from yours truly. I need to hone my skills before I start my internship next week."

"Is it a cyanide pill so I can end my misery?" he grumbled, eyeing her with a small smile as she started laughing.

"You know what, I'm fresh out. But I guarantee you the lunch I made is much better than a cyanide pill." She winked with a quick grin and swept from the room, shutting his office door with a click behind her.

THE MORNING SUN woke him as it broke through the gauzy curtains of her bedroom window, shining directly on his face. Bright red and orange glowed against his eyelids, causing him to pull the pillow over his face to shield him in darkness once more.

But the hand that slid over his back and traveled down his shoulder and arm had him smiling, his system heating almost instantly.

"But it's so early, warden. Can't I just sleep a bit longer?" Linc asked, sleep putting a deep rasp into his voice that was darkened by his immediate, primal response to her hands cruising over his skin.

"Sorry, but I have to send you to work," Lynette replied, planting kisses along his shoulder and biting gently, teasing him.

"Fuck work," Linc growled as he rolled over and pinned her beneath him, kissing her hard and fast on the lips before his own curved into a mischievous grin. "Unless you wanna come in with me today so I can parade you around like the miracle you are."

She snorted, rolling her eyes. "Walter doesn't need any more distractions. Nor do you."

"My whole life is a distraction." He combed his fingers through her hair, enjoying the way the sun glowed bright in the copper strands against the white of her pillowcase. "Come on, I'll buy you lunch."

"That's sweet, but I can't." She lifted her head to kiss his nose, her eyes sparkling. "I have rehearsal today. In..." she glanced over at the digital clock resting on her nightstand and sighed. "Twenty minutes."

"Good. That gives me fifteen minutes to seduce you." He kissed her again with relish, amused when she started beating her hands against his chest. She groaned when his mouth found the soft spot just under her ear.

"Oh, no. No, I need to go," Lynette whined, arching beneath him even as she tried to get free. "Linc, really. I have to go."

"But you don't want to," he ventured, releasing her and meeting her eyes as she sat up, the blankets and sheets in a puddle around her slender body.

She shook her head, her eyes softening.

"I never want to leave you," she said quietly. Her lips parted as he reached for her hand and pressed a kiss to her open palm. His blue eyes were sharp and focused on hers, darkened by an emotion she wished she could understand.

"I love you."

"I know," she whispered, pulling her hand free and racing into the bathroom to shower, needing space from him before she gave in and missed her rehearsal.

Linc fell back against the pillows and sprawled lazily, listening to the hiss of the shower. He closed his eyes and imagined her stepping under the hot spray of water, toying with the idea of joining her.

Instead, he did the noble thing and got dressed, went into her kitchen, and made her breakfast.

As he cooked scrambled eggs and made toast, he thought of the week they'd had together since the fundraiser. Nearly every day they'd both been busier than hell, but they made time for other, more important things during the cool, early spring nights.

He hadn't been to his own apartment other than to grab a change of clothes in days. For some reason she seemed more comfortable in her own space, which he could respect. Her place wasn't as large as his, but it was definitely more cozy.

Which was always a welcome relief after the hectic chaos that was the hotel. With Win on lockdown in his suite, Grant glowering over tanking reservation numbers, and Madison running around barking orders and making demands, it had been a difficult week for everyone. Not to mention Marshall, who bailed out on all of them out of spite. The few times he was at the hotel, he was in his office packing up his stuff like he'd been fired.

Shaking his head, Linc dumped some eggs onto a plate for Lynette and frowned. The only person who seemed to be in high spirits was his mother, who'd been parading around announcing Madison's new gig to anyone who would listen. It was equally as despicable as what Marshall was doing. It seemed like, for once, Win was the only one staying relatively out of trouble.

Which, Linc knew, was a goddamn blessing.

"Oh, you cooked," Lynette said as she swept into the kitchen, her gym bag hanging over one shoulder. Her hair was tied back in a bun at the nape of her neck. Her eyes shot from the eggs and back up to his face, a smile curving her lips. "Praise the Lord, the Yankee can cook."

"I have a small set of domestic skills, thank you very much," Linc mused as he plopped a couple slices of wheat toast down on the plate and handed it to her. "But I don't do dishes."

"Of course you don't," Lynette said dryly, accepting the plate with raised eyebrows. She glanced down at her watch and let out an anxious huff of breath. "Looks like I'll be eating this on the road. Thanks for feeding me."

"No problem." Linc grinned as she kissed his cheek and raced from her apartment, plate in hand. He stared after her and bit into a piece of wheat toast, wondering when she was going to let him give her a goddamn ring.

THE GUARD NODDED politely to the maid as she sidled down the hallway, pushing her cart of cleaning supplies like she had done nearly every day for the last twenty years. She paused before the door of the suite and knocked.

"Housekeeping," she announced, wiping her hands on the apron of her uniform while she waited for the guest to answer. It was strange for her to have a guest be present while she cleaned his room, but this particular guest had not been allowed to leave. Not even to go downstairs. It was very odd, and likely scandalous, but she was too good and too loyal of an employee to say a word about it to the press or to her own family. Instead, she kept her head down and made sure not to get in the man's way while she changed the sheets and tidied the bathroom.

But on this particular morning, he wasn't answering. She knocked again before glancing up at the guard. "Maybe he is sleeping. He gets drunk and doesn't wake up. It happens sometimes."

The guard snorted, then turned and pounded on the door himself. "Mr. Vasser, please open the door. The maid is here."

When there was still no answer, he sighed and reached for his card key, swiping it in the slot and pushing open the door.

"Go on in. He's probably on the toilet or something." The guard stepped back and let the maid enter the room. As she did, her eyes scanned around curiously, noting the man was nowhere in sight.

She bit her bottom lip and wandered toward the bathroom of the suite, seeing the door cracked open and hearing the shower running. There were no other sounds.

"Housekeeping," she said again, approaching the bathroom door. Her nerves got the best of her as her hands began to tremble. "Mr. Vasser?"

She pushed open the door slowly. Steam from the shower poured out into the bedroom, hot and hazy, clouding her vision. When she faced the shower, she spotted him. His body was lifeless and limp, hanging from the frame of the shower door.

Her scream could be heard throughout the entire thirtieth floor.

TWENTY

W hat do you mean you don't like it?" Raoul snapped, his temper blazing as he glared at his boss, a plate of *scallops alla bordelaise* in his hand.

Madison frowned, her gaze mild and dispassionate. "It has too much spice, Raoul. You're letting the Spanish in your blood influence this classic French dish. It needs to be fixed."

His nostrils flared as he sucked in a furious breath, struggling to contain his anger. "It is perfect the way it is."

"No, it's not." She turned and rested her hip against the stainless steel table between them, folding her arms. With one eyebrow raised, she spoke again, her voice level and controlled. "Next dish, please."

Though he wanted nothing more than to hurl the dish with the scallops into the wall, he tossed it carelessly into the sink instead with a loud crash and handed her the next dish, filled with a carefully seared chunk of prime choice beef and sprigs of asparagus.

"Well?" he grunted, crossing his arms and glaring at her as she sampled the steak.

She took a bite and slowly chewed, measuring the texture and flavor with each bite. Satisfied, she swallowed and bowed her head graciously. "Exquisite. We'll add that to the new menu."

Though his temper was cooling, Raoul grabbed the plate from her and scowled anyway. "You better. I work hard on all of this for you, *cariño*. I expect appreciation."

"And I appreciate you, darling, more than I think that thick head of yours will ever understand." She glanced down at her watch. "Everyone should be flying in soon. We'll have a whole herd of people to feed tonight."

Raoul grunted as he finalized the plating on the next dish. "They do not come out of respect. They come for money."

Madison eyed him curiously. "Is that so?"

"Of course it is," he spat, thrusting the next dish at her, his dark eyes meeting hers. "They come to take advantage of you, *cariño*. Those who know about the will, they think you are weak, that you have been given something that you cannot handle. They will try and take it from you, and once the others know the truth, they will too."

"Pity they don't know me very well, then," she mused, pleased and a little surprised that Raoul was so rabidly defending her. Then again, he'd been one of the few people to always stay by her side, through thick and thin. "I have no intention of letting this go. Don't worry yourself over me."

He rested his hands on the table and met her eyes, his own filled with sympathy and unhappiness. "You are still grieving, old friend."

"Of course I am," she replied easily, though the look on his face and his words had shaken her. She'd managed to ignore the worst of the grief for the last few days, suffering only when she was alone, in solitude, confined to her own misery. But at work she usually pushed aside her feelings toward her grandfather. Her love for him, the sharp sting of betrayal, the emptiness of his loss, and the fear of filling his shoes. It was, even for her, too much to handle all at once. "I loved him, Raoul. With everything I am. And in the end he fooled me just as badly, if not worse, than Wyatt Bailey did."

Raoul cursed under his breath, rage in his eyes as he glared at her. "If Bailey had shown his face in here, he would have found my butcher knife in his chest."

"I had the same idea," Madison mused, though her eyes darkened with anguish. "But I refrained. There's been enough death around this place for the time being."

Raoul sniffed disdainfully and wiped his hands with a nearby kitchen towel. "Your *padre* needs breakfast, *cariño*. Should I poison his food today or tomorrow?"

"Very funny," she replied dryly, reaching over to take another bite of asparagus. Her eyes clouded with irritation. "That bitch Jorja Hale has been coming to see him all week. She's bringing him his vices."

"He was always a weak man. He can't handle this life," Raoul said conversationally, turning around to begin scrambling some eggs.

"Well, we know the reason for that now, don't we?" She released a long sigh and hugged her torso, feeling suddenly cold. "Somehow it doesn't make me understand him any better, though. I feel only pity."

"Man makes no choice in what he is given, only what he does with what he has."

"And he chose to cower in the corner like a scared puppy," she grimaced, rubbing her temple. "I shouldn't feel sorry for locking him up. This week has gone smoother without me worrying about him making a scene at some bar or winding up in jail again."

"Then don't. You did what you thought was best," Raoul reasoned, facing her with a plate of breakfast food in his hands. He quietly assessed the woman who was, strangely enough, his oldest friend. He had a tendency to burn his bridges with most other people, but never with her. "My advice, *cariño*?"

She met his eyes, feeling lost. "Yes?"

He handed the plate to her, his mouth curving in a slow smile. "Speak to him. Make him see reason. Then ship him off to someplace where he won't be a distraction."

She nodded, accepting the plate and staring down at its contents dully. Before she could say anything, however, the security guard rushed into the kitchen, looking pale as a ghost.

Madison lifted her head, her lips firming into a grim line at the glassy look of panic in his eyes.

"What happened?" she demanded, setting the plate aside and straightening. She approached him in a few quick steps.

"You need to come upstairs, Ms. Vasser. Immediately." He shot a nervous glance over her shoulder at Raoul, who was glaring at him through narrowed, suspicious eyes. "Now, please."

"Alright." She glanced at Raoul before following the security guard, wondering what in the world could have gone wrong now.

Moments later, she stood over her father's body and had the alarming realization that she was relieved he was gone.

THEY STOOD SILENTLY in the hallway just outside the door of the suite while the police, medics, and coroner did what needed to be done. Grant had one arm wrapped around his sister and his other hand on the shoulder of his brother.

Madison was stonily quiet, her face revealing nothing. She wasn't sure what her brothers were feeling, but knew in her heart there was only a mountain of pity for their father inside of hers. She felt sorry that Win had gone down the road of self-destruction and that it had killed him, but there was little she could've done. He was a grown man capable of making his own choices and, no matter how hard she tried, he never listened to her. Instead he continued feeding his addictions until they ultimately killed him. It was pitiable and tragic, but certainly not unexpected. The only thing they could do was play down the story in the media and hope his death went unnoticed. The Vasser reputation had already suffered enough from Cyrus' actions. She'd be damned if they would suffer any more because of Win.

Grant watched the EMTs wheel out the stretcher with the black body bag on it and had to grit his teeth and force himself to watch. It was closure, he knew, to play out all stages of death. The minute Madison had called him on his cell an hour before, he'd raced immediately upstairs to see the body himself, to make sure he was truly gone. Now he would watch his father be wheeled away to the morgue.

Suicide. Sadly, it didn't surprise him. He'd known for a while now that his father would likely attempt something of this nature. It didn't make the fact that it happened any easier to swallow, but at least it wasn't completely out of the blue.

One of the cops emerged from the room after the body and made his way toward them, his expression professionally distant and unreadable. He nodded politely before speaking.

"We found this in the bedroom." He held up a clear plastic evidence bag with a mostly used joint in it. "We need to wait on the toxicology report, but from a quick test it appears as though this joint may have been laced with PCP or some other substance, which may explain your father's actions."

"You're saying the drugs made him commit suicide?" Grant asked doubtfully. "He'd been under a lot of pressure recently, as we all have. Don't you feel that's likely the reason he did this?"

"It's possible, Mr. Vasser. I'm just letting you know all the possibilities before we dig in and find the truth."

"Just don't let this drug thing slip to the goddamn press," Linc charged, staring pointedly at the cop.

The cop frowned as he met Linc's eyes, but kept his remarks to himself. "We'll need to close off this area. Are there guests in any of the rooms nearby?"

"No. Though the rooms have been on reserve for our family members who are flying in this afternoon," Madison told him. "I suppose I'll find other rooms for them."

"See that you do." The cop headed back into the room, leaving them alone in the hallway.

"I swear, the saying 'when it rains, it pours' should be our new family motto." Linc sneered, rubbing his face before letting out a heavy sigh. He turned to his siblings and shook his head. "What are we supposed to do now, guys?"

"We should be grieving," Grant pointed out flatly.

"Yeah, well, we don't really have time for that, do we?"

"Would we grieve, though? If we had the time?" Madison asked, her eyes honing in on her brothers, darkly serious.

They considered her words for a moment, neither sure what to say.

When they said nothing, she continued. "The man has been a thorn in our sides since we were children. I'm not ashamed to say that I'm relieved he's gone."

"You don't mean that." Grant stared down at her disbelievingly.

"That's harsh, Mads," Linc put in, eyebrows raised. "Thorn or not, he was still *our* thorn. He was the only father we'll ever get, and yeah, I spent most of my life resenting him, but that never made him any less my father."

"He's not coming back this time. He's gone for good," Grant murmured, the first signs of dark grief showing in his eyes. "Eventually you'll come to terms with that, and then you'll mourn him."

He took off down the hallway, eager to get back to his office.

Linc stared at his sister, disappointment clear in his eyes. "You're good at doing the 'I'm a cold, distant bitch' thing, Mads, but there's a time and a place. This isn't it."

He followed Grant, leaving her alone with her thoughts and regrets.

When he made it down to his office, Linc ran into Walter, who shoved a stack of call notes into his hands.

"Your phone has been ringing off the hook. The press wants a comment."

"Tell them to fuck off," Linc spat, tossing the stack of little papers into the garbage can.

"Can I do that?" Walter asked, looking hopeful.

Linc sighed and collapsed into his desk chair, resting his head against the cool black leather and shutting his eyes. "No. I wish, but no. Just tell them the family has no comments at this time. Until I can draft up a proper press release, that's what we'll have to go with."

"Sounds good, boss." Walter nodded and started to leave, only to stop as Linc called him back in.

"Wait, stay here. And grab a notepad and a pen. I wanna brainstorm a bit."

Walter did as he was told and sat down in one of the chairs facing Linc, notepad in hand.

Linc grabbed his slinky and began playing with it, rolling it from one hand to the other, his mind working over ideas and details. Whatever it took to keep from thinking about his father. He wasn't ready to come to terms with that cold, hard truth. "Alright, so our reservation numbers are down by about fifteen percent from this month last year at this hotel alone, which means we're in trouble. For all five hotels combined, we're down about eight percent. If it continues to slump into next month, as we get into summer, then we're really fucked. So we're gonna have to revamp things a bit, try out some new ideas to keep our profit margins steady."

"Like what?" Walter asked, eyes wide. "You're not thinking of downsizing, are you?"

"You're an intern, buddy. You work here for free, remember?" Linc grinned. "If I was thinking of downsizing, why the hell would I let the one guy I don't pay go?"

"Good point." Walter smiled, feeling better. "Okay, so then what's your idea?"

Linc leaned over his desk, eyes flashing with anticipation. "The same one I've been working on for months. I think the time has finally come to implement it."

"Appeal to the middle class market? Offer some good deals?"

"Precisely." Linc nodded, smacking his fist on the desk. "Write this down, Wally. We're gonna shake things up."

GRANT STOOD ALONE in the elevator hours later, resting his head against the upholstered wall as he shut his eyes tiredly. It had been, to say the least, a trying day.

There were still reporters outside the hotel, hoping for more information on his father's suicide. Despite their best efforts, they wouldn't get any. Not yet, anyway.

The rest of the Vasser clan had arrived that afternoon, arrival flights layered over the span of a few hours from varying parts of the country and the world. Eventually they all came, some in stretch limos and others in sleek black town cars, home to where their family legacy had begun some hundred years earlier.

Fifty-four people in total, all of whom were staying in the hotel until the weekend, after Cyrus' funeral. Some might even stay until Win's funeral the following Thursday.

It was stressful trying to get everyone situated, greeting family members he barely recognized, meeting their young children who he'd never met. It seemed the family only got together when there was a funeral or a wedding to attend, a fact that both saddened and relieved him. He didn't think he could deal with the stress of pulling everyone together more often than he already had to.

They'd badgered him with questions, fears, and concerns, few of which he could actually answer or do anything about. It left him feeling frustrated and guarded, which only made his mood sour and his patience short. But if he'd snapped at them or been callously short, then to hell with it. He wasn't a saint. He had as much a right to be angry and upset as any of them.

Many of them still expected *him* to have all the answers, seeing as he ran the New York operation and had been center stage when the shit hit the fan.

Sometimes wearing the crown was one of the biggest and heaviest burdens. Now it was Madison's turn to wear the mightiest crown of all, which made him realize he no longer envied her.

Marshall had showed up to welcome his four remaining brothers and their families, but the reunion was dismal and melancholy. Despite the bad choices Win had made in his life, he was still their brother. And Cyrus was still their father. The fact remained that they'd lost them both in a tragically short period of time.

Oddly enough, Win's sudden death had lit a fire beneath Marshall, who was eager to assist and talk with anyone who sought him out. He helped sort out room keys and arrange for bags to be brought upstairs. He even sent Walter out to get baby formula from a nearby drugstore because one of Grant's cousins, who just had a baby, had run out.

Then, somewhere in between all of the bustling and gossip and frantic arranging, Marshall pulled Grant aside and apologized for his behavior. It was short and sweet, but good enough.

Grant was just happy not to have a reason to dislike his uncle any longer.

The elevator came to a stop at the second floor and the doors slid quietly open. Grant's eyes opened and he pushed back from the wall of the elevator, making his way toward his office. He spotted Quinn seated at her desk, the phone pressed to her ear as she hurriedly jotted down notes on a piece of paper.

As he approached, she glanced up and smiled, speaking into the phone. "Grant's right here, hold on."

She held out the receiver as she continued to write down more notes. "It's Linc, he wants to know if we can draft up a press release for him. He's busy with other things."

Grant accepted the phone. "Should I assume you told Quinn all the important details you want in this release?"

"Yep. Just get a draft done, I'll finalize it in the morning. I'm swamped right now. I might even bring in a gallon of Red Bull and pull an all-nighter."

"Go home, get some sleep," Grant sighed, rubbing his left temple. "The work will still be there in the morning."

There was a long, dead silence on the other line.

"Alright, who are you and what have you done with my brother?" Linc asked, dumbfounded. *"Because he would never utter those words, I can guaran-fucking-tee it."*

Grant chuckled, eyeing Quinn as she smiled up at him. "Let's just say I'm looking at things through fresh eyes these days. I'll see you tomorrow."

As he hung up the phone, Quinn grabbed the notes and rose to her feet.

"Why don't we go sit on the couch in your office? We can spread out on the coffee table. Plus, seeing as I am always prepared for any situation that may require food, I brought snacks and stowed them away in your fridge."

"What kind of snacks?" he asked, perking up at the thought.

She grinned as she rounded her desk and reached up to tug playfully on his tie, bringing his face down to hers for a quick kiss. "That's for me to know and for you to find out."

He smiled after her as she wandered into his office, stack of notes in hand. He remembered he had a bottle of Pinot Noir stashed in one of the kitchenette cabinets, a gift from a client several months back. He'd never had someone to enjoy it with. Until now.

"They may not be as elegant as the *hors d'œuvres* you're used to, but trust me, they are plenty tasty," Quinn was saying as she pulled a few Tupperware containers from his fridge and set them on the counter. She reached into a lower cabinet to grab an elongated blue platter.

"I'm not as sophisticated as you assume," he said as he came up behind her and reached over her head into a cabinet. He grabbed the bottle of wine and two plastic cups, showing them to her. "See, I even drink wine from Solo cups."

She laughed. "Reminds me of college."

"Oh, this wine will be better than anything you had in college," he mused, shifting to the side of her so he could uncork the wine and pour a generous amount into each cup. "You're stuck with the Pinot, however. I'm afraid it's all I have."

"You know what, it's perfect. The smoky flavor of the Gouda paired with the cherry and oak notes of the wine will be exquisite," Quinn informed him cheerfully, arranging water crackers, slivers of crusty rye bread, gouda cheese, prosciutto, and a combination of green grapes, fresh figs and blackberries on the plate in an artful presentation.

They made their way to the sofa, she with the food and he with the wine, and settled in. Quinn curled her legs beneath her and grabbed her notes and a fresh notepad, her cup of wine in her free hand. Before she tried it, however, she lifted her eyes to meet his, an odd mix of sadness and hesitation on her face.

"I didn't get to say this earlier since you were so busy today. But I'm really sorry about your dad."

He let out a long breath and sipped at his wine, wondering what to say to her. He hadn't had much time to think about his father, or what it meant now that the man was dead. "I'm sorry too, I suppose. Sorry that he gave up."

"He seemed just fine the other day when I saw him eating dinner with your uncle. Did anything else happen?"

Grant frowned, staring down into his cup as he considered her question. "Maybe. The police suggested he may have been on drugs."

"Oh." She bit her lip, feeling sorry for him and a bit annoyed at his dead father. "That's awful."

He shrugged, leaning over to sample a thick slice of Gouda. "I knew he'd used in the past, but I guess I didn't realize he was still into it."

"It isn't your fault, Grant," she asserted, reaching out to hold his hand. "He wanted to go, felt it was best. And so he did."

Grant stared at her silently for a moment, emotions swirling uncomfortably inside of him. The feel of her hand on his was comforting, as was the look of support and concern in her eyes. She cared about him, for some odd reason.

God, it'd been so long since he'd had that from someone outside his family.

"I know what will cheer you up," she said, pulling her hand from his and rising to her feet. She went to his desk and grabbed a tiny box from behind his computer monitor, bringing it over to him. He accepted the box numbly, lifting off the lid to expose the harmonica that lay inside.

Quinn sat back down and smiled sweetly. "Play me something."

He sat still for a long moment, wondering if he could. Then again, it was a simple enough request. What reason did he really have, other than dealing with the demons of his past, to not give her what she wanted?

"What would you like to hear?" He pulled out the tiny instrument and set the box aside, his fingers finding placement over the holes.

"Surprise me."

He shot a quick glance over at her and smiled, before setting his fingers and pressing his mouth against the cool metal.

He launched into an old Irish tune he'd picked up somewhere years ago, one that had been Madison's favorite. It was a hauntingly soft melody that soothed and chilled all at once, reverent to a land of ancient and timeless magic.

Quinn sat back and watched him play, noting how his eyes closed as he lost himself in the music. She knew he ran himself ragged without giving himself time for release, a habit that had made him cold and hardened over the years. She hoped to change that, to help him see that he needed rest as much as he needed his work.

Hopefully, in time he would see just how much she could offer him. Wanted to offer him.

Grant gave in to the song, grief pouring from his subconscious and into the melody. Grief for his dead fiancé Erin, for his father, for his grandfather, for the hotel and his family. Then, as if it had never been, his grief was smoothly replaced by hope. His heart ached, not used to feeling so much. His mind reeled and gave up trying to process it all, gave up trying to fight it. There was nothing left in him that had the strength to beat it back any longer.

He finished on a long and haunting note, then pulled the instrument away from his mouth, set it aside, and buried his face in his hands. He let out a heavy, burdened sigh before tilting his head up to face her.

"Can I share something with you?" he asked, his expression dark and filled with emotion.

She nodded, tears brimming in her eyes from the song and the display of emotions on his face. This time he'd let his walls down for her, and she'd never been more honored.

"A few years ago, I was with this woman. Her name was Erin." His eyes flashed with an old, long held despair as he spoke her name, the wound tearing open as he brought the memories to the forefront of his mind. "I met her at Harvard. She was a law student and I was in business. She was intelligent, beautiful. She also came from a powerful family, one that ran one of the wealthiest steel factories in the country. It made sense for us to be together, and so we were. Within a few years we were engaged. Everything seemed perfect. Until she was killed in a car accident on the New Jersey Turnpike."

Quinn pressed her free hand to her mouth, shock waves of grief shivering through her. "Grant, I'm so sorry."

"Wait, please." He stopped her, fighting back the echoes of pain. "After Erin died, I assumed I would never have what she and I had ever again. To be honest, I didn't want it because I didn't want to ever go through losing it again. But then you came in, and as much as I wanted to resist you, I couldn't. I can't."

Quinn managed a small smile, but there was an immense sorrow in it that destroyed him. Yet she had to know the truth. Had to understand why he was so cautious, why he didn't give in to her the way most men would, the way he knew he should.

It was because he was just as scared of her as he was in love with her.

"I'm not the best with words, and I usually say a lot less than I should." He paused, his lips twitching. "Then again, you often say more than you should. So maybe we balance each other out."

She let out a watery laugh, a tear slipping down her cheek. Knowing his pain made her see him in a much clearer light. And hearing the affection in his voice for the woman he'd lost only made her respect him even more than she already did.

He continued, the amber in his eyes shining in the soft yellow light of the floor lamp behind her. "The only reason I've been able to sleep these last several nights is because I've had your voice to fall asleep to. I know it sounds stupid—"

"Are you kidding? That's the most romantic thing anyone's ever said to me," she interrupted, her eyes dancing even as she wiped away more tears.

"Well, I can do better than that." Slipping off the sofa, he knelt down in front of her, reaching for her hands. He pushed aside the awkwardness he felt and tried to focus only on her, on making her see how much he needed her. "When everything around me is crumbling to pieces, all I have to do is look at you and I can keep going. You're warm, Quinn. The warmest person I've ever known. I never realized just how devoid of warmth my life was until you came into it."

She ignored the rest of the tears that fell and leaned in to kiss him tenderly, sweetly, her hands still clutched in his. When she pulled away and smiled, he basked in the light of it.

"You're right, that was better."

She slid into his arms, her hands diving into his dark hair as her mouth found his, desperate and eager. Her heart lifted and fell in one glorious wave as she reveled in the feel of his hands gripping her back, capable and strong. He, who was made of immovable rock and unbreakable steel, had somehow enveloped her like coolly sweet satin, smooth and gentle. This man, so formidable and powerful, wanted her. It shook her to the very core just to think of it.

"God, why did we wait so long to do this?" she gasped, shuddering as he hastily unzipped her dress and pulled the fabric down, exposing her.

"I'm too careful," he managed, his mouth greedily finding the smooth curve of her throat.

"And I'm too patient." She laughed, pushing him down onto the floor, her gypsy eyes alight with passion and humor. Behind her, the lamplight glowed golden in her hair, giving her the appearance of a dark angel, mischievous and divine.

When she spoke again, her words rang out into the night like sacred bells, haunting and spectacular. "There's no holding back now, Grant. Just know that I love you."

Staggered, he rose up to crush her mouth with his, abruptly flipping her so she was beneath him, pressed into the rug. Her answering moan echoed through to his very bones.

No, there would be no holding back, he thought as he swiftly lost himself in her. Not anymore.

TWENTY ONE

The wine soothed the worst of the ache, but did nothing to heal the wounds.

She continued to sip it anyway, enjoying its tartness and rich, velvety texture as it slid smoothly from the glass and onto her tongue. It was a fine bottle of Australian Cabernet, a 2001, aged to perfection.

Madison curled her legs beneath her as she sat on her black leather sofa, wine glass in one hand and her grandfather's letter in the other. Across the room, a fire crackled in the dark slate fireplace. Above it, her television was set on a rock music station, and the husky, sultry voice of Stevie Nicks flowed into the room.

She'd lit candles so that her living room glowed with rich, golden light that flickered shadows off the ceiling. Somehow it helped quiet the restlessness in her heart.

Her father had died today. Tomorrow, she would bury her grandfather.

Most people would crumble under the grief of such awful luck. But not her. She couldn't afford to.

Sipping her wine, she lifted the letter and perused over her grandfather's tiny, scrawling words, considering them thoughtfully. The words in the letter were carefully chosen, deliberately used, and poignant in their efficiency. Cyrus left no loopholes, no doubts as to what he wanted and no room for discussion. She was required to follow his demands to the tee, or lose everything.

It amused her to see Linc's idea, the one she and Grant had over-turned only weeks earlier, as number one on Cyrus' list. According to him, the people who were most likely to shun the Vasser family were those in high society, the elites, people whose allegiances changed direction as easily as a brisk wind in October. So screw them, Cyrus demanded, and revamp the image of the company entirely. Adapta-tion, he said, was key to any creature's survival. And if the hotels were to survive the damage he'd caused, they were going to have to toss tradition out the window and try new things. Hilton did it. So would the Vassers.

Corporatize. It was a word that had been tossed around in her family circle before, usually as a bad joke. Now it was going to be their reality.

They would retain the current hotels as their luxury line and would invest in buying up smaller hotels to convert into Vasser full service and focused service hotels for business class and leisure trav-elers. It was a transition that would take years to implement, but it was required to bring the Vasser Hotels to a new level of prominence in the industry. Otherwise they'd be left to wallow in the dust of dying traditions.

Linc would be pleased, Madison mused, setting aside the letter and staring at the fire. Already he'd mentioned something to her about a fresh proposal for how to revamp the company. It seemed he was more determined than ever to make his ideas a reality, now that it was obvious they needed a drastic change of course.

She would have to find some way of preventing the victory from going to his head. His ego was big enough already.

Grant would be disappointed. But even he couldn't deny the blow Cyrus' sins had dealt to the family empire. Eventually the press would die down and people would forget about the scandal, but their reputation had taken a big hit. As long as people associated the name Vasser with the words *murder* and *suicide*, they were in trouble.

So the best way out was to give people something else to asso-ciate the name Vasser with. Something fresh, something new and improved. Excellence and prosperity. Perseverance. Americans loved a good rising from the ashes tale of success, and Madison was more than ready to give it to them.

The Vasser name wouldn't die a miserable, bloody death on her watch. On the contrary, she planned to breathe as much life into it as her lungs could hold.

Feeling more confident, she downed the last of the wine in her glass. The rest of the list would have to wait until step one was presented and planned for.

As long as the family was willing to work with her on revamping the company image, then she would proceed in disclosing the rest of her instructions, bit by bit, at a pace that wouldn't alarm them more than they could handle.

Because what she needed to do would definitely scare them. That was a fact she couldn't avoid. They weren't going to like the changes she needed to make in order to keep the family empire afloat. Drastic changes that were borderline suicidal.

If corporatizing and restructuring the company meant making enemies of them all, then so be it. She'd never really been a part of them, anyway. Since she was nine years old she'd been trusted with a much harder task. Cyrus had trusted *her*, not his own sons, not her brothers or her mother. He'd groomed *her*, and her alone, for this list, which he must've known was an inevitability all along.

Surely he knew the truth would one day be revealed and the brashness and arrogance of his youth would cost his heirs their entire legacy. So he'd prepared her as his successor and planned and plotted his way to the grave.

Could she blame him? Of course not. If she'd been in his shoes, she would've done the same. They'd always shared such similar minds.

Except she lacked the coldness required to kill.

A dirty bitterness settled into her stomach as she pushed thoughts of him from her mind. In an attempt to distract herself, she grabbed her cell phone from her coffee table and began scrolling through her contact list, all the way to the bottom.

To the Ws.

She found his name and without thinking called him.

Before she could regret her decision he answered, his voice thick with liquor and dark and mean with misery.

"*Yeah?*" Wyatt growled. She heard the sound of him taking a swig of beer and immediately felt her hackles rise.

"You're drunk?"

There was a long pause where she could only hear the background sounds of people talking, laughing. A baseball game was playing and it was the second inning. The bartender called out for more potato skins for a hungry patron.

When he finally spoke, he'd lost all the meanness in his voice. "*Hey, sweetheart.*"

"Hello." She rubbed her left temple as her heart raged violently.

"*Is something wrong? Are you okay?*"

"Where are you?" Her hand fell from her forehead and clutched the silk fabric of her shirt, right over her heart. It couldn't seem to settle down, no matter how hard she willed it to.

"*Atlantic city. I've been here since...well, since I found out.*"

Madison nodded, even though he couldn't see it. "You shouldn't be surprised. He was a weak man."

"*Damnit, woman, he was my friend,*" Wyatt snapped, his temper sparking. She could all but feel the heat of it through the receiver. "*He didn't deserve to go like that. No one does.*"

"But he did. There's nothing we can do to change it." For the first time since she found her father's body that morning, her throat clenched and tears threatened behind her eyes. She breathed out the first sob in silence, not wanting him to hear. Not wanting to accept it herself. "The police said it appeared he was on drugs. We won't know until the toxicology report comes in."

Wyatt sighed and she heard him take another drink from his beer, only to then order something stronger from the bartender. "*What do you want from me, sweetheart?*"

She started to say she didn't know, but stopped herself before she could. Hadn't she decided only days earlier to try and play his game right back on him? Now was as good a time as any. He was clearly weak and intoxicated, grieving and miserable. It wouldn't take much to convince him that she was lonely, get him to drive into the city to her town house, drag him into her bed.

But she'd be damned if she would tell Wyatt the truth, that she missed him. Needed him, even. And that she was horrifically close to crumbling with grief over the death of a father she'd always claimed to never love. But she had. Oh, and the pain of losing him devastated her.

"I wanted to see if you would like to get lunch with me sometime, catch up. Like old times," she lied, struggling to keep the sadness from her voice. The isolation. "You left so abruptly the other night. We barely had the chance to talk."

"*I got the impression you didn't want to talk to me. And it was a pretty crystal fucking clear impression.*"

"I was caught off guard by you being there," she said lightly, even as the hand that held her phone was trembling. "Seeing you...it reminded me of what we had."

He snorted out a derisive laugh and she scowled down at the phone.

"What? You don't believe me?" she demanded hotly, letting her anger take over.

"*Oh no, I believe you one hundred percent.*" He chuckled darkly. "*But I know you, Madison. I know how that sexy mind of yours works. Never in your wildest dreams would you submit to me like this. It isn't in your nature, sweetheart.*"

She pursed her lips and seriously considered throwing the phone into the goddamn fire. Instead, she softened her voice and prepared to lay it on thick.

"I'm not the same girl I was, Wyatt," she began, imagining sliding her hands over his chest and nipping at his jaw line with her teeth. It was an image that helped put the seduction in her voice almost instantly. "And when I saw you, I realized that I wasn't over you. Had never been over you."

He said nothing for a few moments, as if considering her words and trying to figure out her angle. She only rolled her eyes and damned her heart for believing in the words even while her mind laughed in the face of it all.

"I've never met another woman I could trust with my life and yet never for a goddamn minute would I trust any word she says."

Fuming, she clenched the cell phone tightly in her hand until her knuckles were white. "Same goes, then. You promised me you would always be there, but you left."

"I had my reasons."

"Reasons," she repeated in a hiss, the amber in her eyes flaring bright gold. "Well I hope they were good reasons."

"They were," he said simply, darkness hollowing his voice.

She hesitated, a quick release of breath escaping her lungs as her throat clenched again. His causal admission shattered the cold stone of her hardened heart to pieces. Damnit, she couldn't let him do this, not again, not now when she was already weakened, damaged...

But when he spoke again, the pain in his voice haunted her. *"I love you, sweetheart. That hasn't changed."*

She let the phone fall from her cheek as she hung up on him, permitting only a single tear to fall.

THE FUNERAL WAS held on a cool, March day, clouds shadowing the sun as rain threatened to fall. In the distance, thunder rumbled, ominous and dark.

It was, as if by fate, a day that suited the man being laid to rest flawlessly.

Madison stood with Grant and Linc before the dark ebony wood casket as it hovered over the hole that fell six feet deep, her hands grasping a cluster of calla lilies. Her grandfather would have scolded her for daring to put flowers over his casket, but it was her way of paying him back for withholding from her. Childish, maybe, but it gave her an odd sense of closure.

The entire family was there, crowded around the grave like a mass of black clothed statues. The preacher who read consoling words on death from the bible in his hands must have found it peculiar that not a single one of those present was crying.

It said something dark and sinister about a man who could die and no one would shed a single tear at his funeral.

Quinn stood solidly beside Grant, her hand in his, her eyes taking in the family members surrounding her. She'd met a few of them before the service, but there were just too many for her to keep track. Linc hadn't been lying when he'd told her his family was huge.

There were people of all ages, shapes and sizes surrounding her. Some spoke only in French while others clung to their cell phones restlessly and still others looked bored enough to die. It bothered Quinn that the rest of the Vasser family, at least those of the younger generations, seemed to care a lot less about the family empire than Grant and his siblings did. Most of them, she figured, had probably only shown up to find out how much inheritance they were getting. It was a tragic shame.

Those who were clearly of the older generation, notably Marshall's four remaining brothers, appeared the most respectful and saddened. Cyrus had been their father, after all, and had given them each a hotel for their own to manage and a legacy to give their children. There was Clark Vasser from the Los Angeles Vasser Hotel, Duke from Las Vegas, Lyndon from Paris, and lastly Walter from London. Quinn noted the way they stood proudly beside their oldest brother, Marshall, in a show of support and unity.

They, at least, knew the real power that came from standing together in tragedy.

Grant's youngest sister was also there, hovering awkwardly beside Charlene. Quinn watched Kennedy curiously, noting the dark shadows under the girl's eyes that were so very much like her father's. She possessed the same poetic innocence that had made Win seem so childlike and kind.

Charlene had been evasive and rude, but Quinn expected that. Grant somewhat inexpertly alluded to his mother earlier that day that he was now seeing his secretary, causing her to nearly faint with shock in the hotel lobby. Quinn tried to brush off Charlene's obvious disapproval of her, but it still hurt.

She knew what she was and where she came from, and never for one minute would she let someone else make her feel badly about herself. But the fact still remained that Grant could do better, at least by society's standards.

Quinn knew she would live with that nagging at the back of her mind for as long as he chose to stay with her.

Linc stood on Grant's other side, Lynette curled up against him. As he stood there in the graveyard, surrounded by death, he could no longer avoid thinking about his father. He supposed regret was at the forefront of whatever was going on inside of him, regret that he'd let a grudge keep him from rekindling a relationship with the only father he would ever have. Regret that a wicked, asinine woman got between them, and that the last words he'd spoken to the man had been ones of disgust and hate. He couldn't take any of that back now, just like he couldn't change the fact that his grandfather had been a cold-blooded killer. It was a collection of sickening truths that weighed down his very soul.

He shot a quick glance over at his brother, noting that while there weren't tears in Grant's eyes, there were certainly storms of complicated emotions. Anyone watching would assume he was waging a silent war within himself over whether he hated or loved the man being buried. But, hell, weren't they all feeling that way?

The man they'd known and loved was now suddenly something else entirely. He was a murderer, and would forever be just that.

When the service ended, a dozen or so of the family remained to pay their respects one last time as the casket was lowered into the ground. Madison looked off into the distance and spotted Wyatt lingering beside an old, knotted oak tree, waiting for her.

Grant noticed her stiffen and followed her gaze. Disapproval flashed in his eyes even as acceptance settled uneasily into his gut. He knew Wyatt would be able to comfort Madison. He may have despised the man, but no one had ever been able to reach his sister quite like him.

"We'll wait for you," Grant murmured, kissing the top of his sister's head.

Her eyes met his for a long, quiet moment and understanding passed between them as it often did. She nodded and stepped away, her hands digging into the pockets of her black coat.

When she reached Wyatt, she stopped a few feet away and stared at him, her face free of emotion and ice cold. "What are you doing here?"

He leaned against the trunk of the big oak tree, a cigarette in his hand that he drew a long, slow pull from. "I could lie to you, sweetheart. But I won't."

He finished the cigarette and tossed it into the grass, snuffing it out with the toe of his black leather boot. "I wanted to see you. It's that simple."

"Nothing is ever simple with you," she countered, her eyes measuring him frostily. "You always have something planned. What is it this time?"

"I should be asking you the same question. Especially after last night." He grinned, folding his arms casually. "That little seduction act was cute, but kind of a new low for you."

Her eyes narrowed to dangerous slits as she stepped toward him, tilting her head up to meet his eyes. "If I wanted you, Wyatt, you'd be in my bed by now."

He laughed, though there was little amusement in it. "I didn't come here to go to blows with you, sweetheart. I came to make sure you were doing alright."

"I'm fine," she replied haughtily, a refined coldness replacing the hostility in her voice. "You can run along back up to Maine now, or wherever it is you've been hiding these last eight years."

Wyatt shook his head with a dry smile. "You know, when I was in Atlantic City last night, I came across a cute little wedding chapel. It reminded me of us."

Her glare became deadly as she sneered. "Don't you dare bring that up, not now. Not here."

"Why not?" he asked, his voice laced with dark humor and resentment. "We *were* married, sweetheart."

"I had that annulled," she hissed.

"I never signed any annulment papers."

She let out an irritated huff of breath and in a sudden wave of fury lashed out to slap him across the face, only to have him catch her forearm and hold her back, his eyes dangerous as he brought her closer. She struggled, her gaze ice cold and mean.

"That was the biggest mistake I ever made, marrying you," she muttered, her heart rioting as he brought her closer, his face inches from hers. The steel in his eyes heated and softened as he watched her, his lips curving into a grin.

"Like I said, I can never believe a word that comes out of that pretty little mouth of yours." With a movement that was both swift and possessive, he pulled her in and crushed her mouth with his. He gripped her coat to keep her close until he could feel her giving in, loosening up, letting go.

"Damn you," she gasped, her lips hard on his while her teeth nipped and her heart ached. "I hate you."

"I know." His own heart thundered as he lost himself in her, until he almost forgot they were enemies, that they were at war. Until he found a way to settle this with her, to convince her to let him back into her life, they would remain in a constant battle of fire and ice.

He broke the kiss, his eyes dark and haunted, his mouth set in a firm, grim line. "You should go. Be with your family."

She let her hands fall to her sides, her cheeks flushed and her expression dark and unreadable. When she spoke, her voice had the depths of satisfaction that came from a woman who'd gotten what she wanted and enjoyed it.

"I don't give a damn what the state of Nevada thinks, Wyatt. You aren't my husband."

With one last, deadly glare, she turned on her heel and headed back to her brothers, damning Wyatt Bailey to whatever place there was that was worse than Hell.

"I DON'T WANT to go to Lake Pontchartrain."

"Why the hell not? It's great," Linc countered, eyeing Lynette across the butcher-block island in her kitchen. When she only lifted an eyebrow and pursed her lips, he laughed. "Don't tell me you've got something against Louisiana."

"Of course I don't," she insisted, continuing to dice a ripe and juicy tomato, her slender hands diligent and graceful as she worked. He marveled at how she made even the simple act of chopping vegetables look beautiful. "Us southerners stick together, dear Yankee, and don't you forget it."

Her accent thickened as she said the words, which only amused him more. "Then what is it?"

"I don't care much for lakes, if you must know," she said primly, her eyes glued to the task at hand. "I prefer the sea."

"Ah. Well, I can buy us a house on the coast if you'd like." He leaned over the counter, his eyes brightening with the idea. "Cute little beachfront, white siding with bright blue shutters. A dock with a sailboat tied to it. We could walk the beach and gather seashells and you could scatter them throughout the house."

She snorted out a laugh and glanced at him briefly, wearily. "That's a nice dream, Linc, but nowhere near becoming a reality."

"I don't see why not," he countered, reaching for her hand so she would stop cutting, making her look at him again. "I love you, you love me. Just marry me, Lynette. What are we waiting for?"

She hesitated, something haunted in her eyes as she pulled her hand from his and turned away to grab some fresh spinach from the fridge. She was purposely buying time, trying to give her heart a chance to slow down and stop fluttering so damn much. He had this way about him that made her want to run off with him on all his crazy dreams. But she was a realist, and realists always looked at all sides of a decision before making it. In this case she needed more time. Time to arrange the pieces neatly in her own head, to figure out how they were going to fit in her carefully structured life.

But he wouldn't understand that. How could he? He was a spontaneous creature, while she was a cautious one.

"I don't know, Linc." She turned and set the spinach down on the counter, then reached for his hand awkwardly. "I just need more time."

He stared at her, wondering how many more times he was going to have to hear those words from her. "Alright. More time it is. You know I would wait a hundred years for you, but please don't make me do it. I'm not a patient guy."

"I know." She leaned in to kiss his lips softly, sweetly, before backing away with a quiet smile. "I need to grab something from the bedroom, I'll be right back."

She raced off, leaving him alone in her kitchen, lost in thought. When her cell phone beeped from an incoming text message on the counter beside him, he couldn't help but glance over and take a look.

What he read had his heart stalling in his chest.

We need to talk. Stay away from the Vassers.

It was from her father. As quickly as the shock hit him, his temper flooded in to set it vibrantly aflame. It took all he had not to text her father back with a nasty reply, demanding to know what the hell he meant by ordering his daughter to stay away from his family.

When she swept back into the room, she noticed the glare of heat in his eyes and blinked in surprise.

"What's wrong?"

"You got a text message," he growled, nodding his head in the direction of her phone. She hesitated, then walked past him to her phone, lifting it to read the message. Her eyes widened and her heart sank as she read the words from her father.

"Did you read it?" she asked, her hand shaking in a quick spasm. He nodded and approached her, the worst of his anger fading and regret replacing it. He didn't like the look on her face, the obvious embarrassment and bewilderment. He ran his hands down her arms, making sure she looked at him.

"I don't want to get between you and your parents like this, Lynette. I know you said you wouldn't let them control your life, but this is causing you pain. I can't live with myself if I know that being with me ruined what you have with them. I don't want to make you choose like this."

"They're the ones making me choose, Linc." She shook her head slowly, sadness in her eyes. "Not you."

Just then, her phone went off again with another text message from her father. She read it, her brow creasing in anger and shock. "Dear Lord."

"What?" He grabbed the phone from her, reading the text himself. *Hell is coming for the Vassers. You must not be there when it does.*

"Jesus, what the hell does that mean?" Linc growled, thrusting her phone back at her and turning around to pace, his hands diving into his hair. "This is getting ridiculous."

"I don't know what it means," she managed, tears filling her eyes as she watched him. "Really, Linc, I don't."

He faced her, violent storms racing across his features.

"If he says anything to you, if he's planning something, you have to tell me, Lynette." His eyes hardened dangerously as he planted his hands on her shoulders, needing her to understand. "This isn't just about us now. It's about my family. And if he shares something with you, I expect you to betray him and tell me. If you won't do that for me, then this is done."

"What?" she gasped, cringing as her own temper sparked. "How dare you?"

"How dare I what? Try to protect my family?" he snapped, throwing up his hands in frustration. "Either we're together in this or we're not. If you're with me, then you're a part of my family. And if they go down, if I go down, you fall with us. That's just how it works."

"He won't do anything, Linc, he's just angry." She crossed her arms tightly, avoiding his eyes.

"Somehow I don't think it's that innocent." Scowling, he leaned against her kitchen island, considering the situation. "He's the one making waves here. All I can do is look out for me and mine. I want you to be a part of that list, but it looks like you're going to have to choose after all."

"Choose between you and him," she stated flatly, her eyes cold and level as she met his. He nodded, and she inhaled deeply to settle her heart. Indecision waged a ferocious battle inside of her as she weighed all the pros and cons and tested all the angles, searching for compromises, ways out of the inevitable. But there were none, and Linc was one hundred percent right. Her father was making her choose.

For that reason alone, she knew she could never choose him.

"Well then I choose you, Linc," she said simply, eyeing him with raised eyebrows and a haughty frown. "If you'll still take me."

He let out a long, slow release of breath, relief coursing through his veins even as regret raced beside it. He didn't want it to be this way, had never wanted this. But her father was giving them no choice.

"Come here." He beckoned her toward him, his arms held out. She let him pull her close against his chest. When he held her there, could feel her heart beating against his own and smell the scent of lilacs in her hair, he nearly broke down with wild relief.

"Let me finish this," she said softly, breaking away from him and grabbing her phone, typing a message to her father. After she sent it, she held up the phone for him to see. "He won't bother us any longer."

Linc read the words and had to steel his heart against the guilt.

I choose him. If you can't handle that, then I guess this is goodbye.

"You're sure about this?"

She attempted a smile as she tossed the phone aside and went to him again, kissing him slowly, deeply. "I love you."

"Good," he grunted, dragging her closer and savoring her mouth. "That's all we need, Lynette. Just trust me. We'll be okay."

HER GRANDFATHER'S FAVORITE motto had always been: *The King's name is a tower of strength.*

Madison now felt that she fully understood what he had meant.

Cyrus had always strived to make the Vasser name as prominent and powerful as he could, understanding that image and reputation came first before anything else. It didn't matter what happened behind closed doors, as long as it didn't interfere with public perception. The public could make or break you, and keeping them on your side was essential to survival.

When he'd been a much younger man, he'd let his ambition drive him to disposing of his own brothers, knowing he was better suited to run the empire than they were. Then he'd let his arrogance reign the night he murdered his own father in cold blood, knowing his secret would die with the old man and then he would be crowned king.

Despite all that, he went on to lead the Vasser Hotel company through the greatest fifty years of its one hundred and twelve year history. With his sharp and ruthless mind, he cut and chiseled and perfected the empire to form what she and her family enjoyed the fruits of all these years later. It was due to his tireless dedication to the hotels that they had survived recessions, political turmoil, government regulations, and more. The company had been his life, his very heart and soul.

Yet all the years he spent structuring and managing the empire, he must have known that his own actions would eventually be the downfall of all he cared about.

Which was, of course, where she came in.

The will and confession had been read to the entire family earlier that day in one of the largest conference rooms at the hotel. The family's attorney completed the task, explaining in a cold, businesslike fashion what the terms were to all those present.

It hadn't been a pleasant scene to witness. Very few outside of her immediate family had been informed of Cyrus crowning her as his replacement, and so the news sent rippling shockwaves of anger and mortification throughout the group. Nearly all of them were older than her, most of them stemming from lines that came before her own line through her father. So no one could understand nor comprehend the blatant favoritism being thrown her way.

But it was done. They couldn't change it, no matter how hard they fought, kicked and screamed about it. She was in charge, and that was that.

Grant, Linc, and surprisingly Marshall stood by her side, for which she was grateful. Their cooperation would ease some of the hostility and eventually the rest of the family would lie down and accept the cold hard truth.

And as for her, well, she'd always been fabulous at making the best out of a tough situation. This would be no different.

She sat at her desk in her quiet office, darkness claiming the sky out the window behind her. The city lights came on to join what little sunlight broke through the storm clouds. Occasionally, lightning sparkled in the distance, thunder absent as the storm moved east toward the sea.

A stack of mail lay on the desk before her and she grabbed the top envelope without glancing at its face, tearing it open. She removed the letter that lay inside, unfolding it. As she read, her eyes narrowed to slits.

The paper she held was simple and pure white, with a single line of plain black text in twelve point font. There was no header, no signature, and no date.

It simply read: *When empires fall, what becomes of the Queen? Everything will burn, and so will she.*

Nausea settled in to mix with the disgust and anger in her stomach as she read and reread the words a dozen times, her heart thundering in her chest.

Unable to do more, she replaced the letter in its envelope and threw it in the top drawer of her desk, locking it away.

She didn't have time to waste on foolish threats. She had work to do.

I have no spur
To prick the sides of my intent, but only
Vaulting ambition, which o'erleaps itself,
And falls on th'other

— William Shakespeare, *Macbeth* —

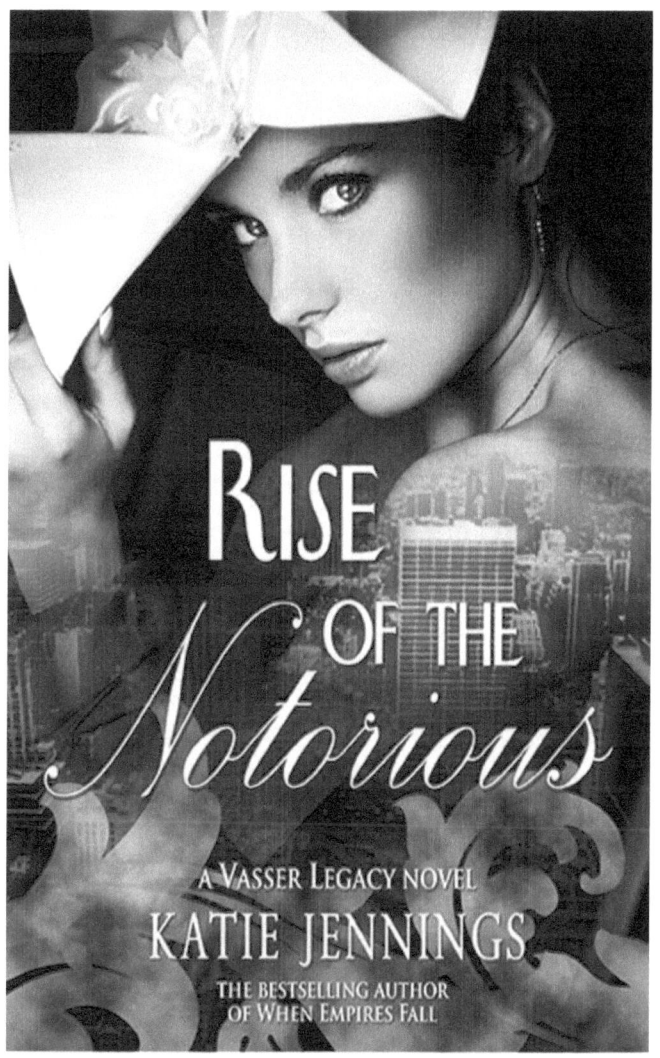

RISE OF THE *Notorious*

A VASSER LEGACY NOVEL

KATIE JENNINGS

THE BESTSELLING AUTHOR
OF WHEN EMPIRES FALL

THE VASSER LEGACY
CONTINUES IN THIS
EXPLOSIVE SEQUEL

Read On For A Sneak Peek

PROLOGUE

LAS VEGAS, NEVADA
JULY 1ST 2004

They say that only clever creatures can survive the desert heat. After all, the desert is nothing more than a sweltering wasteland that has claimed more victims than it has given life, which makes it more of a graveyard than a flourishing habitat. But, regardless of this fact, at some point in time man had either been foolish enough, or maybe greedy enough, to build a playground in the middle of Hell.

Then they'd had the audacity to call it a fertile plain. *Las Vegas*.

What a glorious contradiction.

Madison Vasser despised the desert with all of her being. She was a creature made for colder climates, for snow drifts and icy streets. Her ivory skin welcomed a cool winter chill, and scornfully burned under the red-hot desert sun. But, like many others, she had learned to adapt to her new home, for the reward for staying was much too great to relinquish.

She was nineteen, she was ambitious, and she was in love.

Her smile was instinctive and more than a little wicked as she sauntered through her family's lavish casino, her golden dress fitted to her curves and cropped short above her knees. Men in the casino faltered and stared as she passed, stunned by her radiance, moved by the passion so clear in her expression. She was a woman who knew what she wanted and was taking it without reservation. There was no *asking*, no *begging*. No, there was only ambition and victory. And she was the master of both.

She'd come to Vegas a year before to serve her family's empire. And now, as she walked through the casino, she had to marvel at her grandfather's brilliance to build in the godforsaken desert in the first place. Despite appearances, it really was a powerful city. The money that traded hands there was layered thick with hopeful sweat and anxious tears, but, damnit, the people loved it. They flocked to it, never having fully sated themselves with the escapist thrill of bright lights and lost inhibitions.

The hotel itself thrived, rising like a glittering beacon of refuge out of the dusty sand and drier-than-hell rock. It towered over its neighbors, both larger and taller than anything else within several hundred miles. Cyrus had insisted upon it, had purposely designed it so the sapphire and gold "V" shone boldly and brilliantly from atop the glass walled building for all to see. No one entering Las Vegas would have any doubt who was the top dog in town or who ruled the landscape like a king rules an empire.

The Vasser name was as powerful as it was timeless. And, as her grandfather was apt to say, it was the tower of strength.

She made her way out of the bustling casino and passed by the hotel's premiere French restaurant, *Soleil*, thinking she'd grab a bottle of wine for later. After all, it was somewhat of an anniversary. It had been exactly one year since she had arrived in Las Vegas.

Oh, and how things had changed since then.

She may have hated the desert, but there was no denying that it had given her an incredible gift, one she would have gone to Hell and back for had she known of its existence. Well, *his* existence, really.

Wyatt Bailey, the man who'd come from nowhere and shamelessly set fire to her heart.

He'd been virtually nothing when she had found him, just a blackjack dealer working for her uncle with a mysterious past, no car, and a crappy apartment. Despite his shortcomings, she had taken him under her wing and given him everything.

Within a couple of months, she'd gotten him promoted to Pit Boss, moved his meager belongings into her suite at the hotel, bought him a brand new Mercedes SLR and new designer clothes. Most importantly, she had given him her heart, and in return, he had changed her entire world.

She had never loved any man the way she loved Wyatt, with a fiery passion and a crushing need that consumed her every waking moment until she couldn't stand it unless she was at his side. He was intense and fiercely obsessed with her, emotions she knew only too well as she possessed them herself. They were such similar creatures, which was why it had been so easy to fall in love with him. It had taken barely more than a touch and they were mesmerized by each other, which was exactly how she had always hoped love would be.

Smiling again, she swept through the service entrance and into the restaurant's kitchen, her sultry amber eyes catching sight of Raoul, one of the cooks at the hotel. He was busy whipping up eggs in a large, stainless steel bowl at a furious speed, his dark hair falling into his eyes as he worked.

She and Raoul had become fast friends the moment she had begun working for her Uncle Duke because, like herself, she recognized in him an ambitious and restless spirit. He craved status, power, and the finer things in life as much as she did. And once she had her way she would see to it that they both got what they wanted in this life. Success.

"Darling, I hope that quiche is not for Grant and Erin." Madison smirked as she came up beside him, one hand sliding over his shoulder companionably. "You know she's lactose intolerant."

Raoul stopped whisking and glared down at her, his mouth set in a firm line. "*Sí*, but your brother likes it, no? I will make something else for his woman."

She leaned in to kiss his cheek, coaxing a small smile out of him as she did so. "I can always count on you."

"It's nothing." He brushed her off, reaching for the bowl again to pour the egg into a shallow glass dish layered with pastry dough. "You should go prepare for your brother, *cariño*."

She glanced down at the slim gold watch on her left wrist, pursing her lips. "I have a few hours till they fly in. Enough time to have a glass of wine and take a hot bath."

He smirked and shook his head, sprinkling cheese over the quiche. "There is a nice Moscato in the fridge."

"Fantastic idea." Madison swept over to the kitchen's large wine fridge, opening the glass door and reaching for the Moscato. She checked the date on it and smiled. "Excellent. Wyatt enjoys a good white."

Raoul said nothing as she shut the door and wandered back to him, bottle in hand. "I'll be down in a couple of hours to help you finish with dinner."

"*Hasta siempre*," he murmured without looking at her, his eyes focused instead on the quiche as he finished preparing it.

She paused, her eyes softening as she watched him. It was only when he was feeling emotional that he used that phrase of endearment with her. Just what was bothering him now, she didn't know. But whatever the reason, she would be there for him when he needed her, just as he was always there for her. Loyalty was everything.

"Until forever, darling." She squeezed his shoulder briefly before leaving the kitchen, her mind shifting focus from her friend and instead to her lover, who was waiting for her upstairs.

Since she had begun working at the hotel she had lived in one of the suites. Because the arrangement wasn't meant to be permanent, she figured it was best to be close to the action of the hotel instead of living elsewhere in the city. And, of course, it didn't get any more luxurious than a suite at the Vasser Hotel.

Wine in hand, she made her way towards the hotel's elevators, her head held high and a smooth confidence to her step. The world was hers for the taking. And boy, did she intend to take. Only what she deserved, of course, but she was going to make her grandfather proud. After all, he had entrusted *her* with his most lucrative secrets, trained *her* to be everything he needed her to be. If it wasn't for him, she would be nothing.

She would never, ever let herself forget that.

The elevator she boarded rose slowly towards the upper floors and she gazed at herself in the mirrored gold doors as she waited. Her long, dark brown hair was meticulously straight, its length falling to nearly her mid-back. Eyes of vibrant amber beneath heavy lids stared back at her, sultry and intense. She was proud of the heritage evident in her appearance, proud that she so greatly resembled the man who she respected above all else. It was all a part of who she was, and who she was becoming.

She was a Vasser, and she would go to the grave defending her family and the empire that was her birthright.

When the elevator came to a stop and the doors slid smoothly open, Madison sauntered out and strolled down the long hallway, her heeled footsteps muffled by the ornate gold and sapphire carpet. She reached into the small handbag she carried and pulled out her key card just as she came up to the door of her suite.

She slid the card neatly into the slot and pushed the door open, her smile still in place as she entered the room.

"I brought some wine up, darling. I figured we could have some fun before Grant flies in."

But she paused, taken aback as she noticed the empty living area and the neatly cleaned bedroom beyond. Frowning, she stalked through the bedroom and into the adjoining bathroom, expecting him to be there.

When she found it empty, her heart began to race in her chest as frustration and anger surged through her. Where the hell was he?

She tore back into the bedroom, heading straight for the dresser and ripping out the drawers. When she noticed his clothes were missing, her breathing became shallow and forced, her chest constricting violently.

No, it couldn't be. He wouldn't do this.

She stormed back into the living room, her hand clenching violently around the wine bottle, her vision hazing with red. That was when she spotted the note, written on the hotel's white and gold stationary, sitting atop the coffee table. Beside it lay the key to the Mercedes she had given him.

Her handbag fell to the floor as she grabbed the note hastily and read the words, gripping it so tightly that she nearly tore it to shreds.

It read simply: *I'm sorry, sweetheart.*

"You godforsaken bastard," she snarled, her hand shaking as she crumbled the note into her fist. In a fit of glorious rage, she hurled the wine bottle against the wall, her heart panging at the resounding crash as glass and wine spilled hideously onto the floor.

As the realization that he had left her exploded through her system, she did the only thing that would satisfy the blood lust coursing through her at that very moment. She tore the room to pieces, and cursed his name over and over until her throat was dry and her eyes were bright with tears. The fury she unleashed ripped through the suite like a tsunami; its wake leaving chairs upturned, tables pushed over, vases shattered and draperies ripped from windows. Anything she could grab she did, and as she ruined her pretty possessions she vowed to hunt him down and make him pay.

"Stop it, *cariño*."

Raoul's voice shot out at her from the doorway, causing her to falter for the briefest of moments, her chest heaving. In her hands she held a priceless Baroque statue, the weapon she intended to use to shatter the equally priceless antique mirror over the desk to pieces.

She looked up to meet his dark eyes, and in that instant felt her knees crumble beneath her.

Within seconds he was with her, gathering her close, pressing her face into his chest.

"Don't you dare waste tears on him," he grunted, glaring around at the destruction she had made, an odd, prideful gleam in his eyes. He knew that, while she may be cool-headed most of the time, she was a vindictive devil capable of catastrophe when provoked. "He is not worth it."

As hard as she tried, her fury could only carry her so far. Her emotions were boiling up to overtake her, cloaking her in misery and abject humiliation. Because that's exactly what this was. Wyatt Bailey had used her, led her to believe he loved her, and then left. For as long as she lived, she'd damn him to the darkest depths of Hell for scorning her.

"How dare he leave me," she spat, despising the crack in her voice as the words sank in and enveloped her in despair. When she spoke again, it was more of a whisper and she hated herself for feeling this awful weakness. "How dare he?"

Clutching at Raoul's white dress shirt, she gave in to her emotions and let them drain her dry, her tears painful and horrific.

Never again. Never again would she trust a man with her heart only to have him trample on it this way. She thought of the night only three weeks earlier when she and Wyatt had impulsively gone to a chapel downtown and tied the knot, completely in secret. No one in her family had any idea. Now, it appeared, they never would.

Raoul simply held her, seeking to comfort even as a satisfied smile curved over his lips.

Finalmente. At last. Wyatt Bailey was gone.

ABOUT THE AUTHOR

Nothing can compare to the exhilaration of discovering, at last, a mode of release for the imagination. Mine came, after years of struggling to visualize my creativity, in the form of the written word. I found myself with my nose constantly in a book, absorbing the life of the characters and the beauty of the setting. It was intoxicating, to say the least, and the only thing I knew was that I wanted to give writing a shot, and take the thousands of characters and storylines in my head and put them down on paper and form them into something real and compelling.

In truth, I'm just a girl from a small town north of Los Angeles with an imagination for days and thank goodness a keyboard at my fingertips. And even though my husband thinks I'm a nerd and my mom is undoubtedly my biggest fan, at the end of the day I'm loving life and enjoying giving breath to the characters living in my heart and sharing with others all of the creativity I can harness.

I believe in true love and I've always believed in happy endings. And that is just the beginning of the story.